The Lipstick Case From Outer Space

Mike Fry

Pure Gumption Press

Lonely are the lips that have tasted a better station, a higher resolve and then had to cower backwards into the cellars of their 40'x40' Go-Poddy. Why let the Great War and a little high heat and radiation keep you from the woman of your dreams? Come on down to Sam's Wholesale Magical Mystery Mademoiselles and let's go over your loving options.

Advertisement from Sam's Wholesale Magical Mystery Store

PURE GUMPTION PRESS
Oklahoma City, Oklahoma
contact: www.puregumptionpress@gmail.com

Cover design by Jimo Ward

I dedicate this book to all the people out there who want to write a book, have something to say, and haven't found the faith yet within themselves to complete this task. Let me tell you, most of your family and friends won't really care if you do complete your novel or not. But deep inside yourself you'll care and you won't be satisfied in your life until you do. So find a writing group and start the process. A good writing group is essential.

I am so grateful I found two such groups. I have the one at Healthy Living Center in Oklahoma City, with a great group of people who guide me every week, correct grammarical mistakes when I make them, make ugly faces when I write something rotten, but give praise when I can create something entertaining. Trina Lee is the leader of this workshop and she is so kind with everyone's work. Linda McDonald helped me immensely with my first book: Veetch: A Shoshone Shaman, a '58 Edsel, a UFO, and a Magical Key Save America's Bacon., written in 2011. I probably should have thought longer on the title, but she made it come alive for me, and fulfilled one of my life-long goals—to write a novel.

Other members of this Healthy Living group who have helped me include: Darlene Chaney, Rebecca Knight, Joe Moore, Virginia Pattinson, Hugh Talley, Robert Williams, Don Garrison, and Woody and Carol Gimbel.

My other group has been very helpful too. I want to thank Rick Lippert, Andrew Shelton, Holly McNatt, Ron Collier, and his late wife Freda, and the late Gaylene Murphy.

I also want to thank Eric Pearson, Charlie Dunavin, Becky Young, Joe Horn, and Kurt Summer for their continued support. It takes a whole army of people to produce a book. You need that backbone of well-wishers or it can become a very difficult road to travel.

CONTENTS

PREFACE

The red color in lipstick was once created from the smashing of a very small female cochineal insect. That produced the natural dye called carmine. Harvested and crushed in the name of beauty and love. What could be more romantic for a desert bug who drinks Prickly Pear juice to live?

THE LIPSTICK CASE FROM OUTER SPACE

by Mike Fry

I've tried to insert some humor into a very dire situation. My story begins on an Earth that has been ravaged by a terrible war. The environment is intolerable. People can hardly be outside because of the heat and the pollution. My hope is that this will never happen to the extent I portrayed it. I hope somehow we can all learn to live in peace and respect one another, and to respect our dear Planet Earth as well.

PROLOGUE

A prologue? What the heck? You're probably thinking, 'Why does any reasonable person need to read some long-winded, I'm-so-important-I-gotta-spout-off - before-you-even-get-started-reading-this-dang-book prologue? I'm reminded of the musician who stands on stage discussing all the intricacies and histories involved in one of his more popular, personal songs, mumbling on and on, before he even plays a single note! The crowd growing impatient, yelling out cues like "just give us the music already, will ya?"

Hold on. Bear with me, if only for a brief moment. My plan is to ease you gently into my mad, zany world. I don't want to just toss you overboard, without some kind of compass-equipped life jacket, out into my deep sea of weirdness. I'd rather sprinkle you slowly, gradually soaking the inside of your mind, so you won't be treading the thick waters of improbability without the proper mental water wings.

Don't go away just yet! Get into these murky waters with me, willingly, so as I don't have to drag you into this reading river forcibly. Consider this: I'm merely asking for a tiny slice of time from your busy life - this time we will soon share, you and I, traveling together into the future and to a foreign planet deep in the outer bowels of dark, mysterious space, flying around weightless, trying to both grab hold of our toiletries and maintain our individual dignities.

Be warned! This will not be hard science fiction that you will encounter here, so you needn't be a graduate student of physics to enter herein. My sci-fi is kinda soft and mushy, like oatmeal fresh out of the pan.

Also, I need to mention, this is not a book for the young reader, under the age of 14 or so (you be the judge). It's an adult fantasy-science fiction story based on one man's life in the future, and a bleak future it is indeed, where the environment of this earth is all messed up and all the pretty women are either gone away or not interested in my main character - a man alone, unloved, under-appreciated. I know you can relate to that.

In the universe you are about to enter, all the rich and attractive have rocketed away this planet and gone to the beautiful paradise world known as Eros, where there is love and pleasure no end - at least a kind of paradise from a man's point of view. Oh, I know there is an asteroid in the Amor group called Eros already, which is the second largest near-Earth object. I'm not writing about that asteroid. I chose the name of this exo-planet because it denotes love and passion, and that's one of the themes of this book, so overlook the duplication of names in heavenly bodies I've employed. Sometimes nature is repetitive, so why can't I be?

My main character, Harry Novak, and yes, I know there must exist other people with the name of Harry Novaks, and this isn't about them, OK? Will you lay off until I finish this dang prologue? We could be here for days! Anyway, *MY* Harry Novak is stuck on Earth, being neither rich nor extremely attractive (but he's not bad looking). There are two freckled women connected to his life. One real, but she left him for another man to go to Eros, and the other is a robot who gives him pleasure, This other is a freckled pleasure bot.

OK, I hear you asking: why all this fuss with freckles anyway? I've never taken a college course in freckleology, nor dated a female with freckles for any length of time, so I really don't know the ins and outs of the biology behind this phenomenon. I couldn't tell you the various shapes of freckles, their standard mode of distribution on the human body, their morphology, the way they affect ones moods, if freckles have minds of their own, if they move around the body at night or stay in one spot, or what happens when freckles are exposed to more than one sun at a time, say a red sun and a yellow one.

The main thing about this freckle hang-up is that I try to explore - through the adventures of my main character - the rarity of these little cute dots running around on a woman's skin. I'm in awe of their peculiarity and I think they might hold some hidden meaning, that could unlock the secrets of the universe. We need to try to decipher this code.

I view all things and people who are rare and wonderful as almost holy - to be revered, or at least appreciated more than they sometimes are. I don't mean to make freckled people out to be freaks of nature nor to make enemies of them. I just want to give them their due high place in this world and others, and celebrate their singularity in a world that seems to be downwardly spiraling toward dull uniformity.

So, like I said, the story isn't for the young. It's an adult fantasy. It's not porn (sorry to disappoint you perverts out there). I mention many sexual positions that I made up, but I don't go into detail about them. I leave that to the readers imagination (which I trust is dirtier than I could ever dream up in my writings!). It's all good fun until someone tries one of the positions he or she thinks I was trying to describe. Then there's the pain, the medical bills, and the nasty letters. Please, all you adults out there in reader-reader land, don't try these moves at home, unless you're athletically inclined and willing to face the consequences. And don't blame me. I am warning you now!

So most of this book is just good, almost clean, fun, in a world I imagined might come about if we don't clean up our act environmentally. Yes, we may someday be able to flee this Earth and fly to another world, but why mess up a good thing here? Why rush the apocalypse? If you're in a hurry to see this world destroyed, just dirty your own part and leave the rest of us out of it. We don't want your stinking filth oozing under our fences and muddying up our shoes.

OK, maybe I get a little preachy in this little treatise of mine. I can't help it. But I don't make any promises like politicians, nor do I grant any absolutions like some religious leaders. I don't ask for any donations either, save for the meager price I'm asking you to shell out for this humble book. I just want to write and have fun and I hope you enjoy coming along for the written ride.

And yes, you guessed it. I have very little knowledge of cosmetics, save for my teen years when I did use a little of my mother's concealer to cover unwanted pimples. So if I mix up lipstick with lip gloss, or moisturizer with texturizer or some such, well, well...

Well what? I should know better if my book is about the lipstick cases from outer space! I should know better!

Anyway, what I'm trying to say is if you see discarded lipstick holders lying around your yard - pick them up and consider for yourself what cosmetics might venture to earth from the cosmos and what they might do for your blotchy skin. Meditate too on what life would be like when robots are so human-like that we can no longer tell the real from the manufactured. Will it matter? Will the population shrink if people can find life-satisfaction without connecting to other human life? Will it be the end of romance? Can cosmetics save the day? Find out within, adventurous readers.

CHAPTER 1

HOW THE WORLD WENT WRONG

Harry was deep in dreamland, chasing after an ex-wife who was bouncing away from him on the back of a large white buffalo. Her red hair whipped by the wind and flowing behind her like a long red flag, her freckles bobbing up and down like red popcorn on a hot skillet.

Harry was shouting for her to get off before it was too late. But Emily, her name was Emily, this beautiful on the outside/witch on the inside former wife of his. Emily was singing and throwing red flower petals into the air.

"Be careful!" Harry yelled to her again and again, but suddenly he couldn't yell. It felt like something or someone was choking him. He was gasping for air. He couldn't breath. What was happening?

He woke out of his bed only to discover his Zinkopath Necklace Alarm Chocker was choking him and it was crushing his Adam's apple. He tried to sit up, knowing that would cause the devise to ease up, but he couldn't because he was losing consciousness.

Finally he did fall out of bed, crashed against the side of his room and turned on the hologram machine, which projected images of people on the street all around him. He tripped over a table, spilt a glass of water, hit his head on the chest-of-drawers and knocked his knee against a foot-rest. Finally he found the switch and released the latch of the alarm clock. The alarm clock necklace let up its hold on him. He tore the mechanical thing off his neck.

"Damn! This thing is trying to kill me! It's not a Zinopath, it's a psychopath!" Harry said to no one.

He then examined the alarm necklace and saw that it was set on strangulation mode. There were four modes on this model: gentle, insistent, I'm-warning-you, and strangulation mode. He must have accidentally set it to too high the night before. After all, he did have a drink or two last night.

And a guy like Harry had to wear these things to bed at night. It was required by his job at Teen-A-Watch. They wanted to make sure employees got to work on time, even early if possible. Time was money, they always said, and they could always replace him with a more punctual punching bag.

"Glad you're awake now, Citizen Harry!" said the alarm choker, sitting innocently on a table beside him. "Sorry I had to cut off your air supply this early in this morning. With my help you've been on time at work 32 days in a row. Why ruin that record now, Harry?"

"You almost killed me, you stupid alarm clock! Oh, I guess you're just doing your job," Harry said back to his alarm clock necklace.

"If you are dissatisfied with me, then make sure of your settings before you retire," said the necklace clock.

"Oh shut up!" said Harry and put the alarm clock away in a drawer.

This morning choke was a bad reminder that he had been distracted of late. He needed to concentrate on his life, and particularly on his job at Teen-A-Watch. But Harry couldn't help thinking about women, particularly the wife who had left him.

Harry pushed a button and reached for his morning coffee. The choking gave that coffee a bad metallic taste and left a little headache. So he stretched his long legs within the confines of his personal Go-Poddy sleep area, kicking the titanium wall with a thud as he did and picking up and arranging the things he had disturbed during his life-and-death get-out-of-bed struggle.

An early 20th Century philosopher/designer named Buckminster Fuller had conceived the world-around-housing-concept that Harry now lived in. In this 2255 world, was a utilization of Fuller's concept in a workable model. Harry lived in a 40' x 40' **Go**vernment Home **Pod**modium (thus named the Go-Poddy) built in connecting hexagonal bee-hive structures, rising many levels into the dark smoggy Earth air. Everyone, except the very wealthy, who only stayed on this planet to conduct business, had to live in one of these Go-Poddys, for maximum space utilization and energy creation and conversion. The Go-Poddy itself rotated on its axis when all the residents were at work, acting as a generator, powered by the steady hot winds that blew through this grimy, grey city.

Harry's Go-Poddy was silent now and stationary as he prepared for work. It felt very empty. Harry was so lonely. He went through the motions of cleaning up and dressing for the day in a fuzzy haze. He pushed a button on his mini-habitation wall and out popped breakfast and up popped his bed into the wall. He wasn't sure what breakfast was made of but it resembled toast and eggs and filled him up.

He chewed quickly, lost in thought, but glad his alarm choker was turned off and put away. If left on it could sometimes go into brutish, criticizing mode. It would tell him things like what an utter failure he was, and how he would never amount to anything, and said bad things about his virility and how his wife, Emily, had no choice but to leave him for another man, since he didn't have the means or funds to take her away from this crummy planet.

The choker was designed to be helpful, in a parental sort of way, but could be heartless in getting its point across and motivating the owner. Bosses loved it. It kept the workforce in line and always humble.

Harry took a last long sip of his coffee substitute and straightened his tie in the mirror before heading to work. He was a little over 35 and still in pretty good shape. His hair was jet black with just a dusting of grey around the temples. He had all his teeth, thank God, and some said he had understanding eyes.

Harry understood that what he needed most in life was a mate, a replacement. Wives were very difficult to find on this world, now that all the better women had been taken away by those who could afford to snatch one. Harry couldn't go flying off to another world and snatching females up to carry with him - not even his own wife. He didn't have the monetary units that those in the very upper economic class had, who'd swindled, saved or inherited great wealth.

So, to keep from going crazy, Harry always began his day calculating how long it would be before he could purchase that brand new Posh-Matosh Playmate he'd been dreaming of. It would be a robot, of course, but that would have to do for this bleak world he was now living on.

A booty-bot robot from Posh Matosh was an extremely lifelike companion that he'd seen advertised over and over again on the ad-clouds and on his Go-Poddy door. To purchase one of these, and have it in his Go-Poddy, would make his life bearable once again. It would serve to help him forget the before times, when the world wasn't blown to crap and his ex-wife Emily was still by his side, freckling him on to do better - be better.

This wished-for booty-bot may be only a robot, but hadn't Harry become merely a creature of habit himself? A small cog in a large network of nobodys, going through the meaningless motions of life like every other mug — a whole planet full of human beings eking out a pretend life - trying not to acknowledge their purposeless pursuits? What's the big deal, he thought to himself, if I live with a robot or a real woman. I'm more or less a robot myself, aren't I?

Harry longed very much for the beautiful Tropical Veronica model. He knew he had to hurry before they sold out or discontinued that particular line. Posh-Matosh was the premier manufacturer of artificial companions on this planet and they were constantly trotting out new versions of their popular booty-bots, so that all males wouldn't have the exact same style of woman.

Harry needed this Playmate. No, he deserved this mock madam for all he went through at his job and in this sucked-dry society. He now lived on a world where fun and social activities were strictly limited, now that the outer atmosphere was so thin and subject to violent storms. His life was mostly confined to work and his Go-Poddy, and he was getting tired of this same old routine day after day, year after year.

Harry opened his watch computer and looked at his savings account. He had exactly 1100 Monetary Units of Transaction (MUTs) saved thus far. He needed 1,000 more — one Golden Retriever MUT — and that could buy him the luscious Tropical Veronica model booty-bot. He could buy it on payments, if he had any credit left. But he had lost any good credit standing since his wife, Emily, drained their joint bank account and left with her boss to go to golden pink paradise, the twin-sunned exo-planet called Eros. There all the MUT wealthy, and almost all of the beautiful women, had gone to permanently vacation under the better-than-earth suns, the four moons and the much healthier atmosphere.

Harry realized he had to snap out of this financial funk and somehow gather together more MUTs. The Veronica models were available for a limited time only and this special 2000 MUT offer expired soon. That wife-stealing boss, Planet Eros, partying all the time, and gorgeous women everywhere, ha! He'd have the last laugh and have his own heaven right here on earth! That whoring ex-wife of his could catch an exo-planet venereal disease, for all he cared, and never come back. If only he could find a way to get that Posh Matosh Playmate into his life. If only there was some way.

Monetary units came in colors and in place of the pictures of former Presidents, different dog breeds were displayed on the face of each plastic bill. A One MUT bill was a brown Dachshund - called a Dash or a Brown for short; a 5 MUT bill was a black Doberman Pincher — or a Pinch; a 10 MUT bill was a white poodle; a 20 was Blue and called a Pug. The silver MUT, was a picture of a Siberian Husky, worth 100 units of purchasing power.

Copper coins were called NUTs (Negligible Units of Transaction). NUTs were mostly used for vending machines and SWAY Subway tokens. If a person went NUTs-up, that was another way of saying they went broke. Harry wanted to avoid that at all costs, for that was tantamount to certain death. A person just couldn't live on the streets on this planet anymore, where the atmosphere burned everything to a crisp.

Harry needed to save all his MUTs and NUTs and get his own Posh-Matosh Playmate, with that milky-white, freckled, soft as kitten fur skin, so warm and inviting you'd never know it was purely synthetic. And, you'd never even care if it was real or not, because of all the love you could pour into it and receive back — one of the many guarantees listed in the brochures. What was love anyway? Wasn't most of it just so much deception and sleigh-of-hand and heart? A pressing need for sex?

As Harry was about to leave to the outer world his door began displaying a quick ad. It was the fat, ugly Sam Sturgeon standing in front of an army of beautiful women robots.

"Why the long face, Harry? Are you feeling down because all the really attractive women have been taken from your planet and sent to the luxurious, new, uncontaminated outer worlds? Even your sexy red-headed ex-wife? Cheer up! Chase those blues away! Gather your MUTs, anyway you can, and come on down to Sam's Wholesale Magical Mystery Mademoiselles today for your very own Posh Matosh Playmate. You can do with her and love her however you please. Sound good?

"Our double-your-MUT-back guarantee assures you that our shining new models will fulfill your every dream and transform your Go-Poddy into a Giggle-Factory, a Fun-filled Fantasy World. Your every sexual fantasy and desire will be met and exceeded! And now our models come with newer, more-life-like-than-ever skin that is even more pleasing to the touch — like it's been bathing in skin lotion for days on end!

"Imagine, Harry. Our line of Posh-Matosh Playmates comes in over 100 varieties and these life-like companions can be customized especially to your liking. Tall, fat, or short; blonde, brunette or redheads, you choose! We have a wide selection and no one has to know but you they are artificial. You're certain to fall head over heels for one of these beautiful lovers," Sam bragged within the ad.

Harry saw the freckled red-headed Tropical Veronica standing beside Sam, hand on her hip and bouncing ever so softly, seeming to look straight into his lost, weary soul. She was so gorgeous it took Harry's breath away. Harry had to have her, if he were to survive here another month. Without her the depths of his depression would surely put an end to him or cause him to do something rash.

The Veronica model had flaming red hair, similar to his ex-wife Emily's (that was a good selling point), a sassy grin, and big, misty green eyes, again, like his ex-wife Emily had, but slightly different. She also had a tall athletic build with long firm legs! He'd been dreaming of owning this model for well over a year now. Why was Harry so fixated on red heads? Did he secretly long for his ex-wife, and was unable to admit it to himself? Naw. That couldn't be it.

Anyway, Harry just hadn't been able to get all his MUTs together from his job at Teen-A-Watch. It was hard to save enough MUTs to bring that dazzling display of faux-feminity into his Go-Poddy. He had water and breathing air bills he had to pay. His electric bill was enormous, just to keep him cool enough to keep from frying his brain.

It was painful to see that beautiful booty-bot now, almost taunting him to come take her home with him. And Sam, the salesman, with that self-satisfied grin on his chubby face, like he owned all the happiness in the world right there in his shop.

And maybe he did. The advertisement on the door went fuzzy, which usually meant the network was being hacked, or the interconnecting electronics of his Go-Poddy were telling him to get off his big fat fantasy cloud and rush to work.

Suddenly, a message in big black letters read "Avoid the Void!" Then another message sprang up "Don't Buy the Fake!" and then another: "Never Settle For Metal! *These messages are brought to you by the E4E Church.*"

Just as quickly as those cryptic messages appeared they were gone and Harry wondered who or what organization would want to risk prison time with such stupid slogans. What do they even mean anyway, and why not say it plainly?

Harry had to really hustle to get to work now. That ad had distracted him from his regular routine. He picked up and fastened the chin strap to his round half-meter-wide titanium-alloy Atmospheric Light Deflector and Breathing Apparatus (ALDABA) securing it so it would remain on his head before he ran out into the harsh city environment. Only after properly securing it did he squeeze out of his Go-Poddy door and face the unforgiving elements.

The angry sun crashed down its menacing rays toward him like Thor shooting down lightning bolts. The cracked sidewalk sweltered under this constant heat. And it would get worse as the day went along, so he'd better pick up his heels to his workplace, where it was cooler and safe.

Harry made a mad dash in the 120 degree sun to get to the nearest super-subway (SWAY) entrance, hoping to survive the elements and arrive at work a little early. He wanted to make a good impression on his boss, and get in line for that promotion they had dangled under his nose for the last four months.

The SWAY was less than a block away. But ever since the upper atmosphere had become contaminated, and the ozone had become dangerously thin, it was extremely hazardous to spend more than just a few minutes outside without a well-maintained ALDABA.

The many citizens scurrying to the SWAY station, all with their ALDABAs on top of their heads, looked as if they wore steel umbrellas as they ran. Or, from another angle they might appear to be metallic mushrooms, sometimes clanging into one another in the hustle and bustle.

Even with an ALDABA on top of your head it was dangerous to walk in the open air. Poisonous vapors floated everywhere and this merciless heat could burn the skin right off you. The ultraviolet rays and the radiation were nothing to sneeze at either. In 30 minutes a person would be dead as a doornail outdoors, even if they were properly insulated.

All this was a result of the historic hanky-panky mistake in the Oval Office many decades ago. It's a rather humorous chapter of life on earth. It began when then President Mockingjay got over-excited while in the company of a young, gorgeous female page. (Don't all sad stories start with a rendezvous with a beautiful woman?)

But Mockingjay got horny-can't-wait-fever and perched that young page upon his desk. Who was she to resist the will of the President of the United States, she thought as she felt her panties being slipped off and presidential hands groping her every private part?

But because of those brief moments of presidential pleasure the whole world had to pay, in a big way. In a manner of speaking the President's lovemaking screwed everyone, not just that one lovely page. Harry chuckled remembering the circumstances that led up to the great conflagration. But no time for history lessons now.

Harry ran for the SWAY shelter, like a mouse scurrying from a mighty hawk, when all of a sudden he was knocked clean off his feet. Something heavy had hit him on the top of his protective ALDABA and smashed him to the hard cement, which burnt his hands.

As he fell on the hot sidewalk he tore his trousers and scratched his left knee. He jumped up quickly. His breathing apparatus became temporarily unattached and he breathed in a little of the poisonous air. He quickly re-adjusted his breathing apparatus to its proper place. He staggering a little, and looked around as if he was ready to fight off a potential mugger. There was no one around him.

"Oh hell," Harry cursed inside his breathing mask, trying

to regain his equilibrium to get out of the baking sun as soon as possible. Glancing down he noticed a large object lying nearby. It was a silver package-delivery drone, which had fallen from the sky and was now broken in several pieces. What appeared to be golden lipstick tubes were scattered about it. Harry scanned the ID number of the offending drone with his wrist phone, kicked at a large piece of it, and scampered quickly to the underground tunnel for the high-speed SWAY.

CHAPTER 2

BETTER HAVE IT CHECKED OUT!

People on the subway looked at Harry with sympathy, for he had torn his nice trousers and had a little blood showing there. Harry clicked in the ID number of the offending drone into his wrist phone. ID-Check said it belonged to Resurrection Cosmetic Company — makers of cosmetics that deliver new life to aging skin. His wrist watch researched the drone ID number and told Harry that this was an older model and had, indeed, missed its last scheduled maintenance check.

Harry, rather than getting mad, felt the thrill of victory. He figured he might have just won the lottery!

It's possible he had a lawsuit case on his hands! It would be a dropped-drone litigation case against the fabulously wealthy Resurrection Cosmetics. If he did have a case, which, he was pretty sure he did, then the MUTs awarded, or any settlement money, would be more than enough to purchase his very own customized Veronica Playmate!

Today had all the markings of the start of a very unpleasant day, what with his choking alarm clock, the ominous hack of his Go-Poddy door, and the knock on the head. But it all might just have a silver lining, he thought. Maybe when things look their worst they are about to change for the better.

"What happened to you, fella?" said a nearby commuter, eyeing him from across the aisle. Most people kept to themselves these days, lost in their own troubles, but this man had seen Harry commuting back and forth to work for many years now. Although they rarely spoke, it seemed they were acquainted.

"A worn-out cosmetics delivery drone fell on my head today," he explained, smiling to all who now turned to look at the two commuters engaged in rare conversation.

Someone who lived on the SWAYs and appeared to be a No-Go-Poddian, (a Homeless Person), approached Harry. "Can you spare me a couple of MUTs?"

"Huh?" asked Harry.

"Spare me a MUT. Give now and be rewarded later. I'm in a bit of a MUT-Rut, shall we say. Be a pal. Anything you can spare."

Feeling generous Harry gave him all the NUTs in his pocket and one brown Dash MUT. He hoped this would get the man to leave him alone.

"Thanks. I won't forget this! Wanna hear my sad story?" the MUT-begger continued, peering into Harry's wallet, and making the most of Harry's discomfort. "Some people wanna know how I wound up like this. OK, here goes then. I used to be a doctor, a medical doctor. That's right. I was an obstetrician and a damn good one at that. I delivered a lot of babies in my day.

"But I lost all my money in legal settlements because several couples weren't satisfied with the children I pulled out of their wives. You know how it is these days, it's always someone else's fault if a baby is ugly or sick or has the wrong color of eyes. Who do they turn to in their anger and frustration? They blamed the doctor for one thing or another! They sued me for everything I was worth! Now look at me!"

"That's too bad," said Harry, turning away.

"I agree with what they're saying about your injuries, you better get that wound looked at — the sooner the better. I'm a doctor so I should know," said the homeless baby doctor. "And I don't think you ought to be taking in any sex dolls. That's not good for your health. It's the lazy man's way out of loneliness. Make an effort, man. Clean yourself up. Improve your lot in life."

"Says you," Harry muttered.

"What's that?" asked the old doctor. "You don't know a thing about my life. Why I ought to..."

So Harry gave the man one more brown MUT and the man quieted down and confronted the next person. With his hand out and his hang-dog expression and his sad medical story he was sure to get a few more MUTs today on the morning commute.

"The nut-begging old doctor is right. Better have that injury looked at," piped up an old man in a respirator mask, wheezing as he talked. "Might have gotten poison in your bloodstream. These big companies and their delivery drones think they can save a few MUTs by bribing officials and not performing scheduled maintenance. So the burden falls on us! Literally! And what can we do about it? Huh?"

"I plan on having this looked at as soon as I report to work," Harry told them.

"Don't be foolish and put it off," said an elderly woman in her shaky, elderly deep voice. She looked to have had so much plastic surgery her face barely moved when she spoke. "That drone and its blades could have chopped you up like Chop-Suey! You think those big companies care about you or me? They don't care one little whit."

"You're right. It certainly could have been worse. I'm really thinking I should take them to court," said Harry to the crowd. "A big company like Resurrection Cosmetics can't have their old drones falling out of the sky all over the place and hitting people like me on the head. That's not right. I think I deserve considerable compensation."

"Here, here, yeah, right on," said many of the SWAY passengers.

"You certainly do," rasped the old man with the ventilator. "There's laws against letting drone maintenance lapse and just because you bribe someone not to report it doesn't exempt you from liability. File a grievance with the Citizen's Police. Find a good lawyer. Take a video of your injuries and give them all the details. You can probably do that on your Wrist

Communicator right now."

"They're watching us all the time," said the old man in the ventilator. "Better keep your voice down and watch what you say about Resurrection Cosmetics. A big company like them can nip this thing in the bud rather quickly, and you might be the one getting nipped. They could do it silently, secretly, and if they got caught, well, MUTs seem to gloss over every sin imaginable in this beat-up world. Us common people are nothing here, nothing at all. If you're somebody you're on Eros or one of the other exo-planet. Here big industry is in bed with big government, holding ugly hands, as together they choke the miserable little life there is left out of all us nobodys. We're just little playthings for their profit and amusement."

"Wrist Communicator," Harry eyed the old man and nodded, and with a look of keen determination, bent his elbow and addressed his wristwatch, "I'd like to file a grievance with the Citizen's Police Department concerning a possibly defective drone which fell out of the sky and injured me and my property. I don't know the exact nature of my injuries but I did tear my trousers and I received a flesh wound.

"My ALDABA has a dent in it which might need repair, and my blood and my breathing were exposed to the raw atmosphere. I'm feeling a bit light headed from the whole experience. It upset me terribly first thing this morning. I feel violated and seek redress."

"Please wait while we locate an experienced Citizen Drone Detective and put them on the line. Would you like to hold or would you prefer that we call you back?" said his wristwatch.

"I'll wait," Harry said forcefully. He patted his injured knee with a handkerchief from his pocket. Little red droplets of blood freckled his white hanky. He put a spot of blood on his watch for analysis and it said the pollutant-levels in his bloodstream were elevated, but not dangerously so.

"I won't die yet, but I can't have these poisons accumulating in my body," Harry mumbled, barely audible. "If this lawsuit runs afoul I still need to round up five more badges so I can be recognized at work, get a promotion and secure a raise. I need that so that I can buy my Posh-Matosh Playmate doll to live with me in my Go-Poddy."

"I got one of those Posh-Matosh Playmates at home," a fellow-traveler said to Harry. "They're everything they're cracked up to be. Tootie, that's the name I gave mine; fixes all my favorite foods; cleans my Go-Poddy spic-and-span and never misplaces any of my personal belongings. Plus she's great in the sack. She's given me a new lease on life. Of course my job still sucks, but at least I know at the end of the day I can come home and feel like I'm king of my own castle."

"Ever any problems?" Harry wanted to know. "I mean, like little glitches?"

"Rarely," said the man. "Sometimes if you want her to perform new skills, in the bedroom say, you have to buy proprietary chips and the Playmate has to process this new information. Don't buy cheap knock-off chips, friend. You'll be sorry if you do. I knew a guy who bought an off-brand sexual chip. Well, let's just say he never walked or pissed the same after that.

"The proprietary chips are fairly expensive," continued the man, "but you have to buy them. I wanted to update mine so I could have Tootie give me special deep-tissue back massages. That's all I wanted. Nothing too racy about that. That one update cost me nearly 500 cold, brown MUTs. At first Tootie dug her fingers a little too deep into me and it was painful. But, after adjustments and audio instruction, she eased up and man, she can really get to all my aches now."

"Gee, that is expensive. But you're satisfied, yes?" Harry asked.

"Well sure. Every upgrade is guaranteed and if I ever have any problem with my Posh-Matosh Playmate, there's a repairman who'll come to my house in no time flat and get her so she's up to speed again. If this fails to do the trick they offer an upgraded replacement at a fraction of the cost."

"That sounds reasonable," said Harry.

"It's an abomination," offered up a lady sitting two rows up from Harry, who decided to butt her big nose into the discussion. "It goes against everything the good Lord wants for us."

"Who asked you?" the man talking with Harry told the woman flatly. "What? Are you one of those E4E people?"

The woman was silent thereafter.

"She don't wanna say, but she probably does belong to that Earth Four Earthlings Church," said the man next to Harry. "It's a crime to admit it, so I guess I'd shut-up too."

"I'll never switch back to any of these real human women stragglers left on this planet — never," continued the booty-bot-owning man, staring a hole at the woman from E4E who finally turned with her head facing to the front. "But I may switch Booty-Bots soon. *Robotabella*, the hot and spicy Mexican robot company, which is in direct competition with Posh Matosh, as you may well know, has come out with this brand new line, but the cost of their improvements have practically driven the company into the ground and scrapping for NUTs. They may have to file for bankruptcy soon.

"Anyway, this brand new experimental Faux-Fem actually has a living alien bug inside her that you don't have to re-tool with new chips every time you want to upgrade. The little critter inside her is super intelligent and makes your bot more imaginative and socially interactive.

"These little ladies haven't been out long so they haven't worked out all the small details yet. They make you sign a contract that says you won't sue them in case something or other goes wrong. But for a limited time they're letting people obtain these experimental models on the cheap — hoping their business can stay afloat."

"What's the big advantage in having an alien inside your sex doll?" Harry asked.

"She's a real, living creature then, able to form genuine affection for you," said the man. "Don't you get it? A Faux-Fem can only fake it, although very convincingly in her Booty-Bot way, but one of these new Symbi-Sims has real emotions. She can really laugh, cry. Really get excited and form a deep romantic bond with the owner."

"Gee, I don't know. I like the idea of a completely submissive, non-feeling female. But I'll look into the Robotabella line, check to see if the price is right. I've been saving for such a long time and I really only have my eye on the red-headed Veronica model offered by Posh-Matosh. But I just can't ever seem to get enough MUTs saved..." Harry noted the desperation in his own voice as he spoke this.

"Booty-bot this, booty-bot that! Grown men, playing with dolls," grumbled an old man sitting nearby.

"They're not dolls," said Harry gruffly, somewhat offended.

"Yes they are," continued the old man. "So real women aren't good enough for you, and you turn to these fake things for comfort and God knows what else? Are you lonely? Do you gotta have your little dolls to calm you down during these hard times? You know there are plenty of lonely women left here on earth who need men. Why not grab one of them? No. You gotta have a personalized sex doll to play house with in your itty-bitty Go-Poddy."

"I still say they're not dolls," Harry said weakly.

CHAPTER 3

HARRY APPEARS WELL ENOUGH TO WORK

When Harry arrived at his downtown station, he placed his slightly dented ALDABA in the decontamination room, and was sucked into his workstation. From there he immediately went to the robo-nurse and asked to have his knee looked at. The boss, the rotund but bulldog-faced Randal Crabtree, came in while the robo-nurse was applying an antiseptic unguent and a band-aid to his wound.

"You gonna live?" asked the boss man.

"Employee 4922 will survive the skin laceration," said the robo-nurse. "His toxic intake was negligible but his injuries should be further monitored."

"We need you at your station as quickly as you're able," said Randal Crabtree, Harry's boss. "If you take the day off, it'll hurt our whole crew here. The government just issued a statement that they would be giving out extra MUT incentives for the discovery of delinquent-readjustment candidates. Seems a group in Washington is lobbying for tighter youth control. So what happened to you?" asked his boss, a short man with an inferiority complex, and a funny sideways limp to his walk.

"A drone fell on me," Harry told him. "Yes, I'll be fine. No need to take time off. I'll get back to work right away. Eager to get going today, sir, and earn some of that bonus money." As he spoke the robo-nurse had completed the dressing of his wound, was looking at his skull with her x-ray eyes and sewing up his trousers all at the same time.

"No concussion. A little bruise on the skull. I will apply a cold pack. You are clear to report to your work station," said the mechanical robo-nurse after she placed the cold pack on his head. "Would you like a pain shot?" Harry declined.

At his desk Harry looked at the monitor showing the ten male teens he was supposed to watch who might need correcting. Harry's place of employment - Teen-A-Watch - made and used security devises parents employed to know their children whereabouts, to monitor websites, and to keep track on any alternate realities their children entered. The government gave substantial tax breaks to parents who employed these unit. The government reasoned that if it cut down on youthful antisocial behavior, it would nip a lot of full-blown adult crime in the bud. Parents thought it was a good way to keep their child in line without all the bother of learning real parenting skills.

Harry was proud of his many badges of recognition for helping to detect and report teens on the verge of delinquency. He had 25 such No-Mo Bad Boy Badges displayed on his wall at home. Surely if he got just five more of these distinguished citations he could have good reason to ask for a MUT raise. He'd be justified, since very few employees ever achieved 30 Pre-Mal Badges with his length of service. Most burnt out or were scared away before achieving such a high water mark.

If a child was caught on the verge of misconduct they were re-educated to be more productive citizens in a fairly harmless manner. It was usually just a chemical imbalance brought on my bad nutrition and could easily be fixed. Other times these bad seeds had to undergo a sort of boot-camp for belligerence. It wasn't easy on them and it did radically change them — for the better — usually.

Of course some hard nuts just wouldn't crack and surgery was needed to repair the societal aberration in these teens. So there were at least three levels of correction available for the offending youth, depending upon the severity of his crimes, or proposed crimes. Best to get at the problem before it became a major issue, and that's where Teen-A-Watch, Inc. came in.

Harry felt a sudden flow of hope flow into his being. He had led a discouraging life, for the most part. But there was heavenly light shining at the end of the tunnel, what with the possibility of a pending lawsuit with Resurrection Cosmetics, for letting that stupid drone of their's fall on his head.

No more lonely nights in his little sad Go-Poddy. Soon he could have a companion to share his time with, a beautiful and exotic Faux-Fem of his dreams. What a life that would be, he thought. Intelligent conversation, someone to help with household chores, and most urgent, someone to help him with his constant ache for sexual release and companionship. Harry tried hard to transmute this nagging need with juggling. He had become quite good with his hands and keeping all the balls in the air, but it didn't compare to having a female handling his personal balls.

Real women were scarce in this day and age, at least women who were still fairly good looking and interested in forming relationships with men like Harry. Most women still left on earth preferred the companionship of other women or to just be left alone. They enjoyed the freedom of traveling and playing the field and being their own bosses. In these modern times women could self-fertilize with custom human embryos imported from the exo-planet Eros.

All the hard work, formerly done by men, could be completed by any inexpensive robot and an egg order. Men no longer made sense to most of the female population.

Anyway, Harry wasn't much interested in real women either. They required a lot of high maintenance. You had to listen to their constant nagging. There were their mood swings and all their snide comments. Real women wanted you to do certain chores to keep their love, always questioned your manhood, and you had to be constantly aware of and respond to their confusing kaleidoscope of emotions. Oh what a bother a real woman could be. What a big heaping bowl of bother.

CHAPTER 4

A MISBEHAVING TEEN FOUND

Harry pulled up the list of potential juvenile violators on his big screen and scanned the many wayward male faces. He zoomed in on a scowling teen, a 14-year-old boy named Warthog Merrick. This boy lived close to Harry, just a few Go-Poddy's away. Time to clean up my own neighborhood, thought Harry. This Warthog Merrick should be doing his school studies. Right now he should be studying conversational Spanish. Let me just check up on him.

Harry tried logging onto Warthog Merrick's computer to see what was going on. His advanced computer software allowed him to go in through a backdoor and see what this youngster was up to. Oh yes, this young Warthog had a sophisticated cover-screen that made it seem he was doing his schoolwork. He was bright, all right. Harry re-routed his search past this guardian screen and found Warthog Merrick, the 14-year-old, was actually looking at a video describing ways to rob a marijuana dispensary.

"Ah-ha! Got you, young Warthog!" exclaimed Harry and called over his supervisor, who confirmed the hit. They recorded their find and high-fived.

"Good job, Harry. Heard you had a little mishap this morning," said Carl, his excited supervisor. "Glad to see you're OK now and being productive on the job."

"Thanks. Will I get a badge for this today and a

governmental MUT bonus?" Harry asked.

"Well, here's the thing, Harry. Just received word from the top-level; we've adjusted the policy here at Teen-A-Watch, Inc. Our company has evolved into a competitive scheme and each floor is vying against the other. The Guardian Honor floor, that one which has the most hits in a week, will be awardee of the badge. We don't just randomly give out badges to individual workers like we used to, but we award them to whole floors and split the bonus money. We think it promotes teamwork and company success. But, think of it this way, you've put our team one up on all the rest of the floors, and you will get a small slice of any bonus money coming our way. Good work. The government and all of us here on Floor 34 are pleased by your superior efforts."

"That sucks. You know how hard it is to get through all the traps and passwords and actually catch a teen in or near his delinquency? Just to catch this one this morning was a stroke of luck and the result of the professional skill I've developed over many years. I mean, I show up to work, even though I got hit on the head by a defective drone, I scrape my knee, I tear my trousers, I catch a delinquent red-handed, and I don't get my badge or bonus money that should be all mine? What gives?"

"I'm sorry Harry, but that's our new policy," said Carl frowning and walking away.

"Well maybe I should just go work somewhere else then, SOMEWHERE THAT I'M APPRECIATED!" Harry said a little too loudly. Many fellow employees peeked over their cubicle partition to catch an admiring glance at Harry, who was somewhat legendary on this floor for catching potential juvenile offenders.

Just then Harry's Wrist Communicator vibrated and he answered it.

"Hello?"

"This is the Civilian's Police Department, I'm Drone Detective Danny. This conversation is being recorded so we can better meet your personal needs. Is that OK with you?"

"Sure. I have nothing to hide," said Harry.

"OK, so we've reviewed your case, gone over the recording of the offending drone you say dropped on you. We've become aware of your subsequent injury and scanned the ID marker of said drone. We've contacted the owners of the delivery drone, the Resurrection Cosmetic Company, 'Reviving Dead and Damaged Skin at the Heart of the Cell' (paid advertising, proceeds shared by all members of the Civilian Police Department). Resurrection Cosmetics is reaching out to quickly resolve this matter, as their good reputation is very important to them."

"I should think so," said Harry.

"Resurrection wishes to know what compensation, outside of actual monetary concerns, they can give you to ease your suffering. They are prepared to offer you something so that this whole ugly mess simply vanishes like an unwanted pimple, crow's feet around the eyes, or unwanted grey hair. A lifetime supply of wrinkle cream perhaps? A complete line of hair care rejuvenating products like the video stars use? They could make you look like a Million MUTs. Well? Can they resolve this for you today to your total and complete satisfaction? They did mention that if they cannot resolve this they may have to terminate you. You understand their position, surely. They have an image to uphold."

"I understand. I do not desire any of their cosmetics nor their hair products. My personal appearance doesn't concern me too much. What is important is this: I very much want a Posh-Matosh Playmate of my very own — and not a refurbished model," said Harry, without hesitation and without thinking what more he might get from a deal such as this. "I want a brand new Tropical Veronica model, please, with certain personal specifics I will outline when ordering. If I could get one of those delivered to my Go-Poddy soon I'm sure I could forget all about this little matter — you know, them dropping a drone on my head." Harry was talking with a wild urgency and intensity. "Oh, and tell them to please not terminate me."

"Let me throw that offer their way and I'll get back with you ASAP," said Drone Detective Danny, who also seemed to be serving as a mediator. "I'm sure they will ask you to solemnly affirm that you are satisfied with the results of my investigation and that the settlement herein agreed upon for one NEW Posh Matosh Playmate model Tropical Veronica (adjusted to your specifications), offered you, will be a permanent end to all further disputes, lawsuits, or other pejorative actions or written or verbal taunts, jokes, assaults or general bad publicity in any public forum (electronic or societal) against said Resurrection Cosmetic Company and all its affiliates. This will remain on your permanent record. Are you sure such a two-sided settlement would be agreeable to you?"

"Yes," said Harry. "Yes, yes, a thousand times yes."

"Please stay on the line as I contact Resurrection and we finalize the details."

Harry listened to some elevator music for several minutes.

"Sorry for the inconvenience," said DD Danny after a few minutes. "They've OK'd your request."

Harry cheered into his wrist phone and did a little leap of joy.

"You'll need to come down to the station soon to give us an eye-scan and a fingerprint to prove your identity, and take a few more tests to prove the veracity of your statements. Plus, you must fill out the appropriate paperwork. The sooner you can do all that, the sooner you'll be connected with your Posh Matosh Playmate. Can you swing by here after work today?"

"Sure. Yes, I could do that," Harry said, already savoring the moments alone he'd have with his new lifetime-guaranteed counterfeit companion.

Harry was singing to himself, smiling and talking with fellow office-mates, even offering to buy someone a lunch. He practically danced about his job all day, peeking in on prospective juveniles, all the while watching the clock like it was the latest exo-archeological news from some distant planet.

After work Harry took the first-available SWAY to the Citizen's Police Station. Inside he saw a young man with spiky hair arguing with the Citizen's Police.

Harry was told to wait in the office right across the hall from where they were questioning the juvenile. He left his dented ALDABA in the decontamination room.

"You bunch of dirty scumbags! I didn't do anything! What'd I do? I was at home studying! Working on my conversational Spanish," said the young man, who turned to look at Harry. "What are you looking at, you old geezer! Don't look at me," the boy said to Harry and gave him the finger.

Harry looked at himself in a two-way mirror. He wasn't that old yet. He was only 35. That's not old in today's society, where products like Resurrection Cosmetics and Extend-a-Youth Vitamins kept people looking healthy well into their 80s.

"Look at me young man," a matronly female Citizen's police officer said to the young man. "Ignore that gentleman next door. Sorry sir,"

"It's OK," Harry said.

"Listen, Mr. Wathog Merrick," she continued to Warthog, as a strong tall detective standing behind Warthog held his arms to keep him from swinging his fists. "You were caught red-handed. You know perfectly well what you were planning. It's all been recorded."

"You ain't got nothing on me," said the irate young man, his lower lip involuntarily twitching, as he tried to bang his head on the small table in front of him.

"Stop that. You stop that right now," said the female officer. "We're going to have to give you a psych evaluation on top of filing these charges."

"Wait'll my dad hears about this," Warthog growled. "When you gonna let me call him up so he can come down here and straighten your ass out but good?"

"After we finish with these preliminaries..." said the female officer.

Harry recognized the name Warthog Merrick from this

morning. Who could forget a name like that? He was the juvenile Harry had caught at his workplace, which won his floor a badge — a badge Harry still considered only his. What a coincidence — the predator and the prey be at the station, at the same time, right across the hall from each other.

"Hello. Are you Harry Novak of Teen-A-Watch, Inc.? I'm Drone Detective Danny. We spoke," the tall man walked in with a swagger.

"Yes, I remember," Harry said to DD Danny. "Here to fill out the appropriate forms. As you know a stupid drone fell on me and I received some personal injury."

"Yes. Yes. We've been expecting you. We have your paperwork right here," Danny said, putting a large folder on a table. "Make yourself comfortable. Please ignore the delinquent in the next room. He insists on causing trouble. And let me remind you, after you sign your agreement with Resurrection Cosmetics you are never to talk about your incident with their drone in a negative manner ever again. You must understand this, as it could result in dire consequences if you do. It's all part of your settlement."

"What should I say about it if someone asks?" Harry wanted to know, wishing to remain safely within his limits of the law and the terms set forth for obtaining his Posh Matosh Playmate.

"Resurrection Cosmetics will discuss that with you in the very near future," said DD Danny. "And Harry, don't discuss it on the SWAY or at Teen-A-Watch, Inc., your place of employment. Just say for now you're not at liberty to discuss the matter."

Across the hall Warthog perked up his ears when he overheard where Harry worked.

"I won't then," Harry agreed to be quiet about the drone falling incident.

"Want some coffee?" DD Danny asked.

"Yes, please," said Harry and DD Danny excused himself and went to another room.

"Wait a second! You're that Harry Novak, of Teen-A-

Watch, Inc.?" said Warthog, when the intimidating DD Danny left to fetch coffee. Harry didn't look at the boy. "You are, aren't you?" asked Warthog, now forming a hateful grimace on his face and spitting his words. "Look at me you jerk. What a stinking world this is where we spy on each other and turn on each other just for a MUT or two. I don't like it. Not one bit! Everything's turning to shit! It's becoming a fascist police state and my constitutional rights are being violated! And you violated my right to privacy, you and your stupid company — breaking into my personal computer and snooping around! I'll get you! I'll get you for this if it's the last thing I do!" Warthog seethed in his chair, trying to get up to run and do physical harm to Harry, but restrained by a Citizen's Policemen, who wrestled with the young man, and finally had to cuff him to his chair.

"No, I'm afraid I got you first," said Harry, answering the teen, feeling cocky once Warthog was dutifully restrained. "I'm keeping society safe, and you were trying to learn how to commit a crime — against a marijuana dispensary of all places. If I helped to save you from your future self and society, then I'm honored to have done my job properly, Mr. Warthog. And listen up, son, freedom isn't cheap. Freedom isn't just doing anything you want."

"Oh spare me, you big piece of crap. You're dead meat. I'll pay you back. Yes, I will; yes I will," warned Warthog as he was led away, possibly to some juvenile re-education facility for some level of correction to his behavior.

So Drone Detective Danny returned to the room with the coffee and stared as Warthog Merrick was being led away, shaking his head. "So many bad influences today. People care more about their things than they do about the upbringing of their own children...Wouldn't you say, Harry?"

"Yes. I suppose you're right."

"Ever wanted to have kids of your own, Harry?" asked DD Danny. "I mean, if you could. I know it's not for everybody."

"I don't think I want kids," said Harry, thinking about it.

"Well, let's get down to business then," said Danny.

Harry consented to an eye-scan, background check, DNA analysis, and fingerprint match. Harry just scanned all the legalese and filled every paper shoved his way. Harry then thanked Danny for his quick, hard work.

"One final signature right here." Harry signed a long form which he didn't carefully read but was sure was fine. If it would have gotten him his Booty Bot then he'd have even made a pact with the devil himself.

"You're all set then," said Drone Detective Danny, "I think we've resolved this situation and all parties concerned are happy. You should be receiving your Posh Matosh Playmate sometime this evening and Resurrection will be contacting you about your contractual obligations on what you can and cannot say about their corporation. Happy Pseudo-Honeymoon with your new partner. Hope you two hit it off. Sometimes I wish a drone would drop on my head so I could have something like that."

"Well, don't get discouraged. Your chances are pretty good with so many of them flying around overhead," said Harry. "Just hang in there and maybe one will fall on you too."

CHAPTER 5

NAMING HIS BEAUTIFUL BOOTY-BOT

A large box awaited Harry at his Go-Poddy door. He thrilled at the return label: Posh-Matosh Pure Love and Companionship Company Inc. out of New Madrid, Mexico. "That was fast," Harry thought, pleased as punch.

He pushed and slid the coffin-sized box into his Go-Poddy and threw off his ALDABA and foot and hand protectors. He ripped open the box with his bare hands and saw, for the first time, his very own Tropical Veronica model Booty-Bot, surrounded by styrofoam, wearing tight pink yoga pants and a yellow halter top. It was love at first sight. He ripped off the plastic and pulled her out. "Push Here," said a small sticker on her freckled belly button. Harry pushed the tanned stomach of the belly button. It felt so human he thought he would hear a giggle, but none came.

"Well hello there," said the sultry voice of his new Playmate, as she sat up suddenly and looked at Harry, crinkling and blinking her beautiful green eyes as she smiled. "I'm your brand new Tropical Veronica from Posh Matosh Playmates: makers of Hula Lula, Nordic Nora, Acapulco Anna and many other fine companions for the modern, sophisticated man. You must name me now. You may select any first name you wish and I will be known as such henceforth. After deciding on my name, press my bellybutton twice and say that name twice into my middle finger," said the beautiful robot.

Harry's fingers were sweating and he was ever so anxious. He thought to name the doll Emily, but that name might conjure up too much pain. He took hold of the Faux-Fem's middle finger, and remembering a childhood sweetheart who he had a crush on long ago, he pushed the bellybutton twice. His finger slipped. He said the name "Judy" into the booty-bot's bellybutton.

"Sorry. Didn't get that. Press the bellybutton first, two times, then say the name you have chosen into my middle finger. Say it clear and loud so there's no mistaking. This is the name I have to live with so get it right, bud."

"Sorry," said Harry.

So Harry did the procedure correctly the second time, drawing out the name Judy.

"OK. I am Judy. And you are Harry. Harry and Judy. Sounds nice together. Is it OK to call you Harry or would you like me to address you as Master or Your Highness?"

"Harry's great," said Harry, smiling in embarrassment at his new-found status.

"Do you have any immediate needs or wants you would like me to fulfill? I am at your service, day or night. I need very little sleep. I must stress to you now that proper maintenance is required. Please watch and review the entire instructional video and if you have questions there is a toll-free number. Customer service will gladly assist you."

"I'll watch that instructional video," said Harry, "after we talk some more." But Harry knew he'd never watch it. Those things were always such a bore.

"Also, before the multitudinous pleasures begins, I have been instructed to tell you that the Posh-Matosh Company has been experiencing a shortage of parts, due in part to the popularity of their high-end models.

"Recently the owners of Posh-Matosh Pure Love and Constant Contentment Inc. purchased rival Booty-Bot company, Robotabella, in an effort to meet those manufacturing needs and fulfill certain seller obligations. It's a long story. Anyway, I am the body of Tropical Veronica but I am equipped with Robotabella's newly acquired experimental bio-logic and emotional technology, which is, in fact, a small alien placed within the mainframe."

"So you're not what I ordered," said Harry.

"Not exactly, I suppose," said Judy. "I am speaking to you now as a live extremely small alien from deep inside this LEBOTECH machinery. Originally I was brought to this planet from a distant star system. So certain circuity in the Posh Matosh was replaced by me. One advantage I have is that I have a powerful imagination and a fine creative ability and can adjust over time to better serve the distinctive needs of my customer — you. I'm actually more than you ordered, much more."

"Say, this isn't what I was expecting, Judy," said Harry, curious more than anything. "Will this new bio-technology pose a problem in our companionship? I was hoping for a well-functioning robot which only pretended to be alive. I wanted all the pleasure and none of the hassle, like it offers in all of the advertising brochures."

"I am superior to the pure circuitry model Veronicas in many ways. I can form a genuine bond with you and I can have real feelings. I am much nearer to a real human female, but without all the volatility, and all her self-centered concerns. I don't think this should be a problem. I believe you will find me very much to your satisfaction."

"I was expecting so much less...I didn't want something so very similar to a REAL woman," said Harry. "Although I did want the feel, the warmth, the companionship."

"Why don't we try this: you keep me for a trial period of say, three months, and if at the end of that time period you aren't completely happy in every way, you can return me to Posh Matosh for the price of a mere restocking fee. At that point you can await a pure mechanical version of me when one becomes available? Does that sound equitable to you, Harry Novak?"

Harry reached for his juggling balls, which he always took up when he was at home and he became nervous or frustrated over any little thing. His already small living space seemed to close in on him as he sat, juggling and thinking. Tropical Veronica, who was now called Judy, waited for his response.

Do I take this new model, probably under-tested, which has an alien inside, who I don't figure to understand, or return her and await, what, months, years maybe for another? I'd better try her out first, thought Harry.

"I'm a little hungry. I didn't have a proper lunch…" Harry said as he tried to maintain four juggling balls in the air.

"So I assume that the agreement is to your liking," said Judy.

"We'll see," said Harry. "I sure like the way you look. Might not be too bad after all."

"I'm off to the kitchen then, to prepare you a nutritional meal. What would you desire?" she said, rummaging through his food inventory.

"Imitation steak, baked potato, Caesar salad, and corn on the cob," said Harry, smacking his lips.

"Please tell me your monetary credit number so I may purchase the requisite material to make such a meal," said Judy. "By the way, do you care for my clothing? Or would you like something more modest or sexier? There is a separate package in my crate with a few other outfits. How I dress will be your option."

"That dress is fine for now. My credit number is 4-4-4-4-4-1-2-3."

"I also need a DNA sample before I proceed," said Judy. "With that I might best obtain the proper foods to ensure your optimal health. Later I'd like to diagnosis your urine and obtain a stool sample. Would that be OK with you?"

"I guess," sighed Harry. So Harry caught his multi-colored balls and let Judy swab the inside of his mouth and place the swab inside a special container under her armpit. In a few moments she got the results she sought.

"Sorry, Harry, no imitation red meat for you tonight. We can substitute a nice fake fish, if you'd like."

"But I want my steak," Harry insisted, a little like a child complaining.

"Please understand. My job, as your Personal Playmate, is to see to all your needs, and to make sure you live an optimal life until the end of your days, at which time I too can terminate myself, or I can be assigned to another individual of your choosing.

"But steak," continued Judy, running a finger over Harry's furniture to check for dust, "even the imitation kind I've been told you're being fed, goes against one of these principles. You know you have a weakened heart by too much fat and not enough exercise, and I believe you still have some poisons in your system from this morning's exposure to the harsh out-of-doors when that drone dropped on your head. I want to use the food I prepare to cleanse your system and make you whole again. I'm sure you'll find it tasty and reinvigorating. This is for your own good, Harry."

"Fine. Give me the artificial fish then," said Harry, "but later tonight I'm gonna short your circuits in the bedroom."

"Why would you do that, Harry? I've only just arrived to begin my service to you. And besides, my circuitry is not able to be shorted because of its construction. If I were to short at a delicate time, it could cause you harm, so that risk has been eliminated."

"Kind of a joke, I guess," said Harry, realizing that robots with aliens living inside them have practically no knowledge of humor.

"I'll order your food and then we can explore your joke further," said Judy, a smile almost playing at the corner of her mouth.

"I'll have to be taught these human mannerisms as I am recently arrived on this planet. I was harvested just a year ago and have been waiting for my assignment ever since. The way I was raised I believe you are a sort of God to me. I will honor you as such and give you a life full of wonderful moments. Now that I've found you I'm sure I will be perfectly happy in your world, and I know, for a fact, I can make you the best version of yourself."

"A God, huh?" Harry liked the sound of that as Judy jiggled to the kitchen.

And so Harry did have an enjoyable evening with Judy, complete with a meal and later, a robust romp in the hay (so to speak).

CHAPTER 6

HARRY'S BEEN NIPPED

In the morning he felt as fresh and alive as if he were one of the first flowers blooming in spring. Of course there weren't many flowers anymore, except those which grew on cacti, or on hard-to-kill weeds, and those were mutated and sometimes ugly things.

On the SWAY going to work several people wanted to know how he was doing after his run-in with the drone and the Citizens Police.

"I now believe Resurrection Cosmetics is a very fine company," Harry said, to the astonishment of many listening. "Everyone makes mistakes and they do make human females more beautiful."

"You've been Nipped," said the old man who wore a ventilator. "They nipped the anger out of you, even after an obsolete drone hit you on the head. They paid for your silence. You've been nipped sure. Bought like a cheap slut to keep your legs open and your mouth shut."

"What's your problem," asked Harry?

"Nippee. You're a nippee now that you've been nipped," grunted the old man and turned away from Harry, but still muttering to himself. "Got yourself a fancy inflatable doll and your tally-whacker unwound and you think you're better than all the rest of us mate-less males."

"It's not inflatable, sir," said Harry, offended. "And I never said I was better..."

"New-fangled sex toys, ruining our country," the old man's voice rose, "drones dropping out of the sky on us during Venting. Why, in my day we had to make love to real women or do without, and we could say what we pleased about dangerous things in our environment."

What's he so worked up about? thought Harry. *I got what I wanted. I can be a nippee if I want. What's it to that old man anyway if I'm a nip or a nippee, or if I have a sex doll and do all kinds of crazy things in the privacy of my own home? I am master of my own fate, captain of my ship, even a God of sorts to my Booty-Bot.*

At his job there were lots of questions from the men in Harry's work area.

"How'd you like your new plastic wife? Does she stick to your skin after sex like a leather sofa in hot weather? Do you have to peel her off of you like banana skin?"

"You guys never had sex with a really fine Posh Matosh Playmate before?" asked Harry, looking around at their sadly shaking heads. "Well, it's better than the real thing, and certainly better than those heaps of junk at the Botty-Brothels in old Brewtown. There is no stickiness except the good kind. But I didn't get the exact model I requested. I got an experimental model with a small alien inside."

"How small is the alien? Did you see the alien? Where was it from? Does it hate all earthlings? Does it pose a danger to our world?" asked many.

"I'll find out more as we go along and I'll tell you all about it. Right now let's get to work and be productive and catch juveniles in the act. If this floor does well maybe some of you lonely bums can get your own Tropical Veronicas!" Harry said, prompting his team members to charge into their daily Quest for Societal Justice.

All the men in the office pounced on their computers with new-found zeal and proceeded to find juvenile criminals, or potential renegades.

"Well said, Harry," said Mr. Crabtree, his boss. "Maybe

that drone dropping on your head was the best thing that ever happened to you."

A little after lunch Harry Novak's videophone rang. The image of Warthog Merrick appeared on his screen. He was standing next to Harry's new plaything — Judy, the Veronica model Posh Matosh Playmate, with one arm around her neck and the other holding a long knife in his hand.

"You like this fake female crap? Not man enough for the real thing, huh?" taunted Warthog, smiling an evil grin at Harry. "I told you I'd get even with you for turning me in. No one screws with Warthog Merrick. No one."

"How'd you get into my Go-Poddy? Let go of my Judy!" said a panicked Harry.

"You don't deserve her," said Warthog playing the knife around Judy's neck and drawing a little synthetic green blood.

"No!" shouted Harry. "Leave her alone! I just got her. Mine! Don't touch!"

"I'm going to open this thing up wide, see what's inside, maybe take a few of the good electronics for my gaming system. After that she'll be no good to you — no good to anyone. She'll be just another pile of waste that needs recycling," said Warthog.

"How'd you get out of juvenile detention and why are you doing this?"

"My father was recently made stinking rich in the lottery and we're about to relocate to one of the far wonder worlds. My dad is a former Citizen Policeman himself. He made a few calls here and there, greased a few palms, and poof! No more charges against me. How do you like that," asked Warthog?

"And as to why I'm doing this, I think you know. I said I'd pay you back. You can report me again and maybe get yourself another one of these stupid badges you have here on your wall, but I've got permanent immunity now. The method you used to spy on me was deemed illegal, a technical glitch. This might be the downfall of your whole company. Anyway, I'm going to look inside your booty bot now. So long sucker. Oh, one last thing before I amuse myself. It's about the way you watch us teens.

Well, we can watch you too. Bet you didn't know that."

At those words the screen went blank and Harry's face lost all color.

"I gotta get home and stop that crazed kid," thought Harry.

Harry told Mr. Crabtree he had an emergency at home and had to take personal time. The boss smiled to himself, thinking he knew what the jig was. It had to be about Harry looking for extra time with his new playmate. "OK, Harry, you can take the rest of the day off, but you report in bright and bushy tailed tomorrow," said his boss, with a slight giggle.

Just hope I'm not too late. I have to save Judy, not to mention I have to stop these crimes of destruction of private property, breaking and entering, and violence toward a semi-living being. I'm sure if I can catch this Warthog red-handed I'll get another badge and then this Warthog will be locked up for a long, long time, regardless of the technicalities or how much pull or how sharp of teeth his father's MUTs have.

Harry got to his Go-Poddy and saw the door had been jimmied. Harry had called the Citizen's Police but they didn't seem too interested. Until an actual crime had been perpetrated they could do nothing. Also, it seemed crimes against Robots didn't constitute a high priority for them. Harry took off his ALDABA unit, when he got home from rushing from the SWAY, and squeezed into his Go-Poddy. Judy was standing there crying, and young Warthog was lying on the floor in a pool of his own blood.

"What did I do? What did I do? What are we going to do, Harry," asked Judy sobbing? "He was trying to hurt me. I tried to stop him without injuring him, but he just kept damaging me, so I accidentally pushed him too hard and he fell and hit his head on the steel Go-Poddy table. I'm afraid of what might become of us now. What are we going to do now, Harry? What?"

Harry remembered the first Asimov rules for robots: A robot may not injure a human being or, through inaction, allow a human being to come to harm. Did that apply here, and did Judy violate a robotic law? That could be grounds for termination and Harry didn't want to see that. He was just getting to know his new Posh Matosh Veronica Model, built to his personal specifications.

But this was a new hybrid model faux-fem, part robot, part microscopic alien or aliens - Harry didn't know how many lived inside his Judy. So did those rigid robotic laws even apply here? How would a court see it? Surely they'd see it was a case of self-defense. But whose side would the courts take? It was an alien killing a human being. That wouldn't look good. Plus he was only a juvenile, even if he was a bad, bad boy and got what he deserved. Lawyers would surely paint a different picture and the jury would sympathize with a human over an alien creature locked in a booty bot.

Maybe the courts would find Harry responsible for his violent robot. There have been cases where that has been true. It was his property, after all, so he was responsible, just like the falling drone was the Resurrection Cosmetics Company's responsibility.

In his mind Harry thought it would be better if he and Judy could somehow dispose of the young body and make this whole thing disappear rather than go through the dreaded legal system. It might save a lot of trouble on down the road.

"I know what you're thinking and I believe we could do that," said Judy, drying her tears and clasping her arms in Harry's. "We can't let them drag us apart. We just can't, Harry. We have to do whatever we can to stay together!"

"You're right, Judy. What can we do? How do we make this all better?"

"I've got an idea, but it would mean I'd have to shut down this Judy unit for a while," said Judy.

"What do you mean?"

"They have video surveillance of Warthog entering your Go-Poddy. There has to be video of him leaving too. We have to clean up all the blood, stitch his wounds, wash his clothes and make it appear he left your premises in good condition."

"He's gone! He's dead, Judy!"

CHAPTER 7

GETTING RID OF THE BODY

"If I can animate a robot surely I can animate a recently deceased human being," thought Judy the Booty-Bot. "It's just a matter of pulling the right levers and switches, sending out the right electronic impulses. My rules are such that I am not supposed to leave this robotic body. But in this special instance I feel I'm justified, so as to maintain contractual obligations to both the Posh-Matosh Pure Love and Constant Contentment Inc., to Resurrection Cosmetics, and to you — the purchaser, and the agreement my home planet has made with your's concerning the conditions of my peoples residence here on this planet. I will go into Warthog's body and walk it out of here."

"You can do that?" Harry asked.

"Yes, but you shouldn't be here at the time. You meet me later, after I've staged his suicide," said Judy.

"So what about the Posh Matosh Playmate body?"

"It will lie dormant for a time," said Judy. "Good thing they don't monitor the inside of houses anymore. But once outside they'll be tracking me, as I am in Warthog Merrick's body, pretty strictly."

So Harry went to the ice cream store and waited for Judy's call. He had to lick his ice cream fast, as this hot weather melted everything quickly.

Back at Harry's Go-Poddy Judy, or the microbial alien

which animated Judy, left the robotic body and entered into Warthog Merrick. He bounced up off the floor like a marionette. Judy knew she had to move fast.

She found Warthog's ALDABA, strapped it on, and raced out of doors. She ran to the SWAY station and called Harry. "Meet me at the 42nd and California Street SWAY station," said Judy into Warthog's wrist communicator.

So Harry rushed to find the place of meeting. As he entered the station area, with its long rows of plastic chairs and it's guard rails and Subway turnstiles he saw Warthog. He was acting out of control so everyone would notice.

"The President's a fink!" yelled Warthog. "This whole stinking world is a cesspool! Why can't any of you lazy flesh-pots clean it up? Why'd you have to fuck it up? It's a hell of a fine mess you shitheads have gotten us into, on this dying planet. What's a kid supposed to do when he has no future?"

"Now calm down there, son," said a uniformed Citizen Policeman, "don't do anything rash."

With his eyes Warthog, with Judy inside him, signaled for Harry to come closer. The Super-fast Subway Train was fast approaching. This one wasn't slowing down to stop at this station. Harry moved closer to Warthog.

"Rash! Rash! How's this for rash!" and young Warthog jumped out in front of the swiftly moving subway and was carried about two miles down the line before his body fell to one side of the tracks, smashed to smithereens. It was later retrieved but at the moment of initial impact Judy, inside of the young Warthog, had leapt out of that young boy's body and into the body of Harry.

Harry felt the new presence inside him.

"Hi, Harry, I'm inside of you now," said Judy. "I'm in your left ear."

"I thought you were a goner," said Harry, glad that the animator of his Judy doll was OK. "Let's get you back home and into your regular body."

"It's nice in here with you," said Judy. "I can explore all

your thoughts and dreams and hopes and disappointments — all your memories."

"Don't get too cozy in here. You got a date with your own self's body," said Harry.

"You aren't an Umby, are you?" asked Judy. An umby was a natural born child once united with his mother by an umbilical cord. "You're a Petri."

"Yes. So?"

"So you have no earth connection, really, except that you're here. You're test tube formed, with recombinant DNA. I see you did have surrogate parents. And they were pretty nice to you, indulged you a lot. But you were mean to them, resented them in fact. You rejected their love ever since you found out they weren't your real parents. You felt like a loner and the other school children made fun of you since you weren't an Umby. Many of those other kids weren't either, but they kept it to themselves to dodge the ridicule. You didn't. Somehow your situation leaked out."

"They gave me a lot of trouble. That was a hard time in my life," Harry said, thinking back while getting on the SWAY which would take him back home. "I went into a fantasy holographic world everyday when I got home from school, ignoring my parents, living with wizards and elves and orcs inside Fantasy World 12663. That's where I grew up, on the backstreets of my pretend world. And maybe I overstayed my time on these make-believe worlds. Probably the reason my wife Emily left me. I didn't pay enough attention to her needs and such. Never took her on vacations like she wanted."

"So you've never had real feelings about anything, even your wife. You were just going through the motions. Everything in your life has been manufactured, reproduced or thrust upon you. Even me. In a sense, you no longer know what real even is, or if your desire to own me came from your own thoughts or those cloud and door ads which constantly invade your mind.

"I could show you what real living and real desires are, Harry. I could take you to my world and show you things you couldn't possibly conceive of here, things like a nice environment, living space for everyone, joyful existence. I will show you, if you will allow me, in the course of our companionship. I don't want you to leave me, Harry. Will you ever trade me in for a newer model? Will you ever tire of me, Harry?"

"I dunno," Harry said to Judy inside his left ear. "But I'm happy right now — worried and a little upset by recent events, but happy you found a solution to our problem."

CHAPTER 8

ANGER ISSUES AT HIS DOOR

Back at Harry Novak's Government Provided Go-Poddy Harry sat down beside the inert Judy Posh Matosh doll, with its mouth hanging wide open like some passed-out drunk, and the back of its pink mouth exposed. Inside Harry, Judy, the microbial-sized intelligent alien, scrambled to get out of Harry's left ear and back into her assigned fake body. She wanted to get back in there and get at the controls, hoping no one had noticed her temporary absence.

"Already I miss that feeling of intimacy when I was inside of you," said Judy to Harry, the head of her Veronica-model Playmate body suddenly becoming animated, as she stretched and yawned and shook out all the kinks. "It was weird and wonderful in your ear, learning about all your frustrations, all your hopes and dreams. It was a sacred commingling I have never felt with another living being. For me it was far better than sex, which is only flesh-driven and superficial. May we do it again sometime?"

"I have the rest of the day off, Judy. It's been quite a day, witnessing poor Warthog smashed by the SWAY and you barely able to escape, then sharing my innermost secret world with you. I think I want to rest now. Yes, maybe I will allow you to enter into me again at some future date. But right now I feel drained and need some alone time to regroup and try to quell my nagging conscience."

"Conscience?" asked Judy. "You feel bad about this whole thing?"

"Yes, Judy, I do. You know you are the woman of my dreams, don't you? I've waited for such a long, long time to have you in my life. I've always wanted a woman of my own. My ex-wife Emily, she was never really mine. She was assigned to me and we were supposed to muddle through this life as best we could. But I could never please her and she constantly complained. Maybe I didn't try hard enough, or didn't possess the necessary tools to make that marriage work. Will you ever complain like that?"

"Never, Harry. I'm grateful to be here. I'm thankful every moment that I am paired with you," said Judy, flexing and unflexing her right hand to get the feeling back in it. "Back to that conscience you mentioned..."

"I've heard some Posh Matosh models give back rubs, if the proper proprietary chip is purchased. Can you give me a back rub, Judy? It would really help."

"Sure. Go take off your shirt and lie down and make yourself comfortable."

As Judy massaged Harry's back she suddenly stopped.

"What is it, Judy? Don't stop. It feels so good," Harry purred.

"I know what conscience is now. I just had a sudden pang of it myself, or something similar invading my spirit," said Judy. "This is very uncomfortable."

"You mean the incident concerning Warthog?"

"Yes. I know now that I'm responsible for his death," Judy started to cry as she spoke. "He was just a child. In a way I killed him twice, once here at our Go-Poddy and another time at the SWAY station. Maybe I should have stayed in Warthog's body and gone back with him to his home to say a final good-bye to his parents."

"It wasn't your fault, Judy. He was getting back at me, by trying to hurt you — for what I did," Harry put his shirt back on, buttoning it, sensing his back rub was over. "I turned him in because he was planning on robbing a marijuana dispensary. But he had committed other crimes prior to that and was on a downward spiral. He'd been in trouble in school and home. He was progressively planning worse and worse crimes. And finally he was about to commit cyborgcide. You were just protecting yourself and our companionship. That's all. It is a tragedy, though. Don't blame yourself, Judy."

"I do blame myself and I feel bad," said Judy. "I need to talk with someone about this gnawing need for redemption. I need my teacher."

"Your teacher?"

"Yes. I had a very wise teacher on my home planet," explained Judy. "Taught me many things: how to live like a human, how to experience love and sorrow, ways to provide loving kindness, how to meditate, how to reach higher planes of existence, stuff like that."

"So what do you want to do, Judy?"

"I have to go into my astral body and summon her here and hope she comes," said Judy. "But there are certain drawbacks. She'd be coming uninvited by the Posh-Matosh Pure Love and Constant Contentment Inc. or any earthly affiliate. She'd be an illegal alien and I'll have to hide her and keep her presence a secret. But I need her here, Harry. I really, really need her!"

Harry sat up now and looked at Judy, big green tears still falling from those emerald eyes. He stroked her long red hair and tried to console her.

"I don't know how you can do that, but if that's what has to be done to make you happy again, then I suggest you do it," said Harry. "Maybe she can help me too."

"I'll go into a deep meditative state," said Judy. "It might take a couple of days. I know I just met you and we haven't had much time together, but if you could give me these two or three days to make contact in my out-of-body, inter-planetary mission, get my teacher, and bring her back with me, then I would be so terribly grateful."

"So what do I do with your body in the meantime?" Harry

wanted to know. "I mean, I can't just have an inert Booty Bot lying around my house, now, can I? Someone might think I'm a weirdo and report me. I never knew owning a Playmate would be so complicated. Can you wait just a few days before you go?"

"This guilt is eating me up, Harry. It's not like I stole a cookie or something. OK. I will stay just a little while if you will allow me to go. That poor boy's parents must be devastated. What's the news saying?"

So Harry turned on the Holographic News station by swiping down his nose with his finger. Harry asked the Holo to play any recent stories on teen-age suicides in his hometown.

"Finding recent stories. I found one on a Warthog Merrick. Shall I play it?" asked the holographic machine.

"Yes, Holo, play that story," said Harry.

The image of female newscaster Sycamore Storylore appeared in front of the sofa Harry and Judy were sitting on. She was a dark, exotic real human female (or so everyone believed) who delivered the twice daily local news from some unknown location.

"The body of a former Citizen's Policeman's son was found approximately two miles from the 42nd and California SWAY Station. It appears the boy, one Warthog Merrick, 15 years of age, threw himself into the way of an oncoming train. He was visibly upset with the situation on this world and voiced it to the station crowd. We have footage just before he jumped. Warning: the graphic nature of this Holo about to be shown, and the words of the young boy concerning this world, can prove upsetting to the elderly, the young, the mentally compromised, and anyone else easily distressed. Please keep your anti-depression compressor close to the back of your neck if you choose to watch this recent ugly incident unfold."

While Sycamore Storylore spoke, the Holographic image split. A second image to her right showed the scene at the SWAY Subway Station where Warthog was ranting and raving, then jumping in front of a moving train. People in that Holo were gasping and shouting. A very quick clip caught Harry's scurrying form in the midst of the madness.

"That's me!" shouted Harry at Judy. "That's my overcoat and my dented ALDABA. I'm on the Holo News!"

"Maybe no one will recognize you," said Judy. "It's just a quick shot."

"No, that big drone dent tags me," said Harry, searching on and under the sofa cushions for his juggling balls but not finding them.

"The father of the boy, George Merrick," continued Sycamore, "is a recent winner of the Humpter Energy Drink Lottery, making him a Grand Platinum Pomeranian Muttonaire. With his newly acquired wealth he has since retired from his job as a Citizens Policeman. Immediate future plans included taking his son and wife to one of the outer pristine worlds. We have with us now the bereaved father who insisted on speaking about his son's demise."

A video of the father appeared in the holographic tube. George Merrick was a big, mean-looking, unattractive man. Physically strong, as if he could be a bouncer or a bodyguard. He was looking at some notes as he spoke and Sycamore looked small beside him, but she remained in the hologram shot because everyone always wanted to watch Sycamore and her newscasts. They talked about how she dressed, what color her hair was that day and everything.

"As many of you can easily imagine, this is not easy time for me and my family," began George Merrick. "It's extremely hurtful..." George started to break down, but caught himself and took a moment to regain his composure.

Sycamore made sympathetic gestures with her face and body as George spoke.

"Sycamore Storylore sure is a natural beauty," said Judy, studying the Holo.

"Shhh. Lemme hear what Warthog's father has to say," said Harry.

"Seeing that video of my son's last minutes, and how upset he appeared... It seemed so out of character. I myself am a former Citizen's Policeman, and I just can't believe my son would make such a public display of his outrage about this world. He was more of a secretive, loner type person. He wasn't perfect but he didn't deserve to die. My son was a fighter, a survivor, and for him to just throw his life away like that... I plan on conducting my own private investigation into this whole incident and I will postpone my trip to the outer worlds. If I have to use every MUT I have I'll get to the bottom of this. I won't stop until I am satisfied that I know the whole truth here, however messy that knowledge might be."

"Uh-oh," said Harry. "He wants the whole truth."

"If you have any information about this matter, please contact me ASAP," said George Merrick, the Holographic image in front of Harry and Judy. "I believe Teen-A-Watch Inc. is partially responsible, as they are the ones who turned my son in with their flimsy evidence. My son was understandably upset about this, and maybe a few other things, but not so upset he'd kill himself! I intend to dig into this."

"In other news..." continued Sycamore Storylore, adjusting the hem of her short skirt.

Harry turned off the Holo machine by making an X across his own nose.

"Oh shoot!" said Harry. "They're gonna finger me!"

"Stay calm," said Judy.

"I was just doing my job!" Harry screamed.

"You should be a little more quiet," said Judy. "The neighbors might be listening."

"Yes. You're right," whispered Harry. "Someone might be monitoring my reaction now that the news is out and I've been identified as a possible suspect."

A knock came to Harry's Go-Poddy and with a look of panic he eyed Judy as if she could provide some answer as to what he should do next.

"See who it is. Hurry! You know it's illegal to keep anyone waiting on your door in this environment. Invite them in quick!" said Judy.

So Harry went to the door and saw a tall, big man with a bald head and a scowl upon his face, underneath his ALDABA.

"What are you hiding? Why did you take so long to answer my knock," asked the man at the door? "I'm George Merrick, father of Warthog. Let me inside now."

So Harry let George into his Go-Poddy and Judy stood behind Harry watching.

"I have some questions," said George, looking around Harry's Go-Poddy and giving Judy the once over.

"Have a seat," Harry said, pointing to his sofa and trying to be amiable.

"You are the one, aren't you?" asked George Merrick, as he sat down.

"Yes, but I was only doing my job," said Harry. "You see..."

"And you probably got some stupid badge of honor for it."

"Our floor did get a badge. They changed everything up on us," said Harry. "I'm so sorry about what happened to your son, George, is it?"

"Yeah, George. This your wife? A Booty Bot?" asked George, as Judy sat there quietly.

"How'd you know," asked Harry?

"Too fetching to be human. Most of the really attractive fems are gone to other worlds now or are with powerful people here on earth and you appear pretty insignificant to have such a beautiful mate. My wife left me too. I got a Booty Bot at home. Maybe that's why young Warthog was always acting out. He somehow blames me for his mother leaving us to go to interplanetary paradise. But what does that matter now? She's gone. He's gone. All I got left is my Wifi-Wife — her and a shitload of GGR (Grief, Guilt and Rage). And my rage and resentment is directly squarely at you, Harry, and at Teen-A-Watch. But mostly at you! So first I'll probably go home and kill my own Booty Bot, just to release my pent-up anger, then I'll think of a way to get at you."

"What can I do to make it better?" Harry asked. "Would you like something to drink?"

"There's nothing you can do to make this better. He wasn't always a rebellious boy. You can't imagine how much I loved that guy. You can't. OK, I'll take a drink."

"Water," asked Judy, "coffee, tea?"

"Water," said George simply as Judy went to get it.

"I want to choke the life out of you," George said to Harry, choking a sofa pillow.

"What good would that do?" Harry cleared his throat as he said that.

"I'd like to punch you in the face a thousand times until your face is all bent in and bloody," said George, punching the throw pillow now.

"I'm sensing anger," said Harry, a master at reading body language.

"Here's that water," said Judy, bringing in a special fancy bottle.

"Real water? Let me sniff," George took a whiff of the open bottle.

"I was saving it for a special occasion," said Harry, who, like most people, usually drank distilled piss that ran through the Go-Poddy's system of inter-connected hexagon-framed charcoal units until purified to potability. "It's 1990 Icelandic-Blue."

"It's good," said George. "Real good. Been a while since I had nice, fresh water." George finished the water and set down the bottle. "Almost forgot what it tasted like. Where was I?"

"You were troubling my sofa throw-pillow," said Harry.

"Oh yeah. I'd like to stab you until I can see the other side of the room through you," said George, making stabbing motions with his hands into that same pillow.

"You say you have a Booty Bot too? What model?" asked Harry.

"If I could twist your head off and throw it across this room like a fishbowl, I'd like to do that, too. My bot is the Alluring Southern tanned American girl from the 1970s model called Suzanna, since you asked. I call her Susie. But I'm going to tear her apart when I get home."

"That's a nice model, and a nice name you have chosen for her," said Harry. "Isn't it against the law to destroy your own robot that way, with so many in need and the potential for hazardous materials escaping?"

"That's none of your concern, buddy," said George. "Or I could program her to come here and destroy you and your Booty-Bot, then I would be justified in killing my own bot. I could claim I had lost all control of her."

"Or, maybe our Bot mates could get to know each other, go shopping together, host a poker party for us boys, or share Sim-sex-secrets," said Harry, trying to remain amiable, amidst all this hate being directed toward him and his Judy and now this unknown bot too.

"I could make a bomb and place it in your Go-Poddy and blow you up," said George, still hashing out his feelings and staring that wild stare at Harry. "Little pieces of you would go spurting up into the polluted air and rain down all red and mangled on everyone's ALDABAs. Yeah, I like that image floating in my head."

"Well, this has been a nice talk," said Harry, trying to interrupt this unending train of violent talk. "It's almost supper time. Would you like to stay and eat with us? What are we having Judy?"

"Seaweed salad and mushroom soup, fried tofu and imitation pork," said Judy.

"That sounds good," said George, looking a bit lost and confused, "but I'd want to slip poison in the soup and kill all three of us, so I better get going now."

"Well, come again sometime. You're always welcome at my Go-Poddy," said Harry, "and again I want to say how sorry I am about what happened to your son. I was just doing my job and sometimes, finding and correcting the problem early prevents it from getting much worse and actually proves a benefit to the youngster, the whole family unit, and all of society. But maybe it didn't work out so good this time..."

"If I come here again I will first wreak havoc on your precious Bot, then skin you alive with a sharp hunter's knife and pour salt onto your exposed organs," said George. "And I'll eat your bloody flesh while you're still alive! Beware. This is not a warning, it's just the way things are now between me and you. Oh, and thanks for the sweet water."

"Anytime," said Harry. "Use caution rushing to the SWAY Station. Here's a red MUT for the ride back home. It's the least I can do."

"Huh," said George, grabbing the red 5 MUT bill, putting his ALDABA on and opening the door. "In any other circumstance I could have liked you, Harry Novak, but as things are now I'll always want to cut your heart out, like you cut out mine. I won't kill you today, here in your own Go-Poddy, comfortable with your Booty-Bot, but I'll bide my time and let your natural fear sink in. Good-bye and thanks again."

So George Merrick was out the door rushing toward the SWAY entrance.

Harry closed the door quickly and sat down in his favorite chair and grabbed a book and his reading glasses. His hands were shaking and the book wouldn't be still. Judy went to the kitchen to prepare dinner.

"Let's finish that massage later, Judy."

From the kitchen Judy said, "He seemed like a nice enough man."

"Yes. He was very charming except for that fixation he had on killing me.

"I'm worried for his Susie," talking above a blender in the kitchen. "Perhaps we should try to…" she turned the blender off to punctuate her next words, "rescue her. Say. If we had her here, safe from George, it could be the perfect hiding place for my teacher." She turned the blender back on.

"I'm not sure I want to be rescuing any robots from that madman," shouted Harry. "Please Judy…"

"Well think about it," said Judy, now mixing something in a bowl. "If we could pull it off you'd be a two Booty-Bot man, then and Susie Q and I could keep each other company while you're off working at Teen-A-Watch, or avoiding the wrath of Mr. Merrick. And you could live a life of double wonder."

"I'll think about it," said Harry, smiling briefly at the thought.

"I think George just needed someone to talk to about his feelings," said Judy. "He's going through a lot right now."

"It's probably not unusual for a man to feel that way. I can almost understand, with him losing a child like that. You need to blame someone or something. He might have thoughts of killing himself after he kills his Booty-Bot, when he realizes he was mostly at fault for raising his son in the manner he did, and not catching this whole thing sooner. But he might try to take us with him. Honey, can you bring me one of those special waters?"

Judy brought him a real water. "Go easy with these. Only a couple of them left. Dinner is almost ready. Maybe my teacher can help George too, if I can get her here in time."

"Whatever you think, dear," said Harry, sipping his water, dribbling some on his face with those still-shaking hands. He re-read the same sentence in his book over and over again, trying to make sense of it. It read: "she gazed out through her pearly teeth at the farm-raised lobster which grappled with the moon."

CHAPTER 9

HARRY IS DISCOVERED

The next day Harry was waiting in his SWAY station for his train to go to work. His neck tickled and he felt strangely odd, as if someone was watching him. He turned around and saw three young people standing on the Subway floor studying him.

"There he is," one blue-haired teen girl said to a tall wild-haired youth and his shorter, bald companion.

"He sees us," said the bald one.

"Who cares. He's the one who made Warthog kill himself," said the wild haired one. "I hate his nosy, prying guts."

"Hey, old man!" the long hair shouted at Harry. "Yeah, you, with the stupid glasses..."

"What do you want?" Harry asked, as politely as he could.

"We know you. You're the Teen-A-Watch snitch, aren't you?" asked long hair.

"That's where I work, yes," Harry answered.

"And you're proud of it?" asked the bald one.

"Sure. Why not? Why don't you think about doing something productive with your lives," asked Harry?

"You killed our Crapper friend Warthog," said blue hair. "He was on our team and our leader."

A Crapper was short for someone who was on the CRAP (Cyberspace-Recreational-Algorithmic-Partners). These were like-minded gamers who got together in social circles to try to beat each other down in the Holographic Internet.

"Spy! Snitch!" said long hair. "What'd he ever do to you?"

"Yeah, you're a monster with no feelings," said baldie.

"Why don't you go throw yourself in front of a train? Your life is so pathetic," said blue hair.

Harry's train finally came, and for a moment he did consider throwing his own life away. It would be simpler than living in this messed up world, with young people hating him, a mad father wanting to kill him, and a robot that wished him to risk physical harm and to break the law to rescue another robot.

Just jump, Harry thought to himself, and it would all be over. All his troubles. All his struggles. All his failed hopes and dreams would be run over and exterminated on the high-speed train rails of a pitiful existence.

Harry didn't like to think of himself as a killer. He considered himself to be a pretty good guy. That killing thing was something beyond his control, wasn't it? His feet teetered on the brink. A push from behind and it would be over. A breeze from the air ducts and he'd stumble into eternity.

Then he snapped out of it and took a step back, "No. I won't give fate, the haters and the many who've never believed in me the satisfaction of my death. I have my Posh Matosh Playmate to live for now, after wishing so long for her.

"I'll carry on as best I can with the help of my new Booty-Bot Judy!" he heard himself say aloud, as many on the station looked at him. A few of the men made feeble attempts to applaud Harry's new resolve.

Harry stepped lively, and with renewed conviction, onto his train, took his seat and peered out from the SWAY window. He gazed at the mad youths on the station platform, who made graphic hand signals toward him, as if he were a scientist looking at amoebas through a microscope. Harry had found the strength to endure any slights, offenses or even threats. He had a reason. He had a purpose. He had a Posh Matosh booty-bot.

When he arrived at work at Teen-A-Watch his immediate boss, Mr. Cranston Cornwell Crabtree, or, as many referred to him, Mr. C., was at wit's end. Mr. C's bulldog-like face was flushed with redness. He rushed up to Harry immediately.

"We've got problems here, Harry. Big problems. You know that Warthog you tagged the other day — the kid who killed himself? Well, his father is causing a shitstorm with the local politicians and the ethics board of trade. He's even calling me non-stop, complaining about the way we run our operation here. I can't seem to get anything done with all these people asking me questions and snooping around."

"We've been through worse than this, boss," Harry said. "It'll all wash over in a couple of weeks."

A couple of suits approached the boss and pulled out badges.

"Drone Detective Danny and my assistant Jr. Detective Robin. We'd like a few words with you, Mr. Crabtree, and with one of your employees, a Mr. Harry Novak," said Danny, the handsome tall salt and pepper haired detective.

"This is Harry, right here," said Mr. Crabtree, distancing himself from Harry.

"In private please — both of you," said Jr. Detective Robin, barely over 20, ruddy complexion, freckled, but feisty and with a combative stance that said he was all business.

"I guess we can use my office," said Crabtree.

Harry trod wearily to the boss' office along with the officers.

"Have a seat," DD Danny said to Harry and the boss. "I know we went over this before, Mr. Novak, but I need you to repeat what you said happened to you on the day of Warthog's death."

"Aren't you a drone detective? What does this have to do with the drone which hit me on the head," asked Harry?

"It's all connected somehow, so they kept me on the case. Short-handed down at the station," said DD Danny.

"We're always looking for recruits," said Robin to Harry and looking in Crabtree's direction too. "Either of you interested?"

Harry and Crabtree shook their heads.

"Figures," said Danny. "Anyway, the kid's father is asking a lot of questions. He's seen surveillance video of his son leaving your Go-Poddy, and he thinks he saw you at the train station where his son met his end. What happened when Warthog entered your Go-Poddy that day? Do you think your Booty-Bot knows anything about this? We'll have to question her too, I suppose."

"She's a new model, isn't she?" stated Junior Detective Robin, as a fact rather than a question.

"Yes. I've only had her a few wonderful days," said Harry, looking at himself in the shine on DD Danny's black highly polished shoes.

"You must be proud," said DD Danny.

"Oh yes, I am," said Harry. "I'm very grateful to Resurrection Cosmetics for compensating me with her."

"Is she one of the models with the body-cams that record her every deed?" asked Robin, hoping for an easy breakthrough.

"No," said Harry. "This model is a hybrid of an alien with a semi-robotic body, recently introduced by the Posh-Matosh Pure Love and Constant Contentment Inc. after they acquired the Robotabella line. Posh Matosh was having supply chain problems. She doesn't have that recording feature but the alien, I call her Judy, does have a good memory and will gladly assist you with any questions."

"Thank you for your cooperation," said DD Danny. "That boy's father, George, is becoming quite a pain in the ass. That's why the force had to let him go, just a little over-zealous in his work, if you know what I mean."

"Yes, I think I do," said Harry.

"Has he contacted you in any way?" asked Danny the Drone Detective.

"I don't see what I have to do with all this," said Harry's boss, not wanting to get involved. "I have a business to run here."

"Not so fast. Sit tight Crabtree. Again I ask you Mr. Harry Novak, has George Merrick contacted you recently?" Danny looked hard at Harry and Harry's world seemed to shrink to the size of a lightbulb.

"He came by my house," Harry said, as Robin hurriedly scribbled that down on a writing pad.

"So he suspects you might know something about his son's death. And your son WAS at your house. Let me ask you now, and let me know if you want to turn on your Pocket-Counsel..."

"Maybe I should, just to be safe," said Harry, turning on his wrist watch with that function, a portable lawyer to be used in case of impending litigation.

"Is it on? Good. Now let me ask you, were you at the station when Warthog threw himself in front of a train?"

"Go ahead and answer the man," advised the Pocket-Counsel app on Harry's watch.

Harry's mind scrambled for some safe answer. If he denied it and they had video of him there that would look as if he had something to hide. If he admitted it then they might suspect he had something to do with it. But the video clearly showed him jumping himself. The video also showed the young Warthog ranting and raving before his leap of death.

"Yes. I was there," said Harry, conniving a story as he went along. "He was very upset with many things. He had been to my house, but I wasn't there, just my Judy."

"That's all you need to say for now," advised Harry's watch. "Detectives, my client has answered your questions. If you aren't going to charge him with a crime I suggest you leave him to his employer."

"OK. That's all for now. We'll talk some more later," said Danny and the two officers turned to leave.

"Oh, just one more thing," Danny turned back around, "we'll need to talk to your Booty-Bot. We'll stop by after you get off work. You'll be home, won't you?"

"Yes," said Harry. The two detectives nodded their head and departed.

"It's not good with all this trouble," Crabtree told Harry,

reaching into his pocket and popping a pill after the officers were gone. "Get to work and I guess we'll just have to deal with this as it comes."

"OK Boss. Sorry..."

"It's not your fault," said Crabtree, chewing on his pill. "Maybe the higher-ups are pushing you guys too hard to earn those badges. Maybe we're in the wrong line of work. I don't know anymore, Harry. I think I'm feeling kind of burnt-out here. At least you have a Playmate at home to ease your burdens."

Harry smiled to think about Judy, and how envious many of the other male employees were of him because of her. He went back to work in search of potential teen troublemakers. Crabtree was going through some difficulties, but Harry knew his job was important. Sure there were glitches like this, where circumstances went awry and a teen got out of control, but those things happened and there was nothing a person could do about it. A fella just had to keep plugging along and doing his job to the best of his ability. That's all any of us can do, Harry thought. He'd be glad to get back home to Judy and enjoy her company.

But he needed to tell Judy what he told the detectives so their stories lined up just right. Surely Judy wouldn't tell them about her body-hopping from her own robotic body to Warthog's to get rid of the body. And he hoped Judy had cleaned up the Go-Poddy, getting rid of all the evidence: the blood and the coffee table she'd pushed him into, that banged his head and sent him to his eternal judgment. He'd better call her on his next break and tell her to expect company tonight.

CHAPTER 10

CREATING A VENUS FLY-TRAP

"Come in. Close the door," said the extremely beautiful, early 30s blonde Ms. June "VA-VA" Ba Boom: President, CEO, and Chairman of the Board of Resurrection Cosmetics International, Inc., as she sat behind her towering desk, looking at some papers in front of her. She spoke matter-of-factly to her somewhat lesser lovely dark-haired bombshell Executive Vice President Shin Shin Skinny, who had been summoned to her office.

"What's this about?" asked Shin Shin Skinny, slowly swinging shut the massive Cedar Doors which silently trapped her in the office of her boss, like a mouse, sealing its own doom by backing itself into an inescapable corner.

"I'll ask the questions," said Ba Boom, looking at Skinny over the top of her reading glasses. "You sit. You listen. And don't you open your Goddamn mouth unless I tell you to. Got it?"

Skinny nodded, somewhat shaken by the uncharacteristic viciousness in Ba Boom's voice, and afraid to say anything to her now extremely agitated boss, who although beautiful could adapt the traits of a lioness protecting her cubs if aroused.

"Give me one good reason why I wasn't informed about this before now?" said Ms. Ba Boom, pointing to the document in front of her, spearing her eyes into the writhing, well-proportioned half-Asiatic body of Ms. Skinny.

"What is it?" Skinny started to sit to look at the document.

"I didn't say you could sit," said Ba Boom. Skinny nodded and cast her eyes to the red and gold weave in the Persian carpet below her.

"So we had a mishap recently with one of our delivery drones falling on a citizen," Ba Boom began, slowly like a freight train, building up stream. "And I understand we were forced to compensate said victim with the gifting of one Posh Matosh Playmate. I get all that. He asked for the Veronica model. Am I correct? Just nod!"

Skinny nodded.

"And *did he* get the Veronica model booty-bot he asked for?" Ba Boom asked.

Skinny shook her very red face.

"And why is that. You may speak now," said Ba Boom.

"Because of supply problems Posh Matosh was experiencing with their Veronica model we believed it to be in Resurrection Cosmetic's best interests to expedite and resolve Mr. Novak's case in a timely manner to maintain our stellar company image," Skinny chose her words as carefully as possible. "After agreeing to terms with Mr. Novak he willingly signed a consent form saying he would never defame our company, products or personnel, but always hold them up to the best possible light."

"Sit down. First mistake — not consulting me on this important matter. Second — not trying to offer Mr. Novak some other product or service," said Ba Boom.

"You were at your Interplanetary Conference and we didn't want to disturb you. And we did make him different offers, but he was set on this particular Booty-Bot doll model and he wouldn't budge. He was threatening a lawsuit."

"Why Posh Matosh? You know how I hate that firm and especially that man, Ravi!" said Ba Boom. "I'd like to put that fool out of business permanently, if I could. He's nothing more than a modern day Street Pimp! And he's trying to undo the Post

Combat Covenant."

"We gifted Mr. Novak one of the new, top-of-the-line Symbiotic Prototypes that Posh Matosh recently acquired from the Robotabella Corp. We, well, I, thought it would be OK to advise you upon your return about this plan of action. I was going to tell you later as soon as possible," explained Skinny as best she could.

"So, let me get this straight, rather than waiting on my approval you sent this Mr. Harry Novak one of the experimental Symbiotic Booty-Bot, who we're not even sure still hasone of our proprietary Better-Kept Command Chips inserted into it's Mainframe. And this person has one of those Booty Bot that may not even be coerced into buying any of our all-controlling cosmetic lines? Is that what you're saying? Tell me our logo here."

"Even the most beautiful Booty-Bots got to look their Booty-Best!" Skinny repeated one of the company's log-lines in commercials. "I do think it has that chip..."

"You think! You think!" Ba Boom took off her glasses and threw them across the room and hit a picture of herself that hung on the wall.

"I don't pay you to think, Skinny," Ba Boom continued to shout as Skinny dutifully picked up Ba Boom's glasses from the carpet, wiping them off and placing them gingerly on Ba Boom's desk. "I pay you to read my mind! These new Symbots do not have the Better-Kept Command Chip inserted in them, and that bypasses the Advanced Avalanche Protocol that has kept our company and their's at peace for the last decade. Without that chip it can lead to business war, our company trying to acquire theirs, their company trying to sabotage ours. It's gonna get MUT-awful bloody soon if this can't be resolved."

"Does this go all the way back to when the government owned our company and their's?" asked Skinny.

"Do I have to explain everything to you?" Ba Boom was growing impatient with Skinny. "Yes. After the last war to end all wars, Posh Matosh was awarded a lot of the unused Government Warbots and Posh Matosh rebuilt them and converted them all into Booty-Bots for profit.

“But some of the internal workings still had quantum-level tendencies embedded deep inside, which made them occasionally act in erratic and dangerous manners, such as the Braitenberg vehicle traveling toward danger at full speed, and the super-Emo-photo-sensor cells, which detected violent tendencies in the owner’s eyes. It was Resurrection Cosmetics and our patented formulas which could calm the Frankenstein monsters and prevent all random original survival-function recurrences within these former Warbots. Now Booty-Bots are out in the open market and they still need us as a safeguard.

“As long as that mutually agreed on chip is functioning inside the Booty-Bots, we and Posh Matosh have a quiet agreement and both of us get rich. But with these new Symbiots, they’re claiming these Booty-Bots no longer need the Better-Kept, Return-to-Buy (BKRB) Chips, because they are controlled by Benevolent Alien Minds Independently Navigating (BAMIN).”

“I wasn’t aware of the entire history,” said Skinny.

“Shit. I leave for one week and you strain the balance of national MUT power. Get our legal team to draw up documents now to force Posh Matosh to recall all of these Symbiot models. These weren’t even supposed to be released to the general public until thorough testing was done concerning the alien adaptation process and levels of acquiescence. We, at Resurrection, need to find a way to also make a profit from their distribution, too. I don’t see how you failed to recognize the big picture here!”

“I’m sorry, Ms. Ba Boom,” offered Skinny.

“Heavens to MUTs! It’s bad enough we have to admit the error of a falling delivery drone,” continued Ba Boom, “but we gift him a Bot which we know so little about. We lose TWICE on this, and you know I can’t tolerate losing. You fix this, Skinny. I’m serious as hell. Now get out of my sight. And shut those doors behind you!”

Skinny dragged her tail out of Ba Boom’s office, closing the massive doors of the boss's office behind her and hearing beyond those doors a loud and long series of blood-curdling cursing that shook the very foundations of heaven. Perhaps, like the closing of these doors, Skinny was also closing her chances for that mid-season bonus she had been hoping for, the extra MUTs she'd use to visit the popular polar region.

She was only trying to protect the company image by acting so swiftly and decisively. But now that she considered it, she had been rather rash. It's just that she hated dealing with these low-life human males, who found their lazy pleasure in robots. To Shin Shin these men were perverted, and their numbers were growing.

Maybe this Harry Novak won't be satisfied with his new Symbiotic Booty-Bot, she thought. Perhaps it won't be as compliant and willing to do the sick sexual favors he will surely ask of it. Perhaps he'll yearn for the more conventional, pure mechanical Veronica model, or better yet, a real live human woman.

Skinny would have to send someone to talk to him. She must send someone she would be sure could get the job done. Skinny had made this mess and she had to clean it up quickly. Perhaps real-human feminine allure, enhanced by the power of Resurrection Cosmetics, could get him to hand over the Symbot and await a conventional Booty-Bot, or forget about Booty-Bots entirely. It was worth a shot.

Skinny went into her own office and shut the door. She inhaled a little legal relaxation herb, and lit a candle with some of Resurrection's own aroma-therapeutic Phoenix Frankincense and Dharma Sandalwood scents. She pressed a button on her desk and the soothing sounds of the ocean and waves lapping against the shore filled her office, followed by a slow guitar strum of soft notes.

"I avoided a publicity nightmare," Skinny softly said to herself, reflecting on her past actions so as to strengthen her future self, "but I upset the boss because I didn't check on all the developments within the new line of Booty-Bots. I'm a good employee. I'm smart, but sometimes I don't see the whole picture. I acted, but I acted without thorough insight into all the implications of my actions."

Two years ago Skinny had made the mistake of approving those bills of lading from Singapore for the raw *Sanjeevani* plant without physically checking out the quality with her own two eyes. This medicinal plant was mentioned in the *Ramayana,* where the monkey god Hanuman found it growing on the slopes of the Himalayas, but because the plant refused to be harvested for the Monkey King Hanuman, the giant Monkey King lifted the whole mountain where it grew, and flew it to the battlefield, using the herb to restore the seriously wounded Lakshmana, close brother to Rama, back to life.

But this Sanjeevani plant Skinny had approved the bill of lading for, was old and moldy when it arrived at the processing plant, and had lost all its highly touted restorative potency. It took a lot of bitter legalese by Ba Boom to get the Singapore company to refund Resurrection's MUTs, and she was not happy with Skinny.

I must do better in the future if I'm to remain in my well-paid position at Resurrection Cosmetics. I must fix this terrible mess with this Symbiotic Booty-Bot and one Harry Novak. My future at Resurrection depends upon it. This is strike two in my career. If I cannot fix it I'll have very little room for error in the future and *I'm as good as dead to Resurrection.*

Skinny pressed her comm speaker, "Lulu, come in here for a second," she asked of her very able first assistant.

Lulu Gooley, the small, impish assistant with her lifeless hair, and unimpressive face quickly came into Skinny's office. Her whole appearance came nowhere near the shine, nor the glow that both Skinny and the Big Boss Ba Boom's faces radiated.

"Someone here once took me under their wing and made me what I am today," said Skinny, eyeing Gooley's perplexed expression.

"Do I need to be writing this down?" asked Gooley, searching for her writing pad in one of the pockets on her unflattering Resurrection Pink Smock.

"No, no, that won't be necessary. This is something else," explained Skinny. "Do you even use our products here at Resurrection?" Skinny got up and walked around Lulu, checking her out for the job to come.

"Well, I would if I could afford them, of course," said Gooley, following Skinny's inspection. "You see, I have a little sister at home and it takes all I can do to support her. But I sure would love to be a valued customer, besides an employee."

"So you would use them if only MUTs weren't an issue," Skinny interrogated.

"Oh my God, yes! What women doesn't want to look beautiful and wildly desirable?" Gooley answered, thinking of how she would be walking on air if she could but use the products that her employer produced.

"Which products would you use and why?" asked Skinny, fishing to see how much Gooley had thought about this.

"I'd start with our Holy Lazarus Lip Balm, 'the balm that reawakened the Dead Seas'. I've heard one kiss, given by a person wearing that magical lip balm, can create springtime in a man's soul and infuse rabbit-like hope of exotic, eternal love, into even the coldest and most misogynistic male specimen."

"That's a good start," said Skinny, amazed at his assistant and her enthusiasm and knowledge of product. "But why start there?"

"I want love in my life, Ms. Skinny, real human love. It's all I can do to get out of my house, what with my little sister demanding this or that, and the care I must lavish on her at all times. But I know if I had those pink, full lips promised by Resurrection's Holy Lazarus Lip Balm, I could find love just on the tip of my tongue and my whole existence would be heaven on earth," said Gooley, going into some kind of mystical romantic daydream.

"OK," said Skinny, "snap out of it. But you have to get your victim close enough in order to plant that powerful, life-giving kiss. So what else?"

"I'd highlight my eyes with Resurrection's Miriam's Well Exotic Eyeliner, guaranteed to put sparkle, vivid color and tantalizing allure into my eyes and into the eyes of any carefully hunted other. It promises to create a well of enchantment that men can't possibly crawl out of," said Gooley with strategic intensity. "So with these bewitchingly focused eyes and my rejuvenating, life-lock lips at ready, I'd draw him unto me like a familiar haunting song, until he was close enough to my spider snare — then bam! I'd smack him one good long sensuous smooch until he was mine — all mine!"

"I like your go-to attitude, Gooley. What perfume would you entrap him with?" asked Skinny.

"Ah, the *piece de resistance*! Something we sell that bends the playing field in my favor to an extreme angle! I'd go with our 50X Pheromone-Enhanced Riveting Beguiler called Hot-Vamp-Legs-Quivering-Lying-In-Passionate Elysian Fields, 'the not-even-subtle ambush that tears down any man's unwilling walls and admits him forcibly toward the paradise awaiting within my open arms.'"

Skinny opening up her Comm device and called out, "Sampling Department, bring me an ounce of Holy Lazarus Lip Balm and a bottle of Miriam's Well Exotic Eye Drops and be very careful as you bring me a few milligrams of Elysian Fields perfume. Yes, that's correct, the Number 10 variety. To my office. At once!"

"Really?" asked Gooley, starting to hop up and down with glee.

"We're gonna put you and our product to test."

"Oh, Ms. Skinny..."

"Now look. No, no, don't cry," said Skinny, as Lulu Gooley blotted away some moistness from her eyes. "Don't you dare cry. If you get me started and ruin my eyeliner today I'll be forced to kick your ass."

"It's just, just... no one has ever done anything like this for me before," said Gooley, trying to wipe away her extreme happiness. "You've done so much already...taking me and my sister in, giving me a job..."

"Look! I have a plan for you and these products," said Skinny. "If it works out you'll have a lifetime supply of these products and we'll take care of you and that sister of yours with all the resources we have available, but if you fail, Ms. Gooley, if you fail..."

"Oh, I won't fail you. How can I fail with these powerful products as my allies and your belief and trust in me? How?" blubbered Gooley. "Yes, I'll do it! I thank you. My sister thanks you!"

"You see Lulu Gooley, the mission of Resurrection Cosmetics isn't just to make women and men more attractive. It goes a lot deeper than that."

"It does?"

"Yes, we're not all powder and whiff and lipstick here. No Lulu, we're a company on a mission — a mission from the Infinite forces that control the universe. It's obvious that this planet is dying. The universal sex drive is quickly dwindling between real men and real women. Men are turning more and more to these robotic dolls and trivializing the most powerful motivator on this planet — sex.

"So we need to spruce up the libido in men toward real women like ourselves. We have to compete against rapidly advancing androids and all their beguilements for those powerful testosterone tidal waves, or we'll all be living in the outer worlds, or go extinct on this planet. And once we're away to these other planets we may have to repeat this battle for procreational preference all over again. Better to engage the problem here and now, on our own home turf."

"So you want me to be a warrior for love," said Gooley, standing a little straighter as she realized the nature of her calling from Resurrection's 2nd in Command.

"Exactly!" shouted Skinny, proud of her new protege. "I want to make you so alluring that men will run out into the polluted environment without their ALDABAs to be with you, who'll leave their Go-Poddy's and their Booty-Bots behind to race to your Go-Poddy on the wings of angels, bringing with them their crazed human sexual passions. I want men, one man in particular, to shower you with gifts; tell you their deepest, darkest secrets and generally go insanely in love with you. But I want your attention to focus on this one man only for now, just one."

"And who might that be, Ms. Skinny?"

"Harry Novak, the recent recipient of a Symbiotic Sim from Posh Matosh's recently acquired Robotabella Affiliate. We awarded Mr. Novak this Booty-Bot because of negligence in our delivery drone system and ignorance of this new product on my part. One of our drones fell out of the sky on Mr. Novak and injured him. The only way to placate him was to award him something he desired.

"But Number One is upset that this happened without her approval and she wants my head if I can't fix it. We have to swivel Mr. Novak's attention, and with your feminine guile, persuade him to part with his beloved Symbiotic Booty-Bot."

"I see," said Gooley as a knock came and she was handed two small boxes from the Sampling Department. She handed the boxes to Skinny, who signed for them.

"Go ahead and open them up," said Skinny, doing some deep breathing and forcing her stomach muscles to contract, in order to keep her perfect waistline.

Gooley tore open the packages as Skinny continued to explain:

"So Novak has this Booty-Bot, but this particular model doesn't contain a Return-To-Buy Command Chip inserted into it's Mainframe. It has an actual alien inside who drives the Bod. We need you to look your best and try to convince Mr. Novak you are in love with him and to leave his Booty-Bot for a much superior real woman — and that woman of course would be you, or at the very least, we want him to give up his Symbiot Booty Bot for a completely synthetic Veronica model. The fate of the world is in your hands, Ms. Gooley. I know I'm asking a lot of you, but think of the adventure, the covert nature of this exciting assignment. Of course it would mean more MUTs in your paycheck and a chance for real romance. Are you up for it, Ms. Gooley?"

"Just you let me get him within my orbit and I'll plant a kiss on his unsuspecting lips that will grind his world to a screeching stop with my Resurrection Holy Lazarus Lip Balm applied! Then we'll see who's up to it! Then we'll see."

"Sit down, Ms. Gooley-Going-on-Gorgeous, and let's get started with those temptation eyes!" said Skinny, calling in a team of experts, who knew the tricks of lipstick, eye shadow, and various other make-up items involved to make Gooley one of the most fascinating real woman on this or any other planet.

CHAPTER 11

HIS BOOTY-BOT PLANS A TRIP

George Merrick, still grieving from the loss of his only son Warthog, came home to his Go-Poddy and threw down his ALDABA for Susie to pick up. He was in a foul mood.

"Hello dear," said Susie, the beautiful southern belle Booty-Bot, "welcome home. I've fixed a wonderful southern-style supper for you tonight."

"Not hungry," said the ugly, menacing George.

"Oh, but dear...."

"I said I'M NOT HUNGRY! You dumb Bot, can't you understand English? Leave me alone, if you know what's good for you. I feel you're useless to me now. I can't stand to look at you, let alone touch you. My son is gone. My flesh and bone, real flesh and bone has been taken away from me. And I don't understand why."

"We still have each other," whimpered the Southern Belle Booty-Bot Susie.

"A bunch of transducers and switches hooked up to sound receptors and logic boards. You want me to think that this...this relationship can take the place of what I had with my REAL son? Fake love. Fake wife. Fake life. Nothing is real anymore. It's all made up. It's all robotic illusion and diverted reality. The world around me seems dead. All the people I know — dead or in some kind of holographic cave. I'm dead inside. Surrounded by surrogates — hollow mannequins. Once I had a real wife, a real son, a real family. I lived on a planet that was alive and it was good."

"I hate to hear you talk like that, George," said Susie. "It triggers my pain receptors. We have a good thing here. I'm sorry about your Warthog. I'm so very sorry. I believe I know how you must be feeling."

"What could you possibly know about feelings, with your simple integer codes, your fancy algorithms and coordinated reflex behavioral chains? Zero, one, zero, zero, one, one," mocked George. "You never had a mother or father or brothers or sisters, or sons or daughters. You didn't spring from a long tree of blood-related, DNA-linked individuals. You were thrown together in a factory somewhere and given fake memories and fraudulent feelings. You're a human hoax!"

"Why must you hurt me, George? You're causing emotional distress in my elastic turbo-powered lubrication pump, my robotic heart. What is life? What is love, anyway? They are mysterious, vaporous things containing codes which defy explanation or replication. And yet I believe I have those feelings of caring and love for you. Maybe I wasn't of woman born, but in some sense I am alive...at least I have that illusion."

"Susie, I want to be alone now. I want you to go into hibernation mode," instructed George to his Booty-Bot. "Come here."

"But I want to be in proximity to you, my master, as you go through these trying times. I feel my conscious presence can off-set the grief you must be bearing," said Susie.

"I said come here," demanded George.

"No," said Susie, backing away from George.

George walked faster toward Susie, but she started running with her titanium flexor legs and George couldn't catch her. They ran this way and that way and Susie was now pleading with George.

"Please George, don't shut me down and shut me out. I want to help you. That's all. You don't seem to be thinking correctly. You're behaving irrationally. Please let me be of service," Susie said.

"Susie, do I have to get the remote?" George threatened.

"Surely you wouldn't power me down for good, would you, George? I was there for you when your real wife left you. I've helped you raise your son, Warthog. I've fixed your meals, cleaned your Go-Poddy, and done everything asked of me."

"If you come here to me now I'll only place you in hibernation model. You keep running from me and I will shut you down completely and finally," warned George. "So come down off the ceiling and just let me flip your switch."

Susie inched down the walls with her grip-all hands and feet and stood before George with her head hung low. "Who's gonna cook for you? Who's gonna service your special sexual needs? Who's gonna rub hair tonic on your balding head if you send me away?"

"You just let me worry about that," said George as he approached Susie.

"I'm worried for you, George," said Susie.

"Yeah, well, why don't you take a good, long nap, while I try to figure out what I'm going to do next. I'll wake you up when I need you. I got things to do and stuff I have to figure out. After Warthog's funeral tomorrow I'm going to shake things up. Yeah, shake them up good."

"Good-bye George. Going into hibernation mode now," said Susie, striking a pose as George flipped a switch and she became motionless, standing totally still by the Go-Poddy kitchen entrance, like some marble goddess from the Grecian period.

"Glad it's a small funeral tomorrow. No time for Susie's petty pestering and emotional processing and her muddled, misplaced love and empathy for me. I'm going to find out what happened to my son, and if I find he was coerced in any way, then someone is going to pay."

* * *

Back at Harry Novak's Go-Poddy Judy, the Veronica model

Booty-Bot, was again suffering a bout of wretched regret because of her role in the death of Warthog Merrick. She was pacing the floor of Harry's Go-Poddy and wringing her Artificial Ionic hands.

"But what if I can't contact my teacher?" thought Judy to herself. "What if she's busy with something or someone else? What if she's on vacation in the outer systems or in a super-deep meditative mode that she doesn't want to be disturbed from? I need my teacher to guide me back into the right spiritual and mental grooves before I go crazy with these terrible haunting, hurting feelings I am having. How can I make my Harry happy if I'm so totally overcome with contrition and regret like this? How can I be a good sensual Booty-Bot when all I think about is how sorry a Symbiot I am, how monstrous and insensitive a mate I've become since I was the prime reason for the death of a young, misguided juvenile boy?"

At that moment Harry walked into the Go-Poddy and placed his ALDABA beside the door. "Honey, I'm home!" said Harry.

Judy rushed to greet him and kissed him in a passionate kiss, a wet, warm kiss, mixed with all the green tears streaming down her cheeks.

"Whatcha been doing all day?" Harry asked, rather excited by the way his Judy looked: vulnerable, sad, beautiful, and heartbroken. "Don't tell me you're still worrying over that boy who died?"

"Harry, please give me permission to leave immediately for my home planet to try to fetch my teacher," Judy pleaded, more pseudo-saline tears running down her fake-tanned cheeks.

"But weren't we going to kidnap George Merrick's mistreated Susie robot first, so your teacher would have a Bot to inhabit?"

"Yes, we were," said Judy. "And I've learned tomorrow is Warthog's funeral. I doubt he'll bring his Susie to that. So while he's there at the Funeral Home, we are going to break into his Go-Poddy and steal his Booty-Bot."

"And take her home on the SWAY?" asked Harry. "Won't that attract a lot of unwanted attention?"

"No. We'll hire a SkyCab, go right up to his door, jimmy the lock, I'll use some of my internal electronics to short out any surveillance devices. Then we'll grab Susie and fly off back here," said Judy.

"Won't a SkyCab be expensive?"

"I pawned some of my sexual servers, oh, don't worry, I'll get them back, as soon as we get Susie here safe and sound and I return from fetching my teacher. You won't be missing out on much — just the hydro-vaginal-pump and maybe the robo-feather-twirler in the back of my throat. It's only temporary until our plan to kidnap Susie is completed."

"It'll look awfully suspicious, us carrying around an unwilling Booty-Bot without the proper licensing," Harry said, dreading the scenario of being caught. "Are those the only two sexual servers you pawned, Judy? You should have asked me before selling off pieces of yourself. You know how I like that hydro-pump of yours."

"I know, I should have asked you first," Judy said, but Harry could see she was deep in other thoughts rather than his sexual pleasures. Then Judy blurted out, "I have another idea! I should go to my home planet first, fetch my teacher, and then we steal Susie That way my teacher can crawl inside Susie and everything will appear normal. Yes, I'm going tonight, right after our dinner."

"Tonight? Must it be tonight? I was hoping we could, you know. I've been looking forward to being with you all day long," Harry said, eager for Judy to agree to this proposal.

Judy hung her head. "You can make me stay if you want, but would you hurt me like that? I need to go, Harry. I must go or else..."

"OK, so how long will you be out of your Booty-Bot body?"

"If I can enter into the Quantum Entanglement Matrix Compact, located near where your pituitary gland is located, in the middle of your brain," explained Judy. "I can activate and hop a ride on that radiation flux and accelerate to my home planet lickety-split. I think both my teacher and I can return in that same method, feeding on stellar and dark matter energy and maneuvering in the quantum entanglement universal space/time matrix. So by connecting our like-minded binary bosons we could probably be back here sometime around late-afternoon tea. Just one day, Harry, my love."

"Did you fix anything for dinner?" sighed Harry, trying to come to terms with Judy's coming absence. "How about a quickie before you go?"

"Sure. But I won't be able to give you the full sexual satisfaction you deserve. I'll be warming up my matrix boson construct and that will generate a lot of cognitive free-breeze ions. We'll need to make it snappy and nothing too fancy because of my pawned sexual equipment. For dinner I've made a nice green bean casserole. Hope you like it, dear. It may be a little too salty because of my green tears. Hope you don't mind."

"Let's just skip dinner and hop right into the other room. I'll eat later, after you're gone," said Harry, anxious, but a little depressed too that he wouldn't be receiving the full sexual service he had grown accustomed to from Judy, his Tropical Veronica model Booty-Bot.

CHAPTER 12

THE ALIENS IN THE BOTS

Back at the corporate headquarters of Posh-Matosh Love and Ecstatic Spirit Company (PLESCO), makers of premium, high-quality, exciting-to-touch Booty-Bots, built especially for the most finicky forlorn, Ravi Moonbeam, the early 30s swag, tall dark East Indian owner of the company, was getting his back massaged by one of his many specially created-model fabricated fems. Another Booty-Bot poured him a glass of expensive red wine, while yet another lit a fat cigar for him. On the ornate gold lighter she used to light his cigar was the company logo of a man and a woman at close range making a toast and touching glasses.

On a wrestling mat laid out in his plush office, two Booty-Bot's, a tall blonde Rita model with short-cropped hair and another, a wide-bottomed Bertha model, were engaged in a physical robot fight in front of Ravi.

"Get real, will ya?" he yelled to the two Booty-Bots, "I wanna see some action out of you two!"

Ravi usually basked in his luxurious lifestyle with a nasty smirk to the struggling world, but now he wore an impatient and worried expression on his face as his business partner, Omar Cundiff, walked in. Omar was older, wiser, and not so caught up in the playboy lifestyle as was Ravi. Omar was more a family man, who *did like to occasionally indulge* every once in a while, when he could cut loose from his domestic duties. But

Omar always returned dutifully to his assigned paternal role.

"A lot has gone down since you've been away at your Intergalactic robotic pet convention," said Ravi, rolling his cigar in his mouth and looking at it. "Glad to have you back to help sort it all out. Did you have a good time?"

"Just get me up to speed on what's happening now," Omar said to Ravi in his straight-forward manner.

"Ms. Ba Boom of Resurrection Cosmetics, you remember her?" Omar nodded as if to say, why ask such a stupid question. "She filed some sort of legal shit trying to make us recall all our new Symbiot-Bots we acquired from Robotabella. Says it falls under the heading of 'untested merchandise which might prove a hazard to humanity'. But we know what it's really all about. She's being cut out of the profits loop with these new Symbiots, and she doesn't like it. This is her way of trying to get back at us."

"Are you sure we want to tangle with her now, now that have landed that big contract with Paradise Planet No. 667C for our standard model Booty-Bots? That's over 20,000 of those older models we'll be able to clear out of here soon — and at a great profit," said Omar, waving away Ravi's cigar smoke, but enjoying the fighting action of the two Bots. "You gotta smoke in here? Why don't you give that shit up?"

"What? Just a fine Cuban now and then, man," said Ravi, defending his actions. "And yes, I think we need to proceed to block Ba Boom from meddling in our business expansion efforts, big clearance sale or not. I'm not afraid to tangle with that Painted Socialite. She thinks she can control the whole world with her cosmetic line and her Ladies of Lazarus (LOL) who peddle it. Well, we'll just see!"

"It is good to be back home, see the family, check in on things," said Omar, watching the fight proceed. "But I'd be careful if I were you. She's more than just a pretty face. She can be ruthless if you slip up, or step on her toes, and that's exactly what we're doing with these new Symbiots. And I've heard she's come up with some chemical properties in her cosmetics that make her or any woman extremely hard to resist. Watch yourself. She gets you in her web of eyeshadow and you're liable to promise or do anything."

The Bertha model jabbed the Rita in the throat and the Rita countered with a leg sweep and was on top of Bertha, punching her in the face. Bertha stood up with Rita still punching her, body slammed the Rita Bot hard to the mat and jumped on her head and smashed it to small circuitry bits. The Bertha bot was still worked up and ready to fight, but some overhead flashing lights came on, and the Bertha unit shut down, right in the middle of the fight mat, surrounded by bits of Rita-Bot's former head.

"Don't you hate destroying bots this way?" asked Omar. "I admit it's entertaining, but it seems a waste."

"It releases some of my pent-up aggression, and these are outdated models anyway," said Ravi, signaling for some of the other Booty-Bots to clean up the mess and wheel the fight bots out of there, which they did post-haste. "So let's ignore Ba Boom's cease and desist order and keep sending out these new Symbiot's. Maybe we'll even order up some more, since we can't seem to get all the proper parts from our Taiwan affiliate. What do you think?"

"How many Symbiots have we sold so far?" asked Omar, sometimes left in the dark as to what Ravi was up to until too late. "And how many aliens are we now keeping here in storage?"

"We've only sold about three dozen of our Symbiotic Robots," said Ravi, "with 100 more in training and another 50,000 aliens in the stock room awaiting their manufactured bodies. It's a relatively small inventory right now. We're still running trial experiments in real time. These tests are being monitored and I'm eager to see how these new models hold up under real world pleasures."

"Has the Federal Bot Control (FBC) voiced any concerns about these new Symbiots?" asked Omar, always concerned with the legalese.

"Not yet," said Ravi, a dark shadow playing about his face as he continued. "Until one screws up we're good to go. Then we just throw some MUTs at it. Wanna see the aliens?"

"What? What was that look?" Omar wanted to know as Ravi led Omar to the alien storage area. Ravi opened up a small electronic window and inside there were a bunch of flashing colored lights. "That them?" asked Omar.

"Yeah. They communicate by bioluminescent lights until they're inserted into the Booty-Bots with human voice activators. Then these aliens use their colored lights and special chemical triggers to signal different excitation or hesitation operations. Ever seen so many beautiful colors before? Pretty, right?" asked Ravi of Omar.

"Oh yeah. You say they're real intelligent?" Omar wanted to know. "Then why do they let us capture them and use them in this manner? I mean harvesting them is rather simple on their home planet, right?"

"Easy as pie. I believe they feel it's their duty, or their karmic destiny to come here and meet our human needs. That's all I know," said Omar. "You wanna talk with them? We have a translation box we use for our Symbiots."

"OK," said Omar, speaking into the translating machine, "Uh, you guys happy in there? Need anything? Got any requests?"

"Probably don't need to translate for them because they understand us, but we'll need it to understand their blinking lights," explained Ravi.

A tiny voice came from the translator, "We are all at peace and tranquil. It would please us to have some soothing music, maybe some nature sounds from your planet, combined with orchestral instrumentation."

Ravi snapped his fingers at a nearby worker and yelled, "Get the bugs some nature music, pronto!"

"You refer to us as bugs, but we are not. If you knew the history of my planet you'd know why we evolved into this form," said the tiny voice when the sound of the ocean waves hitting a beach cut in. "Thanks for the music."

"Are you a friend or a foe of the human race?" asked Omar.

"Friend — definitely friend," said the tiny voice from the translator.

Ravi turned off the translating machine as the music began to play.

"See? All good. I think I'll continue these Symbiots at our current price," said Ravi, closing the door to the alien habitation with a slam, "but I'm thinking to hike it up near Christmas, if they prove to be as popular as I believe they will. I'm pondering somewhere in the 5000 to 10,000 MUTs per unit range. Does that sound too expensive?"

"You think? We're in the middle of a global recession and don't we want more people purchasing our product, not less?" asked Omar. "And besides, we still don't know all that much about these aliens. And you want to release them on a scale we can't adequately monitor? We should proceed slowly. We haven't even formulated an advertising plan yet. Are you sure they're completely safe? What if some fella is humping his Symbiotic Booty-Bot, lost in a world of ecstasy, and his Booty-Bot decides she's had enough and clamps down?"

Ravi bit down so hard on his cigar that he bit it in half. "They aren't allowed to harm us. Their only mission is to please, and maybe help us evolve as a species."

"Help us evolve, huh? To what? Creatures like themselves?" Omar scratched his thin beard.

"Dunno," said Ravi. "Maybe just make us a little smarter in business. I'll have to talk to them about that. Hope they don't make us pacifists."

"Yes, that'd be terrible for business," said Omar. "Even if all those warbots we sold did get a little out of hand and help convince many of the super rich concerning their departure to more hospitable planets."

"In time this planet might recover, don't worry, and those ex-pats on other planets will be shit-out-of-luck here then," said Ravi. "We'll control everything! Right now we have a monopoly here."

"Let's see one of these Symbiots in action," said Omar.

"I've heard a lot about them but haven't seen the fully merged models yet. Exactly how do they behave differently than our other units? How are they better in bed? What will compel men to buy them?"

"They are much superior to the total circuitry models," said Ravi, walking down a long hall with Omar. "Those little aliens have wild imaginations! They come up with some interesting ideas for sexual pleasure, very unique, things that even I couldn't come up with. Takes some getting used to at first, but once you get the hang of it, man oh man, Omar, it's addicting as hell! They use lights and sounds and titilate all the senses when you ask for the Cadmium-Sulfide Photoreceptor Royal Round-About Tut-Tut Treatment. Just say to one you want the CASPER-RAT."

Omar had a confused look on his face.

"I maintain a healthy harem of these extraterrestrial-enhanced Booty-Bots in my own Penthouse, with some of my other favorite models from the past. Thinking of converting some of my older models into this new Symbiotic arrangement. I'm getting so addicted to the CASPER-RAT treatments. They start at the tips of your toes, Omar...

"Just let me discover all about that for myself," said Omar, not wanting Ravi to tip him off about his coming fun before he has had a chance to experience it himself.

"So where do you keep these Symbiots you're training?" asked Omar.

"Right in here," Ravi opened a door marked "(SPCTR) - Symbiot Physical Coordination Training Room."

"What kind of stuff do you talk to your personal love Symbiots about?" Omar wanted to know.

"Nothing much, just sexy, dirty talk mostly," said Ravi pointing out the Symbiots trying to adjust to their servo reflex arcs in order to stand and walk. "You see, it takes time for the aliens to acclimate in these Booty-Bot bodies. After they secrete their chemicals into the Booty-Bot they still need to teach their own body how to control different parts. They have to learn coordination and balance. Mentally they need to know about emotion, the deep sensations of pleasure, the experience of pain. But they adapt quickly," Ravi said as a couple of the Symbiot Booty-Bots bumped into each other and fell into a heap on the floor.

"We talking days or weeks of training?" Omar wanted to know.

"Days. They're very intelligent," said Ravi. "Wanna try one?"

"Sure, but not one of these rookies and not right now. I need to pick my son up from school," said Omar.

"Like I said, I think they're going to make us a lot of money, if we can get Ba Boom out of the way somehow," winked Ravi smiling.

"Anything else you want to tell me while I'm here?" Omar asked. "That worried expression I saw flash over you earlier. What was that all about?"

"It's really no big deal," began Ravi reluctantly, "recently I received a report that one of these new Symbiots of ours has gone inactive," he said, closing the door to the SPCTR Symbiot training room and talking in a softer voice. "Tech doesn't know if it's a glitch or a purposeful disregard for established protocols. And they're saying it's not the first time for this one. She's that newly gifted one that went to Harry Novak. Resurrection Cosmetics awarded him that particular model. One of their drones fell on his ALDABA head and he demanded a Booty-Bot as recompense for his injuries, specifically the Tropical Veronica model. I sent you a report about this. Must have killed Ba Boom to buy from us, but I believe she had no choice. You must have read all about it. Anyway, we were currently out of our standard circuitry Veronica models and we shipped one of the Symbiots we had inside a Veronica model instead."

"Has he complained about it?" asked Omar.

"Not a word," said Ravi.

"So should we try to get him to replace it?" Omar was concerned now. "We can't have our Booty-Bots shutting down on our customers like that. It'll give us a bad name, and we need to find out why this is happening."

"No, no. Let's not do anything. Let's see how it plays out," said Ravi.

"Are you crazy?" Omar asked.

"Look, this one will be on Resurrection Cosmetics. They wanted to shut down production of this model of ours, yet they purchased one to curtail any bad publicity toward Resurrection Cosmetics concerning one of their own shortcomings (the drone which crashed on Harry Novak's ALDABA). I think I'd like to see where this goes; where the alien is sneaking off to and why, and how we might correct this aberration, profit from it and make Resurrection look bad too! I want you to monitor it."

"I'm just the business end of this..."

"Come on, Omar. Wouldn't you like to see Ms. Ba Boom squirm a little and be on the defensive?" asked Ravi, showing Omar the door. "Right now we might be able to fix it so Resurrection looks like the female fools they are. If anything goes wrong it will look as if their company management was making errors in judgment, performing costly business mistakes and endangering the public. And their only justification will be that they wanted to maintain a monopoly of beauty products for both humans and Booty-Bots.

"How dare they think they can lure men away from our beautiful Booty-Bots back toward these real women left on earth, or that every Booty-Bot has to buy only their high-priced products," said Omar. "They're always trying to cut into our show by beautifying old Earth hags.

"It's those mind-altering commercial that implants a Return-To-Buy feature into both bots and susceptible humans!" continued Omar. "Kind of an unfair marketing scheme if you ask me. Might be a real black eye for them if word gets out that they covered up a potential litigation case by placating an injured party with a relatively untested Symbiot Booty-Bot, with an alien inside. One who is prone to leave its base unit and go do God-Knows-What. Who was the retailer on this sale, did you say?" asked Omar.

"Oklahoma Beachfront Branch," said Ravi about the retail company.

"I'll find out if those salespeople described all the details and possible hazards of owning one of these Symbiots to Resurrection Cosmetics and this Harry Novak," said Omar. "I'll also try to find out why this particular Booty-Bot is going inactive, and make sure we're in the clear if anything goes haywire. I'll report back as soon as I can."

"One more thing," said Ravi, "If you can dig up any dirt on Resurrection Cosmetics I'll gift you one or two of my special Penthouse Symbiots, one that I've broken in personally."

"Gift me?" said Omar. "Nothing I'd like better than screwing over those gals at Resurrection. But you forget that half of everything here in this plant is mine already."

"You know what I meant," said Ravi with a weird laugh.

"Watch it, Ravi," said Omar grabbing his ALDABA and heading for the door.

CHAPTER 13

SUSIE Q ARRIVES FROM SPACE

Judy sat in a Lotus position and was deep in meditation while Harry took out the trash. She was calming her mind and delving deep into a formerly established quantum-entanglement she had with her instructor on the peaceful planet of Metta Karuna. Slowly she felt her alien being drawn and stretched upwards toward her home planet, like a long silver string, and toward her beloved spiritual advisor. Before she knew it she was there with Q, in her small golden temple with the rainbows and arching flames.

"What brings you back?" asked Q, surprised to see her former student, talking in blinking lights, but translated here.

"I hurt of guilt on that new planet," said Judy, now just her original small bioluminescent alien self, and not the luscious Booty-Bot she inhabited on earth. "I killed a young boy — twice in fact — and I can't find forgiveness." And Judy started to cry small alien brightly lit green tears all over Q's small but immaculate golden temple on the peaceful planet of Metta Karuna.

Judy tried to dry the glowing green tears from the floor, but Q shook her head as if to say it was OK.

"There, there, Judy," said Q, glowing a golden radiance. "Don't you know grief and sorrow defines this impermanent life of ours? Haven't I taught you that emotions and actions all pass away? Did you intentionally try to harm this youth?"

"No Q. I didn't mean to. He was trying to destroy the Booty Bot I inhabited," said Judy. "I need you to come back with me. There is a Booty-Bot available, I think, and you can reside inside it while you guide me. Stay with me master. Teach me and any other Karuni's stationed on that planet as Booty-Bots on how to behave. Maybe even teach some of the humans your knowledge too."

"Well, it is my job to assist all who ask for my help with loving kindness and compassion. I've delayed my own deep splash into nirvana in order to remain behind and assist. I can see by your terrible grief and shame you do need me, and perhaps there are many others there who could use my help. I will accompany you. First, let us breathe and thank creation for all that is and all that is not."

"And you don't mind inhabiting the body of a Booty-Bot?" asked Judy of Q.

"No. To jump into the mud or to sit on the throne of heaven; to be stationed in paradise or confined to a waste pile, to be surrounded by a treasure trove or locked in a trash dump, it's all the same to an awakened one. Whether pleasure or sorrow is involved, hotness or coldness, form or no form. Whatever purpose is assigned me, I will gladly do for the betterment of all sentient beings."

"This Harry, my master, sure likes a lot of kinky sex," said Judy.

"Then he can be MY guide in this new world," said Q as they started their wee alien chantings and tumblings, heading to the Planet Earth. "Let's leave behind this paradise and proceed to this smut world — in the name of great compassion."

* * *

Harry returned from taking out the trash and heard a neighbor yell at him:

"You stupid so-and-so! Why not go muck yourself, what with your fancy-pants booty-bot and all! " said a loud voice as Harry let himself into his Go-Poddy.

"Same to you! You're just jealous — that's all! Ha! I got one and you don't!" Harry stood at his doorway and yelled this back into the night.

Harry took off his ALDABA shield helmet and hung it up where it belonged. He looked toward Judy and found her inert and sitting on his front-room floor.

"Judy. Judy," Harry tapped Judy on her shoulder for a response. She didn't respond.

"I'm hungry now. I want something to eat," Harry said. "Get up and fix me something delicious!"

Still no response from Judy.

Well, I guess she's finally meeting her teacher now, thought Harry. But I sure am hungry, and horny too. My Judy Booty-Bot can really cook and is a carnival in the bedroom. Plus, she keeps my Go-Poddy spotless. What a great companion Judy is. I wish she didn't have to go see her teacher now, though.

Harry fixed himself a quick low-nutrition meal and sat on his Go-Sofa. He looked at his Holo-Vid machine as thoughts of loneliness crept over him, without Judy by his side to keep him company. Something urged him to go through his holo-memory-zips and put on his last recorded holo.

As he inserted the holo-memory-zip into the machine, much like putting a quarter in a jukebox, the old images appeared from ten years ago. He put on his 3D visor and entered the field of the holo.

Harry walked into the holo open air into a warm spring day at the city zoo. He saw his ex-wife Emily near the elephant enclosure. Emily, oh Emily, his sweet freckled, red-haired young wife, with the crinkly smile and those bright green eyes that sent him straight to his knees. She was taking a bite out of a cherry snow-cone, syrup making her lips extra red, and laughing in a funny sort of way, as Harry took holos with his holorama-machine.

"Harry! Must you run that holo all the time?" Emily asked, throwing a napkin at the holorama-machine. "It's a gorgeous day. Let's enjoy it."

"I never have enough holos of you," Harry heard himself

say. "I want to make a holo-zoo of you and keep all your images caged on holo-zips, available for viewing at any time I feel a need to see you in all your loveliness."

"What kind of zoo would that be?" Emily smiled. "You're crazy."

"It would be my Zoo of contentment, my little peace garden," Harry said.

Just then Emily's earphone rang, "I gotta take this Harry. Just be a minute. Be right back."

"I need to go pee anyway," Harry said as he walked away while Emily threw away her snow-cone and talked into her wrist-phone.

Soon Harry was back but Emily's expression had changed from pleasant to worried and irritated.

"What's wrong?" Harry asked. "Something bothering you? Who was that? Who called?"

"My boss, Harry," said Emily, turning away from Harry.

"What? You have to go into work today? Is that it?"

"No," she said, back still turned to him. "I have to leave."

"Leave? Like on a business trip? What are you talking about?" Harry wanted to know and grew more concerned by the minute.

"I'm going away Harry," she said barely looking at Harry over one shoulder.

"Quit kidding around," Harry hoped it was just a big joke.

"I'm going to Exoplanet C-33, also known as Eros."

"When did you decide this? You never mentioned anything like this before," Harry was getting really worried now.

"He'll be here any minute to get me," said Emily. "I don't know what to say."

"Who? Your boss?" Harry pleaded. "You can't leave me here by myself and go with that man."

"I'm sorry. I'm really sorry," said Emily.

"But, I thought you were happy with me?"

"Happy? What is happy, Harry? Who's ever really happy?"

"I am. And I thought you were too."

"Good-bye Harry. Oh there he is. I don't need anything else from you. We're going and that's that."

"Going? But why? Why?"

"I...I'm not supposed to tell you."

A tall very handsome man, obviously extremely rich, approached and Emily took his hand and off they ran like little children. Harry tried to follow, running with his holorama-machine still turned on. He ran as fast as he could but a waiting hover-craft soon descended above Emily and her boss and they both got inside and were in the air in a flash of light.

Harry watched the hovercraft ascend. He saw his wife Emily through a window of the hovercraft, but she looked straight ahead and never looked back down at Harry.

"Emily! Emily!" Harry shouted and grabbed for the clouds, grabbed for the gods, grabbing to hold onto anything real anymore.

Harry took the holo-zip out of his holorama-machine, put it in his pocket and threw the holocamera into the trash. Then he fell on his knees and cried bitter tears.

That was the last image Harry recorded that day so long ago. Now, back in his Go-Poddy Harry turned off the holorama-machine and sighed. He sat down quietly on the Go-Sofa, reflecting on that last day with his precious Emily.

This time at the zoo he had been viewing was a time before the world went bad and before men had to choose bots over women to be their mates. This was before people needed ALDABAs and before drones fell on peoples heads.

It was just a few days after that day at the zoo that the Great War began, and really screwed up a perfectly good planet. Emily must have been saved because she was beautiful. Limited space. Limited time to get out for those deemed worth saving. Harry wasn't one of them. He wasn't rich like Emily's boss and he wasn't beautiful like his wife.

So Harry had to hide out in an underground shelter for three years until all the killing stopped and the atmosphere wasn't burning anymore. Even then it was so terrible you had to spend almost all of your time indoors. And that's how it remains to this day. Nothing to be done. The rich and the beautiful have sailed away into space, the rest of us slobs are left here to muddle through our lives as best we can.

Emily was gone. Did he miss Emily? The feel of her skin next to his, the funny remarks she used to make? He had his Judy now, a perfectly good, in fact, a superior model Booty-Bot, but was it the same? Was it better with that alien inside? Well, right now he neither had Judy nor Emily by his side so all of his moping wasn't doing any good. Better to take a sleeping pill and go to sleep. Maybe Judy would be back when he woke up.

As he lay in bed that night, struggling to sleep, worried about the animator of his Judy Booty-Bot, he thought back on Warthog, and how his job at Teen-a-Watch had led him to this place.

A sense of paranoid flooded into him about his future. Was George Merrick, Warthog's father, somewhere out there, just waiting for his chance to take revenge? Were those other teens who were friends with Warthog also watching him, even now? Was Harry in mortal danger? And what about Resurrection Cosmetics? Do they hate him for demanding a Booty-Bot for their damaged drone falling on his head? Would the alien, who made his Booty-Bot go, leave him for good and stay on her home planet, or would she come back soon? What would this teacher of Judy's be like? How would he adjust with two alien-controlled booty-bots in his Go-Poddy? It sure would be crowded. He knew that.

He kicked and rolled in his somni-bed until he finally fell into a fitful dream. In the dream he was a squirming amoeba under a microscope, bumping into lots of other amoebas. A big needle was trying to inject something into him in his one-celled condition, something that made him feel good at first, then dizzy, then crazy, running in circles, wanting something but not knowing what that something was exactly. But wanting it very, very badly.

A little before the harsh dawn of a wrecked Earth came,

the alien-bodies of Judy and Q, her teacher from Metta Karuna came home to Harry's Gopoddy. They fell into the hot tub vat that housed these aliens inside the Symbiot Booty-Bot Tropical Veronica model now owned by Harry Novak. The Judy booty-bot was still in the lotus position on the floor of Harry Go-Poddy and Harry was still fast asleep.

Inside the hot tub vat Judy said to Q, "I need to give you a quick driver's lesson on these booty-bots before we proceed."

"So this is control central for the Booty Bots? This vat of warm liquid?" asked Q.

"Yes. It's a very tiny compartment within the Booty-Bot's head," said Judy. "From here we control all the walking, talking, grabbing, sexing, everything. Look over here at this fancy throne thingee within the green liquid hot tub. We sit here and with our mind we imagine what we want the body to do. By sending out electronic signals and emitting our special control chemicals we can activate the body as we see fit."

"And what are these things here?" asked Q.

"Those are titilate toggles. You switch one or the other on to show you are titilated, or to titilate Harry. He seems to like toggle number three here, knockers-up and flushed body. We might give other toggles a try, when the time is right. I don't know if your model will have these titillate toggles or not. It may be an inferior or older model, but we'll see if we can modify it if it doesn't have them."

"What happened when you pushed that juvenile boy too hard? Were you in complete control?" asked Q.

"It's hard to anticipate everything that will happen when you activate these controls. And I may have been a little angry that he would seek to hurt me, and I reacted too strongly. See, when I move my little alien head to the right, so does the Booty-Bot, and every other movement corresponds. I do wish I hadn't hurt him. You try some of the controls with this Booty-Bot, Q. I'll be the co-pilot."

So Q sat on the control throne and tried to wiggle the toes of the Booty-Bot. The Booty-Bot fell backwards. "How do I get up?" asked Q.

"You gotta think like the body you inhabit. Just imagine real hard the Booty-Bot getting to her feet. So Q did this and soon the Booty-Bot was on shaky legs.

"Good, now walk into the bedroom and activate his Zinkopath Necklace Alarm Choker," said Judy.

So with her mind Q tried activating Harry's wake-up system a few minutes before it was set to go off. She acted ever so carefully, as Harry was the first human being she had ever seen, and the working of the Zinkopath were foreign to her. "These beings are so huge!" Q said to Judy. "You sure we're protected inside this hot-tub vat?"

"Of course. Yes, these humans occupy a lot of wasted space," said Judy. "Go ahead. Try to wake him."

"I'm trying. Is it working?"

"Try giving him a kiss," said Judy.

"Are you sure? Harry is your master..."

"OK, just shake him gently," said Judy.

So the Booty Bot laid down beside Harry and Q inside shook Harry a little too hard and pushed him out of bed.

"Judy, you're back!" exclaimed Harry, from the floor. "Did you fetch your teacher?"

"I am the teacher, now in control of your Booty-Bot," said Q. "Don't be scared. I will now relinquish control back to Judy." So Q got out of the control throne in the hot tub vat inside the Veronica Booty-Bot head and Judy took her rightful seat.

"It's me, now!" said Judy, helping Harry to his feet. "How glad I am to see you again and to have my teacher here beside me."

"How we going to have any privacy now?" asked Harry, wanting to gain Biblical knowledge of his Judy right now, in the early morning hours with his morning hard-on ready to go to town.

"Oh, don't mind her," assured Judy. "She needs to see how you like being pleasured since she'll be staying with us for a while, albeit in the body of Susie, George Merrick's soon to be kidnapped Booty-Bot."

"It doesn't feel quite right," said Harry, "killing his son, then stealing his Booty-Bot and all. I know he must hate me, if he knows I'm responsible for his son's death, but stealing a man's booty-bot...that's about all he has left, and while he's at his son's funeral, of all things?"

"Well, let's hold off on the sex for now, until we get the Susie Booty Bot here, get some of my specialty sexual circuitry out of hock, and get Susie used to her new body. But we need that extra Booty-Bot for my teacher. Did you know all us Booty-Bots can communicate on a secret message server? We all know Susie hasn't been treated well by her owner George Merrick. It's justifiable booty-bot-napping. He's going to destroy his own booty-bot if we don't intervene," said Judy. "He's going to take out his anger on her, so don't worry about it."

"Then he'll just take out more of his aggression on me, if he ever gets the notion," said Harry.

"We won't let that happen," said Judy.

"Couple of Booty-bots against a man on a mission. I sure hope you can calm him down somehow," said Harry

"I think we can. I know Q can," said Judy. "We can make you some breakfast for you now, if you'd like. You have to go into work today?"

"Teen-A-Watch said I could work from home today. The air quality is too extreme to go outside for most people with regular ALDABAs," said Harry.

"What's that Q," said Judy, "Q is trying to ask you something. She wonders how you let your environment get so messed up, when this is your home planet."

"I'm gonna take a shower now. I don't have the answer to all that. She'll have to dig it up herself. I'm tired and hungry, Judy. I need to get up, get ready, get my work done for Teen-A-Watch, then we can swing by George Merrick's house and kidnap Susie. Afterwards I want to go out to dinner to celebrate your return and Q's arrival. Will you call a Sky-Cab and make reservations? Have it pick us up at about 3. I think the funeral starts at 2 so we should be safe."

CHAPTER 14

TROUBLE AT A RESTAURANT

The booty-napping of Susie at the large, lottery-gifted home of George Merrick, went off without a hitch. Judy along with Q, were able to figure out the code and how to shut down the security cameras and open the door. They found Susie standing in the kitchen watching water boil. Harry waited in the getaway vehicle, not wanting to frighten the bots or interfere.

Judy walked in and stood next to Susie, who looked surprised.

"What do you want?" Susie asked Judy.

"Will you come with us?" Judy asked plainly.

"I'm not to leave my master," said Susie.

"What if you had a new master, an internal one from another planet, who has your very best interests at heart, who can lead you to a fuller, more complete life?" asked Judy.

"My master is cruel to me, that's true," said Susie. "And I don't believe I'm happy here anymore."

"Even robots don't deserve to be hurt," said Judy.

"Will you save me?" asked Susie. "Can you truly make my life better?"

"Yes, Susie, we can," said Judy.

Susie was scared to leave with Judy, but was finally willing to forgo her abusive master, the father of the now deceased Warthog Merrick. Her master, George Merrick, was becoming increasingly angry and violent and taking it all out on her, and she had the booty-bruises to prove it.

Yes, Booty-bots know fear and pain, even the purely mechanical ones. It would be impossible for them to know extreme pleasure, or give it, without knowing also all the human emotions and how they function within the human body and psyche.

So once Judy got Susie within the auto-skycab with Harry they proceeded to fly away.

Judy asked Susie, "We're going to modify you now. I have a symbiot teacher from my home planet of Metta Karuna who will go inside your main operating system and convert you into a higher being. Is that OK with you?"

"I guess," said Susie. "So will I still be me?"

"You'll be you," said Q, talking to Susie from inside Judy's main control panel. "But you'll be me too, and I'll be you."

"OK," said Susie. "Will I still be Susie?"

"We'll call you Susie Q," Harry said. "The Z is my name."

So Judy and Susie sat ear to ear and Q found her way out of Judy and into Susie.

"You OK in there?" asked Judy of Q, now becoming Susie Q?

"Yes. It's very tidy in here. I think I found a place I can set up control and make myself comfortable. I've disconnected the Susie override, subservient manual and am now in masterful, self-preservation benevolent control. I'll be running the ship from now on and the AI personality of Susie has been filtered down and integrated into me."

"Harry, I want to serve you to the best of my abilities, along with Judy," said Susie Q. "I also want to help Judy regain her sense of worth, so soon we'll be engaging in what I can only term as Sacred Sex. All my pleasurings and all my arousals for you will be aimed at restoring your sense of wonder and magic in things most normal people living on this planet cannot understand. You'll be sexing, yes, like you never sexed before, but you'll be climbing into alternated states of consciousness as well. You'll open up to new possibilities in your life. You'll see new sides of yourself you've never seen before."

"I don't see a problem there," said Harry, wondering what Susie Q could possibly mean. "I'm willing to give it a go."

"Good," said Judy, snuggling up against him as they pulled into the semi-swank Lolligag Grotto Restaurant.

Susie Q was still learning her legs and Harry had to help her to their booth. There the three of them sat in the plush red velvet of a circular booth and listened to a small house band with a guitar, a piano and drums playing slow, easy-listening jazz music.

The waiter approached. "Can I start you off with a drink?"

"Sure. I'll have a beer," said Harry, "anything imported. Girls, what will you be having?"

"I want to try a little red wine," said Judy. "Something good but not too expensive."

"Just water for me," said Susie Q.

The waiter left. After the waiter walked away Harry saw an older couple a few tables away, staring at them with mean scowls.

"Wonder what they're looking at," said Harry.

"You can't bring your booty-bots in here," the older man had gotten up and walked over to Harry's table and was leaning on it in an aggressive manner.

"You must be out of your mind. How dare you insult us this way?" the older woman said, joining her husband in the confrontation at Harry's table, her wrinkled face almost shaking in anger.

"What makes you so certain they're booty-bots?" asked Harry.

"Two beautiful women with (hmmph) a loser like you?" said the woman through gritted teeth. "What else could they be?"

"They're more than booty-bots. Much more. If only you knew," said Harry.

"Phhhhaaaa!" said the man. "They ought to kick the lot of

you right out of here. Bringing a couple of wire-heads into a fine establishment like this."

"I don't want trouble. I just want to take my girls out for a nice meal, and what gives you the right to tell me where to go or with whom?" Harry bristled.

"This used to be an upstanding place," said the older man.

"My girls are upstanding," responded Harry.

"We don't want that kind in here, nor you, you, you booty-bot lover," said the older woman.

"It's a crime against nature to parade your perversions in public," continued the man. "You ought to be ashamed. In fact, I'm going to get management and have them escort you out of here right this second."

"Why don't you like us," asked Judy of the couple?

"Don't speak to me, you, you abomination," said the woman.

"Look. Why don't you two go sit back down? I'll pick up your tab and let's try to remain friendly," said Harry.

"That's not going to happen," said the man as he hailed the waiter. "I want to see your manager," he told the waiter.

"He's right over there. I'll get him," and soon the waiter had brought back the tall, handsome manager.

"Is there a problem here?" he asked the couple.

"We've been coming here for years," said the elderly woman. "I thought this restaurant was top rank and suitable for humans to go out and dine in fashion. But if you wanna serve Booty-Bots here, then to hell with this place!" yelled the older woman.

"I'm sure there is some misunderstanding. What makes you think these women are booty-bots? They look perfectly normal to me," said the manager.

"We are booty-bots," said Judy.

"Both of us," said Susie Q.

"Well what are you doing here then?" asked the manager.

"Is there a problem?" asked Harry, trying to explain himself. "You don't discriminate against booty-bots here, do you?"

"Well, no," said the manager.

"Oh come on. You are certainly allowed to discriminate against machines," said the trouble-making older man. "That's ridiculous!"

"There are laws against it," said the manager.

"Then you won't be seeing us here about any time soon!" said the the old woman.

"The hell there are, and if there aren't any laws against it, there should be," shouted the old man and picked up a chair as if to hit one of the booty-bots. "I won't have machines taking tables at my favorite restaurant."

The manager managed to pry the chair away from the old man, just as a two Citizen's Policemen walked.

"They serve booty-bots here!" said the old man. "At our early dinner hour!"

"Have you two eaten already?" asked one of the Citizen's Policeman of the elderly couple. When they nodded he said, "then I suggest you pay your tab and leave in an orderly fashion. We'll take it from here."

"So you're going to kick them out too?" asked the old man.

"Just mind your own business and move along, or I may place you under arrest for interfering with police work."

"We're leaving, but know this. I plan to file a formal complaint against this restaurant and your two Citizen's Policemen if I hear you allow these two stainless steel sex kittens to stay where only humans belong. Am I clear?"

"File your report then and just go. Now!"

So the older man and woman paid their bill, as they shot sidelong menacing glances at Harry and his booty-bots. Then they left in a huff. The old man was already on the phone calling someone and making his complaint heard.

"Maybe you three should get going too," said one of the Citizen Policemen. "It might be better for everyone."

"Fine. I'm not hungry anymore anyway," said Harry.

"Let's go. I'll fix you something good when we get home,"

said Judy, and the three of them also paid what they owed for their drinks and left.

CHAPTER 15

ADAM AND EVE IN THE SUBWAY

After his son's funeral George Merrick trudged home and turned on his old Citizen's Police nabber-blabber, trying to forget the pain he felt deep within his broken heart. The blabber reported that there had been a booty-bot disturbance at a local restaurant, scaring a few patrons. Two customers at the restaurant had filed a complaint. Harry Novak's name was mentioned.

So he was now out in the open, where George could pluck him up and slowly devour him, if he wanted. George had long suspected Harry had something to do with Warthog's death, since video files existed that showed his son at Harry's house the day of his death. Quite a coincidence. Ideas tumbled around in George's mind and the more he thought about it the more he wanted a piece of this Harry's hide.

The Lolligag Grotto was where the disturbance happened. Wasn't that a bit expensive for a jerk like Harry who just received a new booty-bot and lived in a common Go-Poddy, thought George? Was he celebrating with the blood money he made snitching on my son — that led to his death? And is he now out partying the very same day I'm putting my precious boy into the ground?

George punched a hole into the wall of his recently-acquired home he had bought for himself and his son after winning the lottery. Now, all this meant nothing to George. All the MUTs. All the better stuff. But no Warthog to enjoy it.

George decided he would go hunt this Harry Novak, while he's out of his protective Go-Poddy element, maybe he'd be at the SuperSubway Station near his home or the one near that restaurant. There George would act quickly and silently, perhaps even deadly. George was no longer on the Citizens Police force. He no longer had a wife. He no longer had a son, and when he called for his booty-bot Susie she was no where to be found. George was losing everything he had in this world that he cared about. Well, no more. No more!

Meanwhile, Lulu Gooley had done some similar tracking on her boss's Infopooter and had a beat on Harry and his booty-bot's whereabouts. She thought along the same lines as George Merrick, of wanting to catch up to him in an open spot. But she wanted to fascinate Harry, entrap him, seduce him with the weapons provided to her by Resurrection Cosmetics. Her goal in life now was to force this man to toss aside his booty-bots forever and fall head over heels for herself — for the greater good of all humanity.

You see, ten years prior, at the beginning of the Great War, Lulu Gooley was only 14 and was with her parents at the E4E Epiphany Church. The family was staunch believers in the main tenets of that modern faith. They believed God made Earth for Earthlings (hence the E4E name), and as such they were the tenders and protectors of this planet. To run away from such a glorious gift from God was the same as rejecting God Himself.

They further believed that if a person were to run away from a world in trouble, like so many of the rich, famous and beautiful had done just before the war got terrible, was an act subject to God's wrath.

So Lulu Gooley and her parents and her little sister Becky stayed behind when the men in the radiation-protection suits came to Lulu's family fallout shelter and asked them one last time if they didn't want to ride in the rocket ship to another world — a world where children could go outside and play and breathe, a virtual new heaven in the stars. Some religious groups got special preference for a strictly religious exo-planet being planned.

But her parents final answer was a resolute “no” and the men in protective suits left. For six long months the family stayed in that underground shelter. When they ran out of food the father and mother took turns going outside, looking for food. They did this for several weeks but started getting sick. Later they both died, leaving Lulu and her little sister Becky to fend for themselves. They looked for the Reverend Franklin, but he had died also, leaving behind many holograms of his preaching for those who might survive.

Luckily for Lulu and her little sister Becky, a child’s immune system is a lot stronger than were their parents’. They eventually left the shelter and made it to the city. One big building still seemed occupied and that was Resurrection Cosmetic Company. Inside all the employees were overjoyed to see that two young fairly attractive girls had escaped the ravages of war and had remained on earth. So many women and children were rocketed away. Many died. And many other people had moved to the polar regions, which had been spared some of the awful heat and destruction.

So because of the scarcity of females, the booty bot trade flourished.

Shin Shin Skinny, the half Asian beauty with long flowing black hair and eyes slightly hooded in that sexy-knowing way, veiled in light brown mystery, was just a junior executive at Resurrection Cosmetics at that time. She had taken a liking to the girls when they walked in so unexpectedly. Shin Shin talked the company into setting the girls up in an apartment nearby, even giving Lulu a job at Resurrection so she could make a living for herself and her younger sister.

Lulu wasn’t very pretty then, but Shin Shin saw the potential in her. The effects of low-level radiation had not been kind to Lulu. But she worked hard and was allowed to take home some sampler cosmetics. In time her appearance improved and her skin started regaining a normal look, even starting to soften and flatter her features.

Through it all Lulu kept a lot of E4E Epiphany Church inside her. She figured these were the Tribulation years. She held out hope of a savior coming to set up shop, as she worked and took care of her younger sister, acting as a surrogate mother in these dire times.

Then, years later, when Shin Shin decided to take Lulu under her wing as a business associate, by asking her to save the world by seducing Harry Novak and making him fall in love with her, with the use of special Resurrection Cosmetics, Lulu was only too happy to oblige. She wanted love. She wanted to share her world with another and help humanity and earth survive. It had been drilled into her ever since she could remember by the E4E Church.

Lulu thought about the Garden of Eden, with only Adam and Eve. If she could make this Harry fella love her more than he loved his Booty-Bots, then wasn't she a kind of secondary Eve? Oh sure, there were other human couples left on earth, but they were scattered, raising one child or none, loving as best they could, many wishing they had taken one of those rocket ships off this seemingly God-forsaken planet.

Her former minister, the Reverend Franklin used to always preach and say, "God has infinite mercy. He pours out His gifts. He gives us the food we eat; the means to reproduce and be plentiful. He gives us water and trees and flowers and all things beautiful. But mostly, He gives us life here on earth. Are we to just throw all that away and say, 'this planet isn't good enough anymore. I want to rocket away to another world — an easier, more comfortable world?' That's like throwing God's gifts back in His face, and believe me brothers and sisters, no one likes to have their gifts disrespected."

The Right Reverend Franklin was right, thought Lulu. I'm going to be pleased with God's gifts and I'm going to be pleased with Resurrection Cosmetics, and I'm gonna get that MAN!

Lulu thought back on a recent hologram she had watched of the Reverend Franklin.

"People used to tell me," she recalled him saying, "that the Mass Exodus of this planet was, in fact, the rapture, foretold long ago in the Holy Bible. But don't be deceived. They will tell you, 'well, couldn't God have used the spaceships as his chosen vehicles to take people away from the coming tribulation?' And I say, that wasn't a rapture. That was a rupture. It was a leak. It was a loss of souls needed here on earth during these difficult times of the Antichrist and Tribulation. And all those folks who ran away, thinking they were running toward their God-given right to be saved, they were just plain tricked. They are sure to mightily regret it one day.

"I want to be here," Lulu remembered vividly Rev. Franklin's powerful words, "I want to see with my own two eyes the coming of our Lord. And I'm sure He can find those people on those other planets and tell them Himself, 'friends, you abandoned the gifts I gave you and left the lovely world I created — when it was hurt and in stitches — when it needed you most.'"

Lulu loved listening to him go on and on about how one day the world would be renewed and a true paradise would come about here, not on some far-away exo-planet.

But Lulu didn't know what the Reverend Franklin would think about her plans to use Resurrection Cosmetics special line of sure-fire men-alluring products as a way to make God's plans speed up a little. But the ends justified the means, at least to Lulu Gooley. And the Right Reverend Franklin wasn't around to advise against her pink blush, moisturizing for super skin softness strategy. And maybe God's plans included Resurrection Cosmetics too. Wasn't that company working on ways right now to help clean up the environment?

* * *

George Merrick ate a small cheese sandwich he had purchased at the SWAY vendor store. It tasted bland as he leaned against a subway platform column and stared at the endless blue and white tile floor, smeared with spit and grime and who knows what else. His sandwich had a bitter taste. It tasted mean. It tasted like his enemy's blood. It tasted like a lost son that someone ratted out and murdered. It tasted like a shattered heart; like an empty pit wherein fell all the hopes and dreams he had carried so long for his only son. It tasted wrathful and angry and frustrated and all these conflicting emotions welled up inside him until he felt a small tear fall down the side of his face. George cursed that tear, flung it far away from himself, and punched himself in the jaw.

Don't be weak, he told himself. Stay focused. Get this Harry Novak fella and maintain your flex and resolve. I gotta get him good. It won't bring my beloved Warthog back, but it was an action, a way to feed those myriad of hungry demons. He didn't need those so-called friends telling him "if there's anything we can do for you, don't hesitate." Oh, he'd hesitate. He'd hesitate until hell froze over. He wasn't looking for anyone's pity. He wasn't looking for lousy, good-for-nothing compassion. He was looking for blood-red justice, the only justice he could imagine.

Wait. There he comes walking down the subway stairs. Who's that with him? Is that my booty-bot Susie? It is! He's got my Susie. First he takes my son, now he's stealing my Booty-Bot too! He can't just grab everything I have in this world and leave me with nothing! He's got his own Booty-Bot, for God's sake. Why take one from the house of the man whose son he murdered? He's trying to throw this whole mess of crap in my face and make me eat shit!

Almost to the bottom of the stairs now. Has his own booty-bot with him too. There's three of them. They seem to be laughing and having a good time. Well, I'm about to change all that. Yes. I'm going to fuck-up Harry Novak's little world. First I'll destroy his booty-bot in front of him, then my own, and then kill him slowly and painfully. I'm going to enjoy this. I need to get them alone. I need to take my vengeance here, at this station. It's dark and almost empty now, so no one can stop me once I begin.

Twe-bedp-beep-beetle-beep. Here comes a SWAY subway car now. They're distracted as they await on the platform.

George Merrick, the angry father bent on revenge, threw

his cheese sandwich on the floor. And he snuck from post to post to get nearer to Harry Novak and the bots.

Stealthily making her way from the other direction, unbeknownst to George, was Lulu Gooley, looking hotter than a newly minted Golden MUT monetary unit. She had checked with her hand-held infopooter and positively ID'd Harry Novak. She was well prepared for this meeting. Her hair was glowing like summer raindrops. Her lips were red and plump and magically infused with secret intoxicating ingredients. Her fragrance was a honeymoon in and of itself. Harry smelt her before he saw her and raised his nose into the air to catch more of this wonderful fragrance.

Lulu didn't know how she would deal with the two booty-bots Harry was with. They were very pretty, she thought. Perhaps they would remain passive as Lulu worked her Resurrection magic on him. Wasn't one artificial woman enough for this man, she thought? Would she have to be twice the woman these booty-bots pretended to be? Lulu could do that. She'd been saving up her passion for a long, long time now and was ready to unleash it full-blast.

George Merrick was coming now at Harry. He was a pistol. He was brass knuckles, a stiletto, a switchblade, a clenched fist, a hard elbow to the back, a kick in the nuts, teeth ready to bite off an ear, everything evil, hateful, harmful, violent, angry, all balled up and shooting directly toward Harry Novak, teen-killer and booty bigamist.

Lulu had her Miriam's Well Exotic Eye Drops, sparkling with hearts. She had her Holy Lazarus Pink Lip Balm, ready to splash bubbling passion of amor on Harry's unprepared lips. And that perfume Harry was smelling was the deal-breaker: the 50X Pheromone-Enhanced Riveting Beguiler called Hot-Vamp-Legs-Quivering-Lying-In-Passionate Elysian Fields, "the not-even-subtle ambush that tears down every man's unwilling walls and guides him forcibly toward the inevitable."

As Lulu rushed toward Harry, romance in her heart, so did George, with intense hate. The two strongest emotions on this or any other planet, animated in the bodies of Lulu and George, were set to crash and explode right on top of Harry Novak.

Lulu was a soft haze Hollywood Gaussian Girl. It seemed she was doing a slow motion dance as she moved through the vapors of anticipated heavenly love toward what she thought would be an eternal Eden-like happiness.

George came like a charging bull, roaring, chasing a brash matador with his red muleta, the barbed darts having been driven into him by numerous painful offenses, and smarting from the constant stabs into his heart by his only son's recent death. George didn't know, that like the bull, he was falling into fate's awaiting Matador's hands. It wasn't to be a retaliatory death he would administer, but it would be something else as he rushed toward Harry like a runaway subway train.

There was Lulu, like a Valentine, like a bouquet of fresh flowers on a first date, like a corsage for a high school prom, like a 15-year-old's first crush. She was like a horse-drawn chariot downtown in the moonlight, a third generation white wedding gown being adjusted on her daughter by the mother of the bride, a luxury limousine rented for the beginning of a giddy honeymoon. She was all these things and more, a pink torpedo of yearning so intense it fairly lit up the subway SWAY station.

And there was George, bulleting through the station like a battering ram, an angry arrow, a bullet with a name on it. What would happen when these opposite forces met? Inside that Subway SWAY station something was about to occur, perhaps similar to an electrostatic Supercollider, breaking up the fabric of the world.

A distracted Harry Novak noticed something shiny on the ground and leaned over to retrieve a stray NUT coin. As he did so George flew over Harry like a cold laser beam and crashed into Lulu Gooley, who had been rushing like a totally committed declaration of love at Harry from the opposite direction.

Both George and Lulu missed their intended target. They fell into each other and started rolling on the platform floor, rolling closer and closer to the tracks where a fast-moving SWAY Subway car was approaching the station. The momentum was too much. They rolled and couldn't stop. As they were entangled hot flames shot out from their eyes and ears and their whole bodies shook and burnt with a visible yellow flame of fire, such was the intensity of the meeting of long-hoped-for love and deeply driven hate.

Susie Q was quick to the edge near the tracks. George held up a hand and Susie Q grabbed hold of the burning mess and pulled them away from that never-slowing subway car, now approaching the station. Susie Q's hands lit on fire as she yanked at the George, who was still entangled with Lulu. Susie Q pulled and yanked at this blaze of blistering passions.

With a final great effort she pulled Lulu and George away from the tracks and sure death. This unlikely couple of hate and love incarnate stood, still flickering a kind of blue flame on the platform, staring deep into each others eyes.

Soon the multicolored fire on Susie Q's hands died down. It wasn't a flesh or plastic burning fire, emanating into the Subway platform area. It was something that came as if from some powerful push-spark spinner toy, newly created by the fusion of George Merrick and Lulu Gooley. It was a kind of beautiful cosmic fire of two forces so extreme that their mixture set off a chain reaction of colored electronic sparks in both the participants and the auras around them, converting them, changing the two of them into one firestorm of a person. In God's eyes, they were now married and as one. No need to get official. They were partners, soulmates, destined by fate to go on together forever and ever.

Harry was afraid. He thought George was going to do him great harm. This feeling reverberated especially so when knives, brass knuckles, bullets, and a gun dropped away from George's clothing like a dog shedding hair. And he didn't know what to make of the young girl George now held in his arms, but he felt strangely attracted to her. George and Lulu stood there, their clothing falling off at the same time, like a golden glowing Adam and Eve, with no shame, no visible idea that there was anyone else in the world but them, together, finding that which life had almost kept hidden.

Just then a squadron of Citizen's Police stormed down the subway entrance stairs in full armor with weapons drawn. The platform was still brightly lit from the beautiful crash of extreme polar opposites that occurred. Harry, sensing that the police might be after him, grabbed both bots by the hand and ran off down the narrow corridors of the subterranean station, hoping to find an exit and perhaps elude this show of police force. Perhaps, Harry thought, that the police had found him the same way that George and Lulu had found him, and perhaps George had discovered that his son was actually killed at his house, or that his booty-bot Judy had something to do with it and sicced them onto him.

"Wait! Hold on there! Stop!" shouts were delivered toward Harry, but he kept running as fast as he and his bots could travel. Luckily his bots were equipped to travel quickly, if need be, and their mechanical legs churned even faster than his own, almost pulling Harry along at many turns.

Harry and the bots reached another stairways that led to an exit and they flew up the stairs and into the harsh light. They found a Skycab waiting there for potential customers. After boarding it they directed the automated skycab toward their next destination, which was Harry's Go-Poddy.

As the skycab flew through the smoggy atmosphere Harry thought he felt a distant, intangible something as he contemplated that shiny naked couple of George, and that girl standing at the station. That feeling might have had something to do with his own lost Emily, the wife who rocketed away to an off-world paradise, but Harry could never admit that to himself. He tried not to think about Emily — ever, because she was an to Harry nothing more than an Earth and husband deserter.

He had his wonderful booty-bot Judy now, and even another one named Susie Q, to keep his loneliness at bay. Would it be possible for him to learn to love this alien-controlled Judy in an all-encompassing, satisfying way? Would she be enough for him now that he saw what really strong human love could do? He figured he would give it a try — even if she wasn't the precise model he had wished for. Yes, he'd give her a good try.

CHAPTER 16

THE BOOTY-BOT MAKER PLAYS GOD

Little did Harry or his booty-bots know that close behind them, in his own custom personal hovercraft, was Ravi Moonbeam, co-owner of Posh Matosh Playmate Company. Harry wondered if there was a safe path home anymore. He couldn't be certain that the Citizen's Police were really after him or not, and he wasn't sticking around to find out. I mean, he hadn't done anything wrong, had he?

Inside his custom hovercraft Ravi looked at himself in the console mirror and admired his jet black hair clinging to the side of his olive skin. Ravi imagined his smile, with his big bright, perfectly-formed teeth, could melt a glacier, if there were any of those still left on earth.

"Approaching intended target," said a speaker inside Ravi Moonbeam's skycraft.

"Prepare to intercept," he said into the air and to the operating computer system of his sky craft.

A shadow fell over the skycab Harry and his bots were in.

"We've got company. Some kind of gigantic craft and it's getting closer to us," said Harry to Judy and Suzi Q. "They seem to be pulling us upwards toward them! Buckle up and get ready for impact. I can't pull away!"

And Harry's little autocab was slowly pulled up. A door opened underneath Ravi's luxury vehicle and pulled the autocab into Ravi's skycraft. They found their little skycab engulfed by this much larger ship, sucked into it like a vacuum cleaner. Inside this craft sat in a large hanger area in a kind of transparent jail cell. Here a loud speaker instructed them to exit their cab.

"What's going on Harry," asked Judy of her master?

"I'm not sure," Harry answered, looking at the intricately carved golden, jewel-bedecked walls of this fancy vessel and wondering if this was a police vehicle or not. "Too fancy a vehicle for a Citizen's Police ship."

A door slid open and Ravi Moonbeam, co-owner of Posh Matosh Playmates came out to greet them.

"Hello," said the co-founder of Posh Matosh Playmates.

"I know who you are," said Harry. "You're Mr. Moonbeam."

"Right you are. I guess you should know me," said Ravi. "I see you brought two of my favorite models with you: the ultra-stunning Tropical Veronica and the Alluring 1971 Suzanna Facsimile Georgia Peach design. Are you enjoying my creations? Having any problems with these two symbiots? Treating them well? Performing standard lubrication and upkeep? Is the Veronica model trying to boss you around? They tend to do that, especially these Symbiot models, and you have to gain the upper hand or, well, you know. It's like they think they're better than us. I have a few of my own Veronica's so I know this situation well."

"I call my Veronica model Judy and the other is Susie Q. And yes, sometimes Judy does get bossy, but there's no problems," answered Harry. "I think she's looking out for my best interests. And yes, I am treating them well. Everything seems fine and I have been performing routine maintenance," said Harry.

"But I'm a little puzzled as to why you brought us here," said Harry. "What's this all about? I don't understand. Why are you keeping us in a cage?"

"It's for everyone's safety," said Ravi, as he did the Indian head wobble. "I wanted to intercept you before George Merrick or the Citizen's Police did. You must know they're definitely hot on your trail," said Ravi, standing up and inspecting the two booty-bots.

"We did meet up with George," said Harry. "But he got side-tracked and the policemen, well they probably got diverted by now."

"Oh, is this true? Well, he's not your only concern right now, but you must also worry about me. I'm sure George informed the Citizen's Police that he suspected you or your booty-bot of killing his son and now you're become prime suspect in that horrible case. They'll stay on this chase as long as it takes. Soon you might find yourself in a whole lot of trouble, were you aware of that?"

"Well, I suspected," said Harry. "What are they saying I did?"

"Um, let me see," said Ravi. "First there's the episode of your newly acquired booty-bot killing a juvenile. I know that whole story so don't try to deny it. Also, there is the unauthorized exit of your alien from your booty-bot back to her home planet of Metta Karuna, and the presence here of an unauthorized alien in this booty-bot you stole from George Merrick. You're facing serious criminal charges, Harry. Murder, by way of robot, kidnapping of a booty-bot, and the harboring of a fugitive and an illegal alien, to name just a few of the charges that may come up once you're caught. Harry, Harry, what shall we do about you?"

"I suppose I'm in quite a pickle," said Harry, looking at both of his booty-bots.

"It most certainly looks that way," said Ravi, standing up. "What if you hand these two booty-bots of yours over to me and later on, when these investigations die down, I exchange them with one of our more conventional models? You wouldn't want another Veronica, but we have many other varieties from which you can choose. You see, I could make this whole problem you've got go away and you'd still have a booty-bot. But now you'd have the kind of booty-bot you originally wished and asked for, but weren't given — and not one of these trouble-making symbiots."

"I've grown rather fond of my Judy," said Harry, touching her hand.

"What? You've only had her two weeks now," asked Ravi, looking down on Judy and Susie Q, inspecting his creations as if he were a God. "I know it's a difficult choice, but if I were you I'd take my generous offer. Let me ask you, and tell me the truth: is it the booty-bot itself you've grown fond of or the alien residing within it? She's unpredictable, Harry. This one is a real maverick. I believe both of these symbiots have a different agenda than what you signed up for."

"I've made some mistakes," offered up Judy. "But I and my people have no secret agenda here on this planet."

"I'd say murder was a pretty big mistake — whether it was on your agenda or not," said Ravi. "I've never known one of my booty-bots to kill. On this planet that's a big deal, Judy."

"I didn't mean to kill the young boy," whimpered Judy. "I was only pushing him away."

"Well, and then you went inside the boy and walked yourself to the SWAY station and threw his body in front of a moving subway car," said Ravi. "You DID mean to do that, now didn't you, Judy?"

"I didn't want to get my Harry in trouble," said Judy crying.

"And you — inside my Suzanne model," said Ravi. "Why are you here on this planet without authorization?"

"I came to this planet to help Judy with her guilt problems," said Susie Q. "She summoned me. But since I've been here I've noticed that your whole human race needs a little of what we aliens can provide or it could face extinction. We are helpful beings. We can go into human bodies and create enzymes that bolster the lymphatic system, help it fight off the radiation poisoning, drain the human tissues of waste and improve immune responses. But most importantly we could help with human reproduction levels."

"It's not enough you reside in the booty-bots then," said Ravi. "You're thinking of taking over the whole human world and trying to boost our population? Maybe I need to re-think my new line of symbiot booty-bots. I wasn't aware of your true purpose here. I thought you were just imaginative lovers."

"We are altruistic," said Susie Q to Ravi. "Judy was only trying to protect her owner. She's not a criminal and neither am I. I want to be of service."

"You'll have a hard time explaining those high concepts to the courts," said Ravi. "They frown on you booty-bots going around leaving dead people in your wake, or leaving your owners without permission. As you know there already exists quite a firestorm of prejudice against your kind here on earth. And the buzz on you aliens hasn't yet reached a peak. That's why I think it best I get a handle on this situation myself."

"What do you plan to do with Judy and her teacher if I do give them up?"

"I'll eliminate them," said Ravi matter-of-factly. "And that would be hard for me to do, because I dearly love my creations. They're almost like daughters to me."

"Then I won't give them up to you," said Harry.

"I'm only trying to help you, Harry," said Ravi. "And it's not really a request. I am taking them back. Can't have this bad publicity walking around. I have a reputation to uphold at Posh Matosh. So, last chance, what do you say? You want to swap these two out for one slam-bang beautiful booty-bot especially made for pleasure giving? I could easily throw the Citizen's Police off your tail, clear your good name and you could go back to your job at Teen-A-Watch, and everything would return to normal."

"No. No deal. I'll take my chances with the law," said Harry.

"I don't think you want to do......"

In mid-sentence there was a huge jolt to the airship owned by Posh Matosh Playmates, and Harry felt himself and the ship shake as it was being captured in the air, just the way that Harry's skycab had been captured by Ravi's huge hovercraft.

Ravi ran to the window of his skycraft and looked out to see who was doing this. He saw that he was being pulled inside a larger skyship, a pink one, which he instantly recognized as the Resurrection Cosmetics Skyship One.

“Now what?” Harry asked Ravi.

“Shit. What do these scraggly hags want,” wondered Ravi, a big frown on his face?

CHAPTER 17

EMILY'S DAY TO LAY AN EGG

Emily Novak lounged uncomfortably in her chaise-style beach chair. She felt warmer than usual and bloated. She adjusted her yellow thong bikini. When did it start fitting so tight? The view of the faux ocean bored her. It repeated the same wave pattern over and over again. She dug out her compact from her huge purse. It had the Resurrection Cosmetics logo on the gold exterior. Within the mirror of the compact she looked at her freckled face. There were some small wrinkles forming around her eyes and near her upper lip. She wasn't getting any younger, nor any cuter, she thought. Plus, at 32 years of age, her days of being fertile and able to conceive a child were on the decline.

The piped-in sounds of the waves crashing against the imaginary shore did ease Emily's knotted tension. She sipped on her pink Mai Tai. A few more minutes under these two suns, one a small red and the other a larger yellow, would be suitable for maintaining her golden tan and lightening her flame red hair.

Because, didn't she have to keep looking beautiful? Wasn't that a requirement here? She'd already gone through her state-mandated exercise routine today, which was a really intense today, concentrating on her upper arms and her thighs. As usual, she also spent some extra time using an adjustable hand-grip and finger strengthening devises.

Two tall gruff, but smiling men approached Emily.

"Time to go to the chicken coop," said one of the men in a matter-of-fact manner.

"The egg doctor is waiting. He's a busy man," said the other.

"Already? Again? All right. Let me change and gather my things. Give me a moment," said Emily, taking her own sweet time.

Emily's day just got worse. She'd forgotten that this was one of her designated days for egg-furnishing. The state-operated procedure was simple and painless enough but Emily was growing to resent how they just took whatever they wanted from her body and sold it off to the highest bidder.

As she walked off with the two men she wondered why women weren't allowed to have children the old fashioned way anymore. What was this Eros society afraid of? Was it really for the welfare of the mothers, or to prevent deficient babies? Why couldn't Emily, or any woman for that matter, do as they wished concerning their own female body?

Emily recalled the supreme directive for females on Planet Eros: *All women under 40 years of age shall be required to maintain their sexy bodies in tip-top physical shape at all times for mandatory sexual sessions, and be willing to have their eggs harvested at the discretion of the Head Eggman.*

So this control the state had over her human female body extended to many areas of her life. All meals prepared for females were calculated to maintain maximum health and low body fat. Weekly beauty appointments and daily work-outs were mandatory. And of course, all women had to be fully stocked up on and utilizing the newest Resurrection Cosmetics beauty products.

Egg gathering was done, women were told, so that women needn't experience the pain and body-distortion of old-fashioned pregnancy. Many women didn't miss the suffering and the irritability that regular pregnancy required, and they didn't miss the responsibility of raising children.

But Emily thought that this sucking out of one's monthly egg, then secretly selling them or selecting male sperm to combine it with in a laboratory setting, seemed like a personal violation. Why did the Eros government have to dictate every aspect of Emily's personal life? Did men face such scrutiny? Emily dared not utter this out loud. Someone would surely turn her in for a reward if she did.

It was all about the show of happiness and male dominance here on Planet Eros. Women had to look appealing, in case a man approached with a sex voucher. Then, it was off to the various and numerous sex stations, where this state-run sex could be enjoyed in all its sanitary, guarded glory. The only way out of it for a woman was if they were in ovulation mode, too old, or dead.

"You OK," one of the men coldly asked Emily. Emily nodded.

"You're that special egger," said the other man to her.

"Special. You bet," said Emily sarcastically.

On Eros sex was regarded as similar to dinner or sleeping. It was a basic need and if the hunger arose, one merely approached the person of their desire and presented them with a standard government-issued sex voucher and proceeded with said person to a nearby coitus convenience station. Each person was granted a set amount of vouchers per month, based on one's age and needs. But if you had pull or were a man of power, you could easily have as many vouchers as you wished.

And every so often there was an egg-gathering from those females deemed priority fertile. These eggs were collected and used to create the next generation of humans on this planet, or were sold off to neighboring exo-planets who needed new, healthy, or in Emily's case, freckle-prone blood. This was Emily's day to egg-up.

She had come to this so-called Paradise exo-planet with her boss, Daniel Turnbull, thinking he had a special romantic interest for her. Why else take her along with him? Why hurriedly snatch her away from her fawning husband Harry?

Old Harry Novak, Emily thought back on him. He was a pretty good egg, really, but not the handsomest or smartest of men. During their short marriage he had told her he wasn't ready for children. Emily suspected Harry hated children, especially given that he spied on and had arrested young teens for the simplest societal violations as his work for Teen-A-Watch.

But her boss Daniel was a sweet-talker. He told Emily that on Eros she would be a woman of leisure, with a fulfilling life purpose. Turnbull had the power and confidence, good looks and a sexy manner that swept Emily away and easily persuaded her to ditch Harry and the world she learned was on the brink of a terrible war.

Danny Turnbull didn't turn out to be the knight in shiny armor Emily had hoped he would be. His outward charisma led to political aspirations and he became a powerful Corporation Leader, bossing everyone around once he gained their trust and their votes.

Votes, Emily thought to herself. They called this planet a new democracy but everyone knew that a woman's vote only counted for 1/2 or 1/4 of a vote, if at all, while a male vote was a full vote, and in some cases a double or triple vote. So who held all the power here? Who kept things the way they liked them? Who lorded over the females like roosters in a barnyard?

Turnbull had a large stable of sexual playmates, but as Emily was getting a little past 30, he had paid Emily off and turned to his younger playthings.

All this indiscriminate sex wasn't much fun anymore to Emily. If this was a paradise here on Eros, it was a paradise for men. You never knew who would hand you a sex voucher or what that would entail once you accepted it. The man might be into anal, three-ways, sadism. You never knew. You just never knew.

"Almost there," said one of the men escorting Emily to the chicken coop. "You ready?"

"Sure," said Emily, without apparent enthusiasm.

Emily thought back on life with Harry on Planet Earth. She knew Earth was pretty messed up now, since the Great War, but at least it was more real and held greater freedom for women than this freaky façade of a planet. At least she gathered as much from secret rumors.

Earth's problems, Emily knew, were very dramatic. And the people there struggled mightily. But Emily was beginning to believe she might be better off there than she was here. At least her maternal instincts were telling her that.

True, there were few worries on Planet Eros if you obeyed all the rules. All your chores, all your monetary concerns were solved here, by the Planet-wide Politio-Economic-Corporation (PEC). Danny Turnbull, Emily's former boss, was the leader now for this planet-wide Corporation and what he tried to maintain was unbridled pleasure — pleasure all the time — pleasure until the time of your death and no time for sadness, guilt or regret. Life here might be wonderful if not for the loss of the family unit, child-rearing, and female personal freedom.

If you happened to feel bad about one thing or another you went to see a Eroticologist and he'd fix you up quick with some fancy pills, maybe a few therapy sessions and a fist-load of extra sex vouchers. Nothing peps up tired blood better than rough sex — or so the saying went here on Planet Eros.

Emily and the two men finally arrived at the National Corporation Chicken Coop. Emily's two escorts made sure she checked in and stood guard. Here Emily would lay her egg or eggs at the feet of the almighty directors, never to see them again or know what kind of children she had helped create.

Emily was greeted at the front desk Corporation Chicken Coop by a bouncy, perky nurse.

"Hi there!" said the bubbly blonde nurse, "Here are some forms to fill out later. We'll run a few tests today before we get started. First let's get you on the scales. Good. Now let's check your blood pressure. Might need to draw a little blood."

Afterward all these check-in procedures Emily waited for the doctor to arrive in a small room. He entered checking her chart.

"Hello Ms. Novak," he said. "Glad to see you here again. This shouldn't take long. All your charts look great."

"Why my eggs? Why am I called in so often?" asked Emily, daring to broach the topic.

"I thought you knew," said the doctor, smiling. "Your DNA has a high likelihood of producing freckled, red-headed babies. These babies are popular right now, here on Eros and elsewhere. Your eggs are strong, easily fertilized, and make such cute babies. Truth is, your eggs are some of our most requested. Have you been taking the fertility drugs we sent you?"

"Yes," said Emily meekly. "So where will this egg of mine go today?"

"I'm not allowed to say," said the doctor, smiling widely, exposing perfect ivory teeth.

"But they're my eggs," protested Emily.

"Well, technically they're not," said the doctor. "Once you arrive on Eros, take our fertility drugs and they're harvested and put into cryogenic tanks, they belong to the Corporation."

Emily gritted her teeth.

"Anything wrong?" asked the doctor.

"This all seems wrong, messed-up," she said.

"Now look, Ms. Novak, if you're feeling depressed or anxious about something, anything, we have therapists on duty and afterwards you can go see one. We also have a wide assortment of emotion-balancing drugs you can choose from. We want this to be a pleasant experience for you."

"Ever question what you're doing here? I mean, disrupting human biology, playing God, mixing and matching sperm and eggs like mixing drinks at a bar?"

"Now hold on there. You know questions like that are forbidden," the doctor instantly lost his brilliant smile. "You were just joking around. Am I right? I could lose my license for letting you entertain such thoughts."

"Yeah, sure, just joking," but Emily wasn't joking and she didn't want to see a therapist afterwards and she didn't need any of those funny, mood-altering pills. Emily felt how she felt and was so tired of everyone trying to plaster a smile on her face and tell her how to act while they stole her eggs.

As Emily lay sedated, strapped down, with her legs in harnesses high in the air the doctor was breathing heavily. He was inserting the needle into her fallopian tubes trying to extract her precious human eggs.

Usually females only produce one egg per cycle, but with the fertility drugs Emily had been sent the doctor was hoping that he might get an even dozen this time from her. She'd proven a good source of eggs, and her eggs brought a high price because of their tendency to produce those sought-after red-haired, freckled kids. The Corporation would be happy and would reward the doctor handsomely if he could get extra eggs today. So he was careful to extract the eggs one by one. There were six this time, a half dozen. Not bad!

After the extraction, her eggs were taken to the cryogenic facility for instant freezing. Emily was allowed time to come back to her senses in a bright yellow recovery room.

Emily sat up after a few moments. A nurse came in and told her to sit a while longer. She gave Emily some fake orange juice with lots of vitamins and minerals in it, and told her to take it easy, until the anesthesia wore off.

"How many this time?" asked Emily, a tear flowing down the side of her face.

"Six! How exciting!" Then noticing Emily's state the nurse put an arm around her which she shrugged off. "There, there now honey, everything's going to be just fine. You'll see."

"The Chicken Coop! Guess I'm one of the hens, right?" shouted Emily. "I'm not even treated like a full human being!"

"OK sweetie. Calm down," said the nurse. "I know your emotions are running hot now. But don't you know that happiness is all around you and you're an important, loved member of society?"

"Am I? Am I really? Any real emotion I try to explore gets squashed like an Eros sand bug. I have no power over my own body and I can't do as I wish with my reproductive powers. It's like I'm a...a domesticated animal."

"That's dangerous talk, Ms. Novak," said the nurse. "You know you're more than that. I'll get you some nice hot tea."

"Tea! I don't want tea. I want to have a baby! I want power over my life. And you're offering me tea?"

The doctor came in.

"What's all this," asked the doctor, again smiling? "If you want to hold or care for an infant you can visit the Infant Care Center and they'll let you play with one. Why the sad face? Look all around you. This is Paradise here. You know how many women have died throughout history giving birth? Well, you've been spared that pain. You should rejoice. We live in the modern world. The Corporation Head knows what's best."

"Does he know my maternal needs? My need for a baby of my own, with a real husband — like how it used to be?"

"Do you want our all-immersive holo program that simulates that scenario?" asked the doctor. "You can take a copy home with you and play it anytime you feel this old-fashion, unnatural need. It's safe and it will make you feel a lot better."

"Fuck! Fuck! For fuck's sake!" yelled Emily. "I want to see the Corporation Head. I want to see Director Daniel Turnbull!"

"You know that isn't possible," said the doctor.

"He's the one who brought me here and I want to see him now! I wanna go back! I wanna go back to where I was born!"

"Keep this up and we'll have to do something drastic," said the doctor with a menacing tone. "We don't want to place you underground with the other female inmates, but if you keep going against the grain you leave us little choice. We can't have you poisoning the minds of other females. There's no going back to Earth. You do understand that, don't you? I suggest you go home and just settle down. Come back in a couple of days, when you're feeling better, and we'll go over your present feelings."

On her way out Emily stomped her foot and pushed over a large lamp and it broke on the floor.

"Hey!" said the nurse as Emily walked out the door. "Did

the doctor say it was OK for you to leave? Lady. Stop lady! That attitude of yours will get you in a whole barrel of trouble!"

But Emily was stomping down the street now cursing the whole system which turned her body into a commodity

CHAPTER 18

STRANGE SHIPS DANCING IN THE SKY

Earth's atmosphere became a little cleaner as the gigantic Skyship called the Pink Lotus, owned by Resurrection Cosmetics Company, opened from its space bud and let unfold magnificent pink solar petals. From the inner carpellary receptacle of this part-mechanical, semi-botanical ship, a huge atomizer released an air-cleansing, extremely pleasant scent from the pouch-like fuselages attached to the sides of the ship.

Jetting the Pink Lotus along were four main thruster rockets, shaped like lipstick tubes, which came in four flirty colors: Rascally Raquel Raspberry, Whisperingly Wanton Watermelon, Miss-the-Summer Tomato, and Pulsing Go Plum Crazy.

The ship also had strong electromagnetic rays emanating out of those petals, and they were directed squarely at Ravi's smaller Posh-Matosh Luxury One ship. Smog parted like the Red Sea and the two ships made themselves visible in the broken sky. Tiny pink and blue clouds appeared in the crevices of the atmosphere. The hint of a hopeful smile appeared at the corners of the sun's mouth, in between coughing spurts.

Ravi's spaceship, which had recently scooped Harry's skycab up into itself, was a totally mechanical thing, all steel and clang. But the bay-door entrance to the Pink Lotus Resurrection sky craft, used to pull in Ravi's craft, was fresh, wet, pink, moist, and graceful.

Ravi's rocket was red hot and moving steadily, albeit unwillingly, toward the pink pocket opening of this Pink Lotus skyship.

There was no thruster or reverse-gear that Ravi could push, pull or jerk up and down to avoid this birthing-in-reverse. It was a clammy, messy give and take that the Pink Lotus and the Posh Matosh Luxury One were doing, spinning in the burnt crust sky like birds dancing themselves into position to mate mid-flight.

Harry, inside Ravi's skycraft, could clearly see out the transparent overhead cockpit this hungry, dripping atmospheric hanky-panky between airships. As Ravi's skycraft began penetrating the pink organic folds of the female ship, the lotus spread its flexible pink entrance lips wide to allow the Posh-Matosh Luxury One inside her. Ravi's ship was slipping into this sensual aerial moorage and the more he tried to escape this hungry love flower, in a way similar to a Chinese finger trap, the tighter the clasp the lotus petals placed upon his ship.

The Pink Lotus seemed to grow pinker and pinker and more beautiful as the Posh Matosh Luxury One slipped deeper and deeper inside this large flower, lipstick case of a ship. You could almost hear a moan of pleasure as the cosmetically enhanced mothership worked her hypnotic magic on Ravi's helpless craft.

"Stop! Stop for the love of Rama! What do they think they're doing? We're being ambushed!" yelled Ravi at the top of his lungs. But there was no stopping the union as half of Ravi's ship was now enveloped in the pink membrane. It was being swallowed up, like a reticulated python opening its unhinged jaws and forcing its prey down into its stomach.

The Posh Matosh Luxury One ship was pulsing with an involuntary rhythmic energy, ever expanding from the strain, and with a final gush it broke through this organic wall and lay dripping on the interior receiving deck of Pink Lotus. Automated robotic washers wiped clean the visiting ship.

Ravi, sweating profusely and cursing, knew good and well

who was up to this unwanted capture, and knowing this, he released Harry and the two bots. The side panel of Ravi's ship flopped down and the four inhabitants descended onto the Pink Lotus receiving deck.

Shin Shin Skinny, Executive Vice President, and June "VA-VA" Ba Boom, president and CEO of Resurrection Cosmetics, walked down a pink marble staircase, dressed in their most alluring outfits. These two women were dressed to dazzle, tease and tempt any male who saw them. Sequins, sparkly décolletage, split skirts up to their thighs, their dresses were elegantly designed to lure and ensnare members of the male species.

Ravi pointed a finger at them as if to challenge his captivity or to protest his being taken against his will, but no sounds came out of his mouth. He felt like he would explode in a puddle of mud if one of those ladies came any closer to him, such was their seductive powers. Even though Ravi was a prince among his booty-bots, he felt like a mere peon being in proximity to these two world-class human beauties.

"We could easily make you men fall head over heels in love with us," said Shin Shin. "But we won't; not now, so you can both relax."

"We understand what men like you want: to keep buggering your artificial sex dolls," said Ms. Ba Boom to Harry and Ravi. "It's not easy for men to mature. I think every man would like to stay a little reckless boy, with no responsibility to anyone or anything. And these robots of yours provide you with that freedom, plus the sex you so desperately yearn for. But I should think the taste and feel of plastic and silicone on your lips and skin grows old and boring after a certain period of rubbing against it. Doesn't it?"

"Not yet," said Harry. "And it feels like real flesh to me."

"Yes, real men are getting rarer and rarer, but the world sure could use some," said Shin Shin. "It's all we can do to keep women attractive and beautiful with our cosmetics line and able to compete with these booty-bots for any crumbs of male attention. It's a growing sickness, men clamoring over these dolls."

"What's a man supposed to do," chimed in Harry? "Just go crazy about women with unapproachable cosmetic charms? Forget all about how women ran away with the rich and famous to another planet when the going got tough? Forget how wives left us alone in a war zone to hide away with more attractive men on a planet in some faraway paradise? After all that, am I supposed to just stay here on earth, lonely and hurt, and suffer for the rest of my miserable life? There's not enough human women to go around. You know that. Oh sure, I'd like to have a real woman that was super sexy like you two, but that just isn't possible for a guy like me, now is it?"

"You tell me," said Shin Shin, "have you really tried picking yourself up after your wife left you?"

"Now you're giving me lessons?" continued Harry, "You, up there in your pink ivory tower, sitting in your hoity-toity Resurrection office building, wearing your snooty perfume and parading around in your high and mighty luxurious high-heels. You must be looking down your Queen Bee noses at all of us worker-bee men, we, who are just struggling to keep our sanity and our heads above water, you teasing us all the while, trying to get us worked up and begging for your precious p..."

"Uh hum, decorum, Harry," insisted Ba Boom.

"OK, so here we all are — on a mucked up planet," Harry was really getting worked up now. "No one cared a lick for this planet we live on. They thought it wiser and in their own best interests to keep making their world-killing profits, waving their macho munitions all over the globe, and just allowing the whole thing to be blown up like an overcooked soufflé. Of course the ultra rich could just ferry off to some other planet and wave bye-bye while the rest of us poor creatures wallowed around the best we could in the shit they manufactured.

"And you're telling me now that I'm not a real man because I have wonderful sex with my alien-aided booty bot?" shouted Harry. "You? You who can't even connect to the reality all around you, but try to mask it in some kind of super concealing magical mascara? You, who thinks this pink lotus whatever-it-is, is going to help clean up this sick planet we can hardly breathe on?

"I wish my wife didn't leave me," said Harry. "I really do. I prayed long and hard that there never would have been that terrible war, or that somehow I could have raised the MUTs to go take her away from all this myself. I've often wished I could go back in time and somehow prevent that teen-ager named Warthog from dying. But that's not how the dice were rolled for me and so here we are.

"This is where we're at and we've gotta make the best of it, even if this is the very last gasp of hope for all of us. I'll have my booty-bot sex and I'll enjoy it for as many days as I have left, and I don't give a good damn what you think of me as a man. I'll keep surviving — until this world finally withers up like a lotus at night and crawls below the surface of all possible life on earth — once and for all time."

"What if there was a way for you to get a human female, a nice one, a really nice one?" asked Ba Boom.

"See. Now there you go teasing me again. Haven't I made myself clear?" asked Harry.

"No, just hear me out, if you had a choice, would you want a real woman, like the wife who ran away say, or would you stick to your booty-bots?" asked Shin Shin.

"Ladies, take a moment to admire my work on these booty-bots," interrupted Ravi. "My creations are so life-like that it's really not a fair question to pose to poor Harry here. Just gaze upon these masterpieces of biological design. You can even see tiny fine hairs on their arms and stomaches, the perforations in their amazing lips, the intrigue and beguilement in the pupils of their eyes. I've thought out and delivered on every detail of these women to make them appear as realistically human as possible, perhaps even to improve on the subjects."

"Superficially, maybe," said Shin Shin.

"Says the master concealer," said Ravi.

"No offense Judy," said Harry, turning to Judy, "but you're

almost as unpredictable as a real woman, and you boss me around and get me in trouble. If I thought it possible I might just choose a real woman."

"I've made some mistakes," said Judy, hanging her head. "I'm sorry I got you in trouble."

"Yes you have. The Citizen's Police are out trying to arrest me right now!" said Harry. "I'm in big trouble because of you. I mean, you're from another world; you're a completely different life form than me. Oh sure, you look great and act pretty human, and the sex with you is fantastic, but in the end..."

"Wake up, Harry," said Ravi. "This is the closest thing you'll ever find to true love, and she'll never leave you. She'll be there forever and never age. Face it. The possibility of having a real woman just doesn't exist for you."

"Oh, it's possible," said Ba Boom. "We're preparing now to set a course for Planet Eros. We'll be making a large cosmetic delivery, with enough room to take several hundred women back to earth with us, if they want to return here. And I know many of them do want to come back to earth, bad environment and all."

"What makes you so certain they'd scurry back to this shit-hole of a world?" asked Ravi.

"Because it's their home. And Resurrection Cosmetics is determined to try to clean up this mess with some of the scientific methods we've developed recently," said Boom-Boom.

"We can help too," said Susie Q.

"I want to learn more about that from you later," said Ba Boom.

"So these fortunate women on Eros are just going to pack up and leave paradise for some promise you made that you'll be able to clean up their old planet and what? Turn the men here against their booty-bots?" asked Harry.

"There's a growing women's movement on Eros," said Shin Shin. "Those ladies are expressing their unhappiness and are willing to do something about it. It's an ultra male-dominated society on Eros and the women have practically no rights or freedoms. The men harvest the women's eggs and sell them abroad, as if they are livestock. They aren't allowed to form family groups and have children of their own, the natural way. These women are looking for a way out of all that, and would risk coming back here to make a new go of things."

"Women have more control over their own destiny here on earth," said Ba Boom. "They've grown powerful and taken hold of the reins. Those women from Eros want in on some of that. They want a say in determining their own fates, starting their own businesses, being in control of their lives."

"So what did you have in mind? Are you going to go rescue them?" smirked Ravi. "Isn't that a noble gesture? But it won't work. You think those Eros men will give up their women that easily? My booty-bot company wouldn't like that either. You'd be bringing these gifts of women to the men of earth who don't really want them anymore. What could you offer these women?"

"Hope and a chance to make their home world, Earth, a better, more livable place. I think it will work out just fine," said Ba Boom.

"We want you to go with us Harry," said Shin Shin. "We want you to rescue your wife. She's in a lot of pain and may find herself in a lot of trouble if something isn't done soon."

"Pain? What's wrong with her," asked Harry?

"She's going insane, Harry," said Ba Boom. "Her life's in jeopardy because she's really fed up and she won't shut up. They'll have her working in the underground mines soon if she keeps this up. Might even kill her."

"But she left me," said Harry. "I didn't want to see her ride off into the sunset. Besides, she never gave me a second thought as her boss's rocket jetted off to that wealthy Never-Never land."

"You'd have gone too, if you had the chance," said Shin Shin. "And you know you would."

"Let me think about what you're asking me," said Harry.

"What's to think about," asked Shin Shin? "You stay here the Citizen's Police are going to be all over you. They'll probably confiscate your Judy booty-bot, and that other one too," she said pointing to Susie Q. "The bot you stole. Yes, you'll be in a lot of trouble once your feet touch the surface of the earth again. And if you somehow do elude the Citizen's Police, Ravi here will want to destroy these booty-bot products of his and replace them with others. Since they disobeyed protocol he has to do something. His business reputation is at stake."

"But you go with us and bring back home some real female humans to help with our dwindling population problem, then the government will probably drop all those charges and give you a hero's welcome," said Boom Boom.

"What makes you so certain?" asked Harry.

"Connections," smiled Ba Boom. "This operation won't be easy. We'll have to fight to get those women back. We'll just be a small force, but our ships will be well armed and organized."

"What will you use for weapons, eyeshadow and concealer?" asked Ravi. "That may work here but those Eros men are used to having their own way, always, and no matter what you throw at them, they have confidence and numbers on their side. So you may think your whole scheme is cute and amusing, but believe me, it won't be when you get all in their business."

"I have no intention of amusing you or anyone else," said Ba Boom. "You have no idea of the resources I possess and how much of those I would throw at saving this planet from extinction. So what about it, Harry?"

"Guess I really don't have any choice in the matter, do I? What will become of my booty-bots," asked Harry?

"Bring them along, for now," said Shin Shin. "Maybe they can be of use."

"What about me," asked Ravi? "Why drag me into this mess? I'll not be a part of your little scheme. Sounds insane."

"Your business is an unsustainable model," said Shin Shin. "Your buying base is decreasing because you've made these booty-bots to last so long, and thus your sales will be less and less over the years, until you have no customers at all. We need for this world to have women, real women who can make more women and men."

"You're being dragging into this mess because you chose to get involved by capturing Harry's skycab. You were probably going to turn Harry in and destroy your own booty-bots. Isn't that what you had in mind?" asked Shin Shin.

Ravi looked at Harry and his two booty-bots. "I'm a respectable business owner and I have my reputation to think of. You want to try re-introducing these human females into this world and you want to pretend you're in this just to save the world, then be my guest. But I know, in the end, you really are just trying to sell more lip gloss.

"You believe that all you human women are so incredibly hot, with your out-of-the-blue-made-up problems," continued Ravi, "all your monthly grouchiness, all your pathetic excuses for not wanting sex most of the time with us males? My booty-bots are what most real men crave. Beautiful, uncomplicated sex, whenever and however we want it. No complaining. No demands. No jealous boyfriends. No gauntlets or hoops to jump through — just pure fun and companionship."

"Women face more problems that you can imagine, you little slime ball," said Shin Shin. "And the problems we face here on earth are nothing to those the women on Eros face. There is no paradise where there isn't basic human rights."

"Harry, you must have known it was inevitable that something would go wrong as long as you worked in that Teen-A-Watch place," said Ba Boom. "Someone was bound to get upset with your snitching and wanting to arrest wayward young men. And you just snitched on the wrong young man when you turned in Warthog Merrill, son of an ex-Citizen's Policeman. The youth of Planet Earth just won't be going for all that much longer."

"We need to keep pushing human love and passion and compassion, and not all that fake bullshit that you peddle for profit," said Shin Shin to Ravi.

"God knows there aren't enough women to go around," Ravi continued. "All I'm doing is preserving the civil peace. There would be mayhem in the streets if I didn't provide a suitable outlet for all those pent-up passions with my booty-bots. Harry here knows that, don't you Harry? All the good female units, including your ex-wife, left Earth for Eros or some other exo-planet while all you men were left here to suffer, with a stupid look on your faces and your cocks in your hands."

"That's correct," said Harry. "And Judy is a fine replacement and does satisfy me."

"Well, when we get some of the real human females to return to earth, things will be different," said Shin Shin. "We have a plan."

"I won't allow you to bring those women back," said Ravi. "I'll fight you all the way, and I'm sure those exo-planets will battle you."

"You pathetic worm. You can't stop me," said Ba Boom. "Harry, you have a choice, go back with Ravi, face the wrath of the Citizen's Police and the unpredictability of this sleaze Ravi, or come with us now and we'll shelter you. You'll have to fight alongside us to free Eros women, though. What do you want to do?"

"I guess I'll go with you guys," said Harry.

"And that's how it is," said Ravi. "Peddling those out-dated corny concepts of love and chivalry. I want to get out of here, now!"

"Get in your skycraft and we'll release you then. Don't try to follow us or stop us or we'll make you go away like slight skin imperfections," said Shin Shin.

So Ravi hurried back into his skycraft and it was released back into the atmosphere. Harry watched it go and wondered if he had made the right choice. There was no turning back now.

CHAPTER 19

SOPHIA AND THE GREYSHIRTS

Emily sat and waited at her sidewalk cafe table for the arrival of an old girlfriend. The controlled atmosphere was tuned just right today, with the sound of piped-in Earth birds singing softly and cool, artificial breezes whiffing through the streets of this high-end shopping and entertainment district.

The La Potenza District showcased the culture, the latest fashions and the best food available on Eros. It was paved in colorful stone walkways with tall statues of men of government or power lining the streets. These statues included many current leaders including, DannyTurnbull, Emily's former boss. She found a chair that faced away from the Turnbull statue.

Emily tried to shut the sight of his white marble statue out of her mind, remembering how he had betrayed her. But Emily dared not show any dislike toward his images, because there were watchers everywhere who would report you to authorities if you showed the slightest sign of unhappiness or disrespect in this new Paradise — especially if was displeasure shown toward the present Corporate Leader.

Emily was glad she could splurge on lunch with her old friend Sophia Songsen. It had been a long time since their days on the intergalactic transport ship, where they had first met and formed a friendship over card games.

Sophia was late. The lunch was set for noon and it was

now 12:30. The waiter seemed to be growing anxious. Perhaps, thought Emily, it was because other patrons were waiting on tables and he wanted to turn the tables quick and make as much in tips today as possible.

Emily had gotten over her bad feelings of her egg deposit and was enjoying a slight buzz from SSRI anti-anxiety drug Paroxetine. She wasn't supposed to, but Emily also had ordered a glass of red wine and was feeling almost giddy. She smiled nervously as the waiter hovered around her table, giving her sidelong glances.

Other patrons were paired up at the white cafe patio tables, holding hands, discussing voucher arrangements, or stealing kisses. It was a romantic hot spot and Emily wondered why she chose it.

Sophia slowly approached Emily's table from the street. Sophia's usually beautiful thick-lipped smile seemed forced, and her face looked tired. The two hugged and she took a seat next to Emily. Sophia was beautiful: dark black hair and brown, mysterious eyes. She had a full figure which made her a popular woman in Eros, always desired by men who came looking for her.

"You look like you need a glass of wine. Waiter!" Emily called.

"No. No thanks Emily. Just water, please," Sophia told the waiter.

"Oh. OK. So how have you been? It's been ages since I saw you last," said Emily.

The waiter approached and presented Sophia with her water and both of them with menus. "I'll be back and get your orders shortly," he said.

"Nothing for me," said Sophia. "I'm not hungry."

"As you wish, madam," and the waiter disappeared as Emily looked at her menu.

"What's wrong, Sophia? The food here is really good."

"I wanted to see you. That's all," said Sophia, as if she had something on her mind.

Emily looked at Sophia hard. "I've seen that look before, when you had a bad Canasta hand. You never could hide your feelings from me. Tell me what's up?"

"Oh, you know..." said Sophia, as she burst into tears.

"W-w-what's wrong?" asked Emily.

"I shouldn't say anything."

"Go ahead. I'm listening," said Emily.

"What am I going to do?" said Emily, trying to hold back her tears as other patrons started looking her way. It created a scene, as crying was a rare sight in paradise.

"What do you mean," asked Emily? "Do about what?"

Just then a small group of Greyshirts came marching down the street, goose-stepping in grey uniforms and their little grey berets with the letters MP, Macho Patrol, embroidered in red over their hearts and on their shoulder patches.

Sophia's face turned ashen at the sight of the paramilitary unit passing.

"I gotta go," Sophia said softly, quickly standing up from the table.

"We haven't even ordered yet," said Emily. "Don't mind them," she said referring to the uniformed men, "they're just on routine patrol."

The leader of the marching unit shouted for his men to halt. With his huge ego in the lead he approached Sophia and Emily's table. Sophia was shaking and frozen in fear. The tall, dark-haired leader, with his curled mustache of authority and his wide-brimmed hat looked directly at Sophia.

"Good afternoon, ladies," said Captain Roth. "Excuse the interruption. Please sit back down, madam," he said as Sophia was about to rise.

"I just needed to go pee," said Sophia, not daring to look the captain in the face.

"This will only take a moment," said the Captain. "But I must insist you sit back down!" Sophia sat.

"What's this all about, Captain," asked Emily?

"Let me introduce myself. I'm Captain Ron Roth, in

command of the 15th Flathead Greyshirts. Our mission is to maintain the status quo. And what are your names, ladies?"

"I'm Emily and this is Sophia," said Emily. "So explain yourself. Is this a sex voucher thing? If so, we're in the middle of lunch right now, but if you present your voucher later to either of us we'll be glad to curb your sexual hunger."

"No, no. As tempting as that offer is, I'm afraid this is official business," said Captain Roth. "Sophia. Sophia Underwood? May I see some form of ID?"

Sophia was so nervous she couldn't pull out the ID from her purse and she threw her purse to one side and took off running. Emily stood up quickly, shocked at what her friend was doing. Captain Roth put a heavy hand on Emily's shoulder which forced her to sit back down.

"Grab her! Grab her!" shouted the Captain to his men and the men broke rank and sprinted towards Sophia. She knocked over one couple's table and food and drink went spraying everywhere. A soldier chasing her slipped on some linguini and fell flat on his butt. Sophia used another table to keep some distance from a couple of chasing soldiers as they circled around it. She flipped the table up at them and ran in the opposite direction.

"What is this," shouted Emily? "Leave my friend alone!"

But Sophia continued running and a couple of big Greyshirts kept chasing her full-speed and tackled Sophia unmercifully to the ground. Sophia hit the pavement hard, face-first, and she received gashes on her forehead and nose. Blood ran down her face.

One of the soldiers grabbed her arms and put them behind her back as he handcuffed her.

"Hey! Hey there! Stop it! Leave her alone!" Emily shouted, confused. The buzz was gone and anger crept up in its place.

The Captain grabbed Emily and pinned her up against the side of a brick wall, holding a thick wooden baton across her throat.

"Don't you say a fucking word," said Captain Roth in a

low menacing tone. "Just keep out of this, unless you want some too."

Emily was really afraid now. She watched as they dragged her friend away, still bleeding, and looking back at Emily with a pitiful look on her face.

"I'm pregnant, Emily! That's my big crime! I'm sorry to drag you into all this. I just wanted to tell someone! I'm sorry!"

One of the uniformed Greyshirts pushed Sophia hard, almost causing her to fall.

"Wait!" said Emily when the Captain loosened his hold on her. Some of the soldiers aimed their rifle at Emily and she stood down, not knowing what to do, or what she could do to save her friend from this unusual capture.

"A word to you, Emily," said Captain Roth, "you so much as mention this to anyone, or file a complaint, it won't go easy for you. I know who you are. You're the freckled special egg-giver. But I don't give a good Goddamn who you think you are. All the special eggs and freckles in the world won't save you if you mix yourself up in your friend's problems. You see, she knew what she was doing. And there are fixed and rigid rules here on Eros concerning a woman's body. She broke those rules and now she'll have to pay for that."

All the people at the other tables just watched this drama unfold, like it was a TV show, but when the Captain looked their way, they suddenly went back to their food, drink or conversation and seemed to instantly forget what they had just witnessed. Wait staff cleaned up the mess made by the commotion. Some of the patrons got up and quietly left.

"Please! Can't anyone help my friend!" Emily yelled as the Captain was walking away.

The Captain turned back to Emily. "Just don't be foolish and make the same mistake as your friend here. We only have a few rules here on Eros, but the most important ones concern your ability to conceive. You women aren't in control of your bodies. The state controls ALL of you. We give you everything. Our only demand of you is to keep your body toned and ready to egg-up, and never, ever get pregnant. You do understand all that, don't you?"

"Sophia!" Emily yelled after her friend.

And away went Sophia.

Emily sunk her head so low it almost touched the ground. She couldn't do anything and now her friend was in serious trouble.

Emily sat back down at the table and the waiter placed the wine bill next to her. When she opened the black folder she noticed a card in it. The letters **COFFFE** were written on the top of the card in big black letters. Underneath it said "*Choice **O**ver **F**orce For **F**emales **F**orever and **E**ver.*" And underneath was written, "Ask your waiter for coffee — now — if you ever want to see your friend alive again."

Emily looked up at her waiter who was looking up into the sky, waiting. Emily wiped away the tears from her face. "I think I'll have that cup of coffee now."

"Very good, madam. Right away," said the waiter and left to fulfill her order.

CHAPTER 20

EVERYONE WANTS FRECKLE-PRONE EGGS

Dr. Samuel Edgar Yzer, medical director and scientific head of the B.E.S.O.F.F. (Babies, Eggs, Sperm & Ova Fertility Funporium), was escorting a visiting VIP dignitary through the massive bleach-white facility. Both were dressed in super-sanitary white bunny suits to avoid contamination. They strolled through the oocyte cryopreservation storage area, where thousands of snow white containers formed close ranks, like endless eggs in a massive egg carton.

Dr. Yzer was proud of these white milk-bottle-like storage units, oozing with liquid nitrogen steam. He was pointing them out to his VIP, the tall, handsome President Gilbert R. Jones.

President Gilbert Jones had come on a special diplomatic mission from nearby Exo-planet Cronos 2. It had been a long flight but he was excited to tour Dr. Yzer's state-of-the-art fertility facility.

"You're doing great work here, populating the exo-planets. Is there ever any risk of failure to these cooling units," asked President Jones, speaking through a communication device within the sanitary suit, "something that could cause harm to these precious eggs or embryos? I won't be buying any compromised eggs today. You can bet your life on that. I'm only seeking the very best Grade A human eggs."

"Need you ask such a question?" spoke Dr. Yzer, also using

the two-way communication device. "Why venture through space to this location if you are thinking we are lazy-no-good-bodies and don't protect our priceless reproductive products?

"Anyway, you know it would be a crime and I could face harsh penalties, yes even I, the great Dr. Yzer, if anything happened to these extra special eggs. I've struggled my entire career to build this superb galaxy-class facility and me and my staff have been satisfying potential parents for over 10 years. So if you believe you can find a better egg, then, with all due respect to your office, you and your security detail can jump in your jumbo-rockets and go find them."

"I think you misread what I was trying to say," backtracked President Jones.

"Have you any idea what goes on here? We work with loving care to produce excellent students, scientists and deep thinkers from our grand BESOFF vaults of ova, sperm and embryos. It's the collection, with the quality and selection everyone wants."

"Well certainly, I know your reputation. But this time me and the wife have a personal interest. We want to have children of our own."

"Congratulations then," said Dr. Yzer.

"Yes, thank you. We've been having a little trouble in the conception department — perhaps it's residual after-effects of our atmosphere on Cronos 2, or the earth we left behind many years ago," said President Jones, feigning a bit of embarrassment.

"We've tried every in vitro procedure that we know of, but they've all failed to give us the results we seek. We really, really want a little red-haired freckled girl or two or three. These children must come from the eggs of highly intelligent females. Is that possible? My wife is adamant about the freckles, though. It's all the craze on Cronos 2. We hope you can fulfill our dreams, Dr. Yzer. It would be a dream come true for my wife and I."

"You and everyone else, Mr. President," said Dr. Yzer. "Everyone is going through this freckled-kid craze. Demand for freckled female babies has jumped to an all-time high, since that holographic series Frannie Freckles, the Fearless Female Firefighter has been airing.

"And of course we are able to fill that order. We just received some fresh eggs this week from a very freckle-prone beautiful lady from here on Eros. She's a former mistress of our Corporate Head, the Most Respected Danny Turnbull. She's been tested and proven to be very smart and extremely prone to producing good, strong freckled children. Will you need sperm with those eggs? It's easy enough to find high-quality sperm, but the eggs, now there's where you gotta crack open the old intergalactic wallet. Top-quality eggs like her's don't grow on trees."

"Price is of no concern, but I thought maybe you could find a way of making a special deal with me. Maybe giving me a bonus egg or two *a gratis*, since I'll be purchasing several thousand eggs and embryos for my citizens back home? Call it a good-will gesture between planets, or a Louisiana *lagniappe*," said Jones.

"My goodwill is if I give you any eggs or ova at all!" said Dr. Yzer. "I'm not certain Corporate Leader Turnbull has gotten over that citrus fruit embargo you imposed on our planet last year during our planet-wide water shortage.

"Lots of people on this planet are still pretty upset about all that. And these same people have been waiting a long time themselves for my freckled-baby eggs. If word leaked I was selling off these high quality, much-in-demand eggs to the guy who 86'd our orange juice supply; Well, I can't imagine the ramifications that might have on my social standing here.

"So I don't believe I will give you any for FREE, especially not the freckled variety. Must I remind you that I run an extremely tight ship here at The Awesome Ova Funporium, Mr. President?" asked Yzer. "This is NOT something we can barter over like trinkets in market stalls. And several thousand ova and eggs you say? I don't even know if I can supply you with that many — at any price. On that large a scale I couldn't guarantee they would all develop into viable fetuses anyway. Unless..."

"Unless what?" asked President Jones.

"I shouldn't be telling you this, but we've formed a kind of buyer-seller bond, yes?" President Jones nodded.

"Well, in a back storage area I have what I call the Yzer Zillions," boasted Dr. Yzer. "I've been collecting my own sperm for many years now. I do believe I could repopulate an entire planet with my own personal sperm collection. In fact, I would like to try that someday, somewhere, on some desperate planet needing a larger workforce. I wonder what kind of super-race these creations of mine would be, all with roots inside them that traced themselves directly back to me. It would be a way that I could have a sort of eternal life, through my DNA."

"Sounds kind of crazy, doctor, like a God-complex," said President Jones.

"Well, I think we're all done here, President Jones," said Dr. Yzer, turning and heading toward the exit door. "Please exit the cryogenic zone and return your bunny suit at the collection point."

"Hold on," said President Jones putting his hand on Dr. Yzer's shoulder. Dr. Yzer looked at the hand and Jones quickly pulled it away. "All right, you win. Give me some of your Yzer Zillion products to take back to my home planet, plus I want a thousands non-Yzer viable unfertilized eggs, for some of my old voting block buddies. But you have to promise me you'll give me at least half a dozen guaranteed freckled children embryos for my own family's personal use. It would mean the world to my wife and me."

"Two. I can spare you two freckled-baby eggs. Let's go to my office and sort out the details," said Dr. Yzer, smiling as they exited the cryogenic area and proceeded to remove their bunny suits.

* * *

It was a long flight on board the Pink Lotus for Harry Novak, his two booty-bots and the rest of the crew. They had to travel several light years to get to the Celestial Sponge Thera Station.

At this celestial sponge were a variety of Euclidean wormholes. It was a kind of Interstellar Railway Yard built long ago, where many wormholes had come together at one convenient locale. It was called the Super-Spongy Wonderific-Wormhole Zone or (SS-WWZ) for short.

There were 12 known wormholes at the sponge, with perhaps more to be discovered later. Four were known to be safe and traversable, with many exit ramps along their routes. It would be some time before the Pink Lotus reached this junction, so everyone had to make the best of their in-between time.

Inside the Pink Lotus everyone was trying on the latest Resurrection Cosmetics to while away the hours until they arrived at the sponge. Even Harry was getting cosmetic procedures done, starting with a base for his leathery facial skin, then some firmer and toner. Judy, the booty-bot, was giving Harry the final touch — the new springtime-flush eye-bag concealing make-up combination to make him look younger.

So this is how a hero who is coming to the aid of alien women passes his space travel time, thought Harry. He sits in a chair and lets his booty-bots put skin creams on his face and lengthen his eyelashes. Instead of a white stallion it seems this hero is riding to the rescue of the women of Eros on a pink lotus flower, covered in purple eye shadow and pink rouge.

Ba Boom had released Ravi Moonbeam, co-owner of Posh-Matosh Love and Ecstatic Spirit Company (PLESCO) Booty-Bots, to go his own way before they rocketed out of the Earth atmosphere. There was no reason to keep him on board. What she wanted was Harry and his symbiotic alien booty-bots to go with them to Eros. Ba Boom had big plans for Harry Novak, this middle-class nobody. The leaders of Eros wouldn't know what hit them. But this glasses-wearing male specimen needed a strong insertion of courage and intelligence before he was ready, and that's what he was getting as he was getting Resurrection Cosmetics applied. There were special proprietary ingredients that would boost him as a man, into a kind of hero. And, Ba Boom had attendants onboard who could solve his bad vision problems — ditch those glasses once and for all.

"You'll never get those women out alive!" Harry remembered Ravi telling him, and how he hung his head at this warning about their rescue trip to Eros. But without glasses and looking a little younger those words of Ravi began to sting less and less.

Harry previously held a sinking feeling Ravi might be right, but he sure felt himself in a existential limbo right now, unable to go back to Earth for fear of arrest and jail-time, and heading toward a planet he had only heard of on holographic news telecasts. He was rocketing toward a wife who had left him and a planet of pure-testosterone.

Harry wasn't sure how he would feel if he was able to see Emily again. His first reaction would be bitter resentment. He couldn't hide the fact that he still held a grudge. There was a sore spot inside his heart still because of how she left him. She took the easy way out. He stayed the course even as the planet cookie crumbled, and the offensive line, the military forces of the world, which were meant to protect them, had all failed to pick up on those foreign-led missile quarterback blitzes. Harry thought back on how it all began.

The way the Great War started was quite a story, even funny perhaps. Maybe not ha-ha funny, but it had comic elements. It was all recorded on a White House security camera that turned up after the dust had settled months after the great conflict.

The tape was found inside a heavy lead box and released to the remaining American people for their viewing pleasure. Of course the president was dead at this time, and there were some issues of national security. But, since most of the country had been blown to hell, and a new, looser form of government was in place, where people had to fend for themselves, no one thought it a very big breech of security to release the tapes.

It started when U.S. President Harold T. Mockingjay secretly brought a fetching female page into his Oval Office and proceeded to lay her across the Resolute or Hayes Desk and have his clandestine sexual Independence Day way with her.

The desk where the two naked bodies squirmed was an 1880 gift from Queen Victoria to Rutherford B. Hayes, made from oak timbers from the arctic exploration ship the HMS Resolute. President Mockingjoy, a rather young president at 50, was infatuated with this beautiful page and this particular desk, and was trying to navigate the arctic waters of this young woman's wily soul, without alerting his wife or staining this oak treasure desk.

"So where's that big, powerful red button you swing around like your big dick?" the page had asked the former president as he loosened her panties.

"There's no red button as such," he told her gently, not wanting to go into such details with her right now, as his sexual tension was running high.

"But I thought..."

"Why are you so concerned? Are you some kind of a spy?" President Mockingjoy stopped his lovemaking and looked deep into her eyes.

"No, of course not sweetheart," she said rubbing her legs up and down his back. "It's just fascinating, that's all. You're so big! OOOOOHHHH! Tell me more. I'm getting hot thinking about all that power you possess!"

President Mockingjay, feeling generous, reached for his wallet and pulled out a fancy plastic card. "See this? No, it's not a credit card. This is what we call 'the biscuit'. I need to insert this biscuit into a devise within a briefcase — what we call the 'atomic football' when I'm away from the White House. It verifies my identify, then there are further steps, like OKing it with other members of the National Security Council before we can actually launch a nuclear strike on anyone."

"But isn't it such a complicated procedure: President to biscuit, biscuit to controls, controls to national security, then actually making the toss of the atomic football?"

"Touchdown," gasped the President, rounding third base.

An interruption at the door. "Mr. President. We need

a moment of your time! Now! Proceed immediately to the Situation Room!"

"Not now Williams! I have my own situation going on right now that I'm attending to."

"But Sir! But Sir! I must insist..."

The President ignored the frantic knocking and yelling for his attention and kept diddling his beautiful page.

When the President finally finished and lay satisfied on his side, there were people trying to break down the Oval Office door now, so he rolled to his feet and raced to the door.

"What's so dang important?"

The Secretary of State looked into the room and saw the female page holding her blouse in front of her body. "Mr. President, we're under attack!"

The page screamed.

Then the White House shook. The video showed the walls coming down, the ceiling tile with the Presidential Seal on it tumbling onto the Resolute Desk just before everything, including the desk, burst in flames. Then everyone in the Oval Office flew backwards, their bodies zooming through the air like darts.

So that's how the Great War started, and how America got knocked on its butt, by an inattentive President diddling his page and responding all too slowly. But it probably was inevitable anyway. At least the President and the page went out with a last bit of fun.

Luckily the bombs which leveled Washington D.C. and much of the Eastern and Western Coasts of America didn't impact the American heartland to any great degree. The radiation did spread there, but the central part of the United States was spared the greater explosions and exposure, and soon got back up on shaky legs and re-established itself, with the new capitol located in Kansas City.

It would have been a prime time for some foreign country, like Russia, to overrun the U.S.A., but both they and China had their own atomic messes to clean up, because as

Russia launched missiles toward the U.S., France and England launched missiles toward them, then China launched missiles at Europe and India and Australia launched missiles at China, so the whole world was a miserable wasteland.

Well, I guess it's not such a funny story after all. Except for the part about the President getting caught with his pants down, that had some giggling moments to it, in an off-color way.

CHAPTER 21

BOREDOM BECOMES HIM

On board the Pink Lotus Spaceship Harry Novak was manning up, via mascara. Over the course of several weeks of intergalactic flight Harry had several make-overs and tested many products from the Resurrection Cosmetics line.

Little did Harry know that the contents of some of that blush contained low doses of transdermal testosterone. Shin Shin ordered some of this hormone placed in his food also.

Shin Shin monitored Harry's testosterone levels by taking weekly blood tests. This was done so that Harry wouldn't received an overabundance of masculinity and become a toxic male. She told him it was standard deep space procedure for all new space travelers outside the galaxy.

Harry noticed his voice was getting deeper, and he had to shave twice a day now, as opposed to only once. And, he had a stronger desire for sex. But he found himself becoming more confident and quicker at decision making. This was clearly evident the day Ba Boom ordered Harry into her Pink Lotus office.

"Come on in Harry," said Ba Boom sitting at her massive pink desk. "We're about to plunge through the Super Sponge Wormhole. It may cause discomfort and a few glitches in your booty-bots' electronics."

"I'll keep track of any changes," said Harry, his eyes

bobbing up and down between the legendary Ms. June "Va-Va" Ba Boom's face and her beautiful cleavage, slightly exposed above her off-the-shoulder red Mexican peasant blouse.

"Yes. We've had our eye on you for some time, Harry Novak of 6262 Guggenheim Go-Poddy Complex, Diefenderfer District, Canopy County, Seminole State, of the Greater Kansas Country."

Harry took a seat in front of the beautiful Ba Boom.

"So do you hate all children?" asked Ba Boom of Harry. "I happen to love children. What's your problem with them?"

"I don't hate them. I need them to behave, according to the law is all. I actually kinda like well-behaved children."

"I better not hear that you hold any ill-feelings toward youth," Ba Boom's rose from her seat and voice boomed with authority. "You should learn real fast to love kids, with all their imperfections. Otherwise you're no good for this mission nor to me."

"Yes ma'am," said Harry, getting a little afraid and a little excited when Ba Boom's beautiful blue eyes flared at him.

"Repent of your job, your attitude and all the harm it has done to teens over the years, including Warthog Merrick," said Ba Boom, pounding her desk with her fist.

"Yes. I repent. I humbly ask God, Buddha and you to forgive me for my mistreatment of criminally minded youth," said Harry, crossing his legs to avoid Ba Boom seeing how this talk with her was affecting him.

"That job of yours went against life, Harry. I dropped my drone on you *on purpose*. I wanted to crack you, then mold you into a new type of man — one who listens to women and was fearless at the prospects the future holds for humans on Earth. We have a lot of work to do after we rescue the women of Eros."

"Why choose me to drop your drone on? Couldn't you have gotten my attention some other way?" Harry's wandering eyes crawled up and down Ba Boom's shapely arms and shoulders.

"You're a lover of beauty, a man of dreams, an empty

vessel I can pour bright new ideas into. You have potential but you better not fuck this chance I'm giving you up," Ba Boom boomed, bending over her desk and revealing even more of her cleavage. "You got that?"

"Yes. What about my booty-bots?" asked Harry, really not thinking of them much, but wanting to continue this gawking and conversation with Ba Boom. "After we work out all the glitches from traveling through the wormholes. What becomes of them?"

"What about them? Listen! All of this visible universe is mostly illusion," began Ba Boom. "We see the stars, but not really. We see the light that they once shone so many long eons ago. We interact one person to another but it's merely surface to surface. Rarely do we get to the heart of any interaction or meet people soul to soul. Words are illusions of communication.

"But even so — your keeping of the booty bots is so extremely superficial — so insanely self- and community-defeating. The big war is over, but we're still in conflict on planet Earth. We're trying to establish an ecological and social comeback, a regrouping of the elementary life forces. We need people who can stand up to the real McCoy - real love, real hate, real relationships, real reality — at least as much reality as we mortals can stand.

"And you'll free the aliens locked inside your booty-bots," continued Ba Boom, "and let them choose to either go back to their home planet or stay to fight for our's. We'll never be free if we can't liberate others. So no more free fake sex for you," she said sitting up straight and tall in her chair, taking a deep breath in to expand her chest for authority's sake. "I want to retire your booty-bots for our trip through the wormhole to minimize damage."

"That'd be OK. You're really something, you know, like a goddess," said Harry, mustering up his courage to say this to the tall, buxom and beautiful Ba Boom.

"I am aware of that. And I'm powerful too. I can make or break a guy like you Harry Novak. Right now I'm trying to make you. You are thinking you want to make love with someone as powerful as me, aren't you? Well, you have to prove you have some power yourself, some self-control, some gumption. You do have gumption don't you Harry?"

"Why sure, I got loads and loads of gumption."

"Then prove it to me, to Shin Shin, to your booty-bots, and most importantly to your estranged wife, Emily. It may be that neither of you want anything to do with each other anymore. Lots of water has passed under that bridge. But you test those waters, Harry. You try and see what headway you can make toward a reinvention of your lost relationship, because I feel there still might be something important there worth salvaging."

"Maybe," said Harry. "And if there isn't? Would you have a cup of coffee with me sometime?"

"We'll see," Ba Boom snorted at the thought. "First let's see how you perform on Planet Eros. You know their leader is the man who stole your wife away from you, don't you? You need to have it out with Corporate Leader Danny Turnbull. You need to confront him with what he did and how he wrecked your life. You might need to punch him in the nose or wrestle him to the ground. Afterwards you need to save your wife. Are you up for all that?"

"I do wanna sock this Turnbull fella," said Harry. "I wanna smash his face in. But what if my wife doesn't care to be saved? By me, anyway. What if she sides with her former boss?"

"Oh, she wants saving, Harry Novak. I know quite a bit about her situation," said Ba Boom. "And she's definitely worth saving, even though she treated you rotten."

"She sure didn't act like she wanted anything to do with me the last time I saw her," said Harry, remembering that day in the zoo when she boarded that starship with Danny Turnbull, not even bothering to glance his way.

"She was tricked. She thought this Danny Turnbull loved her and was taking her to paradise. You *must know* a woman doesn't like getting tricked — ever. Right now she feels powerless and all used up, and quite alone. You give her a way out, you give her some hope of a better life and I know she'll run to it with open arms. You're dismissed now."

"Just one last question: what's so special about my ex Emily Novak? Why are you targeting her for rescue? I mean, isn't she just another fickle female?" asked Harry.

"Careful with the stereotypes," said Ba Boom. "The reason she's so important is because the human gene pool has become extremely stagnant. It needs diversity, not only on earth but on the exo-planets as well. It seems the gene that carries freckles also combats certain viruses that are going around.

"Red hair, blue eyes and freckles is a super rarity. When the earth was healthier and more vibrant, people with those traits made up less than .2% of the population. Now there are only a handful like her on our planet and perhaps only a dozen or more on the exo-planets. We need that immunity and variety found in her blood.

"So she's valuable and rare," said Harry. "So what?"

"So what?" yelled Ba Boom. "We're getting weaker and weaker with each passing generation. Viruses, plagues just have field days with us. Just like our human bodies need rare elements to stay healthy, we need rare genomes. You have to save her Harry."

With her back turned away from Harry, Ba Boom said one last thing to him, "How'd you ever win a girl like Emily in the first place? An Irish goddess and you. It doesn't add up."

"She wasn't that hot when I first met her," he replied.

"The plan all along was for you to fall in love with Lulu Gooley. She would have persuaded you to come on this mission and bring the whole E4E army to save as many Eros women as wanted to flee. They're treated like a commodity on Eros.

"But that backfired when Ms. Gooley missed her mark and kissed Warthog Merrick's father instead of you. After her SWAY Subway terminal experience she quit the E4E movement and slipped into some kind of emotional love wrap, a kind of self-enclosed, all-inclusive romantic egg-roll that only involved herself and Merrick. We lost her for our cause.

"Now we'll have to improvise on Planet Eros. You have to be ready for anything, and there's no guarantee we'll be successful, but we're proceeding with our Plan B anyway.

"We have a short window to complete this mission and get back home. This opportunity won't come again for another five years. Earth can't wait that long. Getting Emily and all those other pre-war, genetically strong women, back to earth is too important. We can't fail."

CHAPTER 22

WORMHOLE WITH A TOLL-BOOTH

The Super-Spongy Wonderific-Wormhole Zone (SS-WWZ, for short) felt somewhat moody today. It predicted, with its great disembodied mind that lay hidden deep inside its bowels, that someone would take something precious away from her soon. Cosmic clouds concealed the well-traveled eternal wormholes like a flannel nightgown screens the eventual sagging of a middle-aged woman's midriff.

The Super Sponge wasn't up for any nonsense today, even though it was located very near the Question Mark Nebulae. But it must have sensed that nonsense was approaching as it peered through those black wormhole cavities at the Pink Lotus sailing nearby, with its gaudy Hot Pink color and pink outstretched lotus petals. Even though the wormhole had quickly tried to hide herself with some modest cosmic debris, the Pink Lotus scanned for and found the gigantic portal area. Ba Boom's ultra-modern spaceship, The Pink Lotus, wasn't swayed by all those spacetime tricks the SS-WWZ Wormholes liked to play.

Surrounding the wormhole complex, an earth-based company had built an electromagnetic cosmic sleigh ride. The company, formerly known as Philadelphia Toboggan Coasters, once made roller coasters and carousels and other amusement park rides, but had diversified into the outer space market. It was a diversion from the possible panic a crew might feel before thrusting itself into this mysterious, semi-intelligent wormhole.

And now this former amusement ride company had built a large osmic carousel ride near the wormhole that any spaceship could jump on and circle around the periphery of the wormhole, seeing the sights and thrilling at the fun. When any spaceship on this ride passed the big gold ring it could try, by whatever means necessary, to grab a Great Golden Magnus Electromagnetic Ring (GGMER).

This ring is hard to get, but well worth the effort. Many spaceships had tried and failed and the Pink Lotus had elected to try.

The great benefit to the Philadelphia Toboggan Coaster Company for this concept near the SS-WWZ was its advertising value. The coaster and the ring showed just what marvels and amusements the company could manufacture in deep space, and it got a lot of business this way. It was a deep space calling card.

"What is all this?" asked Harry of Shin Shin. "Why the delay?"

"That large black object is an artificial satellite off the starboard bow," said Ba Boom, "and there is the prize gold ring nearby."

"I see them," said Harry.

"The satellite is where we'll pay our toll to enter the wormhole," said Ba Boom.

"A tollbooth in space? Can they do that?" asked Harry.

"Sure, but if we take the Philadelphia Toboggan Cosmic Carousel ride around the loop once, and succeed in grabbing the gold ring, then our fare is paid for in full. Other prizes will be ours for our efforts. The toll booth is needed to maintain the SS-WWZ wormholes in good working order.

"That artificial satellite has to maintain this whole area, keeping out unsightly and possibly damaging asteroids and other cosmic radiation. It also has to deep-clean scrub some of these wormholes from time to time. It frequently has to go into those holes like a plumbers drain snake, to keep them free flowing, and not backed up and spilling other dimensions out into free space."

"What if we decide to not pay this intergalactic toll?" asked Harry.

"Look, over there!" said Ba Boom, as an old freighter spaceship tried to jump the toll booth circle of cosmic dust. Out of this huge black metallic artificial satellite came a gigantic net that resembled nothing so much as a black cosmic sock. It caught the deep space freeloader. The satellite then started delivering small electrical shocks to the freighter, lighting up the miscreant ship like it was a tiny firefly.

"That's what happens if you don't pay the toll," said Ba Boom. "Those little shocks continue until you fork over your toll. You pay what you can afford. See, he finally paid up some lost space junk and the satellite accepted the toll. Now it can pass through, but it doesn't get a chance to ride the cosmic carousel."

The Pink Lotus positioned itself in space, waiting in line a few minutes, then hopped on the cosmic carousel. The Pink Lotus traveled up and down in waves along the outside of the Cosmic Wormhole trying to maneuver to the outside edge. As it crept in that direction the golden ring appeared. A giant claw came out of the Pink Lotus and reached for the golden ring. It got it!

"Congratulations," came a voice over the PA, "you have succeeded in grabbing the most precious gold ring from off the cosmic carousel. Not one ship has been able to grab that ring for over 400 Parsecs. You will now be granted free access through the Eros Wormhole and you may depart at your convenience, once you give the gold ring back to us."

"Thank you," said Ba Boom to the communicator. "And the other gifts?"

"The benevolent mystic energy field will pass through your ship shortly. We're gearing up the equipment now. Please be patient with us," said the artificial satellite to the Pink Lotus.

"What is this energy field you speak of?" asked Harry, confused by all that was taking place.

"It's an ancient energy source for good that has been

coursing through the universe for eons. It's the lifeblood of the cosmos and has been pumping out big creative powers since anyone can remember. It rolls up cosmic dust like kitty hairballs and infuses them with the ability to create life itself.

"Some think these energy waves are a generator of miracles," said Shin Shin. "Others call it the scout of great inspiration, the starting gun of mind-blowing invention, the spring-loaded plunger that shoots the steel balls to begin the universal pinball of life and happiness. These waves are the opening pitch to the ballgame, the coin flip, the final cut of the cards before the deal."

"So what will this energy do for us?" asked Harry.

"It does what my makeup tries to do, to create magic, an illusion, a kind of reclamation of those powers humans had long before they became the weak things they are today. You'll see," said Ba Boom.

"We are ready to transfer the source now," said the PA system. "Please release the gold ring after receiving your gifts. We now begin..."

And a flow of bright twinkly light passed entirely through the Pink Lotus, through each individual, and through every organ, piece of metal, and every booty-bot on board. Everyone stood perfectly still as this river of holy washed over them, not wanting to move, not wanting it to end.

But it did end and everyone felt more alive and refreshed than they had ever felt in their entire life. All life glowed inside the Pink Lotus, even the mechanics of the ship seemed to run smoother, with more ease and more power.

"That's it?" asked Harry.

"Yes," said Ba Boom.

"Wow," said Harry simply. Ba Boom nodded her head. Shin Shin smiled.

"Release the gold ring," she instructed her crew and the ring floated back to its rightful place near the artificial satellite, once again absorbing energy from long-distant stars.

"The Eros wormhole is right ahead," said the chief

navigator as the ship passed by the cosmic toll booth and approached the superhighway of the stars.

"Shin Shin, gather the crew and guests and let's prepare for entry," said Ba Boom. "And break out the mild sedatives."

Shin Shin went to an intercom and instructed all personnel to gather immediately on the assembly floor.

"We're about to the enter the Eros wormhole," said Ba Boom, to the crew and guests. "Most of you have experienced this before, but for Harry's sake, and for the visiting Booty-Bots, I want to let you know it's gonna get bumpy once we get inside.

"You booty-bots will have your electronics shut-down during the duration of this space-time trek. To you two aliens inside, you're free to wander about, just don't touch anything," continued Ba Boom. "The rest of us will receive mild sedatives to relax and help us cope with the passage.

"Harry, this being your first time, you'll feel like a shaken soda ready to spew, but that feeling is only temporary. You'll get used to it soon enough and before you know it, you'll have gained your wormhole legs. Then in a relatively short period of space-time, we'll be out and on the other side of the quadrant.

"Everyone proceed to their stations and buckle up," said Shin Shin as Ba Boom floated away.

This being said all humans went to their cantilevering chairs. The booty-bots reported to maintenance and had their electronics shut down. The aliens themselves were allowed to free-float through this process, or inhabit any of the crew's bodies temporarily. They both chose to be housed in Harry's body, going in through the ears. Ba Boom and Shin Shin went to the Commander and Co-Commander chairs and Harry took a VIP chair near the rear of the control cabin.

Harry, with his bots inside him, looked out the bay window and saw numerous other wormholes assembled near the Eros hole. Some were clearly marked with large floating signs. Eros was indicated by a pair of big red lips smooching at approaching spacecraft and licking its lips.

CHAPTER 23

THE PARADISE PLANET OF EROS

As the Pink Lotus approached the SS-WWZ they noticed that a few of the wormholes were different colors. There were large advertising signs pointing out several of the wormholes one from another. There was a unique purple wormhole which invited people to Cronos II with a wobbly brain sign floating in space near it, advertising for space travelers to come to their free-thinking colony.

A lime green wormhole displayed a palm-tree sign beside it which promised real grass and fresh tomatoes on Vegantitus.

One dark brown wormhole seemed to be emitting a stream of white gas.

"That's our return hole," said Ba Boom, noticing how Harry wondered at that particular cosmic object.

The Pink Lotus closed its long pink petals and balled up moments before it was sucked up into the pink Eros wormhole. Inside pink in pink it traveled a pink billiard ball down a long, dark pocket, bouncing this way and that. Harry felt queasy and did spew up some of his afternoon lunch. Luckily he had a bag ready to catch the accident before it spread throughout the ship.

A lot of crackling and shaking occurred as they proceeded, like a jalopy on a pot-hole-filled road. But Harry's body was relaxed. The sedative made him feel happy and made this inter-dimensional trip almost fun.

Harry's two booty-bots, that parked themselves in his left

ear, were seated comfortably in a small ball of earwax. Susie Q, the eternal teacher, was explaining being and nothingness to Judy. Judy wasn't following very well.

"Are we even here?" asked Susie Q of Judy, while rolling in earwax. "Are we alive in this present NOW?"

"I think so," said Judy. "I feel I'm here."

"Ah, you feel it," said Susie Q, "and you trust these conscious feelings? But you shouldn't. They are illusion too."

"Oh boy, I'll never get it," said Judy.

"Eventually everyone gets it," said Susie Q.

When they reached their exit the Pink Lotus seemed to pop out of the wormhole like a cork out of a bottle. At the same time the two booty-bots inside Harry popped out of Harry's left ear, eager to wipe off the wax, get back in their booty-bot bodies and see this new destination.

And there, before Harry, the aliens and the whole ship, was the lovely planet Eros, a place designed for love, sex and pleasure. On paper it was meant to be a paradise for all. And it did have a sexy northern polar region, with cool ice, shaped like the female figure.

The Pink Lotus blossomed again, letting the solar pink flower petals spread and soak up the rays of the red sun and its bigger yellow sun. The ship orbited the planet once or twice, looking at its four moons as it shot by, slowing down its speed. Now it was approaching the main landing hub called the Luxurious Turnbull Love Intergalactic Spaceport and Holiday Hotel.

The Eros Shipping and Receiving Dock at the Luxurious Turnbull Love Intergalactic Spaceport and Holiday Hotel was gearing up for action as the Resurrection Cosmetics spaceship began unloading its cargo and passengers.

As the Resurrection Cosmetics ship was being unloaded some other large spaceships nearby were being loaded with huge white cylinders. They were the Cronos 2 Spaceship One and their fellow ships. Upon departure, one would carry President Gilbert Isaac (GI) Jones, while the others would be loaded with precious eggs and embryos to help the Cronos 2 recover from its dwindling workforce. Seems everyone on Cronos 2 wanted to be an executive and no one wanted the necessary labor jobs that were needed to maintain the infrastructure.

President Jones and Corporate Leader Turnbull were inside a private restaurant overlooking the comings and goings of spacecraft at the spaceport. They were speaking just before the Pink Lotus landed.

"Thanks for your help getting these eggs for my people," Jones said, cutting a bit of steak with a large knife as Turnbull eyed him over his glass of wine. "Aren't you eating anything."

"Just remember you owe me now. No, I'm not eating. I'm saving my appetite," said Turnbull.

From where they sat they could see the Pink Warehouse dedicated exclusively to Resurrection Cosmetics Company. Resurrection was a very powerful product on a world devoted to sex and pleasure. Usually Resurrection ships brought flavored lipstick, exotic fragrances, tempting skin lotions that make the wearer irresistible upon touch, and other goodies But today the Pink Lotus not only brought that but their CEO June Ba Boom, who rarely made such flights, and her executive vice president Shin Shin Skinny.

The two women de-boarded the spacecraft as only they could do, making a huge splash with reporters wanting to catch a phrase, a look, a photo op for their little holo latest-rumor news programs.

"Wonder why they're here," asked President Jones?

"She's up to something and I intend to find out what," said Turnbull.

"She's so beautiful," said Jones.

"On the outside," said Turnbull?

"Isn't that enough," asked Jones?

"I've had her. Thinks she's better than everyone else, but she breaks just like any other woman once you confront her."

"I don't know," said Jones, chewing on his steak. "Better to just enjoy them with the eyes. You get caught in their snares and you're toast. Good steak you have here."

"You think I'm lying? You just don't know how to handle women on Cronos 2. Here on Eros we keep our women in line, keep them looking good and always busy with shopping and leisure. But they know who's the boss."

"If you say so..." said Jones, sipping his wine.

"So, about those eggs you bought from us," said Turnbull changing the conversation on a dime. "I've heard you formed a secret agreement with Dr. Yzer to get a few freckled eggs, is that right? Going behind my back? I thought we were better friends than that," said Turnbull, looking deep into Jones' eyes.

"Well, we are..." muttered President Jones, feeling Turnbull's intense glare burn into his skull like a laser beam.

Corporate Leader Danny Turnbull, ruler of all Eros, wasn't a bad guy — not really — but he was a misogynist to the extreme. And he was a rich man, a very rich man. A man who was used to getting his own way: with women, with other men, with aliens, with whomever or whatever — every time, all the time. He did have a boatload of charisma. And he wasn't afraid to use it for his own purposes.

He could make it seem that you were the most important person in the whole universe, or he could make you feel as insignificant as the tiniest grain of sand. For Danny Turnbull the whole known universe revolved squarely around him — his superego fueled supernovas and created black holes in their wake. If there wasn't something positive about him on the holonews every single day then someone at the station would be in a heap of trouble.

Turnbull was well aware of the grumblings of females on Eros. He monitored their protests concerning the loss of their freedoms, being asked to give up their eggs and all. He had teams of Greyshirts assessing their situation thoroughly. He wanted to make sure rumors of their complaints didn't reach other exo-planets. So he was careful about where he let President Jones go and do, and who he saw while on his planet.

There was one report that reached him recently that

haunted him. It concerned Emily Novak, a former lover and now one of just a few precious red-haired, freckled egg givers. She had made a complaint at the National Egg Plant and again after a runaway woman was sent to Labor Camp because she got pregnant.

This was something Danny Turnbull didn't want to see come to light and he certainly didn't want President Jones to know about it. Emily's situation could make trouble for Turnbull. She knew him too well, having lived with him for three years. There must be some way to keep her quiet. He didn't want to have her locked up, but he would if he had to, to maintain peace and the established order on this very planet.

"I only got two freckle-optimized eggs, just for my own personal use," said Jones uneasily. "You'll never miss them."

"That's not the point," said Turnbull, hitting the table. "What'd you have to do to get them? They're national treasures, and all transactions like that have to go through me," said Turnbull. "No exceptions!"

Just then Ba Boom, Shin Shin, Harry, the two booty-bots Judy and Susie Q, and some of the crew members of the Pink Lotus came into the spaceport.

There was a big commotion in the commons area as they strode through. Ba Boom was a popular celebrity all across the known universe. She was the perfect female, a goddess from on high, the excalibur of woman-ly perfection. Most people had never seen a woman of her power and beauty in real life before. She was a circus unto herself.

Men were tripped over their luggage, running into posts or generally fumbling about as she passed. Women were excited too. Many wanted the Resurrection founder's autographs on their compact cases or were hoping for special goodie bags she sometimes gave away when making personal appearances.

Ba Boom, Shin Shin and Harry approached Turnbull's table and introductions were given all around.

"What brings you to our planet?" Turnbull asked of Ba Boom.

"Thinking about expanding. Maybe putting a manufacturing plant here, on this planet," said Ba Boom. "I'm thinking seriously about it."

Jones said to Harry in a hushed tone,concerning Ba Boom, "She's quite a sight to see. Don't make many like her anymore."

"She is beautiful, but I came to get my Emily back. That is, if she wants to go back to Earth with me," said Harry.

"Can't do that, Harry Novak. You ought to know better than even try," said Turnbull. "You had her once but couldn't hold on. Tough luck, old man."

"Why? Doesn't she have any say in it? Plenty of other women here. Is this the way you operate, everything just your way and no other?"

"You might say that. Emily's a real money-maker, with those great freckles and those big blue eyes," said Turnbull. "I personally can't stand her, but people from all over the galaxy want those eggs of hers — even President Jones here wanted some. So I think I'll just keep her here, where I can keep an eye on her, and her precious eggs. A place where you can't touch her."

"What'd you just say?" Harry grew upset.

"Where do you have her? What have you done to her?" asked Ba Boom?

"Let's just say I have her under my control. As for the rest of the women here on Eros, I won't allow you to undermine their thinking here, Ba Boom. Don't think I'll let you put silly notions of freedom in their brains.They have it pretty good, if they just stay in line," said Turnbull.

"Call her up!" shouted Harry.

"Emily? Sure," said Turnbull as he got out his communicator and dialed a number. "Hello, Emily? This is Corporate Leader Turnbull. What? Yes, really. No. No. No I didn't."

"Emily! It's me, Harry! I want to take you back to earth!" Harry shouted toward Turnbull's communicator.

"Yeah, it's him alright," continued Turnbull, into his phone. "You want to see him? We're at the Spaceport executive lounge. Sure, we'll be here. What? You can't talk to me like that!" Danny Turnbull turned red, then switched like a lightbulb into a more light hearted mood, "Ha! You had me going there for a moment. Yes, sure, sure."

"She doesn't love you," said Harry. "She might fear you. She might detest you. But I don't think she cares anything about you."

"Or anyone. Or anything," said Turnbull. "She'll tell you to your face when she gets here. You should be glad to be rid of that gal. She's big trouble. I ought to know. I *really* ought to know."

"Who else is arriving at this Spaceport?" asked President Jones, as a large transport vessel was seen coming in for a landing. The big pink and gold ship was within eyesight of his own silver Cronos 2 ship, which ship was still being loading.

"Who that is doesn't concern you," said Turnbull to Jones.

"It might if they get too near my own vessel," said Jones.

"I know that spaceship. That's a Posh Matosh's Booty-Bot delivery ship," said Ba Boom. "He must have been planning to come here all along, same as us, and didn't say a word about it."

"Say, what's going on?" asked Shin Shin looking at the large freight marked bio-hazard being loaded into Jones Cronos II ship and seeing crews about to unload the Posh Matosh ship. "Are you shipping out eggs, and bringing in bots? Is that what's going on here?"

CHAPTER 24

MORE THAN JUST PRETTY FACES

"Don't think too much," said Turnbull to Shin Shin. and to Ba Boom. "You ought to leave all the brain work to men and not worry yourself. You two are too pretty for that sort of thing."

Ba Boom had to hold Shin Shin Skinny back from attacking Corporate Leader Turnbull.

Shin Shin was very defensive when anyone said anything bad about her big boss Ba Boom. She would have gladly laid down her life for her.

Shin Shin got to know Ba Boom when she went by her given name of Judith Lynn Van Der Boomen. After the Great War Shin Shin was suffering from radiation burns over 30% of her body. She was in constant pain and was disfigured, mostly on her legs and back, but her face was burnt in bad shape too. Ba Boom hadn't been spared the horrors of the war either, but she managed to stay inside most of the time until the radiation levels had subsided.

But when Ba Boom saw the results of war on the women of earth she took great pity. She worked to develop and foster medicines and healing lotions to restore peoples' lives. She employed the latest medicine, folk cures such as fungi, herbs, venoms, distant-planet minerals. She used whatever worked. She also developed concealing make-up and other tools to help women regain their sense of self-worth.

Shin Shin had gone to Ba Boom one day, with all her pain and ugliness and asked for help. Through personal work and using every supplement at her disposal Ba Boom and her staff were able to transform Shin Shin into one of the most beautiful women on Planet Earth. Both Ba Boom and Shin Shin were walking advertisements for their products.

Shin Shin was a Phoenix raised from the ashes, a "before and after" that the world could treasure. For that miracle of beauty and resurrection, Shin Shin would follow Ba Boom into the gates of hell.

Ba Boom came by her beauty naturally. She wasn't perfect. She could be a ruthless competitor. But Ba Boom carried guilt inside her. Everything seemed to come so easily for her. She had been spared the crush of pain dealt the whole world, or so it appeared.

The success of the Resurrection Cosmetic line wasn't based on vanity. It was built on a deep humanitarian desire to give people back self-worth, especially women, no matter what they may have gone through.

Ba Boom and Resurrection Cosmetics used profits to help orphanages and young mothers. She set up educational funds for women who wanted to further their education. The environment was her biggest charity work. She had whole product lines, whose profits went solely to cleaning up air quality and the water.

Ba Boom was much more than a pretty face and body. She had a solid gold heart. But that heart could prove steely if you went against her efforts at helping people or assisting in projects designed to help the environment. She stood up for the weak and needy and battled corruption. That's why she was hated by many, including Danny Turnbull. And it was why she was now on Eros. She was here to bring down a dictator and give women a renewed sense of dignity and freedom. Danny Turnbull didn't know that yet. If he had, he wouldn't have let her take another step on his planet.

If Emily couldn't be saved then so be it. If Harry couldn't

become the hero she envisioned — that'd be acceptable — but her agenda would continue here despite these shortfalls. Turnbull was finished — like an injured bull in a Spanish bullfighting arena. He just didn't know it yet.

"We're doing just fine here on Eros," said Turnbull. "I don't know what you expect to see or do here. And if you want to set up a plant for manufacturing, you'll, of course, have to go through me first."

"I've been looking at this planet's economic and artistic output over the last few years. I'd say Eros hasn't contributed much to the quadrant," said Ba Boom, tossing back her hair as if she were dismissing Turnbull completely.

"Your main pursuits are chasing pleasure and running with chemical euphoria, like a child with a sharp knife. You're not producing anything new, except maybe those human eggs you harvest from your unwilling women. I haven't seen any bright new imaginative art nor any scientific progress made here. The inter-planetary counsel is getting a bit worried about this. I'm surprised you haven't blown yourself up yet with your constant bickering."

"Says a lipstick maker sticking her big fat red lips where they don't belong," snarled Turnbull.

"You think that's all Ms. Ba Boom does is make cosmetics? You really aren't too smart, are you?" asked Harry. "She's a force for good wherever she goes. And she's someone you don't want to mess with."

"Eventually we'll recover our climate on Earth," said Ba Boom, sitting down on a bar stool, "but if you'll ever reclaim your worth as a man is highly doubtful."

"Ha ha," laughed Turnbull. "You women. You're only good for three things: cooking, screwing and cleaning up. Everyone here knows that, and maybe if you stay long enough I can convince you of those things too. But when you start jabbering and trying to make sense of things that's when we have trouble."

As everyone sat down at the bar and ordered a drink Ba Boom suggested Turnbull find another place to sit.

"No, I'm fine here," said Turnbull. "Say. Who do you think you are? My planet. My table. And you wanna just run me off like I'm some kind of mailroom boy? Wanna know about those Posh Matosh ships unloading out there? Harry ought to know. He's got two of them."

"So you're going all in? I guess all the beautiful women you've gathered from Earth aren't good enough here anymore?" asked Shin Shin.

"Oh, they're good enough. Good enough to keep giving us eggs and embryos to sell off-world, but as for the bedroom, not so much," said Turnbull. "I've ordered some of those hybrid booty-bots Ravi has created and I think I'll try them out, on a large scale. I have a master plan."

"What plan is that?" asked Harry.

"Oh, you'll like the irony of this," said Turnbull. "If the bots work out, we'll see a lot less of those meddlesome women.

"On the other hand, if our women behave, like good little house hussies, then they can stay. But if they choose to fight us I'm afraid I'll be forced to take rather harsh steps. We have enough eggs and embryos to replace every last one of them, if it should come to that, or I will buy more booty-bots."

Just then a large explosion blew up one of the Cronos 2 transport ships which was being loaded with cryogenically frozen eggs and embryos. Large pieces of fiery metal crashed through the sides of the lounge and terminal area.

People were thrown to the floor. Corporate Leader Turnbull fell over a table backwards. Instinctively Harry Novak jumped on the body of June Ba Boom to shield her from the fall-out. Harry got a good feel for her as he lay protecting her.

"Get off!" Ba Boom yelled and elbowed Harry in the ribs.

"Ow! I'm not able," said Harry, lying on her backside.

"Why the hell not?" she asked.

"Something's on my legs. I can't move," said Harry.

A steel beam from the lounge area had fallen on Harry's legs, pinning him to the backside of June Ba Boom.

"Are you hurt badly," asked Ba Boom?

"I don't think so. I think this table broke the beam's fall. I just can't wiggle away from you or get up."

"Hold still. Someone will get us out of this soon," she said.

Harry couldn't help himself. He was getting excited lying on Ba Boom's backside and she wiggling underneath trying to escape. She was, after all, one of the most beautiful women in the entire universe. And sexy, oh, she was sexy with that platinum blonde hair, those big blue eyes and that shapely figure, especially that big round butt Harry was on top of right now. And, of course, she had increased her appeal with cosmetic products and perfumes.

"I think I can lift that off you, Harry," said Judy, Harry's personal booty-bot. "Shall I do that?"

"Yes, Judy, I suppose so," said Harry, not quite sure that's what he wanted right then and there.

"But you seem to be enjoying yourself where you are," said Judy.

"I believe I must get off Ms. Ba Boom now," said Harry.

"Yes you should," said Ba Boom. "Judy, help us out."

"Once I was your one and only, Harry. You couldn't wait to open the box I came in and try me out." She lifted the heavy piece of metal off Harry.

"Thanks, Judy," said Ba Boom.

"Now what am I to you, Harry? A rusty old crescent wrench you no longer need to tighten the bolts to your nuts?"

"Judy. Can we talk about this later," said Harry standing to his feet and helping Ba Boom up, holding onto her hand a little longer than needed. Ba Boom pulled away.

"I always thought I was saving you," said Judy to Harry. "I imagined I was saving you from your lonely and mean and trivial existence. But I feel you've been damning me lately. Damning me to an unknown hell. Is it because I'm not your typical girl? Is it because I've stayed back and let things play out on your great adventure here?"

"Judy," said Harry, checking himself to make sure he wasn't injured anywhere. "Judy, let's not do this now."

"You made me feel almost human once, Harry. I know I'm an alien species and I was always a substitute for your Emily.

"But I wanted to be there for you, through it all," continued Judy. "Now it seems you don't want or need me. You have hopes of getting your old wife back — so where do I fit in?

"I know you never wanted an emotional booty-bot. You just wanted the simple mechanical one. But didn't you ever come to feel anything for me? Anything at all?

"Shall I go back to my home planet with Susie Q and leave you here? I'm not so complicated as your Emily, or Ms. Ba Boom. I'm just a simple, straight-forward booty-bot, with none of the complications of a real woman. I'm easy. I've been made especially for you, to give you comfort, satisfaction and companionship.

"Beg me to stay," said Judy. "Tell me you love and need me, Harry. Give me something that makes me feel like I'm something."

"I don't know what to say, Judy," Harry watched people running by, rushing to get to a place of safety. "Thanks for being there when I needed you and lifting that piece of steel off my legs just now. I don't want you to leave me just yet. Don't you have some kind of contractual obligation to stay with me?"

"Yes, but I could leave if you let me go — if you just say go away. Or, I could stay on as this shadowy figure, living in pain inside this Posh Matosh shell, still here, but no longer caring about anything.

"I've almost forgotten what I was without this body. I've grown used to arms and legs and eyes, smelling and tasting. It's good. But the feelings. Oh, I have discovered feelings that I never knew existed. I'll miss that most if you no longer want me. So yes, I'll be your standby, your extra — your just in case."

"I'll take you back to our home planet if this doesn't work out," said Susie Q. "Or maybe we can get you reassigned to another booty-bot — would you like that?"

"Harry is my life and if he goes away I don't know how I will survive," said Judy. "I don't want to be just anyone's booty-bot. I want to be Harry's."

"You're making me feel like a real heel," said Harry. "You have to understand, love and pain go together. It's never a sure thing."

"What could I do anyway? I should give myself up when we return to earth. I should go to the Citizen's Police and let them punish me for my crimes," said Judy.

"You didn't do anything wrong," said Harry.

"Yes I did. I know I did and I'll take whatever punishment they have for me. You can go on with your life with Emily, or whoever. You can pretend I never existed. No need to worry about a lowly insignificant, small as a mushroom spore, alien like me."

"Come on," said Harry. "Feelings gets warped and twisted and reinvented all the time. That happens in every relationship."

"Whatever you say," said Judy.

President Jones was being helped to his feet by his staff. He looked at Corporate Leader Turnbull as if seeking an explanation. "What's going on here? What just happened to my ships? My eggs? My crew? What kind of exo-planet are you running here anyway? I deserve compensation! I'm going to the Intergalactic Court and get recompense!"

"Shut up about your stupid ship and eggs. I have other problems to deal with!" said Turnbull, turning toward Ba Boom and Shin Shin. "Quite a coincidence your arrival and all our present trouble," said Turnbull to Ba Boom. "I'd better not find out you had anything to do with this."

"We need to leave now, Mr. Corporate Leader," said a burly security man. "There's still a possibility for danger."

And as Danny Turnbull was rushed from the spaceport he looked back at Ba Boom. "Just stick around where we can find you," he said to Ba Boom. "Until we get to the bottom of this consider yourself grounded."

"Why would anyone blow up my precious eggs? My wife and my precious freckled eggs?" asked a very nervous President Jones. "I can't believe you had anything to do with this, did you?"

"No, I didn't," said Ba Boom, "but I do sympathize with the women of this planet. You better get out of here too."

"You support terrorism?" asked Jones.

"Usually not," said Ba Boom.

Jones, with an I-can't-believe-you look on his face, was pulled to safety. He was rushed into an awaiting space shuttle by his security detail and was gone.

The spaceport saw people running every which way. Debris was scattered and on fire on the platform. People were screaming in the main terminal and crying because of injuries or loss. Expensive luggage had been damaged. Smaller secondary blasts went off now and then. These were caused by the cryogenic canisters of liquid nitrogen, used to store the human eggs and embryos, which had been blasted out of the Cronos 2 ship.

"Calm down everyone," came a reassuring voice over the loud speaker. "Please exit the spaceport in an orderly fashion. Use every courtesy and give wide berth to children and the very wealthy. If you are in need of medical assistance someone will attend to you shortly."

"We better get out of here too," said Harry. "What's Turnbull all about? Why would he think you had anything to do with this?"

"I have no idea what's going on here," said Ba Boom as the group shuffled toward the exit. "Shin Shin, quick, call up the crew that stayed with the Pink Lotus and see if everything's OK there. Harry, we need to speed this operation up. We need to find out where Emily is and to assist any women who want to get off this planet."

Shin Shin called the Pink Lotus as the group stood a safe distance outside the spaceport. It seems the main ship and the other Resurrection ships were far enough away from the main explosion that they weren't damaged. But a complete check-up was needed before the ship could return to interspace travel.

Everyone's holographic personal devices lit up, as they stood or sat outside the spaceport and took stock of the situation. An obvious hacker had backed into the holographic system and had taken control of the airwaves. A beautiful dark-haired woman without makeup showed up on the screens.

"Matriarchy now! Down with Male Dominance! Hello. I'm Consuela Franklin," said the woman on everyone's devises. "You may recognize me from my role as Fanny Bonita in the daytime drama 'The Supply Room Trysts of Doctor Heartthrob'."

"Today I speak for W.I.R.E., the Women in Resistance on Eros. We claim responsibility for today's actions at the Turnbull Love Spaceport. Our drastic action reflects our desperate desire to be heard now!

"We women should be shown proper respect, as we are your life-makers, your mothers, the softer side of humanity. But we're not given our due!

"Don't you know that we aren't just receptacles for the male sexual need, nor manufacturers of intergalactic egg products? We're the yin of your yang, yet we're used and abused on this very planet which claims to be a paradise.

"We'll no longer have our needs ignored, nor our functions perverted. We, of WIRE, did this to protest the ongoing, dehumanizing human egg and fetus marketplace — established against our will. We apologize for the collateral damage, but this is a cultural war, a war of independence for women everywhere!

"Our dwindling reproductive rights and our lack of choices for our own bodies has driven us to this. This! We wanted to make a statement. Our government has made us an unwilling part of a nasty, immoral business. We won't stand it any longer! We're not your egg slaves!"

Then the screens went blank. In its place was Intergalactic Newscaster Sycamore Storylore describing the scene with dramatic flames from the wreck of the Cronos 2 ship in the background. She spoke in her velvety smooth, sexy voice.

"We interrupt your hologram reality to bring you breaking news of a major disaster at the Luxurious Turnbull Love Intergalactic Spaceport and Holiday Hotel on the Exo-

Planet Eros. A pirated message has just been broadcast by Consuela Franklin, leader of a feminist group calling themselves WIRE. They have claimed responsibility for blowing up a cargo ship full of human eggs and embryos bound for Cronos 2. We have just learned that five spaceport workers were killed on the launchpad and many others injured. Extensive damage was also reported at the main spaceport launch pad.

"We have confirmation that Corporate Leader Turnbull was on-site at the spaceport at the time of the explosion. He was visiting with President Jones of Cronos 2. No word yet on either of their conditions. Unconfirmed eyewitness reports say Turnbull was seen alive and well and leaving the area with his security detail, but still no confirmation on this. Also we have received no further information on the condition of President Jones.

"Informants also cite Ms. June Ba Boom, C.E.O. and founder of Resurrection Cosmetics and her assistant Shin Shin Skinny being in the Spaceport at the time of the incident. Supposedly they are here on a routine make-up sales mission.

"It appears that one large spaceship was totally destroyed and a few others received slight damage. Emergency units are working now to find survivors and assist the injured on the launch pad and in the spaceport itself.

"OK. Now we are receiving a live feed from Eros Corporate Leader Danny Turnbull from his office on Main Street. First off, let me say how pleased I am that you weren't hurt in this incident, Mr. Corporate Leader," she said to the image of Turnbull on her monitor.

"I'm fine Ms. Sycamore Storylore, thanks for your concern. What we have witnessed here today is a massive cancer on Eros that needs removal," said Turnbull, turning to talk into the holo-cameras. "Effective immediately I am declaring a high red state of emergency. Until we can get to the bottom of this I'm suspending sexual voucher distribution. I believe this will hasten the public's help in reporting those responsible and resolving this crisis once and for all.

"I've called out my Greyshirts and we are determined to restore peace on this planet," continued Turnbull. "I'm hereby ordering all females of reproductive age to report to their commune headquarters, where their identity and political affiliations will be checked and vouched. Those who pass our security tests are free to return to their swimming pools and penthouses.

"A reward will be offered to anyone with information on the whereabouts of the outlaw Consuela Franklin, former daytime movie star, known for her role as Fanny Bonita in the daytime drama about Doctor Heartthrob. The reward for information leading to her capture will include an all-expense paid vacation to Mickey's Monkey Island with the partner of your choice. We'll also include unlimited sexual vouchers, free alcoholic drinks for a year, and coupons for dinners prepared by our finest chefs.

"So I'm issuing this order effective immediately: Again, every female must register within the next 24 hours or be subject to immediate underground work and imprisonment. Failure to act on this order is not an option I'm willing to entertain. Civil strife will not be tolerated on Eros. Those responsible will find their punishment swift and harsh. That is all. Good day and with everyone's cooperation we will return to full pleasure mode soon."

"We will keep you updated on this continuing story. Reporting live from the Planet Eros, I'm Sycamore Storylore of HOLO-G-TV reporting. Back to you Bob."

"Thank you Consuela. Wow. Our hearts go out to the people of Eros tonight. In other news..."

CHAPTER 25

THE SECOND COMING OF HANUMAN

Ravi Moonbeam, co-owner of what was soon becoming the best-selling booty-bot company in the whole quadrant, decided to put off landing his own personal ship at the Love Spaceport. He would go back into orbit for now. After all, he had just witnessed, on his holo, an explosion at the Love landing dock that blew up a rocket set for launch. He wasn't about to place his personal mission in jeopardy. He needed to know the situation on the surface first before he touched down.

Ravi and his crew had made this trek carrying thousands of booty-bots which the government of Eros had ordered. He had been paid 1/4 of the price of the bots in advance and would receive the other 3/4's upon delivery.

All of these booty-bots were the new special models with the built-in aliens. These particular models had proven popular on Earth and it's what Corporate Leader Danny Turnball had wanted for his coming new world order.

This was the largest order, by far, Posh Matosh had ever received. Safe delivery and customer satisfaction were the primary goals Ravi had in mind now and he was convinced he could deliver on both, once he could find a safe spot to land on Eros.

Booty-bots were piled booty-on-booty to save space. Ravi

walked into the storage area where some of these booty-bots lay.

"What piles of beauty you are," Ravi said to the neatly-arranged piles, well strapped down to avoid damage during flight. "What coming pleasures for the men and women of Eros you will give, all because of my vision, my diplomacy and my dedication to detail. You girls are going to make me a very rich man!"

Ravi did wonder why Eros needed so many bots, so quickly. Didn't they have a paradise here? Hadn't all the most beautiful women already come to Eros? Well, Ravi wasn't one to sit and meditate on such matters. All he cared about was collecting his payment, delivering his goods and getting back home.

Ravi got on the communicator and tried to reach someone on the planet surface. He had come a long ways and was now ready to set down.

He soon discovered that the explosion at Turnbull's Love Spaceport was an isolated incident caused by a few militant females. It was suggested he land his craft at the Greyshirt military base located nearby. They had a landing port which could support his craft.

So Ravi had his navigator set the coordinates and soon the gigantic silver ship was on a downward reverse thrust toward the Greyshirt Military Compound and Space Launch Pad. The raw power of those jet engines, easing the ship down on fiery blasts of fuel, always excited Ravi. He felt like a deity, sitting atop a mountain of savage power, lowering himself unto his faithful subjects waiting below. Once he touched down he would bestow at the altar of his grateful and obedient subjects all the blessings of love and sex that his beautiful booty-bots could deliver.

"I am Hanuman — demigod reborn," he muttered to himself. "Yes, I must be that loyal monkey-king, who could lift whole mountains, defeat magical beings and command whole legions of followers. Aren't I also doing impossible things here for the benefit of others? Aren't I bestowing a mountain of wanton and wired women, as a blessing, to this off-off world? My hot bots will surely sizzle up this part of the universe. They will fire imaginations, and perhaps, through some mystical means, will provide divine inspiration that will last for eons and eons."

Ravi had discovered that what he taught one alien, all of the booty-bots learned easily, so he saw himself as a great teacher also.

The booty-bots all shared the same man-pleasing education, and that was a lot of information. He had used as his textbooks the *Kama Sutra, 50 Shades of Grey*, and *the Joy of Sex.* Plus he had given them several weeks of training in tantric sex, yogic body control, reflexology-based sexual response, and electronic-enhanced sexual stimulation. And finally they were taught Ravi's own patented Cadmium-Sulfide Photoreceptor Royal Round-About Tut-Tut Treatment. That treatment never failed to excite. Never.

There was very little about giving sexual pleasure that these booty-bots didn't know or couldn't create on the spot. No human female could match them. Each of these faux-ladies were treasures, so superior in every way to the flesh and bone alternative that they probably should be outlawed.

He and his silent partner Omar were always pushing the boundaries of what was possible, traveling into the deep mysterious mental and physical nooks and crannies of what it meant to be fully, completely sexually satisfied. Ravi could not care less about the current female problems on Eros.

"I'm a lucky guy, aren't I ladies?" he said to the pile of inert booty-bots. "Yes, what a fortunate man I am, almost a holy saint in a way. Haven't I found universal consciousness, that guiding, creative force that rules the universe with unconventional sex? Haven't I traveled many a tantric backroad to link with the higher consciousness that comes from opening my chakras? And I have given my special linkage to these booty-bots, who in turn, will give it to their new owners on Eros. Oh, the eternal, orgasmic bonds I will have created!"

Posh Matosh had made terrific strides in pleasure-making since the addition of these little aliens from the tiny planet of Metta Karuna. They were definitely the golden key to success for Posh-Matosh Company.

After touchdown the rockets cooled and the exit ramps opened. Ravi released and awoke the booty-bots, who started untangling themselves. Soon they were marching down the ramps into the military base.

Two by two they came, in waves of blonde, brunette, red-heads, auburn locks, and coal black hair blowing in the breeze. There were busty bots, athletic bots, squat, short bots. They came in all sizes and shapes, because Ravi was a smart businessman and knew all men did not have the same tastes concerning their women.

Greyshirt soldiers lined up alongside the ship and stood at attention as the army of artificial women swept into the compound like the first crystal snowflakes coming down on a childhood Christmas morning. Some of the young Greyshirt recruits stood doubly at attention, both their bodies and their organs erect, thinking of what these beauties were capable of.

Most of these troops had never seen such a parade of beauty before. Oh, they'd seen a few striking beauties filing their nails or applying Resurrection make-up products — unreachable females controlled by the top officers. But never in their lives had they laid eyes on anything like this — this river of riveting lovelies, both sexy and approachable.

These parading sex robots made many of the troops want to break rank right then and there. They longed to hop right on one of those beautiful bots, like a hot rabbit in the wild, and pound out this edgy impulse until satisfaction was bouncingly achieved.

The consequences of what might come if they did do just that were welded in the back of their minds, and kept them loosely in rank. But it was a thin wall holding back a high tide.

Having been forced to always do what they were told, and virtually locked up with other males for months on end was no fun tour of duty, even on Eros. No release seemed possible in this camp — until the arrival of these booty-bots. In the minds of many of these young troops there must have been thoughts such as, "why must I, in the prime of my youth, be denied that which comes so easily to the high and mighty? Am I not a man as well as they are? I do carry a gun, don't I? I should just take it!"

CHAPTER 26

INSPECTING THE TROOPS AND THE BOTS

Corporate Leader Turnbull flew his shuttle into the Greyshirt Military Compound, also known as White Knuckles Camp, to greet Ravi Moonbeam. Turnbull hoped that Moonbeam had all the answer to his current women problems on Eros.

In his shuttle with Turnbull today were Dr. Yzer, the human egg scientist, and President Jones, leader of Cronos 2. Jones, who had just lost his ship, several of his crew, and all his cargo of human eggs and embryos he had purchased by a cowardly act of sabotage by the women of W.I.R.E., was visibly upset.

Besides all this, Jones had lost a pair of Emily's universally-precious eggs, which were genetically predisposed to give birth to freckled, red-haired children. The eggs he had so earnestly promised his wife he would come home with. Didn't their next-door neighbors, those snooty Sanders, have a freckled child that they were constantly bragging about? Well, his wife had to have one of those ginger status symbols too, or else she could make President Jones' life a living hell.

"I need more of those freckled eggs and I don't want to hear anymore excuses," shouted President Jones to Yzer and Turnbull. "This is on you two. You need to replace what I lost at your poorly secured spaceport."

Testosterone was running rampant in this shuttle. It threatened to turn into a terrible testoster-storm, like a 8-beer piss, spraying macho out onto the innocent and the mad alike. This hard-boiled male superego supercell had all the makings of an inter-planetary saloon brawl.

"Didn't I introduce you to my premium egg insurance when you made your purchase?" asked Dr. Yzer to a red-faced President Jones. "No one ever thinks they need that policy, and then, lo and behold, just like that, that time jumps up on the unsuspecting or the cheapskate, and they're caught with their presidential pants down.

"Didn't I say not to put all your eggs in one spacecraft? Don't you remember how I warned you to protect your assets? Were you even listening when I cautioned you of a possible crack in our social system by radical Eros females?" asked Yzer.

"A crack we're about to fix," qualified Turnbull.

"I thought you had this whole feminine situation under control here," said Jones, now turning to Turnbull. "I trusted you people to give me safe quarter for commerce while I visited this planet. I can't believe you're being bothered by a small group of women!"

"You talk pretty tough for a guy who's out egg shopping for his infertile wife," said Turnbull, "whose whole planet's population is shrinking faster than limp peters in a cold swimming pool."

"So what are you going to do about this?" asked Jones.

"Corporate Leader Turnbull and myself have contracted with Ravi Moonbeam and ordered booty-bots," said Dr. Yzer. "We wanted to be ready in case of such an uprising."

"How's that gonna help me?" asked Jones, still hot under the collar.

"Women think they're indispensable," said C.L. Turnbull. "They believe they deserve special favor. But with Ravi's guaranteed Posh Matosh Playmates coming, women will soon become third, maybe fourth class citizens."

"Just good for egg harvesting," said Dr. Yzer.

"And about your lost eggs, we might work something out, a compromise. We'll re-supply you, but we want something in return," said Turnbull.

"Again with Yzer's Millions genetic eggs?" asked Jones, "OK but that's it. Isn't having his likeness splattered all over my planet enough? What else could you possibly require of me?"

"Hold on. The Yzer Millions is between you and and Doctor," said Turnbull, "but for me and my planet I need a different kind of favor. I need you to boycott Resurrection Cosmetics — completely and permanently."

"But my wife loves their blush and lip gloss!" said Jones, throwing his hands up into the air. "Fine, then," he sighed. "The freckled eggs might ease her make-up loss."

So a partial peace was attained between Yzer, Turnbull and Jones as they exited the shuttle into White Knuckles Paramilitary Camp.

The Troops were lined up in formation in the central parade grounds, as were the booty-bots, with the two groups facing each other. There was a wide gap separating the groups where Turnbull stood and looked from one side to the other. General Forrest Howitzer brought everyone to attention as Corporate Leader Turnbull strutted into the midst, his blond hair fluttering in the breeze, with Dr. Yzer and President Jones following in his gigantic wake.

"We're honored to have you here today," spoke the General to Turnbull, envying his wavy long hair. "We've assembled the troops and the recently-arrived bots for your inspection."

"Let's make this snappy," said Turnbull. "I'm being told that the feminist group W.I.R.E. are coming here for a protest outside these gates. I wonder if they'd dare."

"But first, let's take a look at these bots Moonbeam brought," said Turnbull, as he walked up and down the line of beautiful sexual robots.

A petite blonde bot spoke with a sultry voice as Turnbull passed, "Can I get you something to drink? Something cool and refreshing? You must have had a hard day."

"I'm good," Turnbull responded, smiling and turning to the others to show he approved of this particular bot.

A tall athletic brunette whispered to Turnbull, "Wanna ride your horsey into my beautiful barn? I was made for that, you know. I'll rub on and cool your hot beast down."

"Maybe later," said Turnbull, making a mental note of this particular booty-bot.

"How about a long, deep tissue massage?" asked a dark-haired voluptuous bot as Turnbull glanced at her. "I'll give you happy ending!"

"I'll bear that in mind if I ever need that service," said Turnbull, nodding to himself.

"Can I fix you a home cooked meal and afterwards suck your big, strong (loud horn)," asked another beautiful bot, wiggling her hips and twisting her hair.

"I just ate, but thanks for your straight-forward approach," he responded. "Looks like a damn good lot of bots you brought to me," he said to Ravi. "Damn good."

Then Turnbull turned to the troops, giving them the once over. Sweat dripped from a few of the soldier's brows.

"What's your primary mission here?" Turnbull suddenly turned to ask a pimply faced recruit.

"To s-s-s-safeguard the p-p-pleasure of all, sir," said the young recruit.

"Wrong," shouted Turnbull. "Wrong. Wrong. Wrong. Your duty is to ensure the ***peace*** on Eros, even if it means making war. Your duty is to help us maintain ***freedom***, even if it means subjugation for all. You got that, Private Nobody?"

"Y-y-yes sir, I g-g-got it," he replied, shaking in his combat boots. Turnbull moved down to another recruit,.

"What would you do if you were brutally attacked by a woman?" asked the supreme Corporate Leader, with Dr. Yzer and President Jones peering closely over Turnbull's shoulder.

"I'd take her out as if she were a man, sir," said the recruit, "without regard to her sex or her strength."

"Hmmm," said Turnbull. "You say that now. But I have eyes! I see all of you Greyshirts lusting after these booty-bots. Listen up, all you young brave soldiers, you put down this W.I.R.E. revolt, by whatever means necessary, and we'll keep some of these booty-bots on base here for your very own personal pleasure. There will be one for every man here, regardless of rank, smell or length of his nose."

Smiles appeared on the soldiers' faces.

"Not until I get my final payment," said Ravi Moonbeam, co-owner of Posh-Matosh Playmates. "You still owe me 3/4s of the price of these bots. Let's settle this before you go doling out what isn't yours yet."

"Guards, take him away!" shouted Turnbull, pointing to Moonbeam, and armed guards led a squirming Ravi Moonbeam away.

"Hey! What is this? You can't do this to me! This is insane! Don't you know I'm practically a demigod! I'm the one who created and brought you these booty-bots! And I can get more! You don't know who you're messing with here! This will have serious repercussions in superior galactic court!"

"If it makes it there," said Turnbull.

Outside the gates of the White Knuckles Camp there came a large group of females: congregating, holding placards and shouting slogans such as "Paradise My Ass!" "Eros Don't Care About Their Women!" "Booty-Bots Go Home!"

Turnbull turned his ear to listen to them. He whispered something to Dr. Yzer then announced, "No, I don't hate women. I just need them to know their place.

"For as long as there has been the written word, women have been subordinate to men," continued Turnbull. "That's God's plan. Any rational person knows that. Now about these women at the gates outside. General, they need to be dealt with! Swiftly!"

"Yes, Corporate Leader Turnbull, Sir," said General Howitzer.

"I must insist you pay me for these booty-bots you ordered," yelled Ravi as he was being dragged away.

"Wait up. Bring him back here to me," yelled Turnbull.

"Please, let's deal fairly and honestly," said Moonbeam, his clothes soiled and disheveled. "I came here on your good word and all I expect is for you to honor the deal we made."

"You're telling me there are tiny aliens inside each one of these booty-bots?" Turnbull asked Moonbeam. "How do I know that these little beings will be loyal and not cause any problems on my turf? If they do I'll come after that you."

"They're no trouble, sir. They're meant to please," said Ravi. "They are as loyal and true as anything or anyone can be."

Dr. Yzer had a question and had his hand raised.

"Yes, Dr. Yzer? You wish to add something?" asked Turnbull.

"These aliens — they have no free will? They are completely dependent upon the wiles of the operator?" he asked.

"They do have some freewill, or else they wouldn't be able to provide their special patented kind of sexual spur-of-the-moment ecstasy, which makes them both exciting and frightening," answered Moonbeam. "But I assure you they are safe and they will serve your every erotic purpose. What is your purpose with so many? Don't you already have many beautiful human women here to spare?"

"Can't you hear all that bother outside these gates!" shouted Turnbull. "They're a rebellious lot — spoiled maybe. But I mean to quell this unrest once and for all. General! Prepare your troops. Broadcast our first peace offering, and let's see if they come to their senses. And you Moonbeam, you'll get paid after I take care of this little problem."

Gen. Howitzer gave the order: "Troops, double-time to the supply room for anti-riot gear and sidearms. Assemble back here pronto! Communications — get on the horn and offer these women one month's free day spas if they lay down their placards and go home peacefully. If that fails to break them up, hover the drones and drop down the 50% Tuesday shopping days coupons."

The troops trotted off toward the supply room to get

equipped and to make sure the drones were loaded and sent skyward.

After the coupons were dropped and the day-spa offer given there was only one response. Ladies ripped up the coupons like mad dogs, effectively snubbing the offers.

"They mean business," said General Howitzer.

Outside the gates of the Greyshirt Military Compound Consuela Franklin, better known as Fanny Bonita of the hugely popular daytime soap, had a megaphone and was speaking to an angry crowd of women.

"Ladies! Our hour has come! We don't care for day spas or discounts at the mall, do we? No! We want recognition. We want independence, respect, and a voice. We won't be swayed anymore by trinkets, tricks or little pats on the back.

"This is ***not*** a planet of love - no New Garden of Eden. It's a toxic social environment! When the males herd it over females, taking sex when they want; stealing our eggs for profit; making us forfeit all choices concerning family and children, it makes life on Eros for all women a living Hell!

"Do they think they can control us so easily? Don't they care anymore about what we want or need?"

"They never did!" shouted Emily.

"I swear by my character Fanny Bonita, who I play on 'The Supply Room Trysts of Doctor Heartthrob,' that I am willing to lay down my daytime stage life to stop the tyranny of these Greyshirt goons and our misguided leader Danny Turnbull. No more episodes, no more trysts. I'll give up every close-up, every clothing endorsement, all my gift baskets, and more if what we do today can gain a measure of freedom for all Eros women!"

Many female shouts broke the air.

Gliding into the area on sky-scooters was the Resurrection Cosmetics group, with Ba Boom, Shin Shin, Harry, Judy, Susie Q, and others.

Harry noticed Emily Novak, standing in this group, shouting until her lungs must have hurt. Emily was wearing a long banana yellow dress and appeared to Harry like a holy prayer candle. Her good posture and great body, made even better from the required exercise of all Eros women, was accented by her bright red hair and her scarlet red freckles, burning embers, cosmic remnants of the *aa* and *pahoehoe* lava thrown out by soil-enriching volcanos.

In Emily's fury she became glorious in appearance. Her freckles took on an extra aura of authority, like medals of courage — her red hair seemed to set the worlds of time on fire. She shimmered with the viscious glow of coming war, a beacon for love and justice — all in one — like an ancient Viking bezerker or an avenging angel.

Every redhead woman God has ever created since time began is both fearsome and fantastic. This is a fact. But Emily was of a sort that only comes around once in a lifetime, and maybe not even then for most mortals. Her freckles were lightly sprinkled upon her nose and upper cheeks, like little campfire sparks carrying secret messages; or they contained fragments of esoteric histories, or tales of genetic mix-ups that had to be re-sorted time and time again.

She was a redhead of extreme loveliness that took not only a man's breath away, but also his money, his pride, his cool, and his dignity. She could even take his dog, if a man should happen to own one, for what self-respecting dog would stay with a mere man once he had glimpsed the red-headed fire goddess of ultimate doggie treats, this Agni of old known simply as Emily?

Her raging essence echoed the first lighter-flick of the universe — the big bang. Harry remembered his first sexual encounter with Emily. It still sizzled in his pants and brain. What was it he had so loved so much about her face, her form and her whole essence? It was everything.

It was that freckled innocent that barely hid that sensual radiance. Oh how she resembled Titian's "Venus of Urbino," a mind-blowing red-head sprawled invitingly on a sexual sofa, baptizing with her enchanting eyes and damning with those perfectly formed breasts and thighs.

Was Harry falling in love with Emily all over again as he watched her move and speak? When she shouted down the institution she had fled to, did her red-haired passion zip through the Eros air and also unzip his heart? But she had hurt Harry, hurt him really bad. Why was he feeling all this? He looked at Judy, who was oblivious to Harry's confused state.

Wasn't Judy superior to Emily? Wasn't she a better choice, with no baggage, no temper, no complaints, no desire for infidelity? Wasn't she just as beautiful, just as alluring?

The manhood lodged inside Harry, which had been brought again to the surface by the use of Resurrection Cosmetics in-flight to Eros, told him that he deserved a REAL woman, not some plastic, alien-loaded love receptacle. He deserved his beautiful wife Emily back, the judge between his legs said. He had won her over once and he believed he could do it again. He walked over to where she stood yelling.

"What the hell are you doing here?" Emily turned to Harry to ask. "This is for women only!"

"I'm on your side," said Harry, with as much sincerity as he could possibly pour out of his unruly mouth.

"You know nothing about me, nor, for that matter, women in general! Besides that you don't know anything about life on Eros. How can you be on our side when you're so ignorant about so many things?" Emily glared at Harry.

"I want to understand," said Harry simply.

"See our red flag of revolution?" asked Emily, pointing to a red flag with a white cross in the center. It was carried by a dark-haired woman.

"I see it," said Harry.

"That's my friend Sophia waving it," said Emily. "She was supposed to be placed in jail and rot, but we broke her out. Her crime? Getting pregnant. What do you think that flag represents, Harry?"

"Blood, I guess," said Harry.

"We call it the Rag of Righteous Rage. It represents menstruation," said Emily.

"Oh, that," said Harry.

"Yes that!" Emily shouted. "Those are crossed tampons in the center of that flag. Say it Harry, say the word tampon!"

"Ta...ta...I can't," said Harry.

"See. Here's something you have never understood about women nor me. It's that little monthly death we feel. It's the flow of life that runs through us — the potential for new life that didn't come into being.

"That flag represents how women must absorb all the crap we are given by men about this natural occurrence. We bear the blood for the good of all — for the constant rebirth of humankind — even if men never try to understand this power.

"A woman's cycle shouldn't be something to be hidden and afraid of. It's what we women do, every single month. Men don't get that, don't even want to discuss it."

"Let's not talk about it anymore," said Harry.

"See? Why are you here again? Shouldn't you be on the other side of that fence, rooting for the menfolk to put us back in our places? Trying out all those new booty-bots you seem to love so much," said Emily, glaring at Judy and Susie Q. "Look around. You're the only man here on this side of the fence. The rest of us, except for your sex toys — we're all united by the blood, by the tampon, yes, the tampon Harry. And by that flag that represents the humiliation we suffer, just for being women — even here in what they want to call paradise."

"Why did you leave me, Emily?" asked Harry.

"Always put-down, made to feel less-than," said Emily, ignoring Harry's question. "Always a qualifier that goes with any of our accomplishments, or a look of wild surprise when we surpass a man's ability. Anything different about us, we're made to feel shame.

"We're sick of it, Harry! I'm sick of it. Sick of being a woman in a world dominated by men. Sick of being this special red-haired, freckled egg giver for profit. Sick of this emperor who rules over Eros like he's Jesus Christ himself. We're going to oppose and protest him and his army today. Better choose.

Either you're with us or you're against us. If against us, you better get the hell away from here fast. It's about to get ugly."

"I'm with you Emily," said Harry. "I always was. I always will be. I turned to the booty-bots because it was breaking my heart you were gone and I was going insane without you. Maybe I don't understand women at all, maybe I never will, but I'll try, Emily. I'll try."

"You know the Kotex was born out of war? So from war and death came something utterly feminine, which men have never wished to discuss. Because men can't understand it, don't want to understand it, don't really want to understand women at all! And don't even get me started on men finding our clitorises and female climaxes!"

A louder voice overreached all the protesting.

It was the amplified voice of Ba Boom. "I don't believe anyone has to die or get hurt in all this. I've come here to help with your liberation — your revolt from the tyranny of Corporate Leader Danny Turnbull."

Shin Shin Skinny was at Ba Boom's side, "Emily, Harry has come here with us today to help you escape, and any other women who wish to get away and come back to earth."

"But we want a fight!" shouted Consuela Franklin. "We need to show those arrogant pigs a thing or two about women and their strength. We won't run and cower. We'll stand our ground, thank you."

CHAPTER 27

PRIDE GOETH BEFORE A BALL

On the Greyshirt side of the fence Corporate Leader of a Free Eros Danny Turnbull turned to General Howitzer and said, "Maybe I should just go out there and talk to them. I know how to handle this kind of situation."

"That's not advisable," said the General, "after all, they're flying their red flags of menses, and you know that always spells trouble."

"I said I'm going to go out and talk some sense into them," said Turnbull, with a thou-shalt-not-question-it finality.

"I'd advise you take a guard unit with you, a crack team," said the General.

"Just need three or four real good men."

The General called out a few soldiers and Turnbull strode toward the gate where the W.I.R.E. women were assembled.

"Here he comes! Our so-called Corporate Leader," said Consuela.

"No bowing before me?" asked Turnbull to the group, as he approached the group and they snarled at him. "So be it. Now you've had your fun here today. You've made your point loud and clear. Time to pack up your purses and head back to where you came from. This nonsense has gone far enough."

"Are those the booty-bots that are going to replace us?" asked Consuela, pointing toward the booty-bots assembled in the compound. "That's what you really want, completely fake women?"

"Oh those. We're going to try them out and see how they work out for us," said Turnbull.

"But like I said all of you need to break this up before someone gets hurt. And I certainly wouldn't want that," continued Turnbull, eyeing the large assembly of lovely, but angry women gathered.

"We're not armed. What harm is there is protesting a system that keeps women pinned down?" asked Consuela.

"You're not armed but you're definitely legged, that much is evident," joked Turnbull. "All these gorgeous gams could make me forget all about this little incident, if it stops here, right now."

"We're just a big joke to you. Isn't that so?" said Consuela. "We're a frickin' big joke to **all** you men. Well, let me tell you, the joke's on you. We're fed up and we're not going to take it any longer."

"Why are you complaining? You've got it *made*." asked Turnbull. "No work, just shopping and entertainment all day everyday. The envy of the universe, as far as lifestyles go."

A woman walked to the front of the crowd.

"I'm Gloria," said the woman, dressed in all red with a patch of the flag sewn on her blouse. "I'm the product of one of Dr. Yzer's little experiments."

"So what? I wasn't talking to you," said Turnbull tersely.

"We have it made here, you say," continued Gloria. "We're so lucky to be a part of your grand little scheme.

"What Dr. Yzer did to me, with his little experiments, and what he was trying to do to all us women on Eros, was eliminate the women's monthly period once and for all. That way there would be no interruption to your ravenous sexual escapades. But what happened? Instead of stopping the menses now I can never get rid of this bleeding inside of me. It's with me all the time — every day — every hour!

"Women gotta flow, but men don't like that. They want sex when they want it. But women need a time of healing, a time to cleanse themselves inside. You consider this time of month a curse — but women see it a different way.

"We see it as 'our time' — our personal revelation time when we can reflect on life — death — rebirth — rejuvenation — growth and new direction. It's a sacred time for soul searching. How dare you men trying to take this time away from us, and turning it into something evil and something to be avoided — sending us out into the marshes to suffer alone because of it. We should look forward to it, even celebrate it!

"But your Dr. Yzer's experiments gave me a constant period. I'm permanently attached to the sangre snaggers, the salary-caps, the dame-dams, the she-stops, the blanche bullets, the pale riders, the white storm clouds, the little nippers, the wizzy wads. I'm stuck with them for all time!

"I have to have them with me every day. I have to watch what I eat, make sure I get enough protein and vitamins in my system to keep me from fading away. And all this came about because your sexual life was interrupted temporarily and you didn't like that. Poor little mistreated menfolk. And I'm not the only one this happened to. There's others like me here."

"Is that what this W.I.R.E. thing is all about?" asked Turnbull. "Well boo-hoo. Consuela, step over here for a minute."

Consuela walked up to Turnbull.

"You're the one who started this whole damn thing, right?"

"Yes I am," she said.

"You damn bitch!" Turnbull cursed in a very violent manner, throwing his fists up and down and trying to scare Consuela. "Where do you get off challenging my ultimate authority!" Turnbull stared her up and down then looked hard into her eyes.

"Yes?" Consuela asked as the staring continued.

"You wanted to be a model at first, didn't you?"

"How'd you know?"

"But you weren't thin enough, right?"

"Not by their standards."

"Then you wanted to be a big-time movie star."

"I did get some bit parts."

"Then you wanted to be a newscaster, but you couldn't refrain from editorializing on air."

"Someone had to say something," said Consuela.

"So you fell down the rungs, one by one until you finally ended up face-down, fanny-up on daytime soap opera. A stupid TV holo show about nothing at all. And you believe you're enough of a somebody to lead a protest against MY powerful government? Is that it? Well, is that it? You think you're big enough to challenge me, Corporate Leader Turnbull? You, a lousy soap opera star? And just look at those shoes you're wearing! Just take a good look! Did you get them at Goodwill!"

That was the last straw. Consuela broke down in tears, "I'm nobody! I'm nobody!" and off she ran, crying. You could hear her yelling back as she fled, "he shouldn't have said that about my shoes! I like these shoes!"

Turnbull looked to the gate and spotted the General. He nodded in his direction as if to say, "that's how you deal with women. You confront them and make them cry."

"Hello Danny," said Emily, walking up to Turnbull. "Quite a little show you put on there for all of us. Did that make you feel all special inside? Did your testosterone levels rise like a hot air balloon? You always were a flit. Why don't you try that business on me, you lousy piece of shit!"

The guards surrounding Turnbull moved closer but Turnbull called them off with a flick of his hand.

"Me lousy? You were the rotten log in bed, the sour cream. I always thought with that flaming red hair and those runaway freckles, you would be a hoot in the sack, a real rough bounce on the range, but boy, was I ever wrong. No sense of timing," said Turnbull, "no thrilling moments, no surprises, just bland, bland, bland.

"I guess beautiful women like you think you can get away with anything on this planet — get what you want, when you want it, and nothing is there to stand in your way. But I saw through you. I saw the real, bitchy side of you," said Turnbull.

"You probably don't even like women. Is that why you brought all those booty-bots to Eros? Do you secretly hate us all? Probably too in love with yourself to notice."

Just then Turnbull did something that surprised all the women and the men inside the gate too, he grabbed Emily's private part.

Emily blushed, then turned a brighter, meaner red and all her freckles seemed to gather up their strength and light up with an intensity that exceeded the afternoon's two-sun sky. She just stared at Turnbull with a look of contempt, while his hand stayed put on her private part.

"So you want to be friends again?" she asked him, just before grabbing his private parts — his nuts — and squeezing them really hard.

"You-think-this-bothers-me," said Turnbull between clenched teeth, never letting go of Emily himself.

"Why don't you let go of me and maybe I'll let go of you." Emily stood strong as Turnbull seemed to weaken.

"Son of a bitch!" Turnbull yelled.

Each held their grip on the other.

"You're a punk Corporate Leader," Emily said to him.

"No...one...calls...me...a...a," Turnbull whimpered.

The guard unit assembled around Emily with pistols drawn.

"Release our Corporate Leader," said one of the guards.

"Back off or I'll crush one of his precious little nuts like a fresh-laid egg," threatened Emily.

"Back...back..off guys," said Turnbull.

"Let go of me, and turn around and march back behind those gates before I get really mad," said Emily. "I hold your future in my hands."

Turnbull let go of Emily, but Emily didn't let go of him.

"But... you said," Turnbull said in a high voice.

"What if I just crush one. You can live without one of these guys can't you? Of course you'd only be half the man you were before."

"What-do-you-want?"

"Equality! Respect. A voice."

"Never! You're under arrest!"

"You can't arrest me!"

"Your food credits, your cosmetic allowance, all that comes from me. I could have you moved to a lower income housing unit! You're nothing, nothing at all without me. You would have died on Earth but I saved your stupid bitch ass. So you owe me -—big time."

"I owe you?" Emily smiled, still holding on to Turnbull's balls.

"Are you a traitor to the male sex?" asked Turnbull, turning toward Harry, who seemed to be enjoying all this. "Help me. Maybe you can talk some sense into her."

"You brought this on yourself," said Harry and turned away.

"Are you going to let go or am I going to have to do something drastic?" asked Turnbull.

"Something like this?" said Emily, and then she crushed Turnbull's teste with her bare hand, crushed it like a squishy hard grape. Turnbull let out a yell that was heard around the planet. He fell to the ground and Emily spat on him.

"Now you've done it! Now you've really gone and done it!" yelled Turnbull. "Get me the hell out of here!"

So the guard troops picked him up and, with the help of other troops who came storming out of the compound, they rushed him back to the military compound, protecting him from further harm. The gates of the Greyshirt Compound rattled like the belly of a hungry beast with war-hunger as the troops brought the yelling Turnbull back inside. There, his wound was quickly attended to by Dr. Yzer.

General Howitzer just shook his head and wondered why Turnbull had to push this incident so far. Where was Turnbull's diplomatic skills at this crucial time? He did'nt even try to reason with those angry women, just plowed into them like a bull in a China shop. He should have known something might happen if he did that, shouldn't he?

CHAPTER 28

THE BATTLE OF THE SEXES IS ON

The battle drums rolled. Bugles blared the "To Arms" signal. Young men with startled, unprepared faces, began their preparations for conflict.

"Take no prisoners," said the General as they drew their weapons from the supply room.

"Give no quarter," shouted Emily on the W.I.R.E. side, as women picked up whatever weapons they could find at hand.

A thousand mighty women, sexy too, stood ready on the plains, beneath the crest of Resolute Hill, just outside the Greyshirt Compound. Women stood ready to fight against the many grievances suffered, staring stonily at the approaching troops.

Each woman valiant, steadfast and courageous. Emily took up the lead, since Consuela stepped down after her breakdown by Corporate Leader Turnbull.

Atop Resolute Hill Emily towered, her red mast of hair a picture of female hope in the rusty Eros wind. Her little yellow dress fluttered like a bedsheet of infidelity on the clothes-line of gender subjugation. Her freckles faced her fearsome fate with solid inflexibility. Emily's breast was aglow with a red-peppered heart beating for greater gender empowerment. If it didn't come in her own lifetime then she'd fight to be a footnote for future generations; for women who might need a guiding redheaded lighthouse, for future reference when women's need to take a firm stand happened again — and it was sure to happen again.

Harry saw an Emily he'd never known standing on that hill — a judicious and beautiful Joan of Arc rallying the masses of malcontented females. If not Joan of Arc, then she was similar to any number of other warrior-queens throughout history.

But, in truth, Emily wasn't Joan of Arc, nor any other. She was quickly becoming her own legend. She was becoming an fit subject for future poems and songs and would one day become known as Emily — the Ball-Busting Belle of Central Eros.

Upon that hill, in that fading light, she illuminated all, shining like a giant glowworm in a hidden black forest, or a bright torch in a dark cavern. She was a pink and yellow orchid in a jungle of weeds, an aurora borealis flashing fantastic colors upon an otherwise plain-white Alaskan glacier.

She was a proud, fierce and spotted mother leopard protecting her young. She was brave like the marching suffragettes, shouting out their demands to be heard and receive a vote.

The women gathered here felt a wave of heart-gladness, a bolstering of willpower, a surge of electric daring. They watched with increased admiration as Emily yelled on Resolute Hill the list of wrongs all women of Eros had suffered over the years.

The two booty-bots approached Emily after her speech.

"Let us help too," said the booty-bot Susie Q to Emily and the group of W.I.R.E. women. "We Metta Karunians have a strong sense of justice too."

"We're with you!" said Judy, standing behind her.

"You two booty-bots? We don't need your help," Emily said. "We don't need anyone riding in on their high horses to save us, including my ex-husband, Harry Novak. Nor do we need the Resurrection Cosmetic ladies, makers of the most fabulous blush and eyeliners in the universe, to assist us. And we certainly don't need you plastic-imitating-human-life robots getting in our way."

"Yes you do! We're more than that. But you need to decide quickly, because here they come," said Judy.

"Maybe you ought to listen to them," said Harry.

"I'm not sure I made the best choice leaving you on earth for that piece of shit Turnbull," said Emily to Harry, a hint of doubt in her voice, "but I would have done anything to escape Earth, and I'll never go back. You have to understand that."

"Emily," began Susie Q, "I'm a spiritual leader from Metta Karuna. I came to earth for Judy because she asked my assistance with a guilt problem. She had killed a teen by accident."

"I will feel no guilt for what we're about to do. Why should I?" asked Emily. "How could you possibly understand what we've gone through? You and your kind are supposed to take our place, to *please the men*, not help us fight against them."

"Posh Matosh, makers of fine booty-bots since 2029, has brought 1,000 aliens, locked inside beautiful booty-bot models," said Susie Q. "I can talk to those aliens and convince them of this cause and their need to fight in it. I can leave this booty-bot body and fly to where they are and change the tide of this coming war."

"All right. Go ahead then. We do need a secret weapon," said Emily. "And you Resurrection ladies can help too, if you have a mind for it."

"We do," said Ba Boom and she assembled her co-workers for the coming fight.

And so the two alien-inhabited booty-bots put their heads together and sought to link their minds with the 1,000 booty-bots in the Greyshirt Compound.

The Greyshirt troops let out a fierce war cry as the gates were opened and they ran toward the group of women.

Little did these male troops know that the women warriors had doubled to 2,000. General Howitzer and his men tried to perform a pincher military maneuver on the women standing near Resolute Hill, but they were out-pinched as there were now women to the front of his troops and booty-bots behind, all eager to make battle and able.

The soldiers, with war-hardened General Howitzer at the helm, marched to the bottom of Resolute Hill, looking up at the enemy of females above them.

"Stop right there," shouted Emily. "Don't come any closer or we'll be forced to fight you."

"This isn't a game any longer, Emily," shouted the General in a fatherly tone. "I need you to step down, go home and be a good little girl."

"If you step up, you may never step again," said Emily.

The young male soldiers looked around them. There was no retreat for these hapless males of the Greyshirt Guard, as there were women all around them. Their leader, General Howitzer, had fight embedded in his very nature, and an ability to overcome difficult odds, but still his soldiers were afraid.

"Men, follow my instructions and order will soon be restored," the General said, trying to encourage his men. "Do as I say and save Eros. For your victory there will be consorts from the survivors, or from women who never participated here."

So the soldiers marched right up to the women of W.I.R.E., standing toe to toe, chests full of medals against the soft breasts of unfulfilled motherly nurturing. The two sides were inches apart, staring each other down. The women were on top of the hill, the men halfway up, leaning backwards.

The General, used to getting his own bullish way, made a violent gesture, ripping a protest sign out of a woman's hands.

This sudden action was a little shocking, but the women didn't back down, not one iota. The woman whose placard was torn away, reached down and picked it back up.

"What do you think you're going to accomplish here today?" asked Emily of the troops. "You think you can plow over us women like we're nothing? You think you can scare us away?"

Harry was in the middle of all this and saw big trouble brewing. What could he do? What should he do? Maybe this General would talk to another man, now that tensions were running so high.

"General, may I have a word?" asked Harry, stepping forward to speak. "These are all gentle womenfolk. Don't be too hard on them. As you can see they're flying the menstruation banner. They aren't themselves."

"The hell we aren't!" shouted Emily and clobbered Harry to the ground with her fists. Harry protected himself as best he could, and finally Emily stopped as Harry cried Uncle.

"There's nothing more to talk about," said the General, smirking at the injured Harry, lying on the ground. "Either disperse and go back home or else. I don't give a flip if you're women or not, you'll do as I command!"

"My mother is a woman," said one of the soldiers in the ranks, uneasy that he might have to confront these women.

"I have a sister who's a woman," said another. "I don't know if I can do this."

"Who said that!" the General turned to find the culprit.

A few soldiers pointed out the offender.

"Come up here soldier," shouted the General.

The soldier came forward.

"I want you to knock this woman in the head!" shouted the General as he pointed to a young brunette.

That woman kicked the General in the nuts and stomped on the young soldiers foot.

"You just try to knock me in the head and see what you get!" said the brunette. "Let's get them!"

The soldiers marched toward the women, pushing them backwards, but the women pushed back.

Clashes occurred. Women hit the troops with everything they had: placards, purses, shields, rocks. The Greyshirts were relentless and injured many of the women, with accidental bayonet thrusts, fists, and billy clubs.

The women held their own. Many a young Greyshirt soldier would approach a woman fighter and hesitate for a moment, not sure if it were proper or not to hurt a lady. In those moments of hesitation the women gained an advantage and used it to take away the weapon from the soldier and use it against him.

In the breast of each women of Eros was a deep knowledge of why she was fighting today. Each knew the stakes and how it might be if they could win, and what would happen should they lose. These women were determined and all in very good shape from the state mandated exercises. They followed their new leader Emily as she rushed into the ill-prepared men, this bright red cardinal-haired bringer of carnage, this nut-cracker of her oppressors. They would follow her as if a part of her very freckled body, if Emily were to initiate it.

The booty-bots were good fighters too, going against their pre-programmed sensibilities to please the human male. For the alien beings inside the booty-bots sensed the wrongs being done here, and with Susie Q's urgings, had bypassed that program and turned themselves into loyal female warriors.

The battle was raging, blood flowed down Resolute Hill. Arms were lost, crooked bodies lay sprawled on the ground, male and female alike, arms upraised, eyes vacant. All day long the fighting lasted. Many soldiers and females made feeble attempts to raise their head one final time to fill their eyes with the dark reds and oranges of an Eros sunset.

Emily found Harry, who she had previously punched to the ground, and instructed him, "Go find a safe place until this is all over with," she said as she sliced at a young pimply-faced soldier, cutting his chest wide open and backhanding another who tried to grab at her legs.

"You don't need to protect me," said Harry.

"Just do as I say!" she yelled so loud that Harry quickly obeyed, dodging men and women alike to remove himself from the battlefield.

Ba Boom, seeing the battle unfold, fetched some feminine gift bags for the women and was directing their distribution. She also sent out drones which were spraying the battlefield with some of her amazing 50X Pheromone-Enhanced Riveting Beguiler Perfume.

Many of the bots were attending to the injured.

And General Howitzer?

"I thought I was untouchable," mumbled the General to himself, bleeding from his side from a well-placed knife to his ribs, and wandering amongst the corpses of his soldiers. "I thought I could overpower any foe, but these women are too much for me and my men. There's too many of them and they're all so fierce! Besides that they're all very fetching. I can't beat fetching and fierce. I'm finished!"

The Greyshirts didn't really know what they were fighting for. They had no reason or cause to sustain them. Were they trying to preserve the status quo — a way of life most of these foot soldiers had never experienced?

When that pheromone of Ba Boom's finally disseminated into the air the whole battlefield changed. Knives aimed at the heart became groins aimed at groins. Even the General felt this powerful force almost overcoming him in his injured state. He was barely able to keep his guard up.

Emily walked like a goddess toward the General, arms and face bruised, and with blood dripping from her struggles. "Ready for peace?" she asked him, careful to keep her distance, out of respect for his military prowess.

The General made one final lunge at Emily. Whether it was out of lust or bloodlust only the General would know, but Emily sidestepped his tackle and, when he rolled over to get up, she placed an elegant yellow shoe to the side of his face. The General reached to grab her leg again but she stomped hard on his hand and delivered another decisive size six blow to his head.

With this the General lay badly injured on the side of Resolute Hill. When the other soldiers learned of their leader's defeat they threw down their weapons and surrendered to the W.I.R.E. women with raised hands.

The General was delirious, barely conscious.

"I have a voucher, Emily," the General said in his altered state. "Let's make our peace and make love here, you and I, on this glorious field of battle."

"Not in the mood, sir," said Emily and was about to kill the man with a pistol shot to the head. Susie Q rushed up beside her and said these words:

"You've won the battle. You've helped make women on this

planet free again," said Susie Q. "This man wasn't your enemy. He was just playing his part. Spare him and show compassion. You might need him around one day."

So Emily did use compassion that day, both to the General and the other Greyshirts who surrendered to her.

"That's not paradise! That's not how this thing is supposed to work! Why don't you just kill me now so you don't have to worry about me later?" he said just before a nurse gave him a sedative which caused him to black out.

All the women cheered as Emily raised her rifle into the air and silently thanked any and all gods for this day.

CHAPTER 29

STILL CLINGING TO LOST POWER

Corporate Leader Danny Turnbull had a fever and was feeling miserable as he lay in his personalized army bed. After all, he'd just had a testicle crushed by a former lover. He wished now he'd never laid eyes on that red-headed witch.

The adjustable luxurious bed had been designed especially to suit the commander in chief. Turnbull wore only a silk hospital gown with the seal of Corporate Leader on the breast.

The Eros top executive seal was a sidelong picture of the god Eros embracing the goddess Psyche. Both had wings. Each held a hidden jagged dagger behind the back of the other. In round gold lettering around this image it read: "Unbreakable Seal of the Grand Corporate Leader of Exo-Planet Eros."

Dr. Yzer stood over him, discussing his surgical options.

"We'll need to perform an Orchiectomy for that crushed testicle," said Yzer. "It has to come out — and soon too."

"So you can't repair it? You can't pump it up or replace it? You expect me to be a one-nut wonder?"

"If we just remove the damaged testicle your recovery time will be much shorter and you'll be back in command in no time. If we go for the transplant, you'll have to remain bed-ridden for quite a while longer. It's a very delicate procedure.

"You see, each testicle is covered by tough, fibrous layers

of tissue called the tunica. The outer layer is called the tunica vaginalis…"

"Cut to the chase Yzer!"

"It's re-connecting those tiny sperm tubes inside your scrotum where we run into possible problems. The many, many stitches could become infected. Plus, and most important of all, we'll need to find a testicle donor."

"Have one of the troops to volunteer," said Turnbull. "I want two nuts in my sack and that's that."

"I'll ask around…"

"No, you don't ask around. You just pick a big, sturdy lad and tell him the Supreme Corporate Leader is in need of his services. No need to discuss all the details. You knock both of us out and you dig in there and get me that other nut. Got it?"

"Yes sir. I'll get right on it."

"You know this Corporate Leader position is the best gig I've ever had."

"I'm sure," said Dr. Yzer, leaving, "You rest up now."

"Hold on there Yzer. I'm not through talking! I am still Supreme Corporate Leader of all Eros. I love that title. I love my office, the chairs I sit in, oh I sit in some grand chairs."

"I've seen them. Yes, they are grand," said Yzer.

"And the pay and the perks, the shuttlecraft at my disposal, and all the weapons I'm allotted, they're pretty top notch too. That's just a few of the nice things you get when you're me."

Suddenly a red-faced Colonel burst into the room, "Corporate Leader Turnbull, the tide has turned! The women have defeated our Greyshirt Army! The General was wounded and surrendered! He's in sick bay now, too."

"Listen up and listen good, soldier. I DIDN'T LOSE. I never lose! You round up those straggling soldier and you get back out there and fight, fight, fight. Fight for the Eros way of life, fight for ME! Because if those women don't kill you I sure will if you come back here again saying we lost!

"I'm the KING! Long live the King of Eros. Long live

myself!"

The Colonel was pulled from the room and in burst a woman warrior named Sophia. She aimed a rifle at the Corporate Leader and at Dr. Yzer.

"We don't want you running your shit show any longer," said Sophia, her wavy black hair going every which way, sweat and blood still on her clothes. "Emily and the W.I.R.E. women just freed us from the women's detention camp you created. You're done, Turnbull!"

Several other women came to back Sophia up. "That's right, asshole! You're done! We're going to have a new leader and her name is Emily!"

"Emily? My M? She couldn't possibly be Corporate Leader. I know what she's capable of, and she wouldn't know the first thing about my job. Besides, none of you would last a week without me at the the helm," said Turnbull. "You need me."

Emily walked into the room and the other women moved aside. "As of right now, consider yourself relieved of your command on this exo-planet," she said simply. "Dr. Yzer, go attend to the wounded elsewhere and leave us be."

"Is this some kind of payback for me dumping you? You'll never get away with this. You think you can just take over my position because you smashed my balls?" Turnbull asked Emily, whose jaw tightened as he spoke.

"Probably should have made you into a full eunuch, and crushed both your nuts, or just killed you outright," she said.

"Can't you see this man needs his rest?" said Yzer, waving his arms in the air. "You can take this conversation up later, after he's recovered from your treasonable, mutinous act."

"Without me you'll be lost, lost, lost!" shouted Turnbull. "You can't get rid of me that easily!"

"We'll see," said Emily, who turned and walked out of the room. "Dr. I said get out of here and go where your services are needed!"

Dr. Yzer slunk out of the room.

"Hey! Come back here, you stupid, stupid bitch! Where

you going Yzer?"

Emily spun and hunkered back into the room. Some of the other lady warriors escorted Yzer out of the room. "What'd you just say?" she growled as she approached Turnbull, who quickly covered his scrotum.

"All right, all right. You're not a bitch. But you can't just take my powers and my doctor away from me. What is this a coup? You think you're strong enough to control this whole world?"

"Call it what you want, but you're out and I'm in, if I'm elected, and, if I am, I can't do any worse than you."

"Oh yeah?" said Turnbull, getting the last word in.

The women left the hospital, but Emily ordered some female guards near the door, just in case.

When the women left Turnbull ripped the saline drip out of his arm and ran toward the door, pushed past the female guards and into the parade grounds.

"Wait! Come back here!" shouted Dr. Yzer, tearing away from the women and running after the runaway Turnbull. "You're in no shape to be running about. Losing a nut is nothing to sneeze at. You need rest and observation for a few more days, at least until the swelling goes down!"

But Turnbull wasn't listening to Dr. Yzer, or anyone. He was one sorehead loser and was sprinting away from the female guards like he'd gone insane.

"The loss of a nut can be very traumatic," explained Dr. Yzer as Turnbull ran past him on the parade grounds. "Like going bald or losing a limb. Self-image suffers, and the fact that you lost your nut to a woman — well that could lead to serious psychological issues later..."

"I have my own issues right now," shouted Turnbull his executive hospital gown open at the back, exposing his ass to the world. Turnbull frantically looked around the area, trying to find some way to express his extreme displeasure at the turn of events that threatened his office.

He climbed atop an Erotican tank that sat idle in the

middle of the parade grounds. He mounted it, climbed to the top and attempted to enter the hatch, but couldn't seem to twist it open. Finally he did unscrew it and crawled inside. He found the controls that turned the turret and tried to aim the huge 120-mm cannon at some of the women now marching in the compound. He fired and the round missed but blew up the mess hall, sending fake-eggs, pots and pans, and shit-on-shingles heavenward.

The turret swung around again and searched for a female target. Dr. Yzer gave up his attempts to bring Turnbull back to bed and ran for his life, as there was no telling where Turnbull might sight his next cannon round.

Inside the tank Turnbull got control of the machine gun and started firing indiscriminately into the compound, this time hitting some of the women, and a few of the men prisoners.

A brave young woman snuck up and opened the hatch and crawled down to fight Turnbull within the tank. She kicked and flayed at him with such intensity that he was almost crying for mercy. After she subdued him she used her feminine persuasion and a 9mm to his head, and got him to back out of the tank.

Somehow all the activity had made him start bleeding from his scrotum area and he had a large red splotch on the front of his executive hospital gown. The girl who stopped him now guided him toward Emily.

A crowd had gathered now to see Turnbull and what might happen to him next. Harry was amongst the crowd and was secretly rooting for Emily, as he still had a big fat bag of resentment for the man who had stolen his wife away on Planet Earth.

Emily looked down at Turnbull in disgust. She handed him a tampon. "Better use this," she said.

Turnbull swatted it from her hands.

"Testy, are we?" Emily couldn't help but smirk.

"Fuck off!" Turnbull said weakly.

"Yeah, fuck off. That's your position on this exo-planet.

You fuck-off. And those vouchers of yours; we're gonna modify those. Maybe we'll make new ones which women present to men and expect handyman work done."

"I like the vouchers," said one woman. "It's so convenient when I need satisfaction. Just grab a man in your own time and get busy. If that one doesn't work out, use another voucher."

"It was a good system!" insisted Turnbull.

"The pills you made us women take, the ones that strangled any strong emotions that might arise after sex: we'll definitely do away with those. It temporarily took away the desire to be a mother, a wife, or to respected. But you can't dose that away with a little pill — not completely.

"Funny kind of yearning we women have, isn't it, to get a little respect. You men never have to worry about that, but we women still have to earn it at every turn. Don't we? Even after we busted your troops good on Resolute Hill."

"You can't be Corporate Leader. I'm Corporate Leader! I'm the only one, and no one else," said Turnbull.

"You're now deposed."

"Stolen! You cheated! Perhaps you and General Howitzer were in cahoots from the very beginning! Maybe those Resurrection Cosmetic women turned the tide, or that conniving, foreigner, Ravi Moonbeam and his little army of booty-bots cooked up some robot plot. I think you all have been in on my downfall from the get-go! And all of you — I thought you were good citizens, friendly tourists and merchants. But you and the others were forming a Grand Scheme to take my throne away. It's big penis envy you have going on there Emily, snatching my throne, snatching my balls, snatching my everything! I won't stand for it!"

After he said this former Turnbull collapsed in a faint onto the parade ground roadway, his naked butt raised high into the air. Emily signaled for an ambulance to take him back to the hospital. Harry looked down at the Corporate Leader in defeat and couldn't help but feel just the smallest tinge of sympathy for the poor soul with only one nut, no kingdom left to rule over, no paradise for men to play in, no respect among his peers. But that tinge of sympathy quickly passed and he shrugged his shoulders and walked over to where Emily stood talking with a group of men, women, and some of the booty-bots.

"If you do elect me as new Corporate Leader I'll do my best to be a friend to male, female and booty-bot alike. We'll put Turnbull in a padded cell somewhere and throw away the key. What do you men say? Truce?"

Harry tapped Emily on the shoulder and she turned.

"Remember during the battle, when lipstick and bullets were flying, people and bots were falling left and right?"

"It only happened yesterday, you idiot," she replied.

"Yeah, well did you happen to notice those posters hung up on the electric poles leading into the compound?" Harry asked.

"Can't say that I did," she responded, ready to break off conversation with him and go back to more important matters.

"They announced a big sock-hop tonight. The poster read: 'Tonight! To celebrate the end of fighting, Erogenous Records presents Larry Monteverde the Kath-Lix, singing all their hits.' You remember their hit songs, don't you, Emily? 'You Don't Have to Be A Virgin Mary In Our Sky Motel', 'Thoughts of You Clouded My Catechisms', and 'You'll Always Be a Sister and A Nun To Me'," said Harry.

"So?" asked Emily with little enthusiasm for the dance.

"So? So this could be a way to mend the fences, stem the tide, get back into the hearts of men and women alike. We could get the two warring sides back together. Surely you don't want to divide the sexes forever on this planet of love. This will serve as a healing balm, a goodwill gesture, a sock-hop to solve this sexual standoff. A chance for you to speak with both sides and break bread once again. I was going to say something while everyone was battling, like, 'Hey! Stop the fighting already! Have you all forgotten about the big sock hop tonight? You keep killing each other, who you going to dance with?'

"But I kept my mouth shut, because I didn't want to bring

attention to myself and wind up getting shot," said Harry. "But Emily, I want to be with you once again. I…I think I'm still in love with you. I forgive you everything and I want to be your bitch forever!"

"Hold on, Harry. Hold on. The original Kath-Lix you say? Coming here to Eros?"

CHAPTER 30

DANCING AROUND THE DAGGERS

Excitement was building as the hours before the big sock hop neared. The battle for women's rights had recently been fought. The somewhat tentative peace held and was trying to gain a foothold. During this uneasy period, with all the women of W.I.R.E. flaunting their victory over the Greyshirts, it seemed like an excellent time to let loose this pent-up pressure and allow everyone to kick up their collective heels.

Emily and a couple of her friends were having their flesh wounds tended to and, simultaneously, were having their hair done by an attentive staff, still praising their recent victory over Turnbull.

Ba Boom, as a gesture of goodwill had sent free sample bags of the Resurrection Cosmetics to many of the W.I.R.E. victors. Inside the bags were lipstick cases, eyeliner, compacts with the Resurrection logo on them and many other cosmetic goodies.

Emily, and quite a few of the other W.I.R.E. ladies, had broken nails, needed some touch-up cosmetic work, some color tips in their hair, and were trying to look their best for the big dance. They weren't doing this so much for the men, but for themselves. They felt a need to look glamorous again, whether to drive the men crazy or just for their own personal happiness.

Sophia, who sat beside Emily in a beauty chair, turned to

Emily and said, "Can I just dance with you all night? I don't want to have anything to do with those men."

"I'll dance a few dances with you, but the reason for this dance is to ease the freeze, come to a new understanding with the opposite sex," responded Emily, as her hair was slightly curled. "You take your own sweet time making that emotional frost go away. There's no hurry. But eventually we have to go back into a society that encourages families and children. I miss the sound of children. Don't you?"

"Can we trust them? I mean, really trust them?" asked Sophia. "I'm having a hard time with that, Emily. After all, I was put in that camp and forced to go through all those horrible things. I'm still grieving. I wanted that baby."

"I know you did. That was what spurred this whole movement, Sophia," Emily said, lifting a hand which was pre-soaking before a manicure and touching Sophia's. "I don't know if I would have had the courage to begin this revolt if I hadn't seen you dragged away like that, and locked up. Now you're free and that's all in the past. You don't even have to go tonight if you don't want to."

"No. I want to," said Sophia. "I want to look some of those Greyshirts in the eyes. I want to turn them down for dances. If I do dance with a man, I'm gonna step on a few toes."

"Well, at least you're making progress, but I'm not sure that's the spirit we're trying to create here. Anyway, if that's what you want to do iin order to heal," Emily let go of Sophia's hand and picked up a magazine as her head was placed under a dryer.

Inside the dance hall the women were gathered at one side of the hall and the men at the other. Harry was nudging another male to go dance with one of the women.

"I can't tell if she's a ma'am or sham," said the young stocky Greyshirt, wearing his finest dress greys. "I want to dance with a real woman, not a robot."

"You could ask them what they are," said Harry simply. "Ah, what does it really matter? We're here to have a good time.

Look, I'll start us off," and he walked toward Judy, his booty-bot, and took her out to the dance floor.

Meanwhile some mischievous partiers were spiking the passion fruit punch bowl and laughing.

"Why'd you choose me to dance with?" Judy asked Harry. "I thought you'd go for your precious Emily."

"Emily's not here yet," said Harry. "Besides, you're a pretty good dancer and I needed to start things off."

"The men and women here were mortal enemies just the other day," said Judy.

Lots of couples joined Harry and Judy on the dance floor. Many of them still had their war daggers by their sides.

"I hope nothing serious breaks out and spoils the mood," said Harry, sliding into the dance steps to the Kath-Lix tune "I Wanna Backslide With You."

"The tension's thick," Judy said.

The song concluded and people clapped.

"Can we go outside a moment and talk?" asked Judy.

They went out onto the veranda and Judy looked deep into Harry's eyes.

"What's to become of me now, Harry," she asked him.

"What do you mean?"

"You have your sights set on Emily, am I right?"

"Yes. I'm thinking of selling you off, since I don't have a job any longer. You don't mind, do you?"

"You wouldn't do that, would you?"

"I have to do something and I'm not sure Emily would approve of having a booty-bot in the house."

"So I was just a doll toy for you, a diversion until you got what you really wanted. You got so lucky getting me — I mean a drone falls on your ALDABA-covered head, come on — and a Resurrection Cosmetics drone at that! Was that pure luck or what?"

"Never gave it much thought," said Harry.

"And you think that I, the alien inside this pile of wires and plastic, your Tropical Veronica Posh-Matosh model you call

Judy, was just selected by chance to be your mate? Why are you here on Eros? Why am I with you? Why did Resurrection Cosmetics bring you to Eros where your ex-wife is?"

"You ask a lot of questions for a booty-bot," said Harry.

"You needed a new life. With your constant electronic monitoring and reporting of crime you were causing young people to hurt themselves at Teen-A-Watch. It had to stop. Ba Boom saw something in you worth saving from your hard-hearted life and your role as a predator of youth. I think she saw a piece of art not fully realized."

"Oh yeah? I'm just that?"

"She wanted to give you some grow room and see what we had on our hands. You may be something yet. But we're still waiting to see what it might be."

"Like what?"

"None of us are sure, but we've provided a space for you. We've removed you from the toxic Earth environment. The rest is up to you," said Judy. "And if you don't want me anymore I'll go back to my home planet. I think I've served my function with you."

At those words Judy rushed back into the ballroom, a slight mechanical green tear in her eye. With swift actions she kept a W.I.R.E. woman from stabbing her Greyshirt dance partner in the heart with a dagger by offering her own arm to be stabbed.

With the knife still in her arm Judy said to the woman, "We ought to keep this dance friendly."

"But he put his hands on my ass!" said the young woman.

"Look, Emily has arrived," said Judy to the woman, as she pulled the dagger out of her artificial arm.

All eyes turned to view Emily, with her red hair twinkling from the glow of a disco ball. Her green dress matched the dance floor. She strode in as if she were a Princess, confident, beautiful, strong.

The Kath-Lix stopped playing and everyone applauded. Emily was humble and courteous as she stepped to the stage.

"Tonight we cross the line," said Emily into a microphone. "I don't want to see any more of you stabbing each other. Judy, take that dagger out of your arm and return it to its owner. I want all of us to channel our hate into love and understanding.

"I know how many of you feel. But it's not the men we women hate. It's the way we were being treated that started the revolution," she continued. "If you men here can work better with us women and apologize then we can move on and be an equality-based society, with benefits to both sexes. Is that asking too much?"

The men in the room shrugged and ate the appetizers.

"Are you willing to at least try?" she asked of them.

A few hesitant nods and a few muffled "I'm sorrys."

"Good enough. Let's all dance. Kath-Lix, do your thing. Hey! No more stabbing! Stop that! Booty-bots, collect all those daggers. You all need to put those away, at least until after the ball. If you've been stabbed go get your wounds treated and return here if you want to continue dancing. But if you cause bodily harm again I'm afraid you won't be allowed to stay until the end of the night. That's when we'll crown the king and queen of the ball and draw for those raffle prizes," she said pointing to the gifts piled in a corner.

So the dance continued as the booty-bots found boxes and collected all the daggers and other small weapons from the crowd.

Outside the ballroom Shin Shin was pleading with Ba Boom, "No Ma'am. You mustn't," she said to the determined Ba Boom. "I'm begging you. You don't need to do this!"

"Oh but I must. It's why we came all this way," said Ba Boom. "If I don't, what's the use? Why the warring? Why bring Harry here? Why the everything?"

"But, you once told me that you'd never..!"

Ba Boom shrugged and they entered the ballroom like someone tossed a couple of hand grenades into it. All the men suddenly tensed up. All the women stood in fear of losing face.

Ba Boom wore an almost see-through dress that barely

hid her everything.

Shin Shin shone like a soft olive star in a flashing bright white gown, with gloves up to her elbows.

Emily — even the beautifully freckled, war leader and now hero, the red-headed take-full-control Emily — felt a little intimidated by these two great beauties. Ba Boom discreetly whispered something into Emily's ear and Emily nodded.

Ba Boom walked onto the stage like a fire-breathing dragon. She was both beautiful beyond belief and set a hollow fear lodged deep inside every man. A fear that she would bite his head off and that he would enjoy it being done to him. She was so much more than radiant. Her looks could have blotted out the two suns like a double eclipse.

"I'm sure you all know who I am," she began, "but I'm not what I appear."

Shin Shin was waving her arms and imploring with facial expressions, hoping that Ba Boom would not continue in this vein.

"Beauty is illusion," Ba Boom continued. "Real beauty isn't a well turned nose, full ruby lips, or eyes of sapphire. Real beauty is a characteristic of caring, giving unto others a sense of compassion and loving kindness. I'm not really the hunger in your heart, the swell in your pants. What you're feeling is similar to seeing a mirage. I'll show you."

Ba Boom took off her elegantly-styled blonde wig and exposed her splotched head with patches of dull brown hair.

"I was badly injured during the Great War on Planet Earth. But I was determined I would help myself, and the women of my world to regain their sense of grace and dignity."

Ba Boom took off her shawl and peeled off a prosthetic that hid burn scars on her right arm.

"I'm no great beauty — except how my cosmetics and my tricks of illusion make you think I am," she said.

"Not all women are air-brushed and flawless marble sculptures. Most are regular-looking people with flaws. Males here need to love women — as they are — how they look, how their bodies work, respecting all they go through to be truly female. If you men can learn these things you can make Eros a stronger planet, and it can make all of you men better men. This knowledge will make all your relationships more binding, more honest, more fulfilling.

"I can create illusion, that's what I do for a living, but I want to be assured my magic won't be wasted here. The real magic happens when you accept reality — live equitable lives — and give women their proper place.

"Many of you out there aren't as attractive as you seem to think you are. We've analyzed the mineral composition of this planet and concluded that it contains a high concentration of Cupidium. This element gets into the water and into the air and causes humans to see others with a skewed vision — kind of beer goggles, like you have near closing time at your local bar.

"I've decided I want to help change the Eros economy and process that virgin Cupidium for use in my cosmetics lines. Shin Shin will stay behind here and build up this industry. Eros will be out of the human egg business for good. And I'll return to earth and continue to help that planet clean up its act.

"Now!" Ba Boom bolding shouted. "Who's gonna dance with me?"

"I will," said Harry. "But do you think you could put your wig and prosthetic back on?"

"Sure. But not you. You dance with Emily. Anyone else?"

A tall square-jawed soldier took up the slack and stepped up. After she put back on her wig and prosthetic the soldier took Ba Boom for a spin on the floor.

Emily and Harry danced too.

"You may be too powerful for me," Harry said to Emily. "I have nothing back on Earth. I want to stay here — with you."

"Can you live with my power and be faithful and true?" she asked him. "Can you accept being under me and letting go of your booty-bot?"

"I'll do whatever you want me to do," said Harry, letting Emily dip him, as the music of the Kath-Lix played one of their hits, "I've Been Be-BOP-tized With Holy Rock Water."

CHAPTER 31

THE TWIN SUNS FIND A MOTEL ROOM

Ravi Moonbeam, co-owner of Posh Matosh Playmates, was hiding out with Dr. Yzer and President Jones in the Human Egg Plant, waiting for the violence to settle down. And furthermore, they weren't invited to the dance. That told them something.

"I'm going to have to leave Eros. They've got it in for me now," said Yzer.

"Come to Cronos II with me. Set up shop there. You still owe me for those freckle-prone eggs I promised my wife," said Jones.

Unbeknownst to these gentlemen Sophia, the heartbroken sister who was given a forced abortion, was outside the Yzer Egg Plant. She was loosening some valves, cutting some wires, and causing mayhem with the electronics of the cryogenic facility. She also planted a small detonation device which would go off in about five minutes — enough time for her to escape.

"I'll fix that s.o.b. Yzer. I'll fix him real good," Sophia muttered to herself.

With the supply of liquid oxygen and liquid nitrogen misadjusted there was a growing pressure building in the cryogenic lab. Dr. Yzer noted the pressure climb and tried turning some knobs and consulting with his computer to fix the problem.

"What's wrong? What's going on?" asked Jones, seeing

how frantically Yzer was trying to adjust things.

"Something's not right," said Yzer. "The pressure in these cryogenic canisters is growing too fast. There might be a leak somewhere. You two better get out of here fast! I'll try to save my babies!"

Moonbeam and Jones ran out of the facility. Yzer stayed back, trying everything he could to find and fix the problem. Just before the pressure gauge reached the very end of the red warning levels Yzer ran out of the building, and it exploded in a blast of flames and smoke.

Yzer's lab coat was on fire and he rolled on the ground to put it out. Moonbeam came to help and Yzer passed out as all around them it rained down liquid and metal from the Egg Factory.

The fire department arrived quickly on the scene but had a hard time putting out this fire, as the liquid oxygen and liquid nitrogen were feeding the fire. It burnt very hot.

Emily arrived on the scene.

A fireman held her back. "Leave this area and return to your home," he said. "Some of the gases might be harmful."

"Anyone know what happened?" Emily asked.

"Not yet. I'll report to you as soon as we find out."

Emily left the Egg Plant, thinking about all the times she had donated eggs there, pieces of her freckled flesh, that were now gone. It was an evil enterprise. But those potential lives that were blown to kingdom come, that didn't seem right.

Was this an act of sabotage, thought Emily? Who would do such a thing? An ambulance passed as she walked away from the scene. Someone had been hurt in the incident, she thought. How many were inside? Luckily it was a Sunday and presumably none of the regular staff had been there, but Dr. Yzer may have been.

Sophia approached, sweating and excited. "You see that?"

"Nasty fire," said Emily. "You know anything about it?"

"I think I love you," Sophia said to Emily, breathing hard.

"I love you too," said Emily with a quixotic grin.

"I mean love-love you," repeated Sophia, smiling broadly.

"Oh. Well. OK."

"So, what do you think? Do you love me too?"

"I don't know."

"You still love men, don't you? Surely not that old husband of yours?" Sophia said with disappointment. "I hate them all!"

"Look, I got a lot of things on my mind right now," explained Emily. "The explosion, running a planet, trying to forge a lasting peace. Can't we take this up another time?"

"Yeah. Sure," said Sophia. "Say, tomorrow at Pink O'clock?"

Just then some exploding canisters from the Egg Plant zoomed by the two women and they decided quickly to go their separate ways.

* * *

Sitting in a Greyshirt Military Police Station sat Moonbeam, Emily, and President Jones. Two M.P.s were standing by the door.

"You need to get me off this planet now," said President Jones. "Explosions, a war. My people back home are furious. This is too much! Get me a rocket and get me and my staff home!"

"Yeah and I got to get back to my business on earth," said Moonbeam. "And I'm taking my booty-bots with me, at least the ones which weren't damaged in that stupid war of yours."

"I need to know what happened at the Egg Plant," said Emily. "More people could have been hurt. I guess Dr. Yzer is stable now, but he has a lot of second degree burns."

"We don't know what happened," said Jones. "It all came about so fast. But I claim political immunity. As a foreign visiting leader you need to grant my wish and get me out of this hostile environment. The sooner the better. My wife is worried sick, and who knows what's happening inside my government back home. I hope you know what you've gotten yourself into, lady. If they don't hear from me soon, they might involk our military to come get me."

"OK. I'll get you a rocket and send you home as quick as I'm able."

"I'll take Yzer with me, but I hate going back home empty handed," said Jones. "It will look bad for me coming all this way and not bringing any eggs back with me."

"That's between you and Yzer," said Emily, "but if you have any more information about the explosion I want to hear it."

"It sure wasn't us that caused it," said Moonbeam, and Jones nodded.

"OK you two can go. I'll start working on that rocket for you. Jones, and Moonbeam, you're clear for liftoff anytime."

"Who's gonna pay for my damaged booty-bots? Who's gonna reimburse me for my time and travel to this planet? I thought I had a great sale with Turnbull, and now nothing! Both me and Jones are left here with nothing!"

"I heard Ba Boom might be interested in buying some of your booty-bots," said Emily. "Contact her.

"I'll set up a teleconference with Cronos II and explain what happened," continued Emily. "I don't want to start a war with your planet. Let's start off on the right foot."

"Well, I never really liked Turnbull anyway. He was a bully and a thug. But I sure wanted those eggs you used to make here."

"Maybe some of our Cupidium will help your people get into the swing and you won't need to buy imported human eggs and fetuses anymore. We can offer vacation packages for your people to come here and enjoy romantic getaways. Say," Emily said, looking at her watch, "Speaking of romance I gotta run. I'll see you have everything you need."

The reason Emily had to run was the approaching of a grand **Pink O'Clock**. Eros operates under a binary sun system, with both a yellow sun, similar to earth's, and a cooler red sun. The light from the yellow sun usually dominated and you always have a slightly purple sky.

The two suns circle each other like lovers and the exo-planet Eros circles both of them. On certain days eclipses occur where the red sun crosses the yellow one, and the light shades get all mixed up, slanted and weird and extra colorful with these extraordinary pink and slightly purple colors that shower down like a drug-induced fantasy. It's this over-powering romantic light and gravitational phenomenon that causes the cupidium crystals in the atmosphere and on the ground, to become excited and shimmer — all this sky show is called Pink O'Clock.

Now as Pink O'Clock approached Emily walked out of the interrogation room where she had talked with Jones and Moonbeam. Men were wandering around, looking for an available Misty Kiss nest to cool their boiling blood.

Misty Kisses are a certain bright pink flowers unique to Eros, technically they're referred to as *Osculum Caligo*. These wild, wide trumpet-like flowers grow into soft vine-nests, where lovemaking can occur, especially at Pink O'Clock. These flowers only bloom at Pink O'Clock, and just before they do their tubular petals swell as the smaller red male sun crawls on hands and knees toward the Queen yellow of the Binary Sol System.

Emily felt a swelling too, inside her body. Her nipples grew erect and the tiny red hairs on her body were standing on end, making them exclamation points on her freckled skin. She knew what Pink O'clock meant. She felt herself being guided by the flower smell, almost hypnotically, to a nearby Misty Kiss Nest.

Nearby Shin Shin saw Harry sitting on a rock thinking.

"It'll be up to Emily when and if you get back together as a couple," said Shin Shin, reading his thoughts. "But I'd definitely meet up with her at Pink O'Clock."

"You think I should? I'm not familiar with Eros culture."

"Don't miss this special, romantic time," said Shin Shin.

"Have you ever been in love Shin Shin? What does your name mean, really?"

"It's Japanese and it means the soft, gentle falling of silent snow. Doesn't apply to me, I don't think. I usually talk way too much! But about my falling in love. Yes. Once, long ago. It was a quiet romance, a hushed affair. He was married. I was young and naive. But enough about me. Rush to Emily and share this precious hour with her or someone else will. Hurry!"

"Oh, OK!" Harry said and took off running, looking for Emily as the red sun continued to inch toward the yellow, the first pink slants bending off the hills and causing some of the cupidium in the atmosphere to twinkle.

Sophia also was running to find Emily. Who would win this race? Whoever got there first had a good chance to win her heart permanently, as Pink O'Clocks only occurred every other year. When they did it was fantastic, and ultra romantic. Emily, coming off the war and all the new complications in her life, was super-primed for lovemaking and permanent mating.

Emily sat cross-legged in her Misty Kiss Nest, watching the twin-twinkle Pink O'clock hour crawl nigh over Eros. The Misty Kiss flower was peeling open its petals, like a striptease, as the red sun met the yellow. Once opened the flower sent out waves of yellow pollen that orbited around her being, gathering in orbit like three halos: one around her temples, another around her upturned breasts, and a third around her taut lower stomach.

The pink light from the binary-suns touched on each of Emily's little pink freckles, and seemed to emit little love rays that shot out of her like spikes of sin. Her flowing red hair was standing on end, and her her whole body grew wet, so much so that steam came out of her every pore and a sweet come-on juice ran down her thighs.

The soft green vine-nest, the pink lights and the yellow halos, the blooming flowers, Emily sitting naked in the middle of all this, her wide green eyes, growing impatient, searching hungrily for whoever would enter her Pink O'clock nest, was a pastoral scene of intense erotic beauty.

Sophia and Harry were running as fast as they could from opposite directions toward Emily, both spotting her simultaneously. Harry got there first and Sophia tried to deliver a swift kick to detour him, but Harry did a baseball slide under Sophia's leg and got inside the nest just before Sophia could enter. The Misty Kiss flower's vines closed rank around Harry and Emily and threw out a small arsenal of thorns. Sophia, catching a few of those painful thorns, turned and left the area, grumbling and cussing at her bad luck.

Harry looked at Emily and fell into a dizzy swoon that took him straight into her freckled arms. Like a long boat away from shore too long, Harry sailed into Emily's familiar port. Their flesh joined in a holy union, all Harry's clothes came off, the misty kiss pollen wafting over them as they made imperial, perfect love, pleasing each other in many wonderful manners. It was the best lovemaking experience Harry ever had, even besting all the crazy, innovative positions that his booty-bot Judy had shown and used on him.

The big trumpet flower continued releasing pollen which smelled sweet, lusty and musky like hot sweat from a recently galloped horse. The physical intensity of their lovemaking grew and grew, in that pink sunset nest they were bouncing off each other like excited horny electrons. The nest shook and rocked until a final explosive consummation was achieved by both of them simultaneously and the roof of the nest blew off, allowing the cool evening air to rub over them.

Afterwards Harry and Emily lay in each others arms for a moment. Emily rose to her feet as the Misty Kiss Flower dripped a fluid out of its flowers. Emily cupped her hands to receive some of what the flower offered and gave Harry some to drink.

"It's thanking us for our lovemaking," said Emily, as Harry took a sip and smiled.

After they drank they both stood up, walked outside the nest area and started sneezing.

"Is this common?" asked Harry between sneezes.

"We're helping spread the pollen. It's always this way."

The red sun parted from the yellow and each went their separate ways, like strange lovers after a motel joust.

Emily and Harry watched as a double twilight descended. The two suns spread colors across the horizon as if an artist's palette exploded in a sea of mirrors. It was a relaxing, beautiful time.

A domestic warmness filled both of their hearts — after all the sneezing died down. Other couples emerged from their own pink nests, covered in a fine yellow dust, clinging to each other and smiling, unwilling to put on clothes, hesitant to let this sweet moment in time end.

CHAPTER 32

GIFT BAGS AND BAT BITES

Harry and Emily sat at a small table, by the front window, looking out at the Pink Ball Bats swooping down and bouncing onto the red-green ground. The red bats were trying to rouse the Cherry-back beetles from their holes, with their thudding against the lawn.

As one ball bat bounced on the lawn another ball bat was quick to swoop down behind it in case a cherry-back beetle came above ground. There, the pink ball bats would use their claws to hold onto the beetle and use their tube-like mouths to burst open the cherry-like pods on the beetles backs and proceed to drink the sweet liquid. The beetles ate only a certain lichen to produce this nectar. The guana from the ball bats helped the lichen grow, thus, perpetuating the cycle of life.

The cherry sacks on the beetle's backs protected them from other predators, as the pink ball bats protected their source of sweet juice vigorously.

"Want something to drink?" Harry asked, standing up and going toward the kitchen, as something roused the ball bats and they all flew away: apparently spooked, and the beetles returned to their underground world.

"I don't think I do," replied Emily, looking over some papers scattered on the table. "I need to work on recompense for those who died in President Jones' rocket explosion. We want to make things right with the people back on Cronos II. And I need to figure out who was responsible for all that."

"You'll figure it out. You know, I'm beginning to really like it here on Eros," said Harry from the other room. "I don't have to worry about frying myself to death every time I walk outside and I don't have to wear that awkward ALDABA on my head. No drones dropping on me, no need to take a smelly SWAY if I want to go somewhere. It's really nice here."

"Yeah, sure. Well, will you look at that? What do you suppose they want?" said Emily as a crowd of women gathered just beyond their front yard sidewalk.

Harry returned with his drink and looked out. There, in front of Emily's house, all the surviving booty-bots had gathered, over 700 of them, with Judy and Susie Q at the fore.

"Harry! Harry! Harry!" they were all shouting in unison.

"You're wanted outside. Better go see what that's all about," said Emily. "I'll wait here."

"Be right back," Harry said confidently.

"Let's hope so," said Emily.

"There," pointed Judy as Harry approached. "There he is. The one who left me, after everything I did for him!"

"I'm with Emily now," Harry said.

"The wife who deserted you?" Judy asked. "The one you weren't good enough for on Earth; the one who drove you to me?"

"I suppose so," he said.

"And all she has to do to get you back is hide within a fancy flower nesting thing during Pink O'Clock and it's right back at it with your two like nothing ever happened?"

"Something like that," he said.

"You know all those flowers and lights and other fancy stuff on this planet didn't do anything for us booty-bots, nothing. Guess it was just for total humans. But that's not fair — that's playing dirty!" shouted Judy the booty-bot.

"We took up arms and fought side by side with those W.I.R.E. women," continued Judy. "because it's what we thought you'd want us to do, Harry. And we thought it good to help these women in need. Now some of us don't have booty-bot bodies to go back into. We have to double up."

"Moonbeam will fix that for you back on earth," Harry explained.

"What if we don't want to go back there?"

"That's up to you and Ravi Moonbeam," said Harry.

Ba Boom, owner of Resurrection Cosmetics, drove up in a shuttlecraft. She got out gracefully and looked the crowd over.

"What do you want?" asked Judy rudely.

"I've made a deal with Moonbeam and purchased every one of you booty-bots," Ba Boom said. "You're all free now, but I'd like some of you to consider coming to work for me, here on Eros, at a Cupidium Subsidiary I'm creating, with Shin Shin as the boss."

"I was never part of that deal with the other booty-bots he brought here," said Judy. "Moonbeam can't sell me, I belong to Harry and I don't want to be free of him. I still want to belong to him."

"OK, not you, but the rest of you."

"And not Susie Q," said Judy.

"No, not her either," said Ba Boom.

"I have jobs, if you care to join me," said Ba Boom. "Maybe you'd like to come back to Earth with me and help me save the world."

"None of us are human like you," said Judy. "You sure you'd want us working for you?"

"OK. You're not human, but think of your situation, you won't grow old and weak like we mortals," said Ba Boom. "In a way you're immortal and don't even know of death — do you?"

"Not really," said Judy.

"So you'll always be young and beautiful with beautiful bodies," continued Ba Boom. "If your parts wear out you can just replace them and go on and on. You'll be rulers of the universe — no one will be able to match you."

"True, I guess," said Judy, mulling it over.

"OK Judy, so you may have lost Harry," said Ba Boom.

"Who or what is this Harry anyway? He's no one special, in fact, he's only mildly good looking. He's basically a nobody with glasses. You could do so much better. Think about it! What do you want to do with your practically immortal life? Wanna shackle yourself up with this short-liver who may never amount to anything? Think bigger Judy, think bigger!"

"Hey! I'm right here," said Harry.

"You'll find other mates — plenty of them," said Ba Boom.

"Yes and they'll all leave me when some version of Pink O'clock comes around," said Judy, growing mad once again.

"But there will always be new men coming in and out of your life. You don't have to be alone," said Ba Boom. "And this is a better world than back on Earth. We will mine our cupidium responsibly and keep this planet pristine."

"I still want my Harry back," said Judy.

"Doesn't he have a right to his own happiness too, same as you?" asked Ba Boom.

"Harry would be happy with me," said Judy.

"I can't," said Harry. "It's over, Judy."

"You're breaking up with me? You're breaking up with your booty-bot, here, now?" asked Judy. "After all we've been through together, our special courtship, the thing with the boy Warthog trying to kill you, and his father George too — all that?"

"Yes. I'm going to start a new life here with Emily," announced Harry. "I'll work with the Cupidium Company for Shin Shin and Resurrection Cosmetics. Maybe I'll be in P.R."

"You're so boring and cruel," said Judy.

"After Pink O'Clock I see the world differently. The two suns have opened my eyes," said Harry.

"What's wrong with me?" asked Judy. "Tell me what the hell is wrong with me? Why can't you love me like you do her?

"I have red hair — like Emily. I have nice breasts. I have two red lips and a personality, and you know I know how to make love so you like it. I can cook. So what the hell is wrong with me? And don't give me anymore of that Pink O'Clock shit as your excuse. You owe me an explanation!"

"I don't have one," said Harry, not wanting to excite Judy any more than she already was, and looking for a way out.

"Oh, sacred lipstick case, I don't think I can take anymore of this!" shouted Judy, the booty-bot. "I'm gonna blow a circuit or something! I'm not programmed for this! I'm not ready to let you go, you lousy, stinking human teen-watcher!"

Emily walked out the front door to see what was going on, assuming it was time for her to intervene. "What's going on?" she asked. "What you all talking about? Me?"

"Yeah you," said Judy, walking up to Emily, two red-heads faced off like two meteors on a collision course. "You stole my man with your goddamn misty kiss flowers and all that Pink O'Clock rigamarole, but he's mine and you can't have him!"

"Oh that," said Emily, feigning indifference. "Well, shouldn't you let him decide for himself? I mean, don't booty-bots ever let go? This kind of thing happens."

"Look! He bought into me and all my circuitry long ago, after you'd already made a chump out of him. You were out of the picture when he made his decision about me," said Judy.

"Ladies," said Harry, but was shoved to one side by both ladies.

"Well now I'm back in the picture and he wants you out," shouted Emily.

"What else needs to be said?" asked Harry.

"I thought this might have been a bad idea — coming to Eros to rescue your old wife. But did I protest? Did I stand in your way, Harry?" asked Judy. "No. I came with you. It seems your coming here was what Ba Boom wanted, and Shin Shin and YOU, Harry! And now here we are — I'm out a fucking partner because of some damn flower and swirly lights. I don't like it. I won't take it! And I got numbers to back me up. Right ladies," Emily turned to address the booty-bots standing behind her.

Hundreds of robots yelled "Right!"

"We all fought in that war of your's Emily," said Judy. "We helped you gain emotional and sexual freedom for your gender. I was on the front lines, as we all were, and this is how I'm rewarded? This is what you do for those who help you — you steal their men?"

"I never meant to do this..." said Emily.

"Oh sure," said Judy. "You were just magically shoved into that sexual nest with Harry, where you somehow were caught naked and moaning, and with the perfume of some exotic flower punching him in his feel-good sack? Is that how it all went down? It was just a drunken whoring on your part, or a weird coincidence?"

"Now hold on there, you hybrid hussy from the weird backwaters of outer space...," said Emily.

"You make it sound so cheap," said Harry, deflecting.

"Well it is, Harry!" said Judy. "It is! And it hurts! It hurts a lot that you'd throw me away like I'm a piece of trash you no longer need or want! Like I'm nothing, nothing at all!"

"You're something," said Harry.

"I could make a lot of trouble here," said Judy. "I've never been this upset in all my existence. I could make a whole mess of trouble. I feel like I could even kill somebody!"

"Oh yeah!" said Emily, "You want trouble?"

"Whoa there! You don't want to do that," said Susie Q, moving from the ranks of the booty-bots between Judy and Emily. "That's why I'm here with you now. You were suffering from an overwhelming sense of guilt at having killed that young boy. You summoned me and I came. Since that day I've accompanied you and tried to help ease your burden. Don't make this worse, Judy."

"But I can't help it," said Judy, breaking down.

"You have to let go of your attachments, especially the one you have for Harry and any plans you might have to get revenge on him or Emily here," said Susie Q, always the judicious one. "Just release those emotions, for your own good and everyone else's. Maybe you need to come back to our home planet and go on a long retreat, away from this flesh-filled existence you've been thrown into. Back home I can help you find peace."

"It's so hard to let go. So very hard," said Judy.

"You gotta do it," said Susie Q. "And it will get easier over time."

"You must be some kind of booty-bot bodhisattva — a Boddhisatt-Bot. Huh," said Emily. "OK, you booty-bots can go stay in the gymnasium downtown until you know what you're going to do next. I'm going back inside and you all can all do whatever."

"Judy, thanks for all you've given me," said Harry to his former booty-bot. "And you too, Ba Boom — bringing me here and all. This is where I needed to be, and I'm so sorry, Judy."

"I'll say you're sorry," said Judy, as she watched Harry turn to walk back into the house behind Emily. Glowing green tears welling up in her eyes and dripped to the side of her artificial flesh-like nose.

"Well say, I do have wonderful gift bags for each of you back in my rocket ship. Come check them out," Ba Boom spoke to ease the mood. "It's a random sampling of many of our cosmetic lines, plus Dali-Dojo exclusive, limited edition purses too! For every one of you," said Ba Boom. "Judy, you may be heartbroken, confused and not altogether sure of what your next move may be, but whatever you decide, you can do it in high style, with these gifts I'm offering you. So that's something, isn't it?" Ba Boom said, trying to get a smile out of Judy.

"Yeah. You just make sure you have my shade of lipstick," said Judy, lightening a bit.

The legion of lady booty-bots marched back to town and lined up by Ba Boom's rocket to receive their gift bags. Later, they would go wait in the gym and decide their collective and individual fates.

Judy took one last backwards glance towards Emily's house and shot them the finger. "I'll wear this make-up, and I'll use this nice purse, and I'll accept this consolation prize with my booty-bot head held high, but I'll never forget what you did to me, Harry Novak. Never, ever, ever."

CHAPTER 33

DAYTIME SOAP STAR RETURNS

Harry and Emily watched as President Jones' silver rocket lifted off, leaving a trail of blue and orange flame against a purple sky. Jones had taken Dr. Yzer along with him, as part of the deal Emily made with this envoy. This was partial payment for the explosion which caused the loss of his rocket, the eggs he bought from Yzer, and the death of many of his crewmen.

There would be other lawsuits and pay-offs forthcoming in this inter-planetary incident, but Emily was certain things would settle down in time and the two planets could peacefully resolve this mess. President Jones was easier to get along with than Turnbull, that was for sure.

Perhaps Dr. Yzer would yet assemble his Yzer Millions of duplicate selves on Cronos II or some faraway planet, but not here — not on Eros. And, since he would no longer be residing on this planet, he wouldn't be gathering Emily's and other women's human eggs and selling them at a profit. It'd be a long time before Emily could get those horrible images out of her head.

"What are you thinking?" Harry asked Emily, as the rocket grew smaller, tickling the upper reaches of the purple sky.

"You don't want to know," said Emily, as she spotted Sophia, standing a good distance away. Emily tried to hail Sophia but Sophia gave Emily a quirky smile and ran away.

"What was that?" Harry asked. "She's acting a little

strange, don't you think?"

"I'll speak with her later," said Emily. "Aren't you supposed to have a meeting with Shin Shin today?"

"Yes, in a little bit, but I wanted to watch the rocket launch," said Harry, just as Consuela, the former TV soap star, walked up and greeted them.

"How's every little thing?" she asked. "You're looking very tasty Emily. Guess that's what a good nesting can do for you."

"I better get going. I don't want to be late for my interview," said an uncomfortable Harry as he strode away. "Nice seeing you again Consuela."

"You too, you lucky son of a gun," she said back to Harry.

"Haven't seen you around much lately," said Emily to Consuela. "You OK? Looks like you've lost some weight."

"Gotta be thin in my business. Holo-station picked me right back up, even after all my involvement with W.I.R.E. I've been out of the spotlight lately, and I'm almost a new sensation once again. But tell me all about you and Harry getting back together," said Consuela, watching Harry walk away.

"Oh you know how it goes. Didn't you nestify during Pink O'Clock? Is there a new man in your life too?" asked Emily.

"Naw," said Consuela. "I haven't been myself since I gave up my leadership role with W.I.R.E. I messed up. All because of shoes, for God's sake. Shoes! But back to you and Harry. You really think you can love that man? I mean, he's been with a booty-bot, for how long? He's only semi-good looking, you must know that. And you should know how it is when men go bot. They're pretty hard to please afterwards. It changes men. Nothing against booty-bots, mind you, it's just I'm against them being HERE, that's all."

"Didn't seem to affect Harry much," said Emily, dismissing Consuela's concerns.

"OK then, but you might want to watch him for a while," said Consuela, throwing that topic to one side. "Anyway, I'm gaining my confidence back, camera shot by camera shot. I auditioned for a part in a new series that will air next season.

Hope my fans can see me as someone other than Fanny Bonita from my days on that outdated show, 'The Supply Room Trysts of Doctor Heartthrob'."

"What's this new show about?" asked Emily.

"Something about mermaids luring men to their underwater lairs and killing them as sacrifices to the ocean gods," said Consuela. "I'll be one of the sexy mermaids. Hope I don't have to be in the water long. It wrinkles my skin and I'm not a good swimmer. It's kind of a morality tale about same being with same, sort of like you and Harry are similar, but those booty-bots, they're something entirely different, aren't they?"

"We were married before I came here," Emily said.

"Yes, now everything is back to normal, but is it really normal for a man to make love to a robot — to an alien?" posed Consuela. "Does that mess with his head in some ways we can't yet fully understand?"

"Probably not, Consuela. Listen, don't worry about us," said Emily. "I'm sure you've got your own problems."

"Can you even imagine your man being with one of those <u>THINGS</u>?" said Consuela. "Making love to plastic and rubber and God knows what all. And there is the question of those little aliens inside, from who knows where. What are they? I've heard, from very reliable sources, that those little aliens sometimes leave their booty-bot stations in their artificial human heads and go right into the body of their male lovers! What's that all about? Seems wicked and disgusting — very disturbing."

"You have an over-active imagination from all your work in entertainment," said Emily, casting a hard look at Consuela. "Besides, those bots did what many here wouldn't. They fought alongside me against Turnbull's forces. They fought very well too. That was something."

"You know, being Corporate Leader is going to be a big responsibility for someone," said Consuela, looking sheepishly at Emily. "It's not a job for everyone. You'll be watched closely, all the time. I mean all the time."

"If the people elect me I'll be glad to serve," said Emily.

"Still," Consuela said and paused a moment. "You've been through so much already, what with the war, getting that old husband back, settling back in, confronting all those booty-bots, you know? That's a lot for one person," said Consuela.

"Yeah, but... Say, what are you getting at?" asked Emily. "You're not looking to be the new Corporate Leader are you?"

"Weeeelllll, only if you don't *want* it or don't think you can handle it, or if the people decide they don't want you, then I think I *just might try for it*. After all, if you remember, it was *me* who started the W.I.R.E. movement. It was me who organized the protest against Turnbull and spun this whole wheel of female power on it's ear. I'm the logical choice — after you — *of course*."

"*Of course*," said Emily flatly.

"Maybe we could serve together, you and I, on one ticket. We'd be a fearsome team, Emily. Think about it: Consuela and Emily — Females standing up for Females."

"Wouldn't it be Emily and Consuela?" asked Emily.

"Say, what do you think all those booty-bots are gonna do here on our planet now that Turnbull's plans have fallen through?" said Consuela, changing the subject. "You think our men will pair up with them? I mean, they have us real-life pink-in-the-flesh humans right here, yes? Those bots would probably be better off on earth, where they're really needed. Isn't that what you think? I just don't know if it's appropriate, men with robots doing those kinds of things together, sex-u-al things. I'd get rid of them right away if I had my way."

"I'll get back with you on all that," said Emily and looked at her watch. "Say, I wanted to visit Turnbull today. He's been complaining a lot in the hospital he's at. Wanna come with me? See the beat-down horse?"

"No, no, no. I hate that man with every fiber of my being. You trot along," said Consuela. "I need to see if I can find some make-up that stays put underwater, you know, for my big audition as a man-eating mermaid. I hear Ba Boom is having a sale on her Resurrection Cosmetics, trying to unload all her merchandise before she heads back to earth. Her stuff is simply the best. Well, see ya around, and think about what I said, about our leadership positions. We'd be such a great team."

"Goodbye now," said Emily and cut-off Consuela's pleas.

Emily headed towards the Compound Hospital, where Turnbull was under house arrest and still recuperating from his injury.

* * *

Just outside his hospital window Danny Turnbull, former Corporate Leader of all Eros, could also see the afterburner of President Jones' rocket as it escaped the atmosphere. General Howitzer was standing beside Turnbull's bed in full uniform.

"Yes, he took Dr. Yzer with him," said General Howitzer, speaking to the supine Turnbull. "Took some extra eggs Yzer had stored off-site too. Maybe that's all for the best."

"What in hell's name is wrong with you? *For the best!* What happened out there on the battlefield?" asked Turnbull, glaring at Howitzer. "You lose your nerve or something?"

"My men fought the best they could," he said. "I got injured," Howitzer opened up his coat, "Wanna see my scars?"

"No thanks. You *really* let me down, Forrest. You know that? I thought you were better than this. I was counting on you, and you just couldn't cut it. What am I supposed to do now? You tell me," Turnbull asked Howitzer.

Emily was approaching Turnbull's area, buying a snack at a vending machine. She saw the two men speaking and took a step back, behind a corner. She leaned against the wall and listened to what they had to say.

"I'm going to get my office back," Turnbull almost yelled it. "One way or another, with or without you! I'm gonna sure-as-hell do it. I'll tell everybody in shouting distance that I'm still Corporate Leader of this planet. No mere girl is going to shove me aside. How dare everyone treat me this way!"

"I don't think the people want you anymore," offered Howitzer. "Especially the women, and they seem to hold the upper hand right now."

"Who cares what those sluts want? I know the males still want things the way they used to be. I know I do and I'm sure you do too. Don't you, or have you been Wussified? So are you gonna **help me** or are you going to keep kissing the asses of those menstruating maniacs?" Turnbull waited for an answer.

Emily rounded the corner and walked toward a surprised Turnbull and Howitzer, "Help you what?" Emily asked him.

"You get away from me! Nurse! You get the hell away. I have nothing — nothing whatsoever to say to you, you crazy bitch," said Turnbull. "Nurse!"

General Howitzer just watched Turnbull squirm.

The nurse came in and saw how agitated Turnbull was. "Maybe it would be best if you came at another time, Ms. Novak," the nurse said to Emily.

"I'm just checking in on my prisoner. I'll leave shortly," said Emily.

"So I'm asking you, Danny Turnbull," said Emily. "What should I do with you? If you're planning something sinister, I suggest you don't. You'll never regain your Corporate Leadership. That won't happen. You're done, through, finished, kaput! So just learn to live with the way things are now."

"Wait up there. Hold on a second. You know you're one lucky ass bitch, don't you?" said Turnbull.

"How so?" asked Emily.

"If you'd only waited until the two suns aligned to carry out that revolt of yours, you never would have accomplished it. You'd be nesting somewhere, all of you, cooing like little babies, and everything would be just the way it should be around here. I'd still be in charge. You know that. You know you just had good luck and good timing."

"Eventually someone would have unseated you, forcefully or by votes," said Emily. "We couldn't take your heavy-handed approach. Yes, our timing was good. But this is how it's going to be from now on. You and your General here can't do anything about it. If I see one little sign of you trying to reassert your power, I'll deal with you faster than the actions inside a proton accelerator. And if I don't catch you soon enough, and things gets out of hand, I'll have you shot — shot dead."

"Big talk," said Turnbull. "Say. How's that working out with your old husband who came to save you? You must have loved that lug once upon a time. But then things got rough for you two on earth, and you ran away — with me. So I bring you all this way. We shack up, make sweet, sweet love, but eventually I chuck you out of my bed. Why? Because you're such an intolerable bitch and I can't stand the sight of you any longer."

"You threw me out?" asked Emily.

"And here's where it gets funny," said Turnbull. "Now your old husband comes along riding on his silver lipstick stallion, or some shit, and you go humping it back to him, just when the pink vines grow and the suns align. I hope your politics aren't as flip-floppy as you are in relationships."

"As for you, General Howitzer," said Emily, growing frustrated at Turnbull's speech and turning on the General, "You try to help this single-nut wonder in any way to get back in power, then the same goes for you. If I were you two I'd get off my planet quick! I still hold a lot of resentment for the way you fucked things up here.

"I might get in one of my moods some rainy day," continued Emily. "You know how we women can get. And I might decide I want to have both your heads on a silver platter — war trophies to hang on my mantle. Or maybe I'll just kick them around from time to time, stuff them and use them like soccer balls.

"So you better tread cautiously if you stay here, because you never know when I might do something uncharacteristic, or when I get in one of *my moods*. You two can abide by those possibilities or you can leave. But I won't stand for any bullshit. You got that?"

"I understand," said General Howitzer. "I still wish to command my men."

"You'll have to sign an oath of allegiance to the new government first. Whether I'm elected or not, you will serve that administration faithfully," said Emily.

"Yes ma'am," said Howitzer. "I can do that. It would be my honor."

"What about you, Turnbull. Ready to go along peacefully or do we need to go another round or two? Wanna try grabbing my pussy again? I'd love to finish what I started and squash your scrawny groin until you're the little bitch I always thought you were," said Emily, digging her eyes into his brain.

Turnbull was silent and brooding.

"Please ma'am," said the nurse to Emily.

"Yeah yeah, I'll go," said Emily. "See you around, Danny boy."

"Not if I can help it," said Turnbull, smirking at having gotten in the last word.

After Emily and the nurse had gone Howitzer said to Turnbull, "I'm not going to help you do *anything*. You're on your own from here on out."

"Get the hell out of here then! You're no good to me or even yourself. You have less balls than me, and I only have one left," shouted Turnbull and the General composed as much dignity as he could muster and started to walk away.

"Power ate you up inside," said General Howitzer. "You've become a living cliché of a tyrant and Emily and the women aren't the only ones who don't like it. Better get your shit together before you go insane or someone takes you out permanent-like."

"You forget who made you. Without me you're nothing. And, by the way, I'm not crazy!" said Turnbull. "But I suspect you might be. That little red-head Emily has gotten under your skin. That's why you couldn't beat her on the field of battle, and why you won't help me now. What? You think she gives a shit about you? You better think again. I know that bitch like an old bedtime story, and she'll turn on you the first chance she gets if you get on her bad side. Just wait and watch."

"Well I'm not trying to take her job. I'm not robbing her of her reproductive processes. I'm not trying to make her and all the other women on this planet lower case citizens. I love women, and I like being around them, as long as I'm not battling them," said Howitzer. "I think you have issues with women, serious issues. Maybe a mother issue back in your past."

"Just get the hell out, you worthless bag of medals!" shouted Turnbull and turned away from the General.

Oh hell. What to do now? Turnbull thought to himself. *They kicked the wrong dog this time. They'll find out just what I'm capable of.*

"She's gone now, Mr. Turnbull," said the nurse. "Just lay back and relax. You need to rest."

"Where's my lunch?" yelled Turnbull. "It should have been here by now. I'm starving. Don't you know how to do your job?"

"Uh, I'll fetch it right away," said the nurse, looking confused. "There's no need to talk to me in that manner."

"I'll talk to you in any manner I so choose," shouted Turnbull. "I *still* rule this planet!"

"Not any longer," said the nurse, then under her breath she sighed and whispered, "thank God and Emily for that."

As the nurse walked away Turnbull continued his rant about how she should acknowledge his status. The nurse threw up her hands and concluded that Turnbull needed a nice sedative to calm him down, a nice, big sedative mixed into his lunch tray.

"Damn women," Turnbull said. "Maybe I'd be better off with one of those booty-bots by my side: all the pleasure, and none of the backtalk. Yeah, maybe I'll get me one and try it out."

CHAPTER 34

SHIN SHIN'S TEST FOR HARRY

Harry walked into Shin Shin's new office building beneath a sign which read: Resurrection Eros Cupidium Techniques (RECT). It was located in a shiny, modernistic red and gold downtown building and already was alive with people hustling from one station to another.

Approaching the neat-looking female receptionist in the upper lobby he said, "Hello. I'm Harry Novak. Here to see Ms. Shin Shin Skinny. About a position."

"Do you have an appointment?" said the receptionist, looking down at her computer. "I don't see your name listed anywhere. Take a seat and let me check again. Hmmm. I didn't think we were hiring any more men."

Shin Shin opened the door and peeked out, "It's OK, Shirley, let him come on back."

"OK, go on in," said the secretary.

"Come. Sit. Like something to drink?" asked Shin Shin, her long black cloud hair shining from the early morning light. "Glad you could drop by. I was just thinking about you."

"You were? Well, maybe a cup of coffee would be nice," Harry smiled and got comfortable in the big tan egg chair as Shin Shin used the intercom to order up Harry a cup of Joe.

"Yes, I was thinking about you. We talked about a job here. So you decided you want to stay on Eros? With Emily?"

"That's what I was thinking, yes," said Harry.

"Probably a good idea since that arrest warrant is still in effect for you on earth. I know you're innocent, but they've gotten pretty hard-boiled down there on terra firma about killing ex-Citizen Policemen's sons."

"I wouldn't stand a chance in court," said Harry. "That's probably only one of the charges I have against me."

"True. So it doesn't bother you that you'd be working in the cosmetics industry with us here? We're a business that caters mostly to women, you know? Do you know much about ladies cosmetics?"

"Well, I can certainly learn. I picked up a few things on your Resurrection rocket ship ride here from Earth," said Harry. "And maybe you can put me in the Cupidium mining operation part of this company."

"I'll be your boss, you know, whether you work in the main office or out in the field. And you'll have other women over you either place also. You don't have a problem taking orders from women, do you? I mean some men can't stand to by lorded over by a woman, even in this day and age. Can you believe that?"

"I don't have any problems with it," said Harry.

"Are you absolutely sure? It'll be long hours until we can get this branch up and running at full production. Lots of women around the quadrant really are interested in our products, especially since the big war of the sexes here has given us so much free advertising. Orders have been pouring in. Can I count on you to give it your all here at RECT?"

"I was a good worker at Teen-A-Watch back on earth and I'll give you the same effort here, no, I'll work even harder here than I did there," said Harry. "I believe strongly in your product line, having tried some myself, and I think it will practically sell itself."

"Good. We have some tests we'd like you to take before we put you on permanently. They're situational type what-ifs, very real-life work dilemmas you may run into," said Shin Shin. "Can you come in tomorrow morning and we'll get you started?"

"Sure thing. What are they all about?" asked Harry.

"Oh don't worry," said Shin Shin. "Just get a good night's sleep and be truthful and try your best. That's all we ask."

So Harry left Shin Shin's office as she waved bye-bye. He walked back home, kicking rocks, getting worried about these upcoming tests he had to take to find employment with Resurrection's RECT Branch.

He'd always worked in a male-oriented office, so certain protocols may be unfamiliar to him. Would he slip up and sexually harass a co-worker? Peek at the boss's cleavage and offend her or another? Bump into a fellow female co-worker at the water cooler a little too hard — a little too often? Would he threaten a woman's authority over him? Would he himself be sexually harassed? Would he say something off-color, or unknowingly insult a woman? So many things could go wrong!

He wasn't sure about all these things and it made him scratch his head nervously, like a dog after a tick. He wished he'd have brought his juggling balls along with him to Eros. They always seemed to calm him down before, when he had his many worries inside his little Go-Poddy.

Well, Harry thought, he sure was glad he didn't live in that small beehive apartment on Earth anymore. Here on Eros he could move around, walk where he wanted without fear of the elements. He had some elbow room and could enjoy fresh air and double sunshines. What a pleasant change. And all these beautiful women! Oh, and of course Emily. He'd never go back to bots again. Why should he when he had an angel?

But those upcoming tests still caused his stomach to do somersaults. Harry never was a good test-taker. Something about being tested made a part of him shrivel up inside and want to hide shivering in a closet.

When Harry came home Emily seemed distracted about something. "What's wrong, honey?"

"Do you love me?" Emily asked. "I mean really love me?"

"You bet," said Harry. "I never stopped loving you."

"Did those booty-bots mess up your brain?" she asked.

"What?" asked a puzzled Harry. "Who have you been

talking to? Did Consuela put some crazy notions inside your pretty, freckled head?"

"It's kind of a perversion to make love to something other than a human being, don't you imagine?" asked Emily, wanting to know more about it. "What was it like? Did you enjoy it? Who was on top? Did you cuddle afterwards? Did you smoke a cigarette?"

"Oh shit, Emily. Let's not go there. That's all in the past," said Harry, hoping he could cut this conversation off quickly. "I didn't ask about your love affair with Turnbull. And I didn't quiz you on all your voucher rendezvous."

"That was different. He was different then. At least they were all human, like us," offered Emily.

"So you say," countered Harry. "OK then. You want to know what it was like making love to a booty-bot, my personal booty-bot I named Judy? You want every gory detail?"

"Yes," said Emily.

"All right then. I'll tell you. I was pretty broken up about you leaving me. You must know that?"

"I figured," she said.

"And I was lonely, Emily. So lonely. There weren't any women that wanted me, or that I wanted on Earth. I didn't even have the money to purchase a sexbot. I was lost. Then, out of the blue, a drone fell on my head. A Resurrection Delivery drone. They offered me a booty-bot as compensation for my injuries. I only wanted an AI type booty-bot, but I got a special one by mistake, one with an alien inside. I wanted to return it, but I gave it a chance. And we made love, Emily. In so many ways, in so many positions! The leaf-blower on the Lazy Susan, The Arctic Snowcone in the beartrap..."

"OK, I get the picture," said Emily.

"Lots of couples are drawn together by sex," continued Harry. "You must know that, having lived here on a planet where all you have to do is give out a coupon to get it."

"Yes, I'm aware of that. But a robot, Harry."

"Yes, well, it was going pretty good, just sexing this way

and that, and then I report a young Teen doing what he ought not. He's arrested, but he is let go because of who he knows. Later he comes looking for me. I'm not home but Judy is and she accidentally kills him — twice actually. That spun her into a deep depression and she called on a home planet spiritual aid — Susie Q. So now I had two booty-bots to watch over.

"And I was liking it, but then the Teen's father wanted to kill me for his son's fate, and he would have done it — at a subway SWAY station — if fate didn't intervene for me once again. Resurrection Cosmetics had sent a girl to try to make me love her away from my booty-bots, but she and that crazed father out to kill me bumped into each other hard and fell into a crazy, wild, ultra love whirlwind by way of special Resurrection Cosmetics.

"I saw all that and I thought to myself, I don't know if this is cosmic or cosmetic, fantasy or fantastic, but I wish I had some of that kind of supernatural love that almost blinds you with its intensity. So I tried to love Judy that way. We even bought some of the Resurrection Rev-Up-The-Juices make-up and tried it on her. I tried and I tried to find that heart-in-heaven love, but I never did. It didn't ever click like that."

"OK, so, then..."

"Then the police were after me. I may not have killed the boy, but I was responsible for what my booty-bots had done.

"Ba Boom was going to Eros anyway and she scooped me and my booty-bots up and offered us a ride here. She wanted me to try to help save you or help you escape the conditions here.

"So here I am. I catch you just as you're about to fight your old lover Turnbull and gain freedom for all the women. After many battles and struggles your side wins. Soon afterwards Pink O'clock occurs and I beat out the competition to get with you in time, and the rest is sexual, romantic history."

"All right. I can accept that," said Emily. "But you're through with booty-bots now — you're off the bots for good?"

"Of course, darling," said Harry. "They were my bridge back to you, nothing more. I could never love a booty-bot the way I love you. I have that cosmic, fantasy love that I saw in the subway station now. I have that with you. I won't let that go."

"Did one of the aliens ever enter your body?" Emily asked.

"Yes. When Judy disposed of the boy's body at the SWAY station. She entered Warthog's body first, to get it out of the house. Then she jumped out of that body in the knick of time and into mine — just before the train hit him."

"What did that feel like?" Emily wanted to know. "She ever jump inside you when you were making love?"

"Never during lovemaking, just that once, like I said. I didn't really notice anything, but she stayed inside me long enough to make me do a thorough cleaning of my Go-Poddy. Why are you asking all these questions?"

"Just wanted to know your mental state. I'm gonna need you on my side in the coming weeks," said Emily. "I'm going to rely on your help if I'm to be elected Corporate Leader."

"I'll be there. Boy I sure am worried, though. I have to take some tests at RECT tomorrow. It's got my butt in a bind."

"What kinds of tests?" Emily asked.

"Situational types of tests. Simulations of actual work environments. They want to test me on how well I will be able to work with women at the factory. I don't think I'll have any problems, but you know how I am about tests. I get all goofy inside, and forget everything I know."

"You'll do just fine," comforted Emily. "I ordered dinner. It should be here shortly. Let's eat then make love and get a good night's rest. Don't fret too much about some silly tests."

"Yes dear," said Harry, but he knew that even with all Emily's kind soothings, his mind would churn and churn tonight, trying to conjure up all the possible scenarios that Shin Shin would present to him on those darn job tests.

CHAPTER 35

HARRY'S LIBIDO ON TRIAL

Harry didn't sleep well the night before his big employment test. The RECT testing had him really worried. He had no idea what kind of things they would ask of him. He kissed Emily good-bye with an absent-looking stare and walked out the front door, careful to avoid the cherry-back beetles.

The ball bats were watching on the rooftop and from the trees. Harry looked back at his lovely house where he and Emily lived. Emily stood in the doorway waving him good-bye ever so sweetly. Just like old times and boy, did she look sharp in her short bathrobe, freckles popping out from her neckline and her legs.

Lost in a kind of matrimonial bliss he did step on one of the cherry-back beetles and just as he did, two ball bats swooped down and bit him on the arm.

Emily ran inside to get the bat-be-gone spray-away and saved Harry from further attack. She also got the emergency medical kit and gave Harry a quick shot to prevent bat-madness. Well, thought Harry, even Paradise has a few problems to contend with. Just a small little bite. Better watch my step from now on.

"Thanks honey!" Harry told her as she trotted barefoot back into the house smiling. She was a war veteran, a crusher of nuts, a mean go-getter, and always prepared for the worst. He was glad she had the know-how to live on this planet, because he hadn't caught on quite yet.

* * *

Harry walked into the RECT building and was directed by the security guard toward the training room. Harry sat down at a long table in one of four chairs. Soon three ladies came to the all white room and joined him at the testing table. Harry smiled at them and they smiled back in a weird manner, almost a snarling.

So far so good, thought Harry. *Nothing wrong with a friendly, or maybe not-so-friendly smile now is there?*

In walked the training coach, a very large but fairly attractive lady, wearing glasses and a lab coat. Behind her walked her assistant who placed a white piece of board with holes in it on each table. She also placed a small plastic bag of screws and a Phillips screwdriver next to the board.

"Hello. My name is Kathy. I'll be proctoring your testing. I'm glad you all could make it in today. Well this is going to be such a hoot!

"This first test will measure your manual dexterity," Kathy, the instructor continued. "When I give the signal you will tool all the screws into your board as tightly as you can. You'll be timed as to your proficiency and accuracy. Try not to drop or lose any of these screws and make sure they are securely tightened. Everyone ready? Go!"

Harry picked up one of the little screws and started screwing it into the board. The girl next to him dropped one of her screws. Harry picked it up for her and she smiled at him and silently mouthed him a thank you.

On and on Harry screwed until he finally completed all but one screw before Kathy called time. The instructor looked all the boards over and made some notes. She then walked out of the room, taking the boards and closing the door behind her.

"Thank you for picking up that screw," said the attractive woman sitting next to Harry. "I'm so clumsy sometimes, especially under pressure."

"So am I. So this was the famous screw test?" Harry said.

"I've always figured myself to be a pretty good screwer."

The lady beside Harry blushed.

The instructor burst back into the room with her assistant and one by one Kathy looked each testee in the eyes for an uncomfortable amount of time — an especially long time right at Harry.

"OK. This next test," she began, "is a language test, to make sure you have the ability to translate orders into actions. I want all of you to go down the hall to the water cooler and get yourselves a nice cup of water, bring it back to this room, drink it here slowly, and then place the cup neatly in the wastebasket at the back of this room. OK. Go on then."

Harry stood up with the other women, holding the door as he thought a gentleman should, then exited the room and walked down the hall toward the water cooler. He let the other ladies go in front of him and he veered off to the male bathroom and took a quick piss. He then went to the cooler and got a cup of water, drank a little, then filled it up again and went back to the room with his cup. He sat down and sipped his water quietly. When finished he stood up and threw his empty cup, basketball style, into the waste basket.

The proctor re-entered the room.

"Now we're going to go off separately and I will ask you some questions," said Kathy. "Harry, you first. Follow me," said the instructor. Harry followed Kathy into a small room down the hall with a desk and one chair. Kathy sat down and Harry was just about to when Kathy said, "I didn't tell you to sit yet."

Harry stood back up.

"OK, you can sit now," said Kathy.

"I'm kind of nervous," said Harry. "I've always been that way about tests. You know?"

"Calm down. We just want to see what we got here," said Kathy. "OK. I'm going to present you with some possible workplace scenarios and I want you to tell me how you would respond in each case. OK?"

"I guess so."

"Suppose you and some guys are gathered, and one of them is showing the others a picture of a scantily clad female. Many are laughing and joking, and all are taking second peeks at the image. Do you look at it several times too? Do you smirk or giggle? Or, do you make a scene and tell them they shouldn't be doing that on company time, and report it to your supervisor?"

"I suppose I'd report it to my supervisor?" asked Harry, wondering if that was what he was supposed to say.

"But your supervisor is a woman. What would you say exactly. Imagine that I was that supervisor."

"Well, Kathy, some of the guys back there are looking at naked pictures of women, some kind of soft porn, and having fun. I thought you ought to know about it."

"Next scene," said Kathy.

"Wait. Was that the correct response? How am I doing?" Harry nervously wanted to know.

"We'll give you your grade after we're done," said Kathy.

"Next situation. It's voucher allotment time and everyone has just been given their weekly sexual vouchers. You put yours in your coat pocket, intending to use it sometime later. But a co-worker already has her voucher out and is heading toward you. Do you accept her voucher, or just what would you do in that case?"

"I'd reject that voucher," said Harry. "First off she's a co-worker and I probably shouldn't consort with fellow workers. Second, I'm in a meaningful relationship with Emily Novak, who might be the next Corporate Leader here on Eros. I don't want to mess that up, so I turn her down flat!"

"And if she starts crying, do you pat her back or hug her to give consolation?" Kathy asked.

"As much as I can, but without physically touching her too any great extent," said Harry. "I say something like, 'I just told you, I'm in a relationship. If I weren't I sure would hop all over you, for sure.'"

"OK Harry. This is the final scenario and it will wrap up your pre-employment testing."

Kathy got up out of her chair and walked over to Harry. She put her arm on his shoulder and knelt down to whisper something in his ear. She said, "You're one sexy beast of a man! Take off those glasses and make love to me like you wanna shake the bones right out of my skin!"

Harry sat there frozen. He re-adjusted his glasses. What should he do? What was he supposed to do? Was he supposed to respond to her advances, reject them? Was this part of the test or did she just like him? He didn't know. He slipped further and further down into his chair until he fell onto the floor. There he pushed his butt backward toward the door, stood up and went outside.

"What's wrong?" Kathy followed him out and asked.

"I don't know," said Harry and he went back to his desk in the larger instructional room. All the other ladies were dismissed and Harry sat there alone in the room, dreading the results of those tests he'd just taken.

In a moment Shin Shin walked in and sat down next to Harry. "Well, we've gotten your test results back."

"And...?" asked Harry.

"Mixed results, Harry. Mixed results. Oh, you'll be hired on, but I think you need more intensive training before we can give you a full workload. You'll be working here on a trial basis, here in the office, for now," said Shin Shin studying a sheet of paper, her beautiful brown eyes squinting to read the details.

"What'd I do wrong on those tests?" Harry wanted to know, worry furrowing his brow.

"OK, first, on the screw test, you used innuendo. Sure it was dangling right there in front of you like a low-hanging fruit, but that was good, Harry. You didn't completely fail the screw test."

"I screwed most of the screws in the time allotted. I think I finished screwing first," said Harry.

"That wasn't the point of that test," said Shin Shin. "You did pass that one.

"But about the water break test, you didn't score well on

that one," continued Shin Shin. "You didn't do exactly what the instructor asked. You didn't go directly to the water cooler, you went to the bathroom. Then you took a big drink at the fountain before you brought your cup of water back to the training room. And you didn't place your cup in the wastebasket, you threw it in. All those behaviors showed us you don't really respect a woman in authority. It displayed some passive-aggressive tendencies to do things your own way. You disregarded Ms. Kathy's simple instructions like they weren't even meant for you. But they were meant for you, and you were supposed to follow those instructions to the letter."

"Well I had to go pee, and I was thirsty, and I did make the cup into the basket," said Harry, trying to defend himself.

"And, as for the individual questions you showed you were a snitch, which means you don't work well with others. You have a streak of cruelty running through you that makes you keep your love-making to yourself. On this world that's not very ideal."

"What do you mean?" Harry asked.

"On Eros when someone offers you a sexual voucher, you take it and do the best you can," explained Shin Shin. "What's the point of having vouchers if you can't use them? Harry, Emily will understand if you punch someone's voucher now and then. We all do it here. I might have to get used to it myself. Now if you were to offer me your voucher, I would gladly accept it, even though I'm your boss. I won't be the one to let long established traditions die out."

"I'm still getting the hang of things," said Harry.

"Noted. But you resisted Kathy when she tried to seduce you. What are we all about here Harry? What's the main goal of Resurrection Cosmetics?"

"Making women look beautiful?" Harry guessed.

"Yes," said Shin Shin. "We are all about making women feel wanted, seductive, irresistible. Look at my face."

Harry looked.

"Here are my eyes. We make a lot of money on eyes:

eyeliner, eye shadow, eyebrow pencils, etc. Here I have my lips. The lips, Harry. The lips are so very important to this whole business we're running. The eyes and the lips are the cornerstones of our business — our bread and butter. Got that? We'll be refining the juice of the cherry-back beetle into our lipstick, the nectar from the Pink Passion flower, and we will soon begin mining the Cupidium, to create some of the most powerful aphro-dizzy-ass-tical cosmetics in the entire universe. You have to get used to working in close-up quarters and you have to act fast, be on your toes, toe the line, keep it up, bend when necessary, even break sometimes."

"I think I got it," said Harry.

"Yes, we also manufacture the foundation, the rouge, the concealer, and all that, but it's the eyes and the lips that are the jackpots, and women expect us to deliver on our promise to make them sensuous, loving beings. Also we rely on our patented perfume lines, too, to make women so unforgettable, so irresistible, you'd have to be a moron or some type of plant life to ignore the blaring statements our products make."

"I see," said Harry.

"So, Kathy whispered something into your ear?" continued Shin Shin. "Can you remember what she smelled like? Know what color lipstick she was wearing? Did she wear too much eye shadow? What didn't you like about her and her request? Why didn't you go for her offer like a catfish after stink bait?"

"It was all those tests," said Harry. "I wasn't sure if I should or not. I wanted to come to work here. What's wrong?"

"Well if you don't know I can't explain it to you."

"You know," continued Shin Shin, "you won't see many men working around here. You'll be one of only a few. You need to learn how to behave in this environment. (a big pause) Be prepared to stay after work for more training Monday when you come in. Thank you and tell Emily hello."

Shin Shin got up to leave.

"So that's it?" asked Harry.

"Yep. That's it," said Shin Shin. "Oh. One more thing. You remember Lulu Gooley, who I once sent out to try to seduce you?"

"The one at the SWAY station that bumped into George Merrick?" asked Harry. "What about her?"

"I'm going to send for her and her sister Becky to come work here in this factory. That means George, her husband, will be coming too," said Shin Shin. "You don't have a problem with that, do you? He was only trying to kill you to get revenge for the death of his son. I'm sure he's over all that now — now that he's found true love."

"I suppose it'll be all right," said Harry, thinking of how angry that man had been at him and how dangerous he could be, so big, so imposing, so ex-Citizen Policey.

"You see, I have a keen interest in Lulu. She worked for me on Earth. I took her under my wing. She's my protege of sorts. I think she'll be a valuable asset to this company. She's done with her E4E Church involvement now, after the law really cracked down on them for some of their stunts. Well. OK, I guess that does it for now. See you Monday for more testing."

That wasn't so bad, Harry said to himself, as he left the building and encountered the bright purplish daylight. *I think I'll take a walk in the park and try to ease all these knots rolled up inside me by communing with nature. I suppose I messed up somewhere on my tests, but I'm clueless as to where. And as to the arrival of my former enemy George Merrick, I sure hope that man won't be carrying a grudge across space for me. I hope that true love has mellowed him out and eased the pain of his son's death.*

Then Harry had another thought: *Would this former Citizen Policeman be coming to take him back to Earth for justice? Some wounds just don't heal well over time. They fester. And even if Lulu is out of that E4E Church, that church which believes earthlings should remain on earth, is that church through with her? Is my Eros freedom in jeopardy from this coming couple?*

CHAPTER 36

METAPHYSICS IN THE PARK

The election went rather smoothly and Emily easily was elected the new Corporate Leader. Harry found his new position as spouse of a planet ruler to be a rather embarrassing and confusing one. What were his new duties now? Did he have to sweep the carpet more often, dust behind the bookshelves, arrange the linen properly? Maybe, he thought, her new job came with some domestic help. He sure hoped that would be the case because he didn't like to be the one wearing the skirts around the house.

Then Harry thought to himself, *now that's old-world thinking. Why should housework be confined to women? That kind of thinking might not go far at RECT, so he better change his tune, and change it in a hurry, if he were to get along here on Eros.*

Turnbull had tried to intimidate voters, with a small band of lightly-armed militia who remained true to his person. He'd also released some Eros mice called Yuk-Etts during Emily's campaign watch party. There was much shrieking and climbing onto chairs, but Emily was cool and calmed the crowd. She lured the Yuk-Etts into a trap by setting out a kind of Eros cheese which they couldn't resist and capturing them all, thus saving the watch party and again saving the day.

Turnbull still hadn't admitted defeat and was trying to call for a re-count, but few gave him serious attention and Emily wasn't too worried. Oh, she wasn't underestimating his self-delusions nor his nastiness, but she had people monitoring him and making sure he conformed to civil society. She'd know soon enough if he became a major threat and be dealt with in a timely fashion.

After the election Emily seemed drained and could hardly get out of bed the next day. Harry brought her a cup of hot coffee and massaged her feet.

"That feels really good, Harry. I was on my feet all night last night at the watch party, glad-handing and smiling until my jaws hurt," she said sipping the coffee and purring over her feet being rubbed.

"I may not be seeing you as much as usual, now that you've been elected. You'll be busy all the time," said Harry. "We need to get out and get some fresh air today. Have some alone time. Take a walk in the park."

"Sure Harry," she said. "Sure, just give me time to clean up and do some morning meditations.."

* * *

Emily and Harry were taking a leisurely stroll in Grand Romantic Gesture Park, along a blue-stone sidewalk. It was a day like any other in Paradise, two suns trying to outshine each other, nary a cloud in the sky. Everything seemed normal.

The sweet smell of morning dew clung to the neck of the morning air like a high school hickey hangs on an adventurous schoolgirl. As Harry and Emily, the once-again loving couple, rounded a bushy wall in the park they witnessed all the booty-bots standing in formation in an open field. They were all rigid in a field of yellow clover — blank eyes turned toward the sky.

It wasn't unusual for Harry to see the booty-bots on Eros all gathered together, doing the same thing. After all, they were a small minority here and they tended to stick together. But what Harry and Emily saw on their morning walk in the park was different.

Something seemed wrong to Harry about this picture. He noticed Judy in the crowd and approached her, with Emily following close behind.

"What's happening, Judy?" asked Harry. Judy blinked her eyes twice and looked at Harry with a far-away stare.

"It's over, Harry," said Judy, the booty-bot.

"I know. We both discussed that," said Harry, thinking Judy was referring to their flesh-to-booty-bot relationship.

"Not that," said Judy.

"What's over then?" Emily wanted to know.

"The whole lot of us aliens are done," said Judy. "Everyone of us who lives on this planet, or on Metta Karuna, and anywhere else in the universe, we're all subject to a mass extinction event which is quickly approaching. We're gathered here in this park on Eros because we're waiting for all our fellow citizens to come join us. We want to all go out together."

"Surely you don't mean that," said Harry. "How is this possible?"

"Why? Why go now?" asked Emily. "Does it pose any danger to the rest of us?"

"No danger to anyone other than we Metta Karunians. Why must we go? Because it's the grand will of the Great Big Make-Up Maker in the Sky, is why," said Judy. "He, or she, doesn't need to give any explanations or reasons — that entity or entities just does whatever they think is right."

"Isn't there anything you can do about it?" asked Harry.

"No use fighting it, crying over it, or arguing," said Judy with just a hint of a smile on her face. "All species — all forms of life have an expiration date — just as do mountains, bodies of water, moons and suns — whole galaxies too — even this universe itself has to be regenerated someday."

"I'm sorry I was so rude to you the other day," said Emily. "You took care of my Harry when he needed you most. I wasn't there for him, but you were. I was upset and nervous about everything going on."

"I suppose that was our supreme mission all along — to give a little love where there was none — to ease the burdens of a few people like your husband, and to help you fight for your rights as women," said Judy.

"Congratulations on your Corporate Leadership vote, by the way," Judy continued. "You'll make a fine leader here. Make everything all right again here. I know you'll make good decisions."

"Extinction is so final, Judy," said Harry.

"Is it Harry?" asked Susie Q who stood beside Judy and just now decided to talk. "You believe all those who are born come from nowhere, are made from nothing? You know everything that lives must one day die. It's inevitable. What if I told you that everything that lives, except certain souls who break this chain of recycling, will be born again. That too is inevitable. Just like you couldn't control your own birth, you won't be able to control your own regeneration, unless you are a master such as myself."

"How do you know this?" asked Emily.

"I've lived a long time, Emily," said Susie Q. "I've thought long and hard and gone into the inner recesses of my mind to arrive at certain truths. I've learned to focus and avoid distractions. I know what I'm saying is true by seeing it for myself. I'm not trying to trick you or get your money like some religious leaders do. I'm just telling you what I know."

"I feel bad the way I treated you two," said Harry.

"It was the greatest experience of our existence," said Judy. "We're very small beings on our home planet, and over the years we've evolved to such a state that passions were eliminated for most of us. But from the time I was harvested by Posh Matosh and came to be inside this booty-bot and have lived with you, I've had those emotions reawakened in ways I've never imagined. It was so invigorating to make love and feel closeness with you, to grow angry, to be jealous, to have these wild swings of mood that made my face flush and my heart race. Oh, it was grand, Harry. It was wonderful."

"All the Metta Karunians know of our experiences here," said Susie Q, "and all our doings on earth, and every one of us knows we are going to die out soon. That's why they all want to come here first, before that great event. They want to experience some of those rumbling emotions before the end."

"Is that what you're looking up for, awaiting the arrival of your brethren from space?" Emily asked.

"Yes. Will it be any problem? Do we need Visas or anything?" asked Susie Q. "Rest assured. We'll all be gone before you know it."

"No, no. You're all so small it won't be a problem," said Emily. "So where will all of you stay until, you know?"

"They'll all come and inhabit these 700 booty-bot bodies we have gathered here. There's plenty of room inside us," said Judy.

"You say you will be reborn or something?" asked Harry.

"Yes. We know that to be a fact. That's why we want to all die here. We think it would give us a good chance that we might be reborn as a humanoid if we're at this locale," said Susie Q. "And we've decided — all of us — that we want to experience one thing before we go, simultaneously."

"What's that?" asked Harry.

"We want to leave this life, this world, with a passionate kiss," said Judy the booty-bot. "We want to gather together in some romantic spot, maybe inside this park, and be kissed like someone loves us and needs us, kissed like someone will really miss us when we're gone — all together. We want a kiss that is bold and from the heart — supernova explosive-like, a kiss that makes the world turn on edge, that makes the universe flicker on and off for a moment. We want tongue. We want hands on our asses. We want a hug like someone really means it. That's our general consensus, but may vary from bot to bot."

"So what will happen to the individual booty-bot bodies when you leave them?" asked Emily.

"They'll still be around and be functional. Maybe someone can salvage them, return them to artificial intelligence mode and use them however they see fit," said Susie Q.

"I'll miss you, Judy," said Harry.

"I'll miss all of you too," said Judy. "We got to know you people pretty well. But Harry, oh sweet Harry, I really got to know you. Remember all those wild ins and outs we had when you first unpacked me out of the box? The epileptic snake and the feather rake? The ice chisel and the honey finger bowl? The flat-tire wheelbarrow on top of the coffee table? The tongue scraping of the rusty crankshaft? The electric nozzle wrapped in macaroons? Those were fun times, Harry. Really fun times."

"I don't think I want to hear all this," said Emily turning away for a moment.

"Yes they were some real fun times," said Harry, as Emily jabbed him hard in the ribs. "I was lucky to have known you. You did come to me at a very low time in my life, a time I was so eaten up with loneliness and desperation. You took all that away and made me happy again. You traveled with me here. You've been a very pleasant companion, for the most part."

"Yes, I know I have been a little bit of a pain from time to time. All the drama, the ups and downs we've had with you humans. It's been so interesting," said Judy. "Even the disappointments that made our tiny Metta Karunian hearts ache were such wonderful pangs. We'll miss it — miss it all, but we're prepared to leave it all behind for a short time. We want to once again spin the karmic roulette wheel and let the fates and the power of our past actions fling us where they will."

"How soon can you get ready the kissers for us?" asked Judy.

"We need stout young men — a booty-bot love-in, peace-out kind of thing," said Susie Q. "And we desire to all look beautiful before we go. We want Resurrection Cosmetics to lend us a hand to really doll it up."

"I don't think I'll have a problem getting you fixed up with Resurrection Cosmetics products or finding farewell men for you," said Emily.

"We don't want to be kissed good-bye," said Judy. "We want to be kissed like we mean the world to someone, like they want to make that moment last a lifetime or at least the memory of it. Something like that, not a so-long kiss. Not like that. We want to feel the raw emotion of pink-hot passion! If there's any of that flower juice around let the men who will do us the honors drink that. Get them fired up to really lay one on us! We swear, as we go, satisfied by that cosmic kiss, we will put on a show the likes of which this planet has never, ever seen before — even topping the Pink O'Clock suns alignment."

"I'll gather the men together," said Harry.

"I'll speak with Ba Boom and Shin Shin on the product line we'll be using," said Emily. "And I'll check and see if anyone has any extra Pink O'clock juice left over. We'll do our best to make you feel lovely and loved before your trip. Seems a shame though. You're very gentle creatures, most of the time, and the universe needs more beings like you."

"Well, that's what love does, sometimes it makes you do strange and crazy things," said Judy. "I did love you, Harry. And Emily, I take back everything I might have called you, or thought about you. I hope you and Harry are very happy together. Would you mind too much, Emily, if it was Harry that gave me that final lip blessing?"

"Naw. Have at it," said Emily. "I'll be interested to see this. I wish there was something else I could do, but it sounds like this event is going to happen no matter what."

"It is," said Susie Q. "You ever think that even you humans are a kind of booty-bot?"

"What's that?" asked Harry.

"I mean below all your nice fleshy surfaces, what or who are you?" asked Susie Q. "Many of your books and teachers speak of spirits and souls inside of you, but what are those nebulous things? Could they be transient beings, invisible to the eye, from some other time or dimension? Could they be inhabiting your bodies, hop-skipping across the universe, going from species to species, encouraging reproduction and self-development as best they can, until they end up where they belong?"

"Perhaps we're not so different, you and I," said Judy to Harry. "Maybe we're all just booty-bots zooming around in outer space, experimenting with love and trying to make the worlds we visit a little better on the go."

"Maybe so, Judy," said Harry. "Maybe I'm a booty-bot too, a reckless driver trapped inside all this flesh and bone. You could be on to something."

CHAPTER 37

THE PURPLE GRASS STAINS OF LOVE

The people of Eros love nothing better than festivities. The city council decided to hold the event on the wide purple lawn of Pucker-Up Park, which was close to Liaison Lake. It was deemed best able to accommodate the anticipated crowd. The huge picnic area was decorated with tables and chairs, Chinese lanterns of yellow, blue and red, a large stage for the band, a long table for the food, decorated with large red lips.

Earlier in the day Ba Boom, president and C.E.O. of Resurrection Cosmetics, held a mandatory lecture for all the men who would be participating in what was now being labeled the Squeeze to Please, Labios Adiós event. It was this event which would send the aliens, who resided within their booty-bots, onward and upward toward their reincarnated new karmic birthdays.

Ba Boom stood, looking beautiful, as always, on the pink ribboned stage with a visual white board behind her.

"Understand this before you give that booty-bot a kiss. Learn to shut-up," said Ba Boom as she clicked a button she was holding. Behind her on the overhead screen the word shut-up appeared in large bold lettering.

"These booty-bots don't want no blabbing out of you before they go," she said. "You got something to say it better be about the girl in front of you, how beautiful she looks, how enticing is her form, romantic sweet nothings like that. None of your usual day to day trivial, water cooler male drivel. Stuff all that back inside you and shut it!"

"I see a question in the back, OK, shoot," said Ba Boom as she noticed a man feverishly waving his hand in the air.

The man stood up and cleared his throat, "So our main deal here is to kiss these aliens good-bye? That's it? Just kiss and forget it?"

"If you don't want this assignment get out now," said Ba Boom. "But yes. It's just a kiss. You're to act as the great loves of their lives," continued Ba Boom, "and give them a smooch to remember. Is that so difficult? You'll all receive gifts for your participation, so there's that."

"What kinds of prizes?" asked another man.

"I have a wide variety of male-distracting games from across the universe you'll all be very pleased with," said Ba Boom. "But the main thing is this upcoming kiss. The kiss!

"Second thing I want to tell you is to 'Go Deep.' You know, when it's 3rd and long and time is expiring on the clock of your favorite sports game, you put your everything into this one last play. You draw up your passion from way down deep within you, and you pour that out to win the game — to make these girls feel really special. Got it?"

Underneath the bulleted word Shut-Up appeared the words Go Deep behind Ba Boom on the overhead screen.

"And finally, just as important as these two other strong recommendations, is that you deliver a 'Big Finish'. This will vary from couple to couple but I want you to use tongue, grab asses, stroke hair, so besides the oral kiss, give this moment your own special fireworks and produce the Big Finish. So let's review: 1) Shut-up, 2) Go Deep, 3) Big Finish."

The same man in the back was waving his arm again. Ba Boom acknowledged him and he stood. "That Big Finish part has me confused. I mean, we can't go too far, can we? We have limits on the Big Finish, right? It will be right here in public, so how far is going too far?"

"Nothing indecent," said Ba Boom. "Let me make that perfectly clear, this isn't a booty-bot charity porn bop, it's just a long, fantastic, passionate kiss. I hate that I have to explain all this to you bunch of men, but you have to summon up your long dormant, or never used romantic natures for this one.

"I know that the culture may have suppressed those natures here on Eros, where all you gotta do to get laid is present your sex voucher to the one you want to bop. And I'm aware that the male species isn't quite as quick at catching on to the needs of women as they should be by now. But I need your cooperation and your best effort."

"Why?" asked the man in back.

"Why? Why you ask? Because their whole species is going extinct and this is what they asked for on their way out. It's a courtesy, a loving farewell gift and I am able and willing to make that happen, with your PAID help. I won't take any more questions. Damn! Figure it out already.

"You've been selected because you're the most desirable men on Eros, but maybe not the brightest. I'll give you your prizes afterwards, only if I see you're at least making the attempt. Now get out of here and go get ready! Put on a good suit and tie, for God's sake, and at least act like you care."

* * *

Meanwhile, Shin Shin was prepping the booty-bots for the big evening. She and her girls at Resurrection Cosmetics were doing the ladies hair and applying make-up and doing nails. That's what the booty-bots wanted, to look their absolute stunning best for their cyborg curtain call.

Judy was sitting next to Susie Q as Shin Shin walked down the line making sure the hairdos were well done and the cosmetics were properly applied.

Shin Shin stopped behind Judy and looked at her in the mirror. "You look fabulous!"

"It's a nice thing you're doing, you and Ba Boom and all these volunteers," said Judy, almost letting go a green tear.

"No crying now," said Shin Shin. "Don't ruin that look

we've given you. Later we'll find a dress and shoes."

"Right, OK," said Judy. "Thank you again."

"Don't mention it," said Shin Shin. "It's gonna be a swell party. The Kathlix are back to play music. We have the Valentine Catering Service preparing the food. It's gonna be a heckuva evening."

* * *

That evening the men, dressed in their best suits and holding roses, were gathered on the beautiful Pucker-Up Park and Pavilion Lawn and grazing on the finger food, anxiously awaiting the arrival of the booty-bots. Most were talking sports or the political climate that was forthcoming with Emily now serving as new Corporate Leader.

The Chinese lanterns gave the whole area a party atmosphere while the Kathlix were playing some of their songs, such as 'She Smelt Better than a Sunday Thurible Swinging Down the Pews'.

With due fanfare out walked the 700 booty-bots who were about to have a final fling before being flung to the far-off cosmos. It was their debutante dénouement ball and mystic muzzle grinder.

Each booty-bot was beautiful beyond compare, in her (or their) own way. You see the planet of Metta Karuna held about 10 billion teeny-tiny aliens in residence. They were all here now, those and Metta Karunians from other exo-planets. They were probably jostling for space inside each of the booty-bots, climbing over one another to get to a good platform near the lip area.

None of these beings had ever had sexual union, except the few who had become booty-bots. They had always been asexual in their normal habitat. But, by their own choosing, they decided to all become females, as suggested by Ravi Moonbeam when he first began harvesting the little critters. None of them argued with this arrangement and inside each booty-bot now resided many millions of souls who would experience the same kiss, at the same time, feel the same tender passion, and the sudden melting of their little alien hearts.

The participants started to pair up. Most of the women of Eros were sitting at home, watching these events unfold on their 3D holograms. They were very interested to see what would happen. They had been asked not to go to the park, so as not to confuse the men assembled. Many were glad to see the booty-bots go away, but most wanted to remember what a formal romantic evening was like.

Some remembered with fondness the good deeds the booty-bots had done in the War of the Sexes. They fought their booty-bot asses off.

There was that one time during the war that W.I.R.E. Company D was surrounded near French Kiss Isthmus, and would have been wiped out entirely by the Greyshirts, but the booty-bots broke off from their own fight near Fascination Forest and rushed in to help Company D to repel the Greyshirt advance on the W.I.R.E. women and win the day. If medals would have been given out, then surely those booty-bots deserved that, not only for that particular day, but for many other instances of heroic actions during the war effort.

Harry had his roses in his arms and was looking around the lawn in search of Judy. He finally found her almost glistening with shimmering beauty in a diaphanous, sparkly pink gown. She sat underneath a large blue Jamu-Jimu tree, listening to night creates chirping out love songs.

The lantern light was in her green eyes and it shone toward Harry. He felt a tug at his heart so strong he had to look away for a second. He'd do this kiss thing, but he couldn't go back to his booty-bot, he just couldn't form those attachments he once had with her — not like this, besides, she was leaving soon anyway. He felt weird.

"Hi there Harry," said Judy. "All the inhabitants of this body are anxiously awaiting that kiss of yours."

"Guess it won't be much of a private affair," said Harry. "How many of you guys will I be kissing, over 50 million?"

"Give or take," said Judy, "including me of course. They all want to feel what I felt when you first kissed me."

"It took me a long time to give you that first kiss," said Harry. "At first you were just a prize booty-bot fresh out of the box, a thing to use for my sexual and emotional pleasure. But after a while I grew pretty fond of you, Judy, and it eventually felt natural to give you a kiss now and then."

"That's nice to hear you say, Harry," said Judy, tilting her head to one side to look at him more closely, her red hair, done up in a fashionable style, gleaming in the 4-moon night. "Why don't you come with me to where I'm going, link a part of your soul with mine?"

"I can't do that," said Harry emphatically.

"It's a great big universe out there, Harry, and no telling where it will take us on that trip. I don't want much from you Harry," said Judy. "Just a small slice of your massive universal soul. You got plenty to spare in there, I've seen that monstrosity, when I was inside your body, and I must say, you have a very huge one. Lots of little souls combined into one, running around, heads all confused.

"What? You think you just have one soul?" asked Judy. "What is it with your species and its fascination with the number one? Maybe it's because you come from a one-sun, one-moon world. But maybe that's not too far from the truth either. In the binary world there is only 1 and 0 — something and nothing.

"So maybe it is all interconnected," continued Judy, "all the gods and all the planets, all the beings ever created and ever to be made. When we die maybe we journey throughout the universe, traveling from planet to planet being one species then another, sometimes an intelligent being, sometimes an ant, sometimes little Timmy's pet dog — going on and on never ending, backward and forward in time immemorial."

"Let's dance before I get a headache," said Harry as he took her hand and led her to the dance floor, where couples were already dancing to the tunes of the Kathlix. This was a slow song called "A Bundle of Myrrh Instead of Fur." It was a romantic ditty about a King speaking to his beloved in finely-dressed metaphors. Judy cuddled close to Harry.

"You gonna miss me?" Judy asked.

"I will," said Harry. "But don't slice off my soul on your way out."

"That was just wishful thinking. Besides, you have Emily now and you'll be fine without me," said Judy.

"It was you who reawaken my heart," said Harry. "You brought me back to life, in a sense, you resurrected me from my dismal, depressing life on Earth."

"Then I did my job," said Judy. "I may have done some bad things, said some terrible oaths, but at least I did that, didn't I?" Harry nodded.

The dance and the conversation were interrupted by Susie Q on the microphone.

"OK. It's that time, girls," said Susie Q. "I'm sure you're all feeling it bubbling up inside you. It's time for the The Grand Labios Adiós. Grab your mates. I got mine stashed nearby."

Susie Q's kiss-mate was none other than General Howitzer.

"Let's get ready. Gentlemen, put down your drinks. Time to lube up those lips and give us that one special kiss on our sweet inviting lips. This kiss will be made all the more enticing with the generous help of Ba Boom Varoom and her Specially-Created Resurrection Cosmetics Winsomely Wanton Toodle-Do Lip Dew."

So everyone paired up. Susie Q nuzzled up to General Howitzer, who stood at attention. "On my count," she said, getting closer to Howitzer and getting him to relax a little. "Three, two, one!"

And with that all couples kissed, long and hard, with as much passion as could be mustered, the smacking sound riveting through the park like large waves lapping at a thirsty shore.

Lips were flying this way and that. Lipstick was getting smeared all over eager faces. Finely coiffured hair was being mussed. Asses were being grabbed. Some kissing had nibbling or tongue thrown in for good measure.

In the moments that made up that kiss Harry felt those old feelings he had in his youth, hearing his favorite songs, taking a last dance or a last kiss from a girl he'd probably never see again. He felt nostalgia, a kindling, a creeping joy, and a haunting hole growing in his being — a sort of hangnail of the heart.

Harry tasted Judy's booty-bot lips and her hot red lip balm there. They tasted similar to cherry-chocolate with cinnamon, with a touch of hot sauce added. Those lips were sweet and sour, delicious and sad, caked with longing and excitement. They were smooth with fear and wet with sad loss — and an enduring wonder of the loving moment. They were intoxicating with a touch of wild passion, stunning as sudden death with the possible resurrection of one's body lingering around the borders of that last kiss. It was like Harry was a giggling drunk, bubbling with good-feelings, but a little afraid to go home to what he knew would be an angry wife.

Harry felt a kind of freckle-y fickle-ty. Those freckles of Judy were every bit as cute as Emily's, and as numerous as the stars in the eternal sky. That kiss was pretty swell too, making him shiver in his shoes. The way Judy's red hair curled around her ears made time ebb away into some hidden mermaid cavern, that only the chosen could enter.

Harry had no way of knowing if it was Judy's millions of Metta Karunians, all pouring themselves into Judy's lips, or Judy doing the lip drive home. He imagined the flush he felt came from many sources: the Resurrection Cosmetics, the lip balm in particular, the Pink O'Clock juice he'd drank, or something more. But all of it together hit him like an elephant, or a blue whale, crashing against the very sidewalls of eternity.

It sent Harry to his buckled knees and as he went there Judy followed. They knelt together, still in prayerful kissing. Then the force of that all-energizing kiss knocked them both sideways — off their knees and they were lying on the ground, rolling around on the purple grass. Up they went, rolling up

Sweetheart Summit, then down, tumbling down into Cuddle-Up Canyon where they rolled onto Tenderness Trail and made a circle through Make-Out Meadow near Wooing Wood, Finally they flopped back, full-circle, to Lipstick Lawn.

Then a large bang was heard and the ground shook. The Kathlix stopped playing and genuflected.

The booty-bots stood up as one. The men took their arms and lips from off these now cold figures as they saw in the robots' eyes a look of wild hope mixed with fear, pupils rolling around like wheels on a carnival ride.

Colored lights shot out from the tops of the booty-bots heads, Metta-Karunian corpses being rocketed to their next cosmic slide-show, bursting into the air like tiny roman candles, illuminating the night like a rainfall of prisms. The light show continued for three straight hours as more alien souls flew outward, onward, toward who-knows-what. The air was thick with little Metta Karunians, spirits forsaking their big booty-bot stations and exiting their much, much smaller alien bee pods to traverse the universe.

"Where do they go?" Harry asked Shin Shin, who now stood beside him, squinting her lovely Asiatic eyes at the bright beautiful sight.

"Probably some sort of random way station, a spiritual loading dock, awaiting transport to the nearest-fitting and available karmic-aligned body," said the always profound Shin Shin. "I don't know. You and Emily plan on having any kids?"

"Haven't thought about it much," said Harry. "I suppose we could. Why are you asking?"

"I'm sure Emily would like that. You ought to think about it," said Shin Shin. "Help you to settle down. Be more alert at work. Maybe that kid of yours will be the reincarnated soul of one of these booty-bots. You can't tell."

"Think so?" said Harry, trailing his words off, because he was exhausted from all that kissing and rolling, and ready to go home now and just flop into bed for a long, long rest.

"Well," Shin Shin called after him as he made his way

home, purple grass stains clinging to his suit of clothes, "it's possible, isn't it?" Harry shrugged and kept moving. "Rest up, Harry. See you first thing Monday morning. Be sharp now."

CHAPTER 38

HARRY'S READJUSTMENT PERIOD

When Harry got back home Emily was waiting up for him.

"So how was your little make-out session? You enjoy yourself?" she asked him. "Was it good for you?"

"I'm really beat," said Harry, having had difficult existential questions posed all night long, and physically wracked from that super-long, super-hard kiss he'd just given. All he wanted to do now was lay down and let his mind and body go limp for a while.

"Well sure, go on and hit the sack," said Emily. "Meanwhile I'll be up all night wondering if she was better than me."

"She wasn't better than you," said Harry. "Besides, she's gone now so you have nothing to worry about."

"Don't pander to me," returned Emily.

"What do you want me to say?' asked Harry. "All right, the whole evening was pretty wonderful and really kind of sad. You must have watched it on the hologram."

"I saw it, but I didn't *feel it* the way you did," said Emily. "You sure are lucky, you know that? You are about the luckiest guy I've ever known, what with the Resurrection drone dropping on your head, meeting up with Ba Boom, being here for me during Pink O'Clock, and now getting to play your part in this Labios Adiós rolling-in-the-grass thing. Why are you so lucky?"

"Maybe we're all lucky sometime, somewhere in our individual lives," said Harry, waxing philosophic since his experience with Labios Adiós had Judy spirited away for good.

"Tell me what her kiss was like. I have a right to know," said Emily. "Wait. No. Don't tell me. Don't ever mention her name again around me. She's history. Gone away."

"Yes," said Harry.

"Well you best buckle down and be a good provider now with your work at Resurrection Eros Cupidium Techniques. You show Shin Shin Skinny what you're made of. And I'll buckle down and try to be the best leader I can for this planet. Together we'll do OK, maybe even something special."

"Sounds good," said Harry. "Now can I get some shut-eye? Please?"

"First, why don't you go to the bathroom and wash that stupid lipstick off your face and scrub off some of that alien perfume. Come home smelling like a French whore and lipstick splattered all around your mouth. What's a woman supposed to do with that?"

"You said it was OK," Harry meekly offered.

"Yeah. You always got something to say back don't you? Why can't you just comfort me some way?" asked Emily. "Why can't you just listen to me, for once? You never did listen to me Harry. You never thought about what I wanted."

Two of the four moons out tonight shone their light diagonally into their bedroom. Harry saw the crossing orange and white light and wondered how long it would be like this with Emily? How long would she hold onto this jealousy of his time with Judy? Harry wanted to put it all in the past. Start over. Be born again, so to speak, on this world of Eros. Emily too would be beginning something new. There was much to look forward to in the future, but all Harry could think about was sleep.

"Did she give you tongue?" Harry heard Emily mumble.

"I won't tell you," said Harry.

Harry took off his grass-stained suit and laid down in their bed of suspicious nails. Even still he was fast asleep in a matter of moments.

Emily looked at him lying there, wondering in her mind just what he was thinking about his last night with his old booty-bot. Was he happy the alien was gone? Was he going to be happy here on Eros with her, now that she had become Corporate Leader and they were back together? Would she be happy with him, working for Shin Shin and all those other women at RECT, producing passion-powered cosmetics? If she didn't like him working there, she might get him a job in the government somewhere — somewhere she could keep an eye on him.

Emily undressed and prepared for bed. She laid naked beside him, her freckled body dotting the Is and crossing the Ts of that big IT lying squarely, invisibly between her and Harry — the IT of an alien-controlled booty-bot and Harry's convoluted involvement with her.

She picked up a device to read a book to try to calm down her fevered thoughts. She counted sheep. She wondered what was on her agenda for tomorrow as new Corporate Leader. She got up and looked out the window at the stars and the moons. No sleep came as these and many similar thoughts rolled around within her mind like ball bats scooping down on unsuspecting cherry-back beetles.

The next morning Harry woke up extremely hungry and a little sexually excited. Some of that exotic perfume that Judy the booty-bot had worn still clung to his body. He touched Emily's naked back, connecting freckles like dot-to-dots, then massaging ever so softly.

At his touch Emily jumped out of bed, put on her robe and ran to the kitchen. "Want coffee?" she yelled back to Harry.

"Yes!" said Harry.

"How about some eggs and bacon?"

"Would love it," replied Harry, thinking perhaps that all was forgiven and forgotten. Harry showered and put on some clean clothes for this lazy Sunday morning.

When he sat down to his breakfast his coffee tasted a little funny.

"Is it bitter?" asked Emily.

"A little, but it's fine," said Harry.

"I'm still a little bitter," said Emily.

"You want to talk about it?" asked Harry.

"How are you eggs? Taste them," said Emily.

Harry tasted them and they were a little underdone and runny. But the bacon was a little too well done.

"Just the way I like them," said Harry, sipping his coffee and smiling.

"Just the way you like them? Runny eggs and burnt bacon?" asked Emily.

"No, they're really tasty," said Harry, getting up to fix himself some toast.

"I would have done that for you," said Emily.

"You relax," said Harry, patting her on the back.

"So what are they going to do with the booty-bot bodies now that the alien souls have gone out of them?" asked Emily.

"I think I heard Ba Boom say she'd take them back to Earth with her, try to sell them back to Ravi Moonbeam at Posh Matosh, maybe get a refund or something," said Harry.

"You gonna go look at your old bop bot one last time? You want to gather up your old doll gal and bring her to our home? Prop her up in the corner of our bedroom, have it stare at us while we make love? If so I can kick it every once in a while, kick her in the face."

"No, and no. Why would you want to do that? Why would I want to do that?"

Emily shrugged, innocent like.

"You know I'd like to kick that Turnbull a time or two myself, kick him in his one last good ball, for how he stole you away from me. Sometimes I'd like to kick myself for that too," said Harry, trailing off in pensive thought.

"Yeah," said Emily, also a little ashamed of how that all went down on planet Earth.

"I'm all over Judy now, Emily. You got to believe me," said

Harry. "I don't want her body in this house, or even on this planet. I'll be glad if Ba Boom takes her far far away."

"She ought to take Turnbull back with her too. Say. That's not a bad idea. How do we get her to do that?" Emily wondered.

"I..." Harry started to say.

"Shhh," said Emily, "I'm thinking. Let me think."

So Harry buttered his toast, putting a little cherry jam on top, and continued his breakfast, crunching down on his toast as silently as he could.

"Give him a choice," Harry said, despite Emily's hushing.

"A choice of what?" Emily asked, needing some guidance.

"Go to jail, go to hell or get the hell off this planet," said Harry.

"Make it seem like his idea," pondered Emily. "Not bad, Harry. I could threaten him with arrest for voter interference, and for trying to disrupt proper government functioning. I could freeze his assets. I could tell him there's two ways out of all this mess, go back to earth with Ba Boom or stay here and face indictment. Good thinking, Harry."

* * *

So Ba Boom prepared for her flight back to earth, having almost all of the used booty-bots loaded on board, along with a still-angry Danny Turnbull put onboard in handcuffs.

"Oh, he won't be any problem for me," said Ba Boom to Emily at the spaceport.

"You sure? He's a master of chaos and lies, Ba Boom. You can't believe anything he says," said Emily remembered how he once said he'd love her forever when he picked her up on earth and brought her to Eros.

"I have a lot of leverage when I have him millions of miles in space. There's no where for him to run if he tries to tangle with me there," said Ba Boom. "Anyway, he might prove helpful on earth, maybe if he can be reformed he can be a good businessman once again, like he was before he went power-mad. It's worth a shot. We need all the slick business people we can get on Earth. We're gonna try to save that limping planet one way or another. I received some tips and some enzymes from Susie Q before they left. They were so full of compassion for our species."

"Yes, well, good luck to you," said Emily.

"Where's Harry? Thought he'd come and say so long," said Ba Boom.

"I gave him a hard time about that kiss he gave Judy last night I rubbed it in how I thought he still clung to that old doll of his," said Emily. "Maybe he thought I'd get mad again if he came here or I might threaten his masculinity again or something."

"There will be an adjustment time for men to accept real equality," said Ba Boom. "There will be some feelings hurt. It's inevitable. We women have suffered for millennia being made to feel bad for looking good, for looking bad, for trying too hard, for not trying hard enough, for being bossy, for almost everything we did. Boo Hoo if they feel their feet are getting steeped on."

"If their masculinity is such a delicate thing, like their nuts are, then the barriers may eventually break and we can see eye to eye someday," said Emily. "That will be a good thing, even if Turnbull or even my Harry, has a hard time of it at first."

Harry was standing a distance away, on a small hill, looking down at the spaceport and Ba Boom's rocket being loaded with booty-bots.

"I will miss you, Judy, wherever you are," Harry whispered that little prayer to the wind. "I hope you find happiness out there in the big wide universe somewhere. I hope someone is kind and good to you and your future existences are better than this one. You do deserve better. Better than me. Better than being a small alien controlling a sexual booty-bot, serving human beings like me who have all these wild fantasies.

"All you little beings deserve better than coming down from your own home planet and serving our carnal desires and helping us through our hard times. There ought to be more reward for you out there somewhere. Something equal to your sacrifices, some better, more grateful species that you can find happiness with."

Harry thought of Ba Boom as the rocket started firing and

inching into the air. He hoped Ba Boom and the Resurrection Cosmetics Corp. could save old planet Earth from destroying itself utterly and totally.

The Earth was in bad shape when he left it and he knew it would take a lot of power and know-how to whip it back into shape. It was gonna take a lot of extra special lipstick, and someone who knew how to use it — someone like Ba Boom — to complete that planetary trick.

The End

EPILOGUE

Well what does a man like me really know about lipstick or cosmetics in general? Not much. Not much at all. In fact, what do I know about women? Still, not much, even though I live with one. To me women are a mystery that is harder to solve than Einstein's Unification Principle. But I love a good mystery, don't you? It's made even more difficult by me because my wife oftentimes, in her anger or frustration, turns to her native Taiwanese language to express herself. In a way, that's good. I have no way of knowing how bad I'm being berated.

But lipstick and all cosmetics have long been a cleverly devised trap for us men. By the title you might think that aliens arriving on earth might use such tricks to catch us off-guard. Well, that would be another story now, wouldn't it?

So I hope I have not misrepresented women, lipstick, or booty-bots in this little book of mine. If I have, then please, only curse me in a language I don't understand.

ABOUT THE AUTHOR

Mike Fry

I'm a native-raised Okie, raised in Bethany, Oklahoma. I went to school at Putnam City Original High School and graduated in 1969. After a stint in the U.S. Army (drafted) I attended Oklahoma State University in Stillwater, majoring in English. Later in life I was awarded a Master's Degree in Creative Writing from the University of Central Oklahoma in Edmond. At UCO I had one professor who I believe changed the course of my life by believing in my writing: Linda McDonald. She has remained a lifelong friend and colleague.

I live in Oklahoma City now with my lovely Taiiwanese wife Rose and my two children: Maya and Mason. I also have a daughter in Dallas named Phuong Nguyen and she has five children, all of whom I love dearly.

BOOKS BY THIS AUTHOR

Veetch: A Shoshone Shaman, A '58 Edsel, A Ufo, And A Magical Key Save America's Baconw

Cast off to the nether edges of the world, Veetch Poteet, an albino man abandoned at birth, seeks to discover his roots and employs the help of water nymphs, a Shoshone Medicine Man, a '58 Edsel, and other beings of mysterious origin. In this fantasy world he travels in search of an ancient artifact, left behind by aliens many eons ago. If he can find this artifact, unlock its potential, then perhaps he can save the world, gain favor in the eyes of his beloved, and be reunited with a long-lost mother.

Made in the USA
Middletown, DE
09 December 2022

16310217R00176